THE CONFESSOR

DANIEL SILVA

✦

THE
CONFESSOR

✦

G. P. PUTNAM'S SONS ✦ NEW YORK

This book is a work of fiction. Names, characters, places and incidents
are either the product of the author's imagination or are used fictitiously,
and any resemblance to actual persons, living or dead, business establish-
ments, events or locales is entirely coincidental.

G. P. Putnam's Sons
Publishers Since 1838
a member of
Penguin Putnam Inc.
375 Hudson Street
New York, NY 10014

Library of Congress Cataloging-in-Publication Data

Silva, Daniel, date.
The confessor / Daniel Silva.
p.   cm.
ISBN 0-399-14972-4
I. Title.
PR6069.I362 C6   2003   2002031905
823'.914—dc21

Printed in the United States of America
1   3   5   7   9   10   8   6   4   2

This book is printed on acid-free paper. ∞

Book design by Stephanie Huntwork

For David Bull, *il restauratore*,
and as always,
for my wife Jamie and
my children Lily and Nicolas

"Roma locuta est; causa finita est."

Rome has spoken; the case is closed.

ST. AUGUSTINE OF HIPPO

PART ONE

✦

AN APARTMENT IN MUNICH

✦

·1·

MUNICH

THE APARTMENT HOUSE at Adalbertstrasse 68 was one of the few in the fashionable district of Schwabing yet to be overrun by Munich's noisy and growing professional elite. Wedged between two red brick buildings that exuded prewar charm, No. 68 seemed rather like an ugly younger stepsister. Her façade was a cracked beige stucco, her form squat and graceless. As a result her suitors were a tenuous community of students, artists, anarchists, and unrepentant punk rockers, all presided over by an authoritarian caretaker named Frau Ratzinger, who, it was rumored, had been living in the original apartment house at No. 68 when it was leveled by an Allied bomb. Neighborhood activists derided the building as an eyesore in need of gentrification. Defenders said it exemplified the very sort of Bohemian arrogance that had once made Schwabing the Montmartre of Germany—the Schwabing of Hesse and Mann and Lenin. And Adolf Hitler, the professor working in the second-floor window might have been tempted to add, but few in the old neighborhood liked to be reminded of the fact that the young Austrian outcast had once found inspiration in these quiet tree-lined streets too.

To his students and colleagues, he was Herr Doktorprofessor Stern. To friends in the neighborhood he was just Benjamin; to the occasional visitor from home, he was Binyamin. In an anonymous stone-and-glass office complex in the north of Tel Aviv, where a file of his youthful exploits still resided despite his pleas to have it burned, he would always be known as Beni, youngest of Ari Shamron's wayward sons. Officially, Benjamin Stern remained a member of the faculty at Hebrew University in Jerusalem, though for the past four years he had served as visiting professor of European studies at Munich's prestigious Ludwig-Maximilian University. It had become something of a permanent loan, which was fine with Professor Stern. In an odd twist of historical fate, life was more pleasant for a Jew these days in Germany than in Jerusalem or Tel Aviv.

The fact that his mother had survived the horrors of the Riga ghetto gave Professor Stern a certain dubious standing among the other tenants of No. 68. He was a curiosity. He was their conscience. They railed at him about the plight of the Palestinians. They gently asked him questions they dared not put to their parents and grandparents. He was their guidance counselor and trusted sage. They came to him for advice on their studies. They poured out their heart to him when they'd been dumped by a lover. They raided his fridge when they were hungry and pillaged his wallet when they were broke. Most importantly, he served as tenant spokesman in all disputes involving the dreaded Frau Ratzinger. Professor Stern was the only one in the building who did not fear her. They seemed to have a special relationship. A kinship. "It's

Stockholm Syndrome," claimed Alex, a psychology student who lived on the top floor. "Prisoner and camp guard. Master and servant." But it was more than that. The professor and the old woman seemed to speak the same language.

The previous year, when his book on the Wannsee Conference had become an international bestseller, Professor Stern had flirted with the idea of moving to a more stylish building—perhaps one with proper security and a view of the English Gardens. A place where the other tenants didn't treat his flat as if it were an annex to their own. This had incited panic among the others. One evening they came to him en masse and petitioned him to stay. Promises were made. They would not steal his food, nor would they ask for loans when there was no hope of repayment. They would be more respectful of his need for quiet. They would come to him for advice only when it was absolutely necessary. The professor acquiesced, but within a month his flat was once again the de facto common room of Adalbertstrasse 68. Secretly, he was glad they were back. The rebellious children of No. 68 were the only family Benjamin Stern had left.

The clatter of a passing streetcar broke his concentration. He looked up in time to see it disappear behind the canopy of a chestnut tree, then glanced at his watch. Eleven-thirty. He'd been at it since five that morning. He removed his glasses and spent a long moment rubbing his eyes. What was it Orwell had said about writing a book? *A horrible, exhausting struggle, like a long bout of some painful illness.* Sometimes, Benjamin Stern felt as though this book might be fatal.

The red light on his telephone answering machine was blinking. He made a habit of muting the ringers to avoid unwanted interruptions. Hesitantly, like a bomb handler deciding which wire to cut, he reached out and pressed the button. The little speaker emitted a blast of heavy metal music, followed by a warlike yelp.

"I have some good news, Herr Doktorprofessor. By the end of the day, there will be one less filthy Jew on the planet! Wiedersehen, Herr Doktorprofessor."

CLICK.

Professor Stern erased the message. He was used to them by now. He received two a week these days; sometimes more, depending on whether he had made an appearance on television or taken part in some public debate. He knew them by voice; assigned each a trivial, unthreatening nickname to lessen their impact on his nerves. This fellow called at least twice each month. Professor Stern had dubbed him *Wolfie*. Sometimes he told the police. Most of the time he didn't bother. There was nothing they could do anyway.

He locked his manuscript and notes in the floor safe tucked beneath his desk. Then he pulled on a pair of shoes and a woolen jacket and collected the rubbish bag from the kitchen. The old building had no elevator, which meant he had to walk down two flights of stairs to reach the ground floor. As he entered the lobby, a chemical stench greeted him. The building was home to a small but thriving *kosmetik*. The professor detested the beauty shop. When it was busy, the rancid smell of nail-polish remover rose through the ventilation system and enveloped his flat. It also made the building less secure than he would have preferred. Because the *kosmetik* had no separate street entrance, the lobby was constantly cluttered with beautiful Schwabinians arriving for their pedicures, facials, and waxings.

He turned right, toward a doorway that gave onto the tiny courtyard, and hesitated in the threshold, checking to see if the cats were about. Last night he'd been awakened at midnight by a skirmish over some morsel of garbage. There were no cats this morning, only a pair of bored beauticians in spotless white tunics smoking cigarettes against the wall. He padded across the sooty bricks and tossed his bag into the bin.

Returning to the entrance hall, he found Frau Ratzinger punishing the linoleum floor with a worn straw broom. "Good morning, Herr Doktorprofessor," the old woman snapped; then she added accusingly: "Going out for your morning coffee?"

Professor Stern nodded and murmured, *"Ja, ja, Frau Ratzinger."* She glared at two messy stacks of fliers, one advertising a free concert in the park, the other a holistic massage clinic on the Schellingstrasse. "No matter how many times I ask them not to leave these things here, they do it anyway. It's that drama student in 4B. He lets anyone into the building."

The professor shrugged his shoulders, as if mystified by the lawless ways of the young, and smiled kindly at the old woman. Frau Ratzinger picked up the fliers and marched them into the courtyard. A moment later, he could hear her berating the beauticians for tossing their cigarette butts on the ground.

He stepped outside and paused to take stock of the weather. Not too cold for early March, the sun peering through a gauzy layer of cloud. He pushed his hands into his coat pockets and set out. Entering the English Gardens, he followed a tree-lined path along the banks of a rain-swollen canal. He liked the park. It gave his mind a quiet place to rest after the morning's exertions on the computer. More importantly, it gave him an opportunity to see if today they were following him. He stopped walking and beat his coat pockets dramatically to indicate he had forgotten something. Then he doubled back and retraced his steps, scanning faces, checking to see if they matched any of the ones stored in the database of his prodigious memory. He paused on a humpbacked footbridge, as if admiring the rush of the water over a short fall. A drug dealer with spiders tattooed on his face offered him heroin. The professor mumbled something incoherent and walked quickly away. Two minutes later he ducked into a public telephone and pretended to place a call while carefully surveying the surroundings. He hung up the receiver.

Wiedersehen, Herr Doktorprofessor.

He turned onto the Ludwigstrasse and hurried across the university district, head down, hoping to avoid being spotted by any students or colleagues. Earlier that week, he had received a rather nasty letter from Dr. Helmut Berger, the pompous chairman of his department, wondering when the book might be finished and when he could be expected to resume his lecturing obligations. Professor Stern did not like Helmut Berger—their well-publicized feud was both personal and academic—and conveniently he had not found the time to respond.

The bustle of the Viktualienmarkt pushed thoughts of work from his mind. He moved past mounds of brightly colored fruit and vegetables, past flower stalls and open-air butchers. He picked out a few things for his supper, then crossed the street to Café Bar Eduscho for coffee and a *Dinkelbrot*. Forty-five minutes later, as he set out for Schwabing, he felt refreshed, his mind light, ready for one more wrestling match with his book. His illness, as Orwell would have called it.

As he arrived at the apartment house, a gust of wind chased him into the lobby and scattered a fresh stack of salmon-colored fliers. The professor twisted his head so he could read one. A new curry takeaway had opened around the corner. He liked a good curry. He scooped up one of the fliers and stuffed it into his coat pocket.

The wind had carried a few of the leaflets toward the courtyard.

Frau Ratzinger would be furious. As he trod softly up the stairs, she poked her head from her foxhole of a flat and spotted the mess. Predictably appalled, she glared at him with inquisitor's eyes. Slipping the key into his door lock, he could hear the old woman cursing as she dealt with this latest outrage.

In the kitchen, he put away the food and brewed himself a cup of tea. Then he walked down the hallway to his study. A man was standing at his desk, casually leafing through a stack of research. He wore a white tunic, like the ones worn by the beauticians at the *kosmetik*, and was very tall with athletic shoulders. His hair was blond and streaked with gray. Hearing the professor enter the room, the intruder looked up. His eyes were gray too, cold as a glacier.

"Open the safe, Herr Doktorprofessor."

The voice was calm, almost flirtatious. The German was accented. It wasn't Wolfie—Professor Stern was sure of that. He had a flair for languages and an ear for local dialects. The man in the tunic was Swiss, and his *Schwyzerdütsch* had the broad singsong accent of a man from the mountain valleys.

"Who in the hell do you think you are?"

"Open the safe," the intruder repeated as the eyes returned to the papers on the desk.

"There's nothing in the safe of any value. If it's money you're—"

Professor Stern wasn't permitted to finish the sentence. In a swift motion, the intruder reached beneath the tunic, produced a silenced handgun. The professor knew weapons as well as accents. The gun was a Russian-made Stechkin. The bullet tore through the professor's right kneecap. He fell to the floor, hands clutching the wound, blood pumping between his fingers.

"I suppose you'll just have to give me the combination now," the Swiss said calmly.

The pain was like nothing Benjamin Stern had ever experienced. He was panting, struggling to catch his breath, his mind a maelstrom. *The combination?* God, but he could barely remember his name.

"I'm waiting, Herr Doktorprofessor."

He forced himself to take a series of deep breaths. This supplied his brain with enough oxygen to permit him to access the combination to the safe. He recited the numbers, his jaw trembling with shock. The intruder knelt in front of the safe and deftly worked the tumbler. A moment later, the door swung open.

The intruder looked inside, then at the professor.

"You have backup disks. Where do you keep them?"

"I don't know what you're talking about."

"As it stands right now, you'll be able to walk with the use of a cane." He raised the gun. "If I shoot you in the other knee, you'll spend the rest of your life on crutches."

The professor was slipping from consciousness. His jaw was trembling. *Don't shiver, damn you! Don't give him the pleasure of seeing your fear!*

"In the refrigerator."

"The refrigerator?"

"In case"—a burst of pain shot through him—"of a fire."

The intruder raised an eyebrow. *Clever boy.* He'd brought a bag along with him, a black nylon duffel, about three feet in length. He reached inside and withdrew a cylindrical object: a can of spray paint. He removed the cap, and with a skilled hand he began to paint symbols on the wall of the study. Symbols of violence. Symbols of hate. Ludicrously, the professor found himself wondering what Frau Ratzinger would say when she saw this. In his delirium, he must have murmured something aloud, because the intruder paused for a moment to examine him with a vacant stare.

When he was finished with his graffiti, the intruder returned the spray can to his duffel, then stood over the professor. The pain from the shattered bones was making Benjamin Stern hot with fever. Blackness was closing in at the edges of his vision, so that the intruder seemed to be standing at the end of a tunnel. The professor searched the ashen eyes for some sign of lunacy, but he found nothing at all but cool intelligence. This man was no racist fanatic, he thought. He was a professional.

The intruder stooped over him. "Would you like to make a last confession, Professor Stern?"

"What are you"—he grimaced in pain—"talking about?"

"It's very simple. Do you wish to confess your sins?"

"*You're* the murderer," Benjamin Stern said deliriously.

The assassin smiled. The gun swung up again, and he fired two shots into the professor's chest. Benjamin Stern felt his body convulse but was spared further pain. He remained conscious for a few seconds, long enough to see his killer kneel down at his side and to feel the cool touch of his thumb against his damp forehead. He was mumbling something. *Latin?* Yes, the professor was certain of it.

"*Ego te absolvo a peccatis tuis, in nomine Patris et Filii et Spiritus Sancti. Amen.*"

The professor looked into his killer's eyes. "But I'm a Jew," he murmured.

"It doesn't matter," the assassin said.

Then he placed the Stechkin against the side of Benjamin Stern's head and fired one last shot.

· 2 ·

VATICAN CITY

FOUR HUNDRED MILES to the south, on a hillside in the
heart of Rome, an old man strolled through the cold shadows
of a walled garden, dressed in an ivory cassock and cloak. At seventy-two years of age, he no longer moved quickly, though he came
to the gardens each morning and made a point of walking for at
least an hour along the pine-scented footpaths. Some of his predecessors had cleared the gardens so they could meditate undisturbed.
The man in the ivory cassock liked to see people—*real* people, not
just the fawning Curial cardinals and foreign dignitaries who came
to kiss his fisherman's ring each day. A Swiss Guard always hov-
ered a few paces behind him, more for company than protection,
and he enjoyed stopping for a brief chat with the Vatican garden-
ers. He was a naturally curious man and considered himself something of a botanist. Occasionally, he borrowed a pair of pruning
shears and helped trim the roses. Once, a Swiss Guard had found

him on his hands and knees in the garden. Assuming the worst, the guard had summoned an ambulance and rushed to his side, only to find that the Supreme Pontiff of the Roman Catholic Church had decided to do a bit of weeding.

Those closest to the Holy Father could see that something was troubling him. He had lost much of the good humor and easy charm that had seemed like a breath of spring breeze after the dour final days of the Pole. Sister Teresa, the iron-willed nun from Venice who ran his papal household, had noticed a distinct loss of appetite. Even the sweet biscotti she left with his afternoon coffee went untouched lately. She often entered the papal study on the third floor of the Apostolic Palace and found him lying face-down on the floor, deep in prayer, eyes closed as though he were in agony. Karl Brunner, the head of his Swiss Guard detail, had noticed the Holy Father frequently standing at the Vatican walls, gazing across the Tiber, seemingly lost in thought. Brunner had protected the Pole for many years and had seen the toll the papacy had taken on him. It was part of the job, he counseled Sister Teresa, the crushing burden of responsibility that falls on every pope. "It is enough to make even the holiest of men lose their temper from time to time. I'm certain God will give him the strength to overcome it. The old Pietro will be back soon."

Sister Teresa was not so sure. She was among the handful of people inside the Vatican who knew how much Pietro Lucchesi had not wanted this job. When he had arrived in Rome for the funeral of John Paul II, and the conclave that would choose his successor, the elfin, soft-spoken patriarch of Venice was not considered remotely *papabile,* a man possessed with the qualities necessary to be pope. Nor did he give even the slightest indication that he was interested. The fifteen years he had spent working in the Roman Curia were the unhappiest of his career, and he had no desire to return to the back-biting village on the Tiber, even as its lord high mayor. Lucchesi had intended to cast his vote for the archbishop of Buenos Aires, whom he had befriended during a tour of Latin America, and return quietly to Venice.

But inside the conclave, things did not go as intended. As their predecessors had done time and time again over the centuries, Lucchesi and his fellow princes of the church, one hundred thirty in all, entered the Sistine Chapel in solemn procession while singing the Latin hymn *Veni Creator Spiritus.* They gathered beneath Michelangelo's *Last Judgment,* with its humbling depiction of tormented souls rising toward heaven to face the wrath of Christ, and prayed for the Holy Spirit to guide their hand. Then each cardinal stepped forward individually, placed his hand atop the Holy Gospels, and swore an oath binding him to irrevocable silence. When this task was complete, the master of papal liturgical ceremonies commanded, *"Extra Omnes"*—Everyone out—and the conclave began in earnest.

The Pole had not been content to leave matters solely in the hands of the Holy Spirit. He had stacked the College of Cardinals with prelates like himself, doctrinaire hardliners determined to preserve ecclesiastical discipline and the power of Rome over all else. Their candidate was an Italian, a consummate creature of the Roman Curia: Cardinal Secretary of State Marco Brindisi.

The moderates had other ideas. They pleaded for a truly pastoral papacy. They wanted the occupant of the throne of St. Peter to be a gentle and pious man; a man who would be willing to share power with the bishops and limit the influence of the Curia; a man who could reach across the lines of geography and faith to heal those corners of the globe torn by war and poverty. Only a non-European was suitable to the moderates. They believed the time had come for a Third World pope.

The first ballots revealed the conclave to be hopelessly divided, and soon both factions were searching for a way out of the impasse. On the final ballot of the day, a new name surfaced. Pietro Lucchesi, the patriarch of Venice, received five votes. Hearing his name read five times inside the sacred chamber of the Sistine Chapel, Lucchesi closed his eyes and blanched visibly. A moment later, when the ballots were placed into the *nero* for burning, several cardinals noticed that Lucchesi was praying.

That evening, Pietro Lucchesi politely refused an invitation to dine with a group of fellow cardinals, adjourning to his room at the Dormitory of St. Martha instead to meditate and pray. He knew how conclaves worked and could see what was coming. Like Christ in the Garden of Gethsemane, he pleaded with God to lift this burden from his shoulders—to choose someone else.

But the following morning, Lucchesi's support built, rising steadily toward the two-thirds majority necessary to be elected pope. On the final ballot taken before lunch, he was just ten votes short. Too anxious to take food, he prayed in his room before returning to the Sistine Chapel for the ballot that he knew would make him pope. He watched silently as each cardinal advanced and placed a twice-folded slip of paper into the golden chalice that served as a ballot box, each uttering the same solemn oath: "I call as my witness Christ the Lord, who will be my judge that my vote is given to the one whom before God I think should be elected."

The ballots were checked and rechecked before the tally was announced. One hundred fifteen votes had been cast for Lucchesi. The *camerlengo* approached Lucchesi and posed the same question that had been put to hundreds of newly elected popes over two millennia. "Do you accept your canonical election as Supreme Pontiff?" After a lengthy silence that produced much tension in the chapel, Pietro Lucchesi responded: "My shoulders are not broad enough to bear the burden you have given me, but with the help of Christ the Savior, I will try. *Accepto.*"

"By what name do you wish to be called?"

"Paul the Seventh," Lucchesi replied.

The cardinals filed forward to embrace the new pontiff and offer obedience and loyalty to him. Lucchesi was then escorted to the scarlet chamber known as the *camera lacrimatoria*—the crying room—for a few minutes of solitude before being fitted with a white cassock by the Gammarelli brothers, the pontifical tailors. He chose the smallest of the three ready-made cassocks, and even then he seemed like a small boy wearing his father's shirt. As he filed onto the great loggia of St. Peter's to greet Rome and the world, his head was barely visible above the balustrade. A Swiss Guard brought forth a footstool, and a great roar rose from the stunned crowd in the square below. A commentator for Italian television breathlessly declared the new pope "Pietro the Improbable." Cardinal Marco Brindisi, the head of the hard-line Curial cardinals, privately christened him Pope Accidental I.

The *Vaticanisti* said the message of the divisive conclave was clear. Pietro Lucchesi was a compromise pope. His mandate was to run the Church in a competent fashion but launch no grand initiatives. The battle for the heart and soul of the Church, said the *Vaticanisti,* had effectively been postponed for another day.

But Catholic reactionaries, religious and lay alike, did not take such a benign view of Lucchesi's election. To militants, the new pope bore an uncomfortable resemblance to a tubby Venetian named Roncalli who'd inflicted the doctrinal calamity of the Second Vatican Council. Within hours of the conclave's conclusion, the websites and cyber-confessionals of the hardliners were bristling with warnings and dire predictions about what lay ahead. Lucchesi's sermons and public statements were scoured for evidence of unorthodoxy. The reactionaries did not like what they discovered. Lucchesi was trouble, they concluded. Lucchesi would have to be kept under watch. Tightly scripted. It would be up to the mandarins of the Curia to make certain Pietro Lucchesi became nothing more than a caretaker pope.

But Lucchesi believed there were far too many problems confronting the Church for a papacy to be wasted, even the papacy of an unwilling pope. The Church he inherited from the Pole was a Church in crisis. In Western Europe, the epicenter of Catholicism, the situation had grown so dire that a recent synod of bishops declared that Europeans were living as though God did not exist. Fewer babies were being baptized; fewer couples were choosing to be married in the Church; vocations had plummeted to a point where nearly half the parishes in Western Europe would soon have no full-time priest. Lucchesi had to look no further than his own diocese to see the problems the Church faced. Seventy percent of Rome's two and a half million Catholics believed in divorce, birth control, and premarital sex—all officially forbidden by the Church. Fewer than ten percent bothered to attend mass on a regular basis. In France, the so-called "First Daughter" of the Church, the statistics were even worse. In North America, most Catholics didn't even bother to read his encyclicals before flouting them, and only a third attended Mass. Seventy percent of Catholics lived in the Third World, yet most of them rarely saw a priest. In Brazil alone, six hundred thousand people left the Church each year to become evangelical Protestants.

Lucchesi wanted to stem the bleeding before it was too late. He longed to make his beloved Church more relevant in the lives of its adherents, to make his flock Catholic in more than name only. But there was something else that had preoccupied him, a single question that had run ceaselessly around his head since the moment the conclave elected him pope. *Why?* Why had the Holy Spirit chosen him to lead the Church? What special gift, what sliver of knowledge, did he possess that made him the right pontiff for this moment in history? Lucchesi believed he knew the answer, and he had set in motion a perilous stratagem that would shake the Roman Catholic Church to its foundations. If his gambit proved successful, it would revolutionize the Church. If it failed, it might very well destroy it.

THE SUN SLIPPED behind a bank of cloud, and a breath of cold March wind stirred the pine trees of the gardens. The Pope pulled his cloak tightly around his throat. He drifted past the Ethiopian College, then turned onto a narrow footpath that took him toward the dun-colored wall at the southwest corner of Vatican City. Stopping at the foot of the Vatican Radio tower, he mounted a flight of stone steps and climbed up to the parapet.

Rome lay before him, stirring in the flat overcast light. His gaze was drawn across the Tiber, toward the soaring synagogue in the heart of the old ghetto. In 1555, Pope Paul IV, a Pope whose name Lucchesi bore, ordered the Jews of Rome into the ghetto and compelled them to wear a yellow star to make them distinguishable from Christians. It was the intention of those who commissioned the synagogue to build it tall enough so that it could be seen from the Vatican. The message was unmistakably clear. *We are here too. Indeed, we were here long before you.* For Pietro Lucchesi, the synagogue spoke of something else. A treacherous past. A shameful secret. It spoke directly to him, whispering into his ear. It would give him no peace.

The Pope heard footfalls on the garden pathway, sharp and rhythmic, like an expert carpenter driving nails. He turned and saw a man marching toward the wall. Tall and lean, black hair, black clerical suit, a vertical line drawn with India ink. Father Luigi Donati: the Pope's private secretary. Donati had been at Lucchesi's side for twenty years. In Venice they had called him *il doge* because of his willingness to wield power ruthlessly and to go straight for the throat when it served his purposes or the needs of his master. The nickname had followed him to the Vatican. Donati did not mind. He followed the tenets of a secular Italian philosopher named Machiavelli, who counseled that it is better for a prince to be feared than loved. Every pope needed a son of a bitch, according to Donati; a hard man in black who was willing to take on the Curia with a whip and a chair and bend it to his will. It was a role he played with poorly disguised glee.

As Donati drew closer to the parapet, the Pope could see by the grim set of his jaw that something was wrong. He turned his gaze toward the river once more and waited. A moment later he could feel the reassuring presence of Donati at his side. As usual, *il doge* wasted no time on pleasantries or small talk. He leaned close to the Pope's ear and quietly informed him that earlier that morning Professor Benjamin Stern had been discovered murdered in his apartment in Munich. The Pope closed his eyes and lowered his chin to his chest, then reached out and held Father Donati's hand tightly. "How?" he asked. "How did they kill him?"

When Father Donati told him, the Pope swayed and leaned

against the priest's arm for support. "Almighty God in Heaven, please grant us forgiveness for what we have done." Then he looked into the eyes of his trusted secretary. Father Donati's gaze was calm and intelligent and very determined. It gave the Pope the courage to go forward.

"I'm afraid we've terribly underestimated our enemies, Luigi. They are more formidable than we thought, and their wickedness knows no bounds. They will stop at nothing to protect their dirty secrets."

"Indeed, Holiness," Donati said gravely. "In fact, we must now operate under the assumption that they might even be willing to murder a pope."

Murder a pope? It was difficult for Pietro Lucchesi to imagine such a thing, but he knew his trusted secretary was not guilty of exaggeration. The Church was riddled with a cancer. It had been allowed to fester during the long reign of the Pole. Now it had metastasized and was threatening the life of the very organism in which it lived. It needed to be removed. Aggressive measures were required if the patient was to be saved.

The Pope looked away from Donati, toward the dome of the synagogue rising over the riverbank. "I'm afraid there's no one who can do this deed but me."

Father Donati placed his hand on the Pope's forearm and squeezed. "Only you can compose the words, Holiness. Leave the rest in my hands."

Donati turned and walked away, leaving the Pope alone at the parapet. He listened to the sound of his hard man in black pounding along the footpath toward the palace: *crack-crack-crack-crack* . . . To Pietro Lucchesi, it sounded like nails in a coffin.

✦ 3 ✦

VENICE

THE NIGHT RAINS had flooded the Campo San Zaccaria. The restorer stood on the steps of the church like a castaway. In the center of the square, an old priest appeared out of the mist, lifting the skirts of his simple black cassock to reveal a pair of knee-length rubber boots. "It's like the Sea of Galilee this morning, Mario," he said, digging a heavy ring of keys from his pocket. "If only Christ had bestowed on us the ability to walk on water. Winters in Venice would be much more tolerable."

The heavy wooden door opened with a deep groan. The nave was still in darkness. The priest switched on the lights and headed out into the flooded square once more, pausing briefly in the sanctuary to dip his fingers in holy water and make the sign of the cross.

The scaffolding was covered by a shroud. The restorer climbed up to his platform and switched on a fluorescent lamp. The Virgin glowed at him seductively. For much of that winter he had been engaged in a single-minded quest to repair her face. Some nights she came to him in his sleep, stealing into his bedroom, her cheeks in tatters, begging him to heal her.

He turned on a portable electric heater to burn the chill from the air and poured a cup of black coffee from the Thermos bottle, enough to make him alert but not to make his hand shake. Then he prepared his palette, mixing dry pigment in a tiny puddle of medium. When finally he was ready, he lowered his magnifying visor and began to work.

For nearly an hour he had the church to himself. Slowly, the rest of the team trickled in one by one. The restorer, hidden behind his shroud, knew each by sound. The lumbering plod of Francesco Tiepolo, chief of the San Zaccaria project; the crisp *tap-tap-tap* of Adriana Zinetti, renowned cleaner of altars and seducer of men; the conspiratorial shuffle of the ham-fisted Antonio Politi, spreader of malicious lies and gossip.

The restorer was something of an enigma to the rest of the San Zaccaria team. He insisted on keeping his work platform and the altarpiece shrouded at all times. Francesco Tiepolo had pleaded with him to lower the shroud so the tourists and the notoriously bitchy Venetian upper crust could watch him work. "Venice wants to see what you're doing to the Bellini, Mario. Venice doesn't like surprises." Reluctantly, the restorer had relented, and for two days in January he worked in full view of the tourists and the rest of the Zaccaria team. The brief experiment ended when Monsignor Moretti, San Zaccaria's parish priest, popped into the church for a surprise inspection. When he gazed up at the Bellini and saw half the Virgin's face gone, he fell to his knees in hysterical prayer. The shroud returned, and Francesco Tiepolo never dared to raise the issue of removing it again.

The rest of the team found great metaphorical significance in the shroud. Why would a man go to such lengths to conceal himself? Why did he insist on setting himself apart from the others? Why did he decline their numerous invitations to lunch, their invitations to dinner and to the Saturday-night drinking sessions at Harry's Bar? He had even refused to attend the cocktail reception at the Accademia thrown by the Friends of San Zaccaria. The Bellini was one of the most important paintings in all Venice, and it was considered scandalous that he refused to spend a few minutes with the fat American donors who had made the restoration possible.

Even Adriana Zinetti could not penetrate the shroud. This gave rise to rampant speculation that the restorer was a homosexual, which was considered no crime among the free spirits of Team Zaccaria and temporarily increased his sagging popularity among some of the boys. The theory was put to rest one evening when he was met at the church by a stunningly attractive woman. She had wide cheekbones, pale skin, green catlike eyes, and a teardrop chin. It was Adriana Zinetti who noticed the heavy scarring on her left hand. "She's his other project," Adriana speculated gloomily as the pair disappeared into the Venetian night. "Obviously, he prefers his women damaged."

He called himself Mario Delvecchio, but his Italian, while fluent, was tinged by a faint but unmistakable accent. He explained this away by saying he had been raised abroad and had lived in Italy only for brief periods. Someone heard he had served his apprenticeship with the legendary Umberto Conti. Someone else heard that Conti had proclaimed his hands the most gifted he had ever seen.

The envious Antonio Politi was responsible for the next wave of rumors that rippled through Team Zaccaria. Antonio found the leisurely pace of his colleague infuriating. In less time than it had taken the great Mario Delvecchio to retouch the virgin's face, Antonio had cleaned and restored a half-dozen paintings. The fact that they all were of little or no significance only increased his anger. "The master himself painted her in an afternoon," Antonio protested to Tiepolo. "But this man has taken all winter. Always running off to the Accademia to gaze at the Bellinis. Tell him to get on with it! Otherwise, we're going to be here ten years!"

It was Antonio who unearthed the rather bizarre story about Vienna, which he shared with the rest of Team Zaccaria during a family dinner one snowy evening in February—coincidentally, at Trattoria alla Madonna. About ten years earlier, there had been a major cleaning and restoration project at St. Stephan's Cathedral in Vienna. An Italian called Mario was part of that team.

"Our Mario?" Adriana wondered over a glass of *ripasso*.

"Of course it was our Mario. Same snobbery. Same snail's pace."

According to Antonio's source, the restorer in question had vanished without a trace one night—the same night a car bomb exploded in the old Jewish quarter.

"And what do you make of this, Antonio?" Again, it was Adriana, peering at him through the ruby *ripasso*. Antonio paused for dramatic effect, spearing a piece of grilled polenta and holding it aloft like a scepter. "Isn't it obvious? Clearly, the man is a terrorist. I'd say he's *Brigate Rossa*."

"Or maybe he's Osama bin Laden himself!"

Team Zaccaria erupted into such laughter that they were nearly asked to leave the restaurant. The theories of Antonio Politi were never again given any credence, although he never lost faith in them himself. Secretly, he hoped the quiet restorer behind the shroud would repeat his performance of Vienna and vanish without a trace. Then Antonio would step in and finish the Bellini, and his reputation would be made.

The restorer worked well that morning, and the time slipped rapidly away. Glancing at his wristwatch, he was surprised to see that it was already eleven-thirty. He sat down on the edge of the platform, poured more coffee, and looked up at the altarpiece. Painted by Bellini at the height of his powers, it was widely regarded by historians as the first great altarpiece of the sixteenth century. The restorer never tired of looking at it. He marveled at Bellini's skillful use of light and space, the powerful pulling effect that drew his eye inward and upward, the sculptural nobility of the Madonna and child and the saints surrounding them. It was a painting of utter silence. Even after a long, tedious morning of work, the painting blanketed him with a sense of peace.

He pulled aside the shroud. The sun was out, the nave was filled with light streaming through the stained-glass windows. As he finished the last of his coffee, his attention was drawn by a movement at the entrance of the church. It was a boy, about ten years old, with long curly hair. His shoes were soaked from the water in the square. The restorer watched him intently. Even after ten years, he could not look at a young boy without thinking of his son.

The boy went first to Antonio, who waved him on without looking up from his work. Next he made his way up the long center aisle to the high altar, where he received a more friendly reception from Adriana. She smiled at him, touched the side of his face, then pointed in the direction of the restorer's scaffold. The child stopped at the foot of the platform and wordlessly passed the restorer a slip of paper. He unfolded it and found a few words, scrawled like the last plea of a desperate lover. The note was unsigned, but the hand was as plain as the brushstrokes of Bellini.

Ghetto Nuovo. Six o'clock.

The restorer crushed the paper and slipped it into his pocket. When he looked down again the child was gone.

AT FIVE-THIRTY, Francesco Tiepolo entered the church and lumbered slowly across the nave. With his tangled beard, flowing white shirt, and silk scarf knotted at his throat, the immense Italian looked as though he had just stepped from a Renaissance work-shop. It was a look he carefully cultivated.

"All right, everyone," he sang, his voice echoing among the apses and the columns. "That's all for today. Pack up your things. Doors close in five minutes." He seized the restorer's work platform in his bear-like paw and shook it once violently, rattling his lights and brushes. "You too, Mario. Give your lady a kiss goodnight. She'll be all right without you for a few hours. She's managed for five hun-dred years."

The restorer methodically wiped off his brushes and palette and packed his pigments and solvents into a rectangular case of var-nished wood. Then he switched off the lamp and hopped down from the scaffolding. As always, he left the church without saying a word to the others.

With his case beneath his arm, he struck out across the Campo San Zaccaria. He had a smooth gait that seemed to propel him ef-fortlessly across the square, though his unimpressive height and lean physique made him easy to miss. The black hair was cropped short and shot with gray. The angular face, with its deeply cleft chin and full lips, gave the impression of having been carved from wood. The most lasting impression of the face was the eyes, which were almond-shaped and a shocking shade of emerald green. Despite the demanding nature of his work—and the fact that he had recently celebrated his fifty-first birthday—his vision remained perfect.

Passing through an archway, he came to the Riva della Schiavoni, the broad quay overlooking the Canale di San Marco. In spite of the chill March weather, there were many tourists about. The restorer could make out a half-dozen different languages, most of which he could speak. A phrase of Hebrew reached his ears. It diminished quickly, like music on the wind, but left the restorer with an unyielding ache to hear the sound of his real name.

A No. 82 *vaporetto* was waiting at the stop. He boarded and found a place along the railing from which he could see the face of every passenger getting on and off. He dug the note from his pocket and read it one last time. Then he dropped it over the side of the boat and watched it drift away on the silken waters of the lagoon.

IN THE fifteenth century, a swampy parcel of land in the *sestieri* of Cannaregio was set aside for the construction of a new brass foundry, known in the Venetian dialect as a *geto*. The foundry was never built, and a century later, when the rulers of Venice were looking for a suitable spot to confine the city's swelling population of unwanted Jews, the remote parcel known as Ghetto Nuovo was deemed the ideal place. The *campo* was large and had no parish church. The surrounding canals formed a natural moat, which cut off the island from the neighboring communities, and the single bridge could be guarded by Christian watchmen. In 1516, the Christians of Ghetto Nuovo were evicted and the Jews of Venice were forced to take their place. They could leave the ghetto only after sunrise, when the bell tolled in the campanile, and only if they wore a yellow tunic and hat. At nightfall they were required to return to the island, and the gates were chained. Only Jewish doctors could leave the ghetto at night. At its height, the population of the ghetto was more than five thousand. Now, it was home to only twenty Jews.

The restorer crossed a metal footbridge. A ring of apartment buildings, unusually tall for Venice, loomed before him. He entered a *sottoportego* and followed it beneath the apartment houses, emerging a moment later into a square, the Campo di Ghetto Nuovo. A kosher restaurant, a Jewish bakery, a bookstore, a museum. There were two old synagogues as well, virtually invisible except to a trained eye. Only the five windows on the second story of each—the symbol for the five books of the Pentateuch—gave away their locations.

A half-dozen boys were playing football between the long shadows and the puddles. A ball bounced toward the restorer. He gave it a deft kick with the instep of his right foot and sent it expertly back toward the game. One of the boys took it squarely in the chest. It was the one who had come to San Zaccaria that morning.

The child nodded in the direction of the *pozzo,* the wellhead in the center of the square. The restorer turned and saw a familiar figure leaning there, smoking a cigarette. Gray cashmere overcoat, gray scarf wound tightly around his neck, a bullet-shaped head. The skin of his face was deeply tanned and full of cracks and fissures, like desert rock scored by a million years of sun and wind. The spectacles were small and round and inadvertently fashionable. The expression was one of perpetual impatience.

As the restorer approached, the old man lifted his head, and his lips curled into something between a smile and a grimace. He seized the restorer by the arm and inflicted a bone-crushing handshake. Then, tenderly, he kissed his cheek.

"You're here because of Benjamin, aren't you?"

The old man closed his crumpled eyelids and nodded. Then he hooked two stubby fingers inside the restorer's elbow and said, "Walk with me." For an instant the restorer resisted the pull, but there was no escaping it. There had been a death in the family, and Ari Shamron was never one for sitting *shivah*.

IT HAD BEEN a year since Gabriel had seen him last. Shamron had grown visibly older since that day. As they set off round the *campo* in the gathering darkness, Gabriel had to resist the urge to take him by the arm. His cheeks had hollowed, and the steel-blue eyes—eyes that had once struck fear into his enemies and his allies alike—were clouded and wet. When he raised his Turkish cigarette to his lips, his right hand trembled.

Those hands had made Shamron a legend. Shortly after he joined the Office in the 1950s, Shamron's superiors noticed that he possessed an unusually strong grip for a man with such an ordinary physique. He was trained in the art of street snatches and silent killing and sent into the field. He preferred the garrote and used it with deadly efficiency from the cobbled streets of Europe to the filthy alleyways of Cairo and Damascus. He killed Arab spies and generals. He killed the Nazi scientists who were helping Nasser build rockets. And on a warm night in April 1960, in a town north of Buenos Aires, Ari Shamron leapt from the back of a car and seized Adolf Eichmann by the throat as he was waiting for a bus to take him home.

Gabriel was the only person who knew one other salient fact about that night in Argentina: Adolf Eichmann had nearly escaped because Shamron had tripped over a loose shoelace. That same edge-of-disaster quality would mark his many stopovers in the executive suite at King Saul Boulevard. Prime ministers never knew quite what to expect when Shamron appeared outside their door—word of another shocking success or a secret confession of another humiliating failure. His willingness to take risks was both a potent operational strength and a crippling political weakness. Gabriel had lost count of how many times the old man had been cast into exile, then recalled to colors with great fanfare.

Shamron's hold on the executive suite had finally been broken, though his exile would never be permanent. He retained the dubious title of special administrative advisor, which gave him just enough entrée to make a general nuisance of himself, and from his fortresslike villa overlooking the Sea of Galilee he still exercised considerable clandestine power. Spies and generals regularly went there to kiss his ring, and no major decision regarding the security of the state could be taken without first running it past the old man.

His health was a carefully guarded secret. Gabriel had heard rumors about prostate cancer, a mild heart attack, recurring problems with his kidneys. It was clear the old man didn't have long to live. Shamron did not fear death—only that in his absence would spring complacency. And now, as they ambled slowly around the old ghetto, death walked beside them. Benjamin's death. And Shamron's. The nearness of death had made Shamron restless. He seemed like a man anxious to settle accounts. An old warrior, desperate for one last fight.

✦ ✦ ✦

"DID YOU GO to the funeral?"

Shamron shook his head. "Benjamin feared his academic achievements would be tainted if it ever became known he'd worked for us. My presence at the burial would only have raised uncomfortable questions, in Israel and abroad, so I stayed away. I have to admit I wasn't anxious to attend. It's difficult to bury a child."

"Was anyone there? He had no other family in Israel."

"I'm told there were some old friends from the overt world and a few members of the faculty from Hebrew."

"Who sent you here?"

"What does it matter?"

"It matters to me. Who sent you?"

"I'm like a parolee," Shamron said wearily. "I cannot move or act without the approval of the supreme tribunal."

"And who sits on this tribunal?"

"Lev, for one. Of course, if it were up to Lev, I'd be locked in a room with an iron cot and bread and water. But fortunately for me, the other person on the tribunal is the prime minister."

"Your old comrade in arms."

"Let's just say we share similar opinions about the nature of the conflict and the true intentions of our enemies. We speak the same language and enjoy each other's company. He keeps me in the game, despite Lev's best efforts to wrap me in my burial shroud."

"It's not a game, Ari. It never was a game."

"You don't need to remind me of that, Gabriel. You spend your time here in the playgrounds of Europe while every day the *shaheeds* are blowing themselves to bits on Ben Yehuda Street and Jaffa Road."

"I work here."

"Forgive me, Gabriel. I didn't mean that to be as harsh as it sounded. What are you working on, by the way?"

"Do you really care?"

"Of course I do. I wouldn't have asked otherwise."

"The Bellini altarpiece in the Church of the San Zaccaria. It's one of the most important paintings in Venice."

Shamron's face broke into a genuine smile. "I would love to see the look on the patriarch's face if he ever found out that his precious altarpiece was being restored by a nice Jewish boy from the Jezreel Valley."

Without warning, he stopped walking and coughed violently into a handkerchief. When he drew a few deep breaths to steady himself, Gabriel could hear a rattle in his chest. The old man needed to get out of the cold, but he was too stubborn ever to admit physical weakness. Gabriel decided to do it for him.

"Do you mind if we sit down someplace? I've been standing on my scaffolding since eight o'clock this morning."

Shamron managed a weary smile. He knew he was being deceived. He led Gabriel to a bakery on the edge of the *campo*. It was empty except for a tall girl behind the counter. She served them without taking their order: cups of espresso, small bottles of mineral water, a plate of rugelach with cinnamon and nuts. As she leaned over the table, a mane of dark hair fell across the front of one shoulder. Her long hands smelled of vanilla. She covered herself in a bronze-colored wrap and went into the *campo,* leaving Gabriel and Shamron alone in the shop.

Gabriel said, "I'm listening."

"That's an improvement. Usually, you start off by yelling at me about how I've *ruined* your life."

"I'm sure we'll get to that at some point."

"You and my daughter should compare notes."

"We have. How is she?"

"Still living in New Zealand—on a *chicken* farm if you can believe that—and still refusing to take my telephone calls." He took a long time lighting his next cigarette. "She resents me terribly. Says I was never there for her. What she doesn't understand is that I was busy. I had a people to protect."

"It won't last forever."

"In case you haven't noticed, neither will I." Shamron took a bite of rugelach and chewed it slowly. "How's Anna?"

"I suppose she's fine. I haven't spoken to her in nearly two months."

Shamron lowered his chin and peered disapprovingly at Gabriel over his spectacles. "Please tell me you didn't break that poor woman's heart."

Gabriel stirred sugar into his coffee and looked away from Shamron's steady stare. *Anna Rolfe . . .* She was a world-renowned concert violinist and the daughter of a wealthy Swiss banker named Augustus Rolfe. A year earlier, Gabriel had helped her track down the men who had murdered her father. Along the way he had also forced her to confront the unpleasant circumstances about her father's wartime past and the source of his remarkable collection of Impressionist and Modern paintings. He had also fallen in love with the tempestuous virtuoso. After the operation, he'd lived for six months at her secluded villa on the Sintra coast of Portugal. Their relationship began to crumble when Gabriel confessed to her that each time they strolled the streets of the village it was the shadow of his wife Leah he saw at his shoulder—and that some nights, while they made love, Leah stood in their bedroom, a silent spectator to their contentment. When Francesco Tiepolo offered him the San

Zaccaria altarpiece, Gabriel accepted without hesitation. Anna Rolfe did not stand in his way.

"I'm very fond of her, but it would never have worked."

"Did she spend any time with you here in Venice?"

"She performed at a benefit at the Frari. She stayed with me for two days. I'm afraid it only made things worse."

Shamron slowly crushed out his cigarette. "I suppose I'm partly to blame. I pushed you into it before you were ready."

As he always did on occasions such as these, Shamron asked if Gabriel had been to see Leah. Gabriel heard himself say that he had gone to the secluded psychiatric clinic in the south of England before coming to Venice; that he had spent an afternoon with her, pushing her about the grounds; that they had even had a picnic lunch beneath the bare limbs of a maple. But while he spoke, his mind was elsewhere: the tiny street in Vienna not far from the Judenplatz; the car bomb that killed his son; the inferno that destroyed Leah's body and stole her memory.

"It's been twelve years and she still doesn't recognize me. To be honest with you, sometimes I don't recognize her." Gabriel paused, then said, "But you didn't come here to discuss my personal life."

"No, I didn't," Shamron said. "But your personal life is relevant. You see, if you were still involved with Anna Rolfe, I couldn't ask you to come back to work for me—at least, not in good conscience."

"When have you ever let your conscience get in the way of something you wanted?"

"Now there's the old Gabriel that I know and love." Shamron flashed an iron smile. "How much do you know about the murder of Benjamin?"

"Only what I read in the *Herald Tribune*. The Munich police say he was killed by neo-Nazis."

Shamron snorted. Clearly, he did not agree with the findings of the Munich police, no matter how preliminary. "I suppose it's possible. Benjamin's writings on the Holocaust made him extremely unpopular among many segments of German society, and the fact that he was an Israeli made him a target. But I'm not convinced that some skinhead managed to kill him. You see, whenever Jews die on German soil, it makes me uneasy. I want to know more than what the Munich police are telling us on an official basis."

"Why don't you send a *katsa* to Munich to investigate?"

"Because if one of our field officers starts asking questions, people are going to get suspicious. Besides, you know that I always prefer the back door to the front."

"What do you have in mind?"

"In two days, the Munich detective in charge of the case is going to meet with Benjamin's half-brother, Ehud Landau. After briefing Landau on the investigation, he will allow him to take inventory of Benjamin's possessions and arrange a shipment back to Israel."

"If memory serves, Benjamin doesn't have a half-brother."

"He does now." Shamron placed an Israeli passport on the table and slid it toward Gabriel with the palm of his hand. Gabriel opened the cover and saw his own face staring back at him. Then he looked at the name: EHUD LANDAU.

Shamron said, "You have the best eyes I've ever seen. Have a look around his apartment. See if there's something out of place. If you can, remove anything that might tie him to the Office."

Gabriel closed the passport, but left it lying on the table.

"I'm in the middle of a difficult restoration. I can't go running off to Munich now."

"It will take a day—two at the most."

"That's what you said last time."

Shamron's temper, always seething below the surface, broke through. He pounded his fist on the table and shouted at Gabriel in Hebrew: "Do you wish to fix your silly painting or help me find out who killed your friend?"

"It's always that simple for you, isn't it?"

"Oh, but I wish it were so. Do you intend to help me, or will you force me to turn to one of Lev's oafs for this delicate mission?"

Gabriel made a show of contemplation, but his mind was already made up. He scooped up the passport with a smooth movement of his hand and slipped it into his coat pocket. Gabriel had the hands of a conjurer and a magician's sense of misdirection. The passport was there; the passport was gone. Next, Shamron reached into his coat pocket and withdrew a mid-sized manila envelope. Inside, Gabriel found an airline ticket and an expensive Swiss-made wallet of black leather. He opened the wallet: Israeli driver's license, credit cards, membership to an exclusive Tel Aviv health club, a checkout card for a local video store, a substantial amount of currency in euros and shekels.

"What do I do for a living?"

"You own an art gallery. Your business cards are in the zippered compartment."

Gabriel found the cards and removed one:

LANDAU ART GALLERY

SHEINKIN STREET, TEL AVIV

"Does it exist?"

"It does now."

The last item in the envelope was a gold wristwatch with a black leather band. Gabriel turned over the watch and read the engraving on the back. *FOR EHUD FROM HANNAH WITH LOVE.*

"Nice touch," Gabriel said.

"I've always found it's the little things."

The watch, the airline tickets, and the wallet joined the passport in Gabriel's pocket. The two men stood. As they walked outside, the long-haired girl in the bronze-colored wrap came quickly to Shamron's side. Gabriel realized she was the old man's bodyguard.

"Where are you going?"

"Back to Tiberias," Shamron replied. "If you pick up something interesting, send it to King Saul Boulevard through the usual channels."

"Whose eyes?"

"Mine, but that doesn't mean little Lev won't have a peek, so use appropriate discretion."

In the distance, a church bell tolled. Shamron stopped in the center of the campo, next to the *pozzo,* and took one last look around. "Our first ghetto. God, how I do hate this place."

"It's too bad you weren't in Venice in the sixteenth century," Gabriel said. "The Council of Ten would never have dared to lock the Jews away here."

"But I *was* here," Shamron said with conviction. "I was always here. And I remember it all."

·4·

MUNICH

DETECTIVE AXEL WEISS of the Munich *Kriminal Polizei* was waiting outside Adalbertstrasse 68 two days later, dressed in civilian clothes and a tan raincoat. He shook Gabriel's hand carefully, as though he were feeling its density. A tall man with a narrow face and a long nose, Weiss's dark complexion and short-cropped black hair gave him the appearance of a Doberman pinscher. He released Gabriel's hand and patted him fraternally on the shoulder.

"It's a pleasure to meet you, Herr Landau, though I'm sorry it has to be under these circumstances. Let me take you somewhere comfortable to talk before we go up to the apartment."

They set off down the rain-soaked pavement. It was late afternoon, and the lights of Schwabing were slowly coming up. Gabriel never liked German cities at night. The detective stopped in front of a coffeehouse and peered through a fogged window. Wood floors, round tables, students and intellectuals hunched over books. "This will do," he said. Then he opened the door and led Gabriel to a quiet table in the back.

"Your people at the consulate tell me you own an art gallery."

"Yes, that's right."

"In Tel Aviv?"

"You know Tel Aviv?"

The detective shook his head. "It must be very hard for you now—with the war and all."

"We make do. But then, we always have."

A waitress appeared. Detective Weiss ordered two coffees.

"Something to eat, Herr Landau?"

Gabriel shook his head. When the waitress was gone, Weiss said, "Do you have a card?"

He managed to pose the question in an offhand way, but Gabriel could tell his cover story was being probed. His work had left him incapable of seeing things as they appeared to be. When he viewed paintings, he saw not only the surface but the underdrawings and layers of base paint. The same was true of the people he met in his work for Shamron and the situations he found himself. He had the distinct impression Axel Weiss was more than just a detective for the Munich *Kriminal Polizei*. Indeed, Gabriel could feel Weiss's eyes boring into him as he reached into his wallet and produced the business card Shamron had given him in Venice. The detective held it up to the light, as if looking for the marks of a counterfeiter.

"May I keep this?"

"Sure." Gabriel held open his wallet. "Do you need any other identification?"

The detective seemed to find this question offensive and made a grandiose German gesture of dismissal. "*Ach,* no! Of course not. I'm just interested in art, that's all."

Gabriel resisted the temptation to see how little the German policeman knew about art.

"You've spoken to your people?"

Gabriel nodded solemnly. Earlier that afternoon, he had paid a visit to the Israeli consulate for a largely ceremonial briefing. The consular officer had given him a file containing copies of the police reports and clippings from the Munich press. The file was now resting in Ehud Landau's expensive leather briefcase.

"The consular officer was very helpful," Gabriel said. "But if you don't mind, Detective Weiss, I'd like to hear about Benjamin's murder from you."

"Of course," the German said.

He spent the next twenty minutes giving Gabriel a thorough account of the circumstances surrounding the killing. Time of death, cause of death, caliber of weapon, the well-documented threats against Benjamin's life, the graffiti left on the walls of his flat. He spoke in the calm but forthright manner that police the world over seem to reserve for the relatives of the slain. Gabriel's demeanor mirrored that of the German detective. He did not feign grief. He did not pretend that the gruesome details of his half-brother's death caused him pain. He was an Israeli. He saw death nearly on a daily basis. The time for mourning had ended. Now was the time for answers and clearheaded thinking.

"Why was he shot in the knee, Detective?"

Weiss pulled his lips down and tilted his narrow head. "We're not sure. There may have been a struggle. Or they may have wanted to torture him."

"But you told me that none of the other tenants heard any sound. Surely, if he was tortured, the sound of his screaming would have been audible in other parts of the building."

"As I said, Herr Landau, we're not sure."

Weiss was clearly frustrated by the line of questioning, but Herr Landau, art dealer from Tel Aviv, was not quite finished.

"Is a wound to the knee consistent with other murders carried out by right-wing extremists?"

"I can't say that it is."

"Do you have any suspects?"

"We're questioning a number of different people in connection with the murder. I'm afraid that's all I can say at the moment."

"Have you explored the possibility that his death was somehow linked to his teaching at the university? A disgruntled student, for example?"

The detective managed a smile, but it was clear his patience was being put to the test. "Your brother was much beloved. His students worshipped him. He was also on sabbatical this term." The detective paused and studied Gabriel a moment. "You *were* aware of that, weren't you, Herr Landau?"

Gabriel decided it was best not to lie. "No, I'm afraid I wasn't. We haven't spoken in some time. Why was he on sabbatical?"

"The chairman of his department told us he was working on a new book." The detective swallowed the last of his coffee. "Shall we have a look at the apartment now?"

"I just have one more question."

"What's that, Herr Landau?"

"How did the killer get into his building?"

"That's one I can answer," Weiss said. "Despite the fact that your brother received regular death threats, he lived in a very inse-

41

cure building. The tenants are very casual about who they let in. If someone presses the intercom and says 'advertisements,' they're routinely buzzed in. A student who lives one floor above Professor Stern is fairly certain she was the one who let the killer into the building. She's still very upset. Apparently, she was very fond of him."

THEY WALKED back to the apartment building through a steady rain. The detective pressed a button on the intercom panel. Gabriel took note of the corresponding name. LILLIAN RATZINGER — CARE-TAKER. A moment later, a small, fierce-looking woman with hunted brown eyes peered at them around the edge of the door. She recognized Weiss and opened the door to them.

"Good afternoon, Frau Ratzinger," the detective said. "This is Benjamin's brother, Ehud Landau. He's here to put Benjamin's affairs in order."

The old woman glanced at Gabriel and nodded. Then she turned away, as if the sight of him made her uneasy.

An acidic odor greeted Gabriel in the lobby. It reminded him of the solvents he used to strip dirty varnish from a canvas. He peered around a corner and saw the *kosmetik*. A fat woman in the midst of a pedicure looked up at him over a glossy German fashion magazine. Gabriel turned away. Benjamin the eternal student, he thought. Benjamin would be comfortable in a place like this.

On the wall adjacent to the door was a row of metal postboxes. The one corresponding to Benjamin's flat still bore his name. Through the tiny window, Gabriel could see it was empty.

The old woman led them up the dimly lit staircase, a ring of passkeys tinkling in her hand. She paused outside Benjamin's apartment. Tattered remnants of crime-scene tape hung from the doorjamb, and a mound of dead roses lay on the floor. Taped to the wall was a sign, scrawled in a desperate hand: LIEBE IST STÄRKER ALS HAB—*Love is stronger than hate*. Something about the idealistic naïveté of the slogan angered Gabriel. Then he remembered it was the same thing Leah had said to him before he left for Europe to kill Palestinians for Shamron.

"Love is stronger than hate, Gabriel. Whatever you do, don't hate them. If you hate them, you'll become just like Shamron."

The old woman unlocked the door and left without looking at Gabriel. He wondered about the source of her anxiety. Perhaps it was her age. Perhaps she was of a generation still uncomfortable in the presence of Jews.

Weiss led Gabriel into the front room overlooking the Adalbertstrasse. The afternoon shadows were heavy. The detective illuminated the room by turning on the lamp on Benjamin's desk. Gabriel glanced down, then quickly took a step back. The floor was coated with Benjamin's blood. He looked up at the wall and saw the graffiti for the first time. Detective Weiss pointed to the first symbol, a diamond resting on a pedestal that resembled an inverted **V**.

"This one is known as the Odin Rune," Weiss said. "It's an ancient Norse symbol that expresses faith in the pagan religion called Odinism."

"And the second one?" Gabriel asked, though he knew the answer already.

Weiss looked at it a moment before responding. Three numeral sevens, linked at their bases, surrounded by a sea of red.

"It's called the Three Sevens or the Three-Bladed Swastika," the German said. "It symbolizes supremacy over the devil as repre-sented by the numbers 666."

Gabriel took a step forward and tilted his head to one side, as though he were inspecting a canvas in need of restoration. To his well-trained eye it seemed the artist was an imitator rather than a believer. Something else struck him. The symbols of hatred were probably sprayed onto the wall in the moments after Benjamin's murder, yet the lines were straight and perfectly executed, revealing no signs of stress or anxiety. A man used to killing, thought Gabriel. A man comfortable around the dead.

He walked over to the desk. "Was Benjamin's computer taken as evidence?"

Weiss shook his head. "Stolen."

Gabriel looked down at the safe, which was open and empty.

"Stolen as well," the detective said, anticipating the next question.

Gabriel removed a small notebook and pen from his jacket pocket. The policeman sat heavily on the couch, as if he had been walking a beat all day.

"I have to remain in the flat with you while you conduct your inventory. I'm sorry, but those are the rules." He loosened his tie. "Take as much time as you need, Herr Landau. And whatever you do, don't try to take anything, eh? Those are the rules too."

GABRIEL COULD DO only so much in the presence of the detective. He started in the bedroom. The bed was unmade, and on the cracked leather armchair was a stack of freshly laundered cloth-ing, still bound in brown paper and string. On the bedside table was a black mask and a pair of foam-rubber earplugs. Benjamin, Gabriel remembered, was a notoriously light sleeper. The curtains were heavy and dark, the kind usually kept by someone who works at night and sleeps during the day. When Gabriel drew them, the air was suddenly filled with dust.

He spent the next thirty minutes carefully going through the contents of the closet, the dresser, and the bedside table. He made copious notes in his leather-bound notebook, just in case Detective Weiss wanted to have a look at his inventory. In truth, he saw nothing out of the ordinary.

He entered the second bedroom. The walls were lined with bookshelves and filing cabinets. Obviously, Benjamin had turned it into a storage room. It looked as though a bomb had exploded nearby. The floor was strewn with books, and the file drawers were flung open. Gabriel wondered who was responsible, the Munich police or Benjamin's killer.

His search lasted nearly an hour. He flipped through the contents of every file and the pages of every book. Weiss appeared once in the doorway to check on his progress, then yawned and wandered back to the sitting room. Again, Gabriel made abundant notes for the benefit of the detective but found nothing linking Benjamin to the Office—and nothing that might explain why he was murdered.

He walked back to the sitting room. Weiss was watching the evening news on Benjamin's television. He switched it off as Gabriel entered. "Finished?"

"Did Benjamin have a storage room in the building?"

The detective nodded. "German law requires landlords to provide tenants with one."

Gabriel held out his hand. "May I have the key?"

IT WAS Frau Ratzinger who took Gabriel down to the basement and led him along a corridor lined with narrow doorways. She paused at the one marked 2B, which corresponded to Benjamin's flat. The old woman opened the door with a grunt and pulled down on the drawstring connected to the overhead light. A moth scattered, brushing Gabriel's cheek. The woman nodded and receded silently down the hallway.

Gabriel peered into the storage room. It was little more than a closet, some four feet wide and six feet deep, and it reeked of linseed oil and damp. A rusted bicycle frame with one wheel, a pair of ancient skis, unlabeled cardboard boxes stacked to a water-stained ceiling.

He removed the broken bicycle and the skis, and began searching through the boxes of Benjamin's things. In several he found bound stacks of yellowing papers and old spiral notebooks, the flotsam of a lifetime spent in the lecture halls and libraries of academia. There were boxes of dusty old books—the ones, Gabriel supposed, he deemed too unimportant to place on the shelves in his flat. Several more held copies of *Conspiracy at Wannsee: A Reappraisal,* Benjamin's last book.

The final box contained the purely personal. Gabriel felt like a trespasser. He wondered how he would feel if the roles were reversed, if Shamron had sent someone from the Office to rummage through his things. And what would they find? Only what Gabriel wanted them to see. Solvents and pigment, his brushes and his palette, a fine collection of monographs. A Beretta by his bedside.

He drew a long breath and proceeded. Inside a cigar box he

found a pile of tarnished medals and tattered ribbons and remembered that Benjamin had been something of a star runner at school. In an envelope were family photographs. Benjamin, like Gabriel, was an only child. His parents had survived the horrors of Riga only to be killed in a car accident on the road to Haifa. Next he found a stack of letters. The stationery was the color of honey and still smelled of lilac. Gabriel read a few lines and quickly put the letters aside. *Vera* . . . Benjamin's only love. How many nights had he lain awake in some wretched safe flat, listening to Benjamin complain about how the beguiling Vera had ruined him for all other women? Gabriel was quite certain he hated her more than Benjamin had.

The last item was a manila file folder. Gabriel lifted the cover and inside found a stack of newspaper clippings. His eyes flickered over the headlines. ELEVEN ISRAELI ATHLETES AND COACHES TAKEN HOSTAGE IN OLYMPIC VILLAGE . . . TERRORISTS DEMAND RELEASE OF PALESTINIAN AND GERMAN PRISONERS . . . BLACK SEPTEMBER . . .

Gabriel closed the file.

A black-and-white snapshot slipped out. Gabriel scooped it off the floor. Two boys, blue jeans and rucksacks. A pair of young Germans spending a summer roaming Europe, or so it appeared. It had been taken in Antwerp near the river. The one on the left was Benjamin, forelock of wavy hair in his eyes, mischievous smile on his face, his arm flung around the young man standing at his side.

Benjamin's companion was serious and sullen, as though he couldn't be bothered with something as trivial as a snapshot. He wore sunglasses, his hair was cropped short, and even though he was not much more than twenty years old, his temples were shot with gray. "The stain of a boy who's done a man's job," Shamron had said. "Smudges of ash on the prince of fire."

GABRIEL WAS not pleased about the file of newspaper clippings on the Munich massacre, but there was no way he could smuggle so large an item past Detective Weiss. The snapshot was different. He wedged it into Herr Landau's expensive wallet and slipped the wallet into his coat pocket. Then he sidestepped his way out of the storage room and closed the door.

Frau Ratzinger was waiting in the corridor. Gabriel wondered how long she had been standing there but dared not ask. In her hand was a small padded shipping envelope. He could see that it was addressed to Benjamin and that it had been opened.

The old woman held it out to him. "I thought you might want these," she said in German.

"What are they?"

"Benjamin's eyeglasses. He left them at a hotel in Italy. The concierge was good enough to send them back. Unfortunately, they arrived after his death."

Gabriel took the envelope from her, lifted the flap, and removed the eyeglasses. They were the spectacles of an academic: plastic and passé, chewed and scratched. He looked into the envelope once more and saw there was a postcard. He turned the envelope on end, and the postcard fell into his palm. The image showed an ocher-colored hotel on a sapphire lake in the north of Italy. Gabriel turned it over and read the note on the back.

Good luck with your book, Professor Stern.
Giancomo

✦ ✦ ✦

DETECTIVE WEISS insisted on driving Gabriel to his hotel. Because Herr Landau had never before been to Munich, Gabriel was forced to feign awe at the floodlit neoclassical glory of the city center. He also noted that Weiss skillfully made the trip last five minutes longer than necessary by missing several obvious turns.

Finally they arrived in a small cobbled street called the Annastrasse in the Lehel district of the city. Weiss stopped outside the Hotel Opera, handed Gabriel his card, and once more expressed condolences over Herr Landau's loss. "If there's anything else I can do for you, please don't hesitate to ask."

"There is one thing," Gabriel said. "I'd like to speak to the chairman of Benjamin's department at the university. Do you have his telephone numbers?"

"Ah, Doctor Berger. Of course."

The policeman removed an electronic organizer from his pocket, found the numbers, and recited them. Gabriel made a point of jotting them down on the back of the detective's card, even though, heard once, they were now permanently engraved in his memory.

Gabriel thanked the detective and went upstairs for the night. He ordered room service and dined lightly on an omelet and vegetable soup. Then he showered and climbed into bed with the file given to him that afternoon by the consular officer. He read everything carefully, then closed the file and stared at the ceiling, listening to the night rain pattering against the window. *Who killed you, Beni? A neo-Nazi?* No, Gabriel doubted that. He suspected the Odin Rune and Three Sevens painted on the wall were the equivalent of a false-flag claim of responsibility. But why was he killed? Gabriel had one working theory. Benjamin was on sabbatical from the university to write another book, yet inside the flat Gabriel could find no evidence that he was working on anything at all. No notes. No files. No manuscript. Just a note written on the back of a postcard from a hotel in Italy. *Good luck with your book, Professor Stern—Giancomo.*

He opened his wallet and removed the photograph he'd taken from the storeroom. Gabriel had been cursed with a memory that allowed him to forget nothing. He could see Benjamin giving his camera to a pretty Belgian girl, feel Benjamin dragging him to the rail overlooking the river. He even remembered the last thing Benjamin had said before throwing his arm around Gabriel's neck.

"Smile, you asshole."

"This isn't funny, Beni."

"Can you imagine the look on the old man's face if he saw us posing for a picture?"

"He'll have your ass for this."

"Don't worry. I'll burn it."

Five minutes later, in the bathroom sink, Gabriel did just that.

DETECTIVE AXEL WEISS lived in Bogenhausen, a residential district of Munich on the opposite bank of the Isar. He did not go there. Instead, after dropping the Israeli at his hotel, he parked in the shadows on an adjacent street and watched the entrance of the Hotel Opera. Thirty minutes later, he dialed a number in Rome on his cellular phone.

"This is the chief." The words were spoken in English with a pronounced Italian accent. It was always the same.

"I think we may have a problem."

"Tell me everything."

The detective gave a careful recitation of the events of that afternoon and evening. He was experienced at communicating over open phone systems and was careful not to make any specific references. Besides, the man at the other end knew the specifics.

"Do you have the resources to follow the subject?"

"Yes, but if he's a professional—"

"Do it," snapped the man in Rome. "And get a photograph."

Then the connection went dead.

· 5 ·

VATICAN CITY

CARDINAL BRINDISI. How pleasant to see you."
"Your Holiness."

Cardinal Secretary of State Marco Brindisi bent over the proffered fisherman's ring. His lips did not linger long. He stood upright and stared directly into the Pope's eyes with a confidence bordering on insolence. Thin, with a pinched face and skin like parchment, Brindisi seemed suspended above the floor of the papal apartments. His cassock was handmade by the same tailor near the Piazza della Minerva who made garments for the popes. The solid gold pectoral cross attested to the wealth and influence of his family and patrons. The glint of white light on the small, round spectacles concealed a pair of humorless pale-blue eyes.

As secretary of state, Brindisi controlled the internal functions of the Vatican city-state along with its government-to-government relations with the rest of the world. He was in effect the Vatican's prime minister and the second most powerful man in the Roman Catholic Church. Despite his disappointing showing at the conclave, the doctrinaire cardinal maintained a carefully cultivated core of support within the Curia that provided him with a power base rivaling even the Pope's. Indeed, the Pope was not at all sure who would prevail in a showdown, himself or the taciturn cardinal.

The two men had a regular lunch date every Friday. It was the part of the Pope's week he dreaded most. Some of his predecessors had relished the minutiae of Curial matters and had spent hours each day slaving over mountains of paperwork. During the reigns of Pius XII and Paul VI, the lights in the papal study had burned well past midnight. Lucchesi believed his time was better spent on spiritual matters and detested dealing with the day-to-day affairs of the Curia. Unfortunately, he did not yet have a secretary of state whom he trusted, which is why he never missed lunch with Cardinal Brindisi.

They sat across from each other in the simple dining room in the papal apartments, the Pope clad in a white soutane and white zucchetto, the cardinal in a black cassock with a scarlet fascia and zucchetto. As always, Brindisi seemed disappointed with the food. This pleased His Holiness. The Pope knew Brindisi was a gourmand who enjoyed spending his evenings partaking of the gastronomic delights of L'Eau Vive. As a result he always asked his nuns to prepare something particularly offensive to the palate. Today the menu consisted of a consommé of indeterminate origin, followed by overdone veal and boiled potatoes. Brindisi pronounced the food "inspired" and made a brave show of it.

For forty-five minutes, Brindisi held forth on a variety of Curial matters, each one more tedious than the last. A staff crisis in the Congregation for Divine Worship and the Discipline of the Sacraments. A dustup in the Pontifical Council for the Pastoral Care of Migrants and Itinerant People. A report on the monthly meeting of the Vatican Bank officers. Allegations a certain monsignor from the Congregation for the Clergy was misusing his motor-pool privileges. Each time Brindisi paused for a breath, the Pope murmured, "Ah, how interesting, Eminence," all the while wondering why he was being informed of a problem at the motor pool.

"I'm afraid I need to discuss a matter of some"—the fussy cardinal cleared his throat and patted his lips with his napkin—"shall we say, unpleasantness, Holiness. Perhaps now is as good a time as any."

"Please, Eminence," the Pope said quickly, eager for any change of subject that might soften the drumbeat of Curial monotony. "By all means."

Brindisi laid down his fork like a man surrendering after a long siege and clasped his hands beneath his chin. "It seems our old friend from *La Repubblica* is up to no good again. In the course of preparing a long profile on Your Holiness for the newspaper's Easter edition, he has uncovered some"—a reflective pause, a glance toward the heavens for inspiration—"some *inconsistencies* about your childhood."

"What sort of inconsistencies?"

"Inconsistencies about the date of your mother's death. How old you were when you were orphaned. Where you stayed. Who cared for you. He is an enterprising reporter, a constant thorn in the side of the secretariat. He manages to uncover things that we've done our best to bury. I have reiterated to my staff that no one is to talk to him without the approval of the Press Office, but somehow—"

"People are talking to him."

"That appears to be the case, Holiness."

The Pope pushed away his empty plate and exhaled heavily. It had been his intention to release the full details of his childhood in the days after the conclave, but there were those in the Curia and the Press Office who thought the world was not ready for a street-urchin pope, a boy who had lived by his wits and his fists until he was drawn to the breast of the Church. It was an example of the very culture of secrecy and deceit Lucchesi so despised about the Vatican, but in the opening days of his papacy he had been unwilling to waste valuable political capital, so he reluctantly agreed to paper over some of the less saintly details of his upbringing.

"It was a mistake to tell the world that I grew up in Padua, in a loving home filled with much devotion to Christ and the Virgin, before entering the seminary at fifteen. Your friend from *La Repubblica* is going to find the truth."

"Let me deal with *La Repubblica*. We have ways of bringing wayward journalists into line."

"Such as?"

"Banning them from accompanying Your Holiness on foreign trips. Locking them out of press briefings. Revoking their privileges at the Press Office."

"That seems awfully harsh."

"I doubt it will come to that. I'm sure we can convince him of the truth."

"Which truth is that?"

"That you were raised in Padua, in a loving home filled with much devotion to Christ and the Virgin." Brindisi smiled and brushed an invisible breadcrumb from his cassock. "But when one is battling this sort of thing, it can be helpful to have the complete picture so that we know what we're up against."

"What are you suggesting?"

"A brief memorandum. It will be seen by no one in the Curia but myself and will be used by me only in the preparation of a defense—should one be warranted."

"Did you learn those tactics studying Canon Law, Marco?"

Brindisi smiled. "Some things are universal, Holiness."

"A memorandum will be forthcoming."

The Pope and the cardinal stopped talking as a pair of nuns cleared the table and served espresso. The Pope stirred sugar into his coffee slowly, then looked up at Brindisi.

"I have something I wish to discuss as well. It concerns the matter we discussed some months ago—my initiative to continue the process of healing the rift between the Church and the Jews."

"How interesting, Holiness." A man who had spent his career climbing the bureaucratic ladder of the Curia, Brindisi's tone was skillfully noncommittal.

"As part of that initiative, I intend to commission a study of the Church's response to the Holocaust. All relevant documents in the Secret Vatican Archives will be made available for review, and this time we will not tie the hands of the historians and experts we select for this project."

Cardinal Brindisi's already pale face shed any remnant of color. He made a church steeple of his forefingers and pressed it to his lips, trying to regain his composure before mounting his challenge. "As you well remember, Holiness, your predecessor commissioned a study and presented it to the world in 1998. I see no need to repeat the work of the Pole when there are so many other— and I dare say more important—issues confronting the Church at this time."

"*We Remember*? It should have been called *We Apologize*—or *We Beg Forgiveness*. It did not go far enough, neither in its soul-searching nor in its search for the truth. It was yet another insult to the very people whose wounds we wished to heal. What did it say? The Church did nothing wrong. We tried to help. Some of us helped more than others. The Germans did the actual killing, not us, but we are sorry in any case. It is a shameful document."

"Some might consider it shameful that you are speaking this way about the work of a predecessor."

"I have no intention of condemning the efforts of the Pole. His heart was in the right place, but I suspect he did not have the full support of the Curia"—*From men like you,* thought Lucchesi— "which is why the document ended up saying little if anything at all. Out of respect for the Pole, I will portray the new study as a continuation of his good work."

"Another study will be seen as an implicit criticism, no matter how you attempt to render it."

"You were on the panel that drafted *We Remember,* were you not?"

"I was indeed, Holiness."

"Ten years to write fourteen pages."

"Consideration and accuracy take time."

"So does whitewash."

"I object to—"

The Pope cut him off. "Do you oppose revisiting the issue because you fear it will bring shame upon the Church, or because you calculate it will damage your chances of taking my place when I'm gone?"

Brindisi lowered his hands and lifted his eyes to the ceiling for a moment, as if preparing himself for a reading from the Gospel. "I oppose *revisiting* the issue because it will do nothing but give more ammunition to those who wish to destroy us."

"Our continued deception and evasion is more risky. If we do not speak forcefully and honestly, the work of our enemies will be accomplished by our own hand. We will destroy ourselves."

"If *I* may speak forcefully and honestly, Holiness, your naïveté in this matter is shocking. Nothing the Church can say will ever satisfy those who condemn us. In fact, it will only add fuel to the fire. I cannot allow you to tread on the reputation of popes and the Church with this folly. Pius the Twelfth deserves sainthood, not another crucifixion."

Pietro Lucchesi had yet to be seduced by the trappings of papal power, but the blatant insubordination of Brindisi's remark stirred his anger. He forced himself to speak calmly. Even so, there was an edge of rage and condescension in his voice that was plain to the man seated on the other side of the table. "I can assure you, Marco, that those who wish for Pius to be canonized will have to pin their hopes on the outcome of the next conclave."

The cardinal ran a long, spidery finger around the rim of his coffee cup, steeling himself for one more assault on the ridge. Finally, he cleared his throat and said, "The Pole apologized on numerous occasions for the sins of some of the Church's sons and daughters. Other prelates have apologized as well. Some, such as our brethren in France, have gone much further than I would have preferred. But the Jews and their friends in the media will not be satisfied until we admit that we were *wrong*—that His Holiness Pope Pius the Twelfth, a great and saintly man, was *wrong*. What they do not understand—and what you seem to be forgetting, Holiness—is that the Church, as the embodiment of Christ on earth, cannot be *wrong*. The Church is truth itself. If we admit that the Church, or a pope, was wrong . . ." He left his sentence unfinished, then added: "It would be an error for you to go forward with this initiative of yours, Holiness. A *grave* error."

"Behind these walls, Marco, *error* is a loaded word. Surely it is not your intention to level such an accusation at me."

"I have no intention of parsing my words, Holiness."

"And what if the documents contained in the Secret Archives tell a different story?"

"Those documents must never be released."

"I am the only one with the power to release documents from the Secret Archives, and I have decided that it will be done."

The cardinal fingered his pectoral cross. "When do you intend to announce this . . . *initiative?*"

"Next week."

"Where?"

"Across the river," the Pope said. "At the Great Synagogue."

"Out of the question! The Curia hasn't had time to give the matter the thought and preparation it deserves."

"I'm seventy-two years old. I don't have time to wait for the mandarins of the Curia to give the matter thought and preparation. That, I'm afraid, is how things are buried and forgotten. The rabbi and I have spoken. I'm going to the ghetto next week, with or without the support of the Curia—or my secretary of state, for that matter. The truth, Eminence, shall make us free."

"And you, the street-urchin pope from the Veneto, pretend to know the truth."

"Only God knows the truth, Marco, but Thomas Aquinas wrote

of a cultivated ignorance, an *ignorantia affectata*. A willful lack of knowledge designed to protect one from the harm. It is time to shed our *ignorantia affectata*. Our Savior said that he was the light of the world, but here in the Vatican, we live in darkness. I intend to turn on the lights."

"My memory seems to be playing tricks on me, Holiness, but it is my recollection of the conclave that we elected a *Catholic* Pope."

"You did, Eminence, but you also elected a human one."

"If it were not for *me,* you would still be wearing red."

"It is the Holy Spirit who chooses popes. We just cast his ballots."

"Another example of your shocking naïveté."

"Will you be at my side next week in Trastevere?"

"I believe I'm going to be suffering from the flu next week." The cardinal stood up abruptly. "Thank you, Holiness. Another pleasant meal."

"Until next Friday?"

"That remains to be seen."

The Pope held out his hand. Cardinal Brindisi looked down at the fisherman's ring shining in the lamplight, then turned around and walked out without kissing it.

FATHER DONATI listened to the quarrel between the Holy Father and the cardinal from the adjoining pantry. When Brindisi had gone, he entered the dining room and found the Pope looking tired and drawn, eyes closed, thumb and forefinger squeezing the bridge of his nose. Father Donati sat in the cardinal's chair and pushed away the half-drunk cup of espresso.

"I know that must have been unpleasant, Holiness, but it was necessary."

The Pope finally looked up. "We have just disturbed a sleeping cobra, Luigi."

"Yes, Holiness." Donati leaned forward and lowered his voice. "Now let us pray that in its rage, the cobra makes a miscalculation and bites itself."

· 6 ·

MUNICH

GABRIEL SPENT THE BETTER PART of the following morning trying to track down Doctor Helmut Berger, chairman of the department of modern history at Ludwig-Maximilian University. He left two messages on the professor's home answering machine, a second on his cellular phone, and a third with a surly secretary in the department. Over lunch in the shadowed courtyard of the hotel, he considered waiting in ambush outside the professor's office. Then the concierge appeared with a message slip in his hand. The good professor had agreed to meet with Herr Landau at six-thirty at a restaurant called the Gastätte Atzinger on the Amalienstrasse.

That left five hours to kill. The afternoon was clear and blustery, so Gabriel decided to take a walk. Leaving the hotel, he wandered up a narrow cobblestone street that led to the southern end of the English Gardens. He moved slowly along the footpaths, beside shaded streams, across broad sunlit lawns. In the distance the thousand-foot spire of the Olympia Tower sparkled against the crystalline blue sky. Gabriel lowered his gaze and kept walking.

Leaving the park, he drifted through Schwabing. In the Adalbertstrasse he saw Frau Ratzinger sweeping the steps of No. 68. He had no wish to speak to the old woman again, so he rounded a corner and headed in the opposite direction. Every few minutes he would look up and glimpse the tower, looming before him, growing larger by degrees.

Ten minutes later, he found himself at the southern edge of the village. In many ways Olympiapark was just that: a village, a vast residential area, complete with its own railway station, its own post office, even its own mayor. The cement-block bungalows and apartment houses had not aged gracefully. In an attempt to brighten up the place, many of the units had been painted in bright tie-dye patterns.

He came upon the Connollystrasse. It was not a street, really, but a pedestrian walkway lined with small three-story apartment houses. At No. 31 he stopped walking. On the second floor, a bare-chested teenager stepped onto the balcony to shake out a throw rug. Gabriel's memory flashed. Instead of a young German, he saw a Palestinian in a balaclava. Then a woman emerged from the ground-floor apartment, pushing a stroller and clutching a child to her breast. For an instant, Gabriel saw Issa, leader of the Black September team, his face covered in boot polish, swaggering about in his safari suit and golf hat.

The woman looked at Gabriel as though she was used to strangers standing outside her home with disbelieving expressions on their faces. *Yes,* she seemed to be saying. *Yes, this is the place where it happened. But now it's my home, so please go.* She seemed to sense something else in his gaze—something that unnerved her—and she quickly strapped the child into the stroller and headed toward a playground.

Gabriel climbed a grassy hillock and sat in the cool grass. Usually when the memories came, he tried desperately to push them away, but now he unchained the door and allowed them to enter. *Romano . . . Springer . . . Spitzer . . . Slavin . . .* the faces of the dead flashed through his memory. Eleven in all. Two killed in the takeover. Nine more during the bungled German rescue attempt at Fürstenfeldbruck. Golda Meir wanted revenge of Biblical proportions—an eye for an eye—and she ordered the Office to "send forth the boys" to hunt down the members of Black September who had plotted the attack. A brash operations officer named Ari Shamron was placed in charge of the mission, and one of the boys he came for was a promising young student at Jerusalem's Betsal'el School of Art named Gabriel Allon.

Somehow, Shamron had come across the file from Gabriel's unhappy compulsory service in the army. The child of Auschwitz survivors, Gabriel was found arrogant and selfish by his superiors; prone to periods of melancholia, but also highly intelligent and capable of taking independent action without waiting for guidance from commanding officers. He was also multilingual, an attribute that had little value in a frontline infantry unit but was much sought after by Ari Shamron. His war would not be fought in the Golan or the Sinai. It would be a secret war waged in the shadows of Europe. Gabriel had tried to resist him. Shamron left him no choice.

"Once again, Jews are dying on German soil with their hands tied behind their backs," Shamron had said. *"Your parents survived, but how many didn't? Their brothers and sisters? Their aunts and uncles?*

Grandparents? They're all gone, aren't they? Are you really going to sit here in Tel Aviv with your brushes and your paints and do nothing? You have gifts. Let me borrow them for a few months. Then you can do whatever you want with your life."

The mission was code-named Operation Wrath of God. In the lexicon of the unit, Gabriel was an *aleph,* an assassin. The agents who tracked Black Septembrists and learned their habits were code-named *ayin.* A *qoph* was a communications officer. Benjamin Stern had been a *heth,* a logistician. His job was to procure transport and lodging in ways that could never be traced to the Office. Sometimes he doubled as a getaway driver. Indeed, Benjamin had been behind the wheel of the green Fiat that carried Gabriel away from the Piazza Annibaliano the night he assassinated Black September's chief in Italy. On the way to the airport, Gabriel had forced Benjamin to pull to the side of the road so he could be sick. Even now, he could hear Benjamin shouting at him to get back into the car.

"Give me a minute."

"You'll miss your flight."

"I said give me a minute!"

"What's wrong with you? That bastard deserved to die!"

"You didn't see his face, Beni. You didn't see his fucking face."

Over the next eighteen months, Shamron's team assassinated a dozen members of Black September. Gabriel personally killed six men. When it was over, Benjamin resumed his academic career. Gabriel tried to go back to Betsal'el and do the same, but his ability to paint had been chased away by the ghosts of the men he had killed, so he left Leah behind in Israel and moved to Venice to study restoration with Umberto Conti. In restoration, he found healing. Conti, who knew nothing of Gabriel's past, seemed to understand this. Late at night he would come to Gabriel's room in a sagging pensione and drag him into the streets of Venice to look at art. One evening, standing before the great Titian altarpiece in the Frari church, he seized Gabriel by the arm.

"A man who is pleased with himself can be an adequate restorer but not a great restorer. Only a man with a damaged canvas of his own can truly be a great restorer. It is a meditation for you. A ritual. One day you will be a great restorer. You will be better than I am. I'm sure of it."

And though Conti did not know it, those were the same words Shamron had said to Gabriel the night before he sent him to Rome to kill his first Palestinian.

GABRIEL WAS standing outside the Gastätte Atzinger at six-thirty sharp. The first thing he saw of Professor Helmut Berger was the headlamp on his bicycle floating above the Amalienstrasse. Then his form appeared, legs pumping rhythmically, his thinning gray hair floating above his large ears like wings. A brown leather satchel hung across his back.

The endearing quality of the professor's arrival evaporated in short order. Like many German intellectuals, Helmut Berger had the put-upon air of a man who had spent the day grappling with beings of inferior intelligence. He claimed to have time only for a small glass of beer, but he invited Gabriel to select something from the menu. Gabriel ordered only mineral water, which the German seemed to find deeply scandalous.

"I'm very sorry about your brother. Excuse me, your *half*-brother. He was a valuable member of the faculty. His death was a shock to us all." He spoke these lines without genuine emotion, as though they had been written for him by a graduate student. "How can I help you, Herr Landau?"

"Is it true that Benjamin was on a sabbatical at the time of his murder?"

"Yes, that's correct. He was working on another book."

"Do you know the subject of that book?"

"Actually, I don't."

"Really?" Gabriel was genuinely surprised. "Is it typical for someone to leave your department to work on a book without telling you the subject matter?"

"No, but Benjamin was very secretive about this project from the very beginning."

Gabriel decided he could not press the issue. "Did you know anything about the kind of threats Benjamin received?"

"There were so many, it was hard to keep them straight. Benjamin's theories about a collective German wartime guilt made him, shall we say, highly unpopular in many quarters."

"It sounds to me as though you didn't share Benjamin's views."

The professor shrugged. "A few years ago, I wrote a book on the role of the German Catholic Church during the war. Benjamin disagreed with my conclusions and said so in a very public manner. It was not a pleasant time for either of us."

The professor looked at his watch. "I'm afraid I have another engagement. Is there anything else I can tell you? Perhaps something more relevant to your inquiries?"

"Last month, Benjamin made a trip to Italy. Do you happen to know why he went there? Was it connected to the book in any way?"

"I have no idea. You see, Doctor Stern didn't make a habit of giving me advance warning about his travel plans." The professor finished the last of his beer and stood up. Class dismissed. "Again, my condolences, Herr Landau. I wish you luck in your inquiries."

Like hell you do, thought Gabriel, as he watched Professor Berger walk outside and pedal away.

ON THE WAY back to his hotel, Gabriel entered a large student bookstore on the southern edge of the university district. He gazed at the store directory for a moment, then climbed the stairs to the travel section, where he searched a display bin filled with maps until he came across one for northern Italy.

He spread it over a nearby table, then reached into his pocket and removed the postcard. The hotel where Benjamin had stayed was in a town called Brenzone. Judging from the photograph, the town was set on the shoreline of one of Italy's northern lakes. He started in the west and worked his way slowly eastward, reading the names of the towns and villages surrounding each of the great northern lakes—first Maggiore, then Como, then Iseo, and finally Garda. *Brenzone.* There it was, on the eastern shore of the Lago di Garda, about halfway between the bulge at the southern end and the daggerlike northern tip.

Gabriel refolded the map and carried it downstairs to the cash register. A moment later, he stepped back through the revolving doors into the street, the map and postcard resting in his jacket pocket. Instinctively, his eyes flickered over the pavement, the parked cars, the windows of the surrounding buildings.

He turned left and started back to his hotel, wondering why Detective Axel Weiss had been sitting in the café across the street the entire time Gabriel was in the bookstore—and why he was now following him across the center of Munich.

GABRIEL WAS confident he could easily evade or expose the German detective, but now was not the time to betray the fact that he was a trained professional. As far as Axel Weiss knew, Gabriel was Ehud Landau, brother of slain historian Benjamin Stern, and nothing else—which made the fact that he was following him all the more curious.

He entered a hotel on the Maximilianstrasse. He made a brief call on a public telephone in the lobby, then went back outside and kept walking. The policeman was still there, fifty meters back, on the opposite side of the street.

Gabriel walked directly to his hotel. He collected his key from the clerk at the front counter and rode the lift up to his room. He packed his clothing into a garment bag of black leather, then unlocked the room safe and removed the file he had been given by the Israeli consulate, along with the envelope containing Benjamin's eyeglasses. He placed the items in the briefcase and closed the lid. Then he switched off the room lights, walked to the window, and parted the curtain. A car was parked just up the street. Gabriel could see the glow of a cigarette ember behind the wheel. *Weiss.* Gabriel closed the curtain and sat on the end of the bed, waiting for the phone to ring.

Twenty minutes later: "Landau."

"It's at the corner of the Seitzstrasse and the Unsöldstrasse, just south of Prinzregenten. Do you know where that is?"

"Yes," Gabriel said. "Give me the number."

Nine digits. Gabriel did not bother to write them down.

"The keys?"

"Standard location. Back bumper, curbside."

Gabriel hung up, pulled on his jacket, and collected his bags. In the lobby he explained to the night clerk that he was checking out ahead of schedule.

"Do you require a taxi, Herr Landau?"

"No, I'm being picked up. Thank you."

A bill slid toward him across the counter. Gabriel paid with one of Shamron's credit cards and went out. He turned left and started walking quickly, garment bag in one hand, briefcase in the other. Twenty seconds later, he heard the sound of a car door opening and closing, followed by footsteps on the wet cobblestones of the Annastrasse. He maintained his steady pace, resisting the impulse to look over his shoulder.

"*. . . corner of the Seitzstrasse and the Unsöldstrasse . . .*"

Gabriel passed a church, turned left, and paused in a small square to take his bearings. Then he turned right and followed another narrow street toward the sound of the traffic rushing along the Prinzregentenstrasse. Weiss was still trailing him.

He walked along a line of parked cars, reading registration numbers, until he came across the one he'd just been given over the phone. It was attached to a dark gray Opel Omega. Without stopping, he bent slightly at the waist and ran his fingers beneath the rear bumper until he found the keys. With a movement so brief and smooth that Weiss seemed not to notice, Gabriel tore the keys loose.

He pressed the button on the remote. The doors unlocked automatically. Then he opened the driver's side door and threw his bags onto the passenger seat. He looked to his right. Weiss was running toward him, panic on his face.

Gabriel climbed inside, rammed the keys into the ignition, and started the engine. He dropped the car into gear and pulled away from the curb, then turned hard to the right and vanished into the evening traffic.

DETECTIVE AXEL WEISS had leapt out of his car so quickly that he had left his cellular phone behind. He ran all the way back, then paused to catch his breath before dialing the number. A moment later, he broke the news to the man in Rome that the Israeli called Landau was gone.

"How?"

Embarrassed, Weiss told him.

"Did you get a photograph at least?"

"Earlier today—at the Olympic Village."

"The village? What on earth was he doing there?"

"Staring at the apartment house at Connollystrasse Thirty-one."

"Wasn't that where it happened?"

"Yes, that's right. It's not unusual for Jews to make a pilgrimage there."

"Is it usual for Jews to detect surveillance and execute a perfect escape?"

"Point taken."

"Send me the photograph—*tonight*."

Then the man in Rome severed the connection.

⋆ 7 ⋆

NEAR RIETI, ITALY

THERE IS AN UNSETTLING BEAUTY about the Villa Galatina. A former Benedictine abbey, it stands atop a column of granite in the hills of Lazio and stares disapprovingly down at the village on the floor of the wooded valley. In the seventeenth century an important cardinal purchased the abbey and converted it into a lavish summer residence, a place where His Eminence could escape the broiling heat of Rome in August. His architect had possessed the good sense to preserve the exterior, and its tawny-colored façade remains to this day, along with the teeth of the battlements. On a morning in early March, a man was visible high on the windswept parapet. It was not a bow over his shoulder but a high-powered Beretta sniper's rifle. The current owner was a man who took his security seriously. His name was Roberto Pucci, a financier and industrialist whose power over modern Italy rivaled that of even a Renaissance prince of the Church.

An armored Mercedes sedan stopped at the steel gate, where it was greeted by a pair of tan-suited security guards. The man seated in the back compartment lowered his window. One of the guards examined his face, then glanced at the distinctive SVC license plates on the Mercedes. *Vatican plates.* Roberto Pucci's gate swung open and an asphalt drive lined with cypresses stretched before them. A quarter mile up the hillside was the villa itself.

The Mercedes eased up the drive and pulled into a gravel forecourt shaded by umbrella pine and eucalyptus. Two dozen other cars were already there, surrounded by a small army of security men and chauffeurs. The man in the backseat climbed out, leaving his own bodyguard behind, and walked across the courtyard toward the bell tower of the chapel.

His name was Carlo Casagrande. For a brief time in Italy, his name had been a household word, for it was General Carlo Casagrande, chief of the antiterrorist unit of *L'arma dei Carabinieri,* who had crushed the Communist Red Brigades. For reasons of personal security, he was notoriously camera shy, and few people outside the Rome intelligence community would have recognized his face.

Casagrande no longer worked for the *Carabinieri.* In 1981, a week after the attempt to assassinate Pope John Paul II, he resigned his commission and vanished behind the walls of the Vatican. In a way, Casagrande had been working for the men of the Holy See all along. He took control of the Security Office, vowing that no pope would ever again leave St. Peter's Square in the back of an ambulance praying to the Virgin Mary for his life. One of his first acts was to launch a massive investigation into the shooting, so that the conspirators could be identified and neutralized before they were able to mount a second attempt on the Pope's life. The findings of the inquiry were so sensitive that Casagrande shared them with no one but the Holy Father himself.

Casagrande was no longer directly responsible for protecting the life of the pope. For the last three years, he had been engaged in another task for his beloved Church. He remained attached to the Vatican Security Office, but it was only a flag of convenience to give him standing in certain quarters. He was now the head of the vaguely named Special Investigations Division. So secret was Casagrande's assignment, only a handful of men within the Vatican knew the true nature of his work.

Casagrande entered the chapel. Cool air, scented with candle wax and incense, caressed his face. In the sanctuary he dipped his fingers in holy water and made the sign of the cross. Then he walked up the center aisle toward the altar. To call it a chapel was an understatement. It was in fact a rather large church, larger than the parish churches in most of the nearby towns.

Casagrande took his place in the first pew. Roberto Pucci, dressed in a gray suit and an open-necked white shirt, nodded at him from across the aisle. Despite his seventy-five years, Pucci still radiated an aura of physical invincibility. His hair was white and his face the color of oiled saddle leather. He appraised Casagrande coldly with a pair of hooded black eyes. *The Pucci stare*. Whenever Pucci looked at you, it was as if he was deciding whether to stab you in the heart or slit your throat.

Like Carlo Casagrande, Roberto Pucci was an *uomo di fiducia,* a man of trust. Only laymen with a unique skill valued by the men of the Vatican were allowed into its innermost chambers. Casagrande's expertise was security and intelligence. Pucci's was money and political power. He was the hidden hand in Italian politics, a man so influential that no government could form without first making a pilgrimage to the Villa Galatina to secure his blessing. But few people in the Italian political establishment knew that Pucci maintained a similar grip over another Roman institution: the Vatican. His power at the Holy See derived from his covert management of a substantial portion of the vast stock and real estate holdings of the Catholic Church. Under Pucci's sure hand, the net worth of the Vatican's portfolios had experienced explosive growth. Unlike his predecessors, he had achieved this feat without a whiff of scandal.

Casagrande glanced over his shoulder. The others were scattered in the remaining pews: the Italian foreign minister; an important bishop from the Congregation for the Doctrine of the Faith; the chief of the Vatican Press Office; an influential conservative theologian from Cologne; an investment banker from Geneva; the leader of a far-right party in France; the owner of a Spanish media conglomerate; the chief of one of Europe's largest automakers. A dozen more, very much in the same mold—all doctrinaire Catholics, all wielding enormous political or financial power, all dedicated to restoring the Church to the position of supremacy it had enjoyed before the calamity of the Reformation. Casagrande found it vaguely amusing when he overheard debates about where true power resided within the Roman Catholic Church. Did it rest with the Synod of Bishops? The College of Cardinals? Did it rest in the hands of the Supreme Pontiff himself? No, thought Casagrande. True power in the Catholic Church resided here, in this chapel on a mountainside outside Rome, in the hands of this secret brotherhood.

A cleric strode onto the altar, a cardinal clad in the ordinary vestments of a parish priest. The members rose to their feet, and the Mass commenced.

"In nomine Patris et Filii et Spiritus Sancti."

"Amen."

The cardinal led them briskly through the introductory rites, the penitential rite, the Kyrie and the Gloria. He celebrated the Tridentine Mass, for it was one of the goals of the brotherhood to restore what it deemed the unifying force of the Latin liturgy.

The Homily was the typical fare of gatherings such as this: a call to arms, a warning to remain steadfast in the face of enemies, a plea to stamp out the corrosive forces of liberalism and modernism within society and the Church itself. The cardinal did not mention the name of the brotherhood. Unlike its close relatives, Opus Dei, the Legions of Christ, and the Society of St. Pius X, it did not officially exist, and its name was never spoken. Among themselves, the members referred to it only as "the Institute."

Casagrande had heard the sermon many times before, and he allowed his mind to drift. His thoughts turned to the situation in Munich and the report he had received from his operative about the Israeli called Landau. He sensed further trouble, an ominous threat to the Church and the brotherhood itself. He required the blessing of the cardinal, and the money of Roberto Pucci, to deal with it.

"*Hic est enim calix sanguinis mei,*" the cardinal recited. "For this is the chalice of my blood, of the new and eternal testament, the mystery of faith, which shall be shed for you and for many unto the remission of sins."

Casagrande's attention returned to the Mass. Five minutes later, when the Liturgy of the Eucharist was complete, he rose to his feet and filed toward the altar behind Roberto Pucci. The financier received the sacrament of Communion, then Casagrande stepped forward.

Cardinal Secretary of State Marco Brindisi held the host aloft, stared directly into Casagrande's eyes, and said in Latin: "May the body of our Lord Jesus Christ keep your soul unto life everlasting."

Carlo Casagrande whispered, "Amen."

BUSINESS WAS never discussed in the chapel. That was reserved for a sumptuous buffet lunch, served in a large gallery hung with tapestries overlooking the terrace. Casagrande was distracted and had no appetite. During his long war against the Red Brigades, he had been forced to live in hiding in a series of underground bunkers and military barracks, surrounded by the rough company of his staff officers. He had never grown used to the luxurious privilege of life behind the Vatican walls. Nor did he share the enthusiasm of the other guests for Roberto Pucci's food.

He pushed a piece of smoked salmon around his plate while Cardinal Brindisi deftly conducted the meeting. Brindisi was a lifelong Vatican bureaucrat, but he loathed the circular logic and duplicity that characterized most discussions inside the Curia. The cardinal was a man of action, and there was a boardroom quality to the way he presided over the agenda. Had he not become a priest, thought Casagrande, he might very well have been Roberto Pucci's fiercest competitor.

The men seated around the room considered democracy a messy and inefficient means of governance, and the brotherhood, like the Roman Catholic Church itself, was no democracy. Brindisi had been entrusted with power and would wield it until his death. In the lexicon of the Institute, each man in the room was a Director. He would return home and hold a similar gathering with the men who reported to him. In that way, Brindisi's orders would be dispersed throughout the vast organization. There was no tolerance for creativity or independent action among middle management. Members were sworn to absolute obedience.

Casagrande's work was never discussed among the Directorate. He spoke only in executive session, which in this case consisted of a stroll through the magnificent terraced gardens of the Villa Galatina with Brindisi and Pucci during a break in the proceedings. Brindisi walked with his chin up and his fingers interlaced across his abdomen, Casagrande on his left, Pucci on his right. The three most powerful men in the brotherhood: Brindisi, spiritual leader; Pucci, minister of finance; Casagrande, chief of security and operations. The members of the Institute privately referred to them as the Holy Trinity.

The Institute did not have an intelligence section of its own. Casagrande was beholden to a small cadre of Vatican policemen and Swiss Guards loyal to him and the brotherhood. His legendary status among the Italian police and intelligence forces gave him access to their resources as well. In addition, he had built a worldwide network of intelligence and security officials, including a senior administrator of the American FBI, all willing to do his bidding. Axel Weiss, the Munich detective, was a member of Casagrande's network. So was the minister of the interior in the heavily Catholic state of Bavaria. At the suggestion of the minister, Weiss had been assigned to the Stern case. He had removed sensitive material from the historian's apartment and had controlled the direction of the investigation. Stern's assassination had been linked to neo-Nazis, just as Casagrande had intended. Now, with the appearance of the Israeli called Landau, he feared the situation in Munich was beginning to unravel. He expressed his concerns to Cardinal Brindisi and Roberto Pucci in the garden of the Villa Galatina.

"Why don't you just kill him?" Pucci said in his gravelly voice.

Yes, kill him, thought Casagrande. *The Pucci solution.* Casagrande had lost count of how many murders had been linked to the shadowy financier. He chose his words carefully, for he had no wish to openly cross swords with him. Pucci had once ordered a man killed for leering at Pucci's daughter, and his assassins were far more skilled than the fanatical children of the Red Brigades.

"We took a calculated risk by liquidating Benjamin Stern, but it was forced upon us by the material in his possession." Casagrande spoke in a measured, deliberate manner. "Based upon the actions of this man Landau, it is now safe to conclude that the Israeli secret service does not believe the murder of their former operative was carried out by a neo-Nazi extremist."

"Which brings us back to my original suggestion," Pucci interrupted. "Why don't you just kill him?"

"This is not the Italian service that I'm talking about, Don Pucci. This is the *Israeli* service. As director of security, it is my job to protect the Institute. In my opinion, it would be a grave mistake to involve us in a shooting war with the Israeli secret service. They have assassins of their own—assassins who have killed on the streets of Rome and slipped away without a trace." Casagrande looked across the cardinal toward Pucci. "Assassins who could penetrate the walls of this old abbey, Don Pucci."

Cardinal Brindisi played the role of the mediator. "Then how do you suggest we proceed, Carlo?"

"Carefully, Eminence. If he is truly an agent of Israeli intelligence, then we can use our friends in the European security services to make life very uncomfortable for him. In the meantime, we must make sure there's nothing else for him to find." Casagrande paused, then added: "I'm afraid we have one loose end remaining. After examining the material taken from Professor Stern's apartment, I've come to the conclusion he was working with a collaborator—a man who's given us problems in the past."

A look of annoyance rippled over the cardinal's face—a stone cast into a calm pond at sunrise—then his features regained their composure. "And the other aspects of your inquiry, Carlo? Are you any closer to identifying the brethren who leaked these documents to Professor Stern in the first place?"

Casagrande gave a frustrated shake of his head. How many hours had he spent sifting the material taken from the flat in Munich? Notebooks, computer files, address books—Casagrande had gone over everything, looking for clues to the identity of the individuals or group who'd given the information to the professor. Thus far he'd found nothing. The professor had covered his tracks well. It was as if the documents had been handed to him by a ghost.

"I'm afraid that element of the case remains a mystery, Eminence. If this act of treachery was perpetrated by someone inside the Vatican, we may never know the truth. The Curia happens to be good training ground for intrigues of this sort."

This remark elicited a flicker of a smile from Brindisi. They walked in silence for a moment. The cardinal's eyes were down.

"Two days ago, I had lunch with the Holy Father," he said finally. "As we suspected, His Holiness intends to go forward with his program of reconciliation with the Jews. I tried to dissuade him, but it was useless. He's going to the Great Synagogue of Rome next week."

Roberto Pucci spat at the ground. Carlo Casagrande exhaled heavily. He was not surprised by the cardinal's news. Casagrande and Brindisi had a source on the Holy Father's staff, a secretary who was a member of the brotherhood and kept them apprised of developments inside the *appartamento*. He had been warning for weeks that something like this was coming.

"He is a caretaker pope," Pucci snapped. "He needs to learn his place."

Casagrande held his breath, waiting for Pucci to suggest his favorite solution to a problem, but not even Pucci would consider such an option.

"The Holy Father is not content simply to issue another statement of remorse over our past differences with the Jews. He intends to throw open the Secret Archives as well."

"He can't be serious," said Casagrande.

"I'm afraid he's very serious. The question is, if he throws open the archives, will the historians find anything?"

"The Archives have been purged of all references to the meeting at the convent. As for the witnesses, they've been dealt with and their personnel files destroyed. If the Holy Father insists on commissioning a new study, the Archives will yield no new damaging information whatsoever. Unless, of course, the Israeli manages to reconstruct the work of Professor Stern. If that happens—"

"—then the Church, and the Institute, will find itself in very difficult straits," said the Cardinal, finishing Casagrande's sentence for him. "For the greater good of the Church and all those who believe in her, the secret of the covenant must remain just that, a secret."

"Yes, Eminence."

Roberto Pucci lit a cigarette. "Perhaps our friend in the *appartamento* can advise the Holy Father to see the error of his ways, Eminence."

"I've tried that route already, Don Pucci. According to our friend, the Pope is determined to proceed, regardless of the advice of his secretaries or the Curia."

"From a financial point of view, the Holy Father's initiative could be disastrous," Pucci said, switching his focus from murder to money. "Many people wish to do business with the Vatican because of its good name. If the Holy Father drags that good name through the mud of history . . ."

Brindisi nodded in agreement. "In private, the Holy Father often expresses a desire to return to the days of a poor church."

"If he's not careful," said Pucci, "he'll get his wish."

Cardinal Brindisi looked at Casagrande. "This *collaborator,*" the cardinal said. "You believe he poses a threat to us?"

"I do, Eminence."

"What do you require of me, Carlo? Other than my approval, of course."

"Just that, Eminence."

"And from Don Pucci?"

Casagrande looked into the hooded black eyes.

"I need his money."

✦

PART TWO

A
CONVENT
BY THE LAKE

✦

✦ 8 ✦

LAKE GARDA, ITALY

I T WAS EARLY AFTERNOON by the time Gabriel reached the northern end of Lake Garda. As he made his way southward along the shoreline, the climate and vegetation gradually changed from Alpine to Mediterranean. When he lowered his window, chill air washed over his face. The late-day sun shone on the silver-green leaves of the olive trees. Below, the lake was still and flat, like a slab of polished granite.

The town of Brenzone was shrugging off the drowsiness of the *siesta,* awnings opening in the bars and cafés along the waterfront, shopkeepers placing goods in the narrow cobblestone streets rising up the steep slope of Monte Baldo. Gabriel made his way along the lakeshore until he found the Grand Hotel, a saffron-colored villa at the end of town.

As Gabriel pulled into the courtyard, a bellman set upon him with the enthusiasm of a shut-in grateful for company. The lobby was a place from another time. Indeed, Gabriel would not have been surprised to see Kafka perched on the edge of a dusty wing chair, scribbling away at a manuscript in the deep shadows. In the adjoining dining room, a pair of bored waiters slowly set a dozen tables for dinner. If their languorous pace was any indication, most of the tables would not be occupied this evening.

The clerk behind the counter stiffened formally at Gabriel's approach. Gabriel looked at the silver-and-black nametag pinned to the left breast of his blazer: GIANCOMO. Blond and blue-eyed, with the square-shouldered bearing of a Prussian military officer, he eyed Gabriel with a vague curiosity from behind the dais.

In labored but fluent Italian, Gabriel introduced himself as Ehud Landau from Tel Aviv. The clerk seemed pleased by this. When Gabriel asked about a man who had visited the hotel two months earlier—a professor named Benjamin Stern who left behind a pair of eyeglasses—the clerk shook his head slowly. The fifty euros that Gabriel slipped into his palm seemed to stir his memory. "Ah, yes, Herr *Stern*!" The blue eyes danced. "The writer from Munich. I remember him well. He stayed three nights."

"Professor Stern was my brother."

"*Was?*"

"He was murdered in Munich ten days ago."

"Please accept my condolences, Signor Landau, but perhaps I should be talking to the police about Professor Stern and not to his brother."

When Gabriel said he was conducting his own investigation, the concierge frowned thoughtfully. "I'm afraid I can't tell you anything of value, except that I'm quite certain Professor Stern's death had nothing to do with his stay in Brenzone. You see, your brother spent most of his time at the convent."

"The convent?"

The concierge stepped around the counter. "Follow me."

He led Gabriel across the lobby and through a set of French doors. They crossed a terrace overlooking the lake and paused at the balustrade. A short distance away, perched on an outcropping of rock at the edge of the lake, was a crenellated castle.

"The Convent of the Sacred Heart. In the nineteenth century it was a sanatorium. The sisters took over the property before the First War and have been there ever since."

"Do you know what my brother was doing there?"

"I'm afraid not. But why don't you ask Mother Vincenza? She's the mother superior. A lovely woman. I'm sure she'd be very happy to help you."

"Do you have a telephone number?"

The hotelier shook his head. "No phone. The sisters take their privacy very seriously."

A PAIR of towering cypress trees stood like sentinels on either side of the tall iron gate. As Gabriel pressed the bell, a cold wind rose from the lake and swirled in the courtyard, stirring the limbs of the olive trees. A moment later, an old man appeared, dressed in soiled coveralls. When Gabriel said he wished to have a brief word with Mother Vincenza, the old man nodded and disappeared into the convent. Returning a moment later, he unchained the gate and gestured for Gabriel to follow him.

The nun was waiting in the entrance hall. Her oval face was framed by a gray-and-white habit. A pair of thick glasses magnified a steadfast gaze. When Gabriel mentioned Benjamin's name, her face broke into a wide genuine smile. "Yes, of course I remember him," she said, seizing Gabriel's hand. "Such a lovely man. So intelligent. I enjoyed the time we spent together."

Then Gabriel told her the news. Mother Vincenza made the sign of the cross and clasped her hands beneath her chin. Her large eyes seemed on the verge of tears. She took Gabriel by the forearm. "Come with me. You must tell me everything."

The sisters of Brenzone may have taken vows of poverty, but their convent surely occupied one of the most coveted properties in all of Italy. The common room into which Gabriel was shown was a large rectangular gallery with furniture arranged into several separate seating areas. Through the large windows, Gabriel could see a terrace and balustrade and a bright fingernail moon rising over the lake.

They sat in a pair of threadbare armchairs near the window. Mother Vincenza rang a small bell, and when a young nun appeared, the Mother Superior asked for coffee. The nun moved away so smoothly and silently that Gabriel wondered whether she had a set of casters beneath her habit.

Gabriel then told her about the murder of Benjamin. He carefully edited the account so as not to shock the religious woman seated before him. Even so, with each new revelation, Mother Vincenza sighed heavily and crossed herself slowly. By the time Gabriel finished, she was in a state of high distress. The tiny cup of sweetened espresso, brought by the silent young nun, seemed to calm her nerves.

"You knew Benjamin was a writer?" Gabriel asked.

"Of course. That's why he was here in Brenzone."

"He was working on a book?"

"Indeed."

Mother Vincenza paused as the groundskeeper entered the room with a bundle of olive wood in his arms. "Thank you, Licio," she said as the old man laid the wood in a basket by the fire and crept out again.

The nun continued: "If you are his brother, why do you not know the subject of this book?"

"For some reason, Benjamin was very secretive about his project. He kept the nature of it from his friends and family." Gabriel recalled his conversation in Munich with Professor Berger. "Even the head of Benjamin's department at Ludwig-Maximilian University didn't know what he was working on."

Mother Vincenza seemed to accept this explanation, because after a moment of careful appraisal she said, "Your brother was working on a book about the Jews who took refuge in Church properties during the war."

Gabriel considered her statement for a moment. *A book on Jews hiding in convents?* He supposed it was possible, but it didn't really sound like a subject Benjamin would embrace. Nor would it explain his unusual secrecy. He decided to play along.

"What brought him here?"

Mother Vincenza studied him over the rim of her coffee cup. "Finish your drink," she said. "Then I'll show you why your brother came to Brenzone."

THEY DESCENDED the steep stone staircase by flashlight, the nun's warm hand resting lightly on Gabriel's forearm. At the base of the stairs the smell of damp greeted them, and Gabriel could see his breath. A narrow passageway lay before them, lined with arched portals. There was something of the catacombs in this place. Gabriel had a sudden vision of hunted souls moving about by torchlight and speaking in whispers.

Mother Vincenza led him along the passageway, pausing at each portal to play the beam of her flashlight over the interior of a cramped chamber. The stonework shone with damp, and the smell of the lake was overwhelming. Gabriel thought he could hear water lapping above their heads.

"It was the only place where the sisters thought the refugees would be safe," the nun said finally, disturbing the silence. "As you can feel for yourself, it was bitterly cold in the winter. I'm afraid they suffered terribly, especially the children."

"How many?"

"Usually about a dozen. Sometimes more. Sometimes fewer."

"Why fewer?"

"Some moved on to other *conventi*. One family tried to make it to Switzerland. They were caught at the border by a Swiss patrol and handed over to the Germans. I'm told they died at Auschwitz. I was just a little girl during the war, of course. My family lived in Turin."

"It must have been very dangerous for the women living here."

"Yes, very. In those days, Fascist gangs were roaming the country looking for Jews. Bribes were paid. Jews were denounced for money. Anyone who concealed Jews was subject to terrible reprisals. The sisters accepted these people at great risk to themselves."

"So why did they do it?"

She smiled warmly and squeezed his arm. "There is a great tradition in the Church, Signor Landau. Priests and nuns feel a special duty to assist fugitives. To help those unjustly accused. The sisters of Brenzone helped the Jews out of Christian goodness. And they did it because the Holy Father told them to do it."

"Pope Pius instructed the convents to take in Jews?"

The nuns eyes widened. "Indeed. Convents, monasteries, schools, hospitals. All Church institutions and properties were ordered by the Holy Father to throw open their doors to the Jews."

The beam of Mother Vincenza's flashlight fell upon an obese rat. It scurried away, claws scratching against the stones, yellow eyes glowing.

"Thank you, Mother Vincenza," Gabriel said. "I think I've seen enough."

"As you wish." The nun remained motionless, her unfaltering gaze lingering on him. "You should not be saddened by this place, Signor Landau. Because of the sisters of Brenzone, the people who took shelter here managed to survive. This is no place for tears. It is a place of joy. Of hope."

When Gabriel made no response, Mother Vincenza turned and led him up the stairs. As she walked across the gravel forecourt, the night wind lifted the skirt of her habit.

"We're about to sit down for our evening meal. You're welcome to join us if you like."

"You're very kind, but I wouldn't want to intrude. Besides, I've taken enough of your time."

"Not at all."

At the front gate Gabriel stopped and turned to face her. "Do you know the names of people who took shelter here?" he asked suddenly.

The nun seemed surprised by his question. She studied him a moment, then shook her head deliberately. "I'm afraid the names have been lost over the years."

"That's a shame."

"Yes," she said, nodding slowly.

"May I ask you one more question, Mother Vincenza?"

"Certainly."

"Did the Vatican give you permission to speak with Benjamin?"

She lifted her chin defiantly. "I don't need some bureaucrat in the Curia to tell me when to talk and when to keep silent. Only my God can tell me that, and God told me to talk to your brother about the Jews of Brenzone."

MOTHER VINCENZA kept a small office on the second floor of the convent, in a pleasant room overlooking the lake. She closed and locked the door, then sat down at her modest desk and pulled open the top drawer. There, concealed behind a small cardboard box filled with pencils and paperclips, was a sleek cellular telephone. Technically, it was against the strict rules of the convent to keep such a device, but the man from the Vatican had assured her that, given the circumstances, it would not constitute a violation, moral or otherwise.

She powered on the phone, just as he had taught her, and carefully entered the number in Rome. After a few seconds of silence, she could hear a telephone ringing. This surprised her. A moment later, when a male voice came on the line, it surprised her even more.

"This is Mother Vincenza—"

"I know who this is," the man said, his tone brusque and businesslike. Then she remembered his instructions about never using names on the telephone. She felt a fool.

"You asked me to call if anyone came to the convent to ask questions about the professor." She hesitated, waiting for him to speak, but he said nothing. "Someone came this afternoon."

"What did he call himself?"

"Landau," she said. "Ehud Landau, from Tel Aviv. He said he was the man's brother."

"Where is he now?"

"I don't know. Perhaps he's staying at the old hotel."

"Can you find out?"

"I suppose so, yes."

"Find out—then call me back."

The connection went dead.

Mother Vincenza placed the telephone back in its hiding place and quietly closed the drawer.

GABRIEL DECIDED to spend the night in Brenzone and return to Venice first thing in the morning. After leaving the convent, he walked back to the hotel and took a room. The prospect of eating supper in the dreary hotel dining room depressed him, so he walked down to the lakeshore through the chill March evening and ate fish in a cheerful restaurant filled with townspeople. The white wine was local and very cold.

The images of the case flashed through his mind while he ate: The Odin Rune and the Three-Bladed Swastika painted on Benjamin's wall; the blood on the floor where Benjamin had died; Detective Weiss tailing him through the streets of Munich; Mother Vincenza leading him down the stairs to the dank cellar of the convent by the lake.

Gabriel was convinced Benjamin had been killed by someone who wished to silence him. Only that would explain why his computer was missing and why his apartment contained no evidence at all that he was writing a book. If Gabriel could recreate Benjamin's book—or at least the subject matter—he might be able to identify who killed him and why. Unfortunately, he had next to nothing—only an elderly nun who claimed Benjamin was working on a book about Jews taking refuge in Church properties during the war. Generally speaking, it was not the type of subject matter that could get a man killed.

He paid his check and started back to the hotel. He took his time, wandering the quiet streets of the old town, paying little attention to where he was going, following the narrow passageways wherever they happened to lead him. His thoughts mirrored his path through Brenzone. Instinctively, he approached the problem as though it were a restoration, as though Benjamin's book were a painting that had suffered such heavy losses that it was little more than a bare canvas with a few swaths of color and a fragment of an under-drawing. If Benjamin were an Old Master painter, Gabriel would study all his similar works. He would analyze his technique and his influences at the time the work was painted. In short, he would absorb every possible detail about the artist, no matter how seemingly mundane, before setting to work on the canvas.

Thus far Gabriel had very little on which to base his restoration, but now, as he wandered the streets of Brenzone, he became aware of another salient detail.

For the second time in two days, he was being followed.

He turned a corner and walked past a row of shuttered shops. Glancing once over his shoulder, he spotted a man rounding the corner after him. He performed the same maneuver, and once again spotted his pursuer, a mere shadow in the darkened streets, thin and stooped, agile as an alley cat.

Gabriel slipped into the darkened foyer of a small apartment house and listened as the footfalls grew fainter, then ceased altogether. A moment later, he stepped back into the street and started back toward the hotel. His shadow was gone.

WHEN GABRIEL RETURNED to the hotel, the concierge named Giancomo was still on duty behind his dais. He slid the key across the counter as though it were a priceless relic and asked about Gabriel's meal.

"It was wonderful, thank you."

"Perhaps tomorrow night you'll try our own dining room."

"Perhaps," said Gabriel noncommittally, pocketing the key. "I'd like to see Benjamin's bill from his stay here—especially the record of his telephone calls. It might be helpful."

"Yes, I see your point, Signor Landau, but I'm afraid that would be a violation of the hotel's strict privacy policy. I'm sure a man like you can understand that."

Gabriel pointed out that since Benjamin was no longer living, concerns about his privacy were surely misplaced.

"I'm sorry, but the rules apply to the dead as well," the concierge said. "Now, if the police requested such information, we would be obliged to hand it over."

"The information is important to me," Gabriel said. "I'd be willing to pay a surcharge in order to obtain it."

"A surcharge? I see." He scratched his chin thoughtfully. "I believe the charge would be five hundred euros." A pause to allow Gabriel to digest the sum. "A processing fee. In advance, of course."

"Yes, of course."

Gabriel counted out the euro notes and laid them on the counter. Giancomo's hand passed over the surface and the money disappeared.

"Go to your room, Signor Landau. I'll print out the bill and bring it to you."

Gabriel climbed the stairs to his room. He locked and chained the door, then walked to the window and peered out. The lake was shimmering in the moonlight. There was no one outside—at least no one he could see. He sat on the bed and began to undress.

An envelope appeared beneath the door and slid across the terracotta floor. Gabriel picked it up, lifted the flap, and removed the contents. He switched on the bedside lamp and examined the bill. During his two-day stay at the hotel, Benjamin had made only three telephone calls. Two were placed to his own apartment in Munich—to check messages on his answering machine, Gabriel reckoned—and the third to a number in London.

Gabriel lifted the receiver and dialed the number.

An answering machine picked up.

"You've reached the office of Peter Malone. I'm sorry, but I'm not available to take your call. If you'd like to leave a—"

Gabriel placed the receiver back in the cradle.

Peter Malone? The British investigative reporter? Why would Benjamin be calling a man like him? Gabriel folded the bill and slipped it back into the envelope. He was about to drop it into Ehud Landau's briefcase when the telephone rang.

He reached out, but hesitated. No one knew he was here—no one but the concierge and the man who'd followed Gabriel after dinner. Perhaps Malone had captured his number and was calling back. Better to know than remain ignorant, he thought. He snatched up the receiver and held it to his ear for a moment without speaking. Finally: "Yes?"

"Mother Vincenza is lying to you, the same way she lied to your friend. Find Sister Regina and Martin Luther. Then you'll know the truth about what happened at the convent."

"Who is this?"

"Don't come back. It's not safe for you here."

CLICK.

·9·

GRINDELWALD, SWITZERLAND

THE MAN WHO LIVED in the large chalet in the shadow of the Eiger was a private person, even by the exacting standards of the mountains of Inner Switzerland. He made it his business to learn what was being said about him and knew that in the bars and cafés of Grindelwald there was constant speculation about his occupation. Some thought him a successful private banker from Zurich; others believed him to be the owner of a large chemical concern headquartered in Zug. There was a theory he was born to wealth and had no career at all. There was baseless gossip he was an arms dealer or a money launderer. The girl who cleaned his chalet told of a kitchen filled with expensive copper pots and cooking implements of every kind. A rumor circulated that he was a chef or restaurateur. He liked that one the best. He always thought he might have enjoyed cooking for a living, had he not fallen into his current profession.

The limited amount of mail that arrived daily at his chalet bore the name Eric Lange. He spoke German with the accent of a Zuricher but with the sing-song cadence of those native to the valleys of Inner Switzerland. He did his shopping at the Migros supermarket in town and always paid in cash. He received no visitors and, despite his good looks, was never seen in the company of a woman. He was prone to long periods of absence. When asked for an explanation, he would murmur something about a business venture. When pressed to elaborate, his gray eyes would grow so suddenly cold that few possessed the courage to pursue the matter further.

Mostly, he seemed a man with too much time on his hands. From December to March, when the snow was good, he spent most days on the slopes. He was an expert skier, fast but never reckless, with the size and strength of a downhiller and the quickness and agility of a slalom racer. His outfits were costly but reserved, carefully chosen to deflect attention rather than attract it. On chairlifts, he was notorious for his silence. In summer, when all but the permanent glaciers melted, he set out from the chalet each morning and hiked up the steep slope of the valley. His body seemed to have been constructed for this very purpose: tall and powerful, narrow hips and broad shoulders, heavily muscled thighs, and calves shaped like diamonds. He moved along the rocky footpaths with the agility of a large cat and seemed never to tire.

Usually, he would pause at the base of the Eiger for a drink from his canteen and to squint upward toward the windswept face. He never climbed—indeed, he thought men who hurled themselves against the Eiger were some of nature's greatest fools. Some afternoons, from the terrace of his chalet, he could hear the beating of rescue helicopters, and sometimes, with the aid of his Zeiss telescope, he could see dead climbers hanging by their lines, twisting in the *föhn,* the famed Eiger wind. He had the utmost respect for the mountain. The Eiger, like the man known as Eric Lange, was a perfect killer.

SHORTLY BEFORE NOON, Lange slid off the chairlift for his final run of the day. At the bottom of the trail, he disappeared into a grove of pine and glided through the shadows until he arrived at the back door of his chalet. He removed his skis and gloves and punched a series of numbers into the keypad on the wall next to the door. He stepped inside, stripped off his jacket and powder pants, and hung the skis on a professional-style rack. Upstairs, he showered and changed into traveling clothes: corduroy trousers, a dark-gray cashmere sweater, suede brogues. His overnight bag was already packed.

He paused in front of the bathroom mirror and examined his appearance. The hair was a combination of sun-streaked blond and gray. The eyes were naturally colorless and took well to contact lenses. The features were altered periodically by a plastic surgeon at a discreet clinic located outside Geneva. He slipped on a pair of tortoise-shell eyeglasses, then added gel to his hair and combed it straight back. The change in his appearance was remarkable.

He walked into his bedroom. Concealed inside the large walk-in closet was a combination safe. He worked the tumbler and pulled open the heavy door. Inside were the tools of his trade: false passports, a large amount of cash in various currencies, a collection of handguns. He filled his wallet with Swiss francs and selected a Stechkin nine-millimeter pistol, his favorite weapon. He nestled the gun into his overnight bag and closed the door of the safe. Five minutes later, he climbed into his Audi sedan and set out for Zurich.

✦ ✦ ✦

IN THE VIOLENT history of European political extremism, no terrorist was suspected of shedding more blood than the man dubbed the Leopard. A freelance assassin-for-hire, he had plied his trade across the continent and left a trail of bodies and bomb damage stretching from Athens to London and Madrid to Stockholm. He had worked for the Red Army Faction in West Germany, the Red Brigades in Italy, and *Action Directe* in France. He had killed a British army officer for the Irish Republican Army and a Spanish minister for the Basque separatist group ETA. His relationship with Palestinian terrorists had been long and fruitful. He had committed a string of kidnappings and assassinations for Abu Jihad, the second-in-command of the PLO, and he had killed for the fanatical Palestinian dissident Abu Nidal. Indeed, the Leopard was believed to have been the mastermind behind the simultaneous attacks on the Rome and Vienna airports in December 1985 that left nineteen people dead and 120 wounded. It had been nine years since his last suspected attack, the murder of a French industrialist in Paris. Some within the Western European security and intelligence community believed that the Leopard was dead—that he had been killed in a dispute with one of his old employers. Some doubted he had ever existed at all.

NIGHT HAD FALLEN by the time Eric Lange arrived in Zurich. He parked his car on a rather unpleasant street north of the train station and walked to the Hotel St. Gotthard, just off the gentle sweep of the Bahnhofstrasse. A room had been reserved for him. The absence of luggage did not surprise the clerk. Because of its location and reputation for discretion, the hotel was often used for business meetings too confidential to take place even on the premises of a private bank. Hitler himself was rumored to have stayed at the St. Gotthard when he was in Zurich to meet with his Swiss bankers.

Lange took the lift up to his room. He drew the curtains and spent a moment rearranging the furniture. He pushed an armchair into the center of the room, facing the door, and in front of the chair placed a low, circular coffee table. On the table he left two items, a small but powerful flashlight and the Stechkin. Then he sat down and switched off the lights. The darkness was absolute.

He sipped a disappointing red wine from the minibar while waiting for the client to arrive. As a condition of employment, he refused to deal with cutouts or couriers. If a man wanted his services, he had to have the courage to present himself in person and show his face. Lange insisted on this not out of ego but for his own protection. His services were so costly that only very wealthy men could afford him, men skilled in the art of betrayal, men who knew how to set up others to pay the price for their sins.

At 8:15 P.M., the precise time Lange had requested, there was a knock at the door. Lange picked up the Stechkin with one hand and the flashlight with the other and gave his visitor permission to enter the pitch-black room. When the door had closed again, he switched on the light. The beam fell upon a small, well-dressed man, late sixties, with a monkish fringe of iron-gray hair. Lange knew him: General Carlo Casagrande, the former *Carabinieri* chief of counterterrorism, now keeper of all things secret at the Vatican. How many of the general's former foes would love to be in Lange's position now—pointing a loaded gun at the great Casagrande, slayer of the *Brigate Rossa,* savior of Italy. The Brigades had tried to kill him, but

Casagrande had lived underground during the war, moving from bunker to bunker, barracks to barracks. Instead, they'd massacred his wife and daughter. The old general was never the same after that, which probably explained why he was here now, in a darkened hotel room in Zurich, hiring a professional killer.

"It's like a confessional in here," Casagrande said in Italian.

"That's the point," Lange replied in the same language. "You can kneel if it makes you more comfortable."

"I think I'll remain standing."

"You have the dossier?"

Casagrande held up his attaché case. Lange lifted the Stechkin into the beam of light so the man from the Vatican could see it. Casagrande moved with the slowness of a man handling high explosives. He opened his briefcase, removed a large manila envelope, and laid it on the coffee table. Lange scooped it up with his gun hand and shook the contents into his lap. A moment later, he looked up.

"I'm disappointed. I was hoping you were coming here to ask me to kill the Pope."

"You would have done it, wouldn't you? You would have killed your Pope."

"He's not *my* pope, but the answer to your question is yes, I would have killed him. And if they'd hired me to do it, instead of that maniacal Turk, the Pole would have died that afternoon in St. Peter's."

"Then I suppose I should be thankful that the KGB *didn't* hire you. God knows you did enough other dirty work for them."

"The KGB? I don't think so, General, and neither do you. The KGB wasn't fond of the Pole, but they weren't foolish enough to kill him, either. Even you don't believe it was the KGB. From what I hear, you believe the conspiracy to kill the Pope originated closer to home—within the Church itself. That's why the findings of your inquiry were kept secret. The prospect of revealing the true identity of the plotters was too embarrassing for all concerned. It was also convenient to keep the finger of unsubstantiated blame pointed eastward, toward Moscow, the true enemies of the Vatican."

"The days when we settled our differences by murdering popes ended with the Middle Ages."

"Please, General, such statements are beneath a man of your intelligence and experience." Lange dropped the dossier on the coffee table. "The links between this man and the Jew professor are too strong. I won't do it. Find someone else."

"There is no one else like you. And I don't have time to find another suitable candidate."

"Then it will cost you."

"How much?"

A pause, then: "Five hundred thousand, paid in advance."

"That's a bit excessive, don't you think?"

"No, I don't."

Casagrande made a show of thought, then nodded. "After you kill him, I want you to search his office and remove any material linking him to the professor or the book. I also want you to bring me his computer. Carry the items back to Zurich and leave them in the same safe-deposit account where you left the material from Munich."

"Transporting the computer of a man you've just killed is not the wisest thing for an assassin to do."

Casagrande looked at the ceiling. "How much?"

"An additional one hundred thousand."

"Done."

"When I see that the money has been deposited in my account, I'll move against the target. Is there a deadline?"

"Yesterday."

"Then you should have come to me two days ago."

Casagrande turned and let himself out. Eric Lange switched off the light and sat there in the dark, finishing his wine.

CASAGRANDE WALKED down the Bahnhofstrasse into a swirling wind blowing off the lake. He felt an appalling desire to fall on his knees in a confessional and unburden his sins to a priest. He could not. Under the rules of the Institute, he could confess only to a priest who was a member of the brotherhood. Because of the sensitive nature of Casagrande's work, his confessor was none other than Cardinal Marco Brindisi.

He came to the Talstrasse, a quiet street lined with graystone buildings and modern office blocks. Casagrande walked a short distance, until he arrived at a plain doorway. On the wall next to the doorway was a brass plaque:

BECKER & PUHL

PRIVATE BANKERS

TALSTRASSE 26

Next to the plaque was a button, which Casagrande pressed with his thumb. He glanced up into the fisheye of the security camera over the door, then looked away. A moment later, the deadbolt snapped back and Casagrande stepped into a small antechamber.

Herr Becker was waiting for him. Starched, fussy and very bald,

Becker was known for absolute discretion, even in the highly secretive world of the Bahnhofstrasse. The exchange of information
that took place next was brief and largely a needless formality. Casagrande and Becker were well acquainted and had done much business over the years, though Becker had no idea who Casagrande was
or where his money came from. As usual, Casagrande had to struggle to hear Becker's voice, for it rose barely above a whisper even in
normal conversation. As he followed him down the corridor to the
strongbox room, the fall of Becker's Bally loafers on the polished
marble floor made no sound.

They entered a windowless chamber, empty of furniture except
for a high viewing table. Herr Becker left Casagrande alone, then
returned a moment later with a metal a safe-deposit box. "Leave it
on the table when you're finished," the banker said. "I'll be just outside the door if there's anything else you require."

The Swiss banker went out. Casagrande unbuttoned his overcoat and unzipped the false lining. Hidden inside were several
bound stacks of currency, courtesy of Roberto Pucci. One by one,
the Italian placed the bundles of cash into the box.

When Casagrande was finished, he summoned Herr Becker.
The little Swiss banker saw him out and bid him a pleasant evening.
As Casagrande walked back up the Bahnhofstrasse, he found himself reciting the familiar and comforting words of the Act of Con-
trition.

·10·

VENICE

GABRIEL RETURNED TO VENICE early the following morning. He left the Opel in the carpark adjacent to the train station and took a water taxi to the Church of San Zaccaria. He entered without greeting the other members of the team, then climbed his scaffolding and concealed himself behind the shroud. After an absence of three days, they were strangers to each other, Gabriel and his virgin, but as the hours slowly passed they grew comfortable in each other's presence. As always, she blanketed him with a sense of peace, and the concentration required by his work pushed the investigation of Benjamin's death into a quiet corner of his mind.

He took a break to replenish his palette. For a moment, his mind left the Bellini and returned to Brenzone. After taking breakfast that morning in his hotel, he had walked to the convent and rung the bell at the front gate to summon Mother Vincenza. When she

appeared, Gabriel had asked if he could speak to a woman called
Sister Regina. The nun's face reddened visibly, and she explained
that there was no one at the convent by that name. When Gabriel
asked whether there had *ever* been a Sister Regina at the convent,
Mother Vincenza shook her head and suggested that Signor Landau respect the cloistered nature of the convent and never return.
Without another word, she crossed the courtyard and disappeared
inside. Gabriel then spotted Licio, the groundskeeper, trimming
the vines on a trellis. When he tried to summon him, the old man
glanced up, then hurried away through the shadowed garden. At
that moment Gabriel concluded that it was Licio who had followed
him through the streets of Brenzone the previous night and Licio
who had placed the anonymous call to his hotel room. Clearly, the
old man was frightened. Gabriel decided that, for now at least, he
would do nothing to make Licio's situation worse. Instead, he would
focus on the convent itself. If Mother Vincenza were telling him
the truth—that Jews had been sheltered at the convent during the
war—then somewhere there would be a record of it.

Returning to Venice, he'd had a nagging impression that he was
being followed by a gray Lancia. In Verona he left the *autostrada*
and entered the ancient city center, where he performed a series of
field-tested maneuvers designed to shake surveillance. In Padua he
did the same thing. Half an hour later, racing across the causeway
toward Venice, he was quite confident he was alone.

He worked on the altarpiece all afternoon and into the evening.
At seven o'clock, he left the church and wandered over to Francesco Tiepolo's office in San Marco and found him sitting alone at
the broad oak table he used as a desk, working his way through a
stack of papers. Tiepolo was a highly skilled restorer in his own
right, but had long ago set aside his brushes and palette to focus his

attention on running his thriving restoration business. As Gabriel entered the room, Tiepolo smiled at him through his tangled black beard. On the streets of Venice, he was often mistaken by tourists for Luciano Pavarotti.

Over a glass of *ripasso,* Gabriel broke the news that he had to leave Venice again for a few days to take care of a personal matter. Tiepolo buried his big face in his hands and murmured a string of Italian curses before looking up in frustration.

"Mario, in six weeks the venerable Church of the San Zaccaria is scheduled to reopen to the public. If it does not reopen to the public in six weeks, restored to its original glory, the superintendents will take me down to the cellars of the Doge's Palace for a ritual disembowelment. Am I making myself clear to you, Mario? If you don't finish that Bellini, my reputation will be ruined."

"I'm close, Francesco. I just need to sort out some personal affairs."

"What sort of affairs?"

"A death in the family."

"Really?"

"Don't ask any more questions, Francesco."

"You do whatever you need, Mario. But let me tell you this. If I think the Bellini is in danger of not being finished on schedule, I'll have no choice but to remove you from the project and give it to Antonio."

"Antonio's not qualified to restore that altarpiece, and you know it."

"What else can I do? Restore it myself? You leave me no choice."

Tiepolo's anger quickly evaporated, as it usually did, and he poured more *ripasso* into his empty glass. Gabriel looked up at the wall behind Tiepolo's desk. Amid photos of churches and *scuolas* restored by Tiepolo's firm was a curious image: Tiepolo himself, strolling through the Vatican Gardens, with none other than Pope Paul VII at his side.

"You had a private audience with the Pope?"

"Not an audience really. It was more informal than that."

"Would you care to explain?"

Tiepolo looked down and shuffled his stack of paperwork. It did not take a trained interrogator to conclude that he was reluctant to answer Gabriel's question. Finally, he said, "It's not something I discuss frequently, but the Holy Father and I are rather good friends."

"Really?"

"The Holy Father and I worked very closely together here in Venice when he was the patriarch. He's actually something of an art historian. Oh, we used to have the most terrible battles. Now we get on famously. I go down to Rome to have supper with him at least once a month. He insists on doing the cooking himself. His specialty is tuna and spaghettini, but he puts so much red pepper in it that we spend the rest of the night sweating. He's a warrior, that man! A culinary sadist."

Gabriel smiled and stood up. Tiepolo said, "You won't let me down, will you, Mario?"

"A friend of *il papa*? Of course not. *Ciao,* Francesco. See you in a couple days."

AN AIR of desertion hung over the old ghetto—no children playing in the *campo,* no old men sitting in the café, and from the tall apartment houses came no sounds of life. In a few of the windows, Gabriel saw lights burning, and for a fleeting instant he smelled meat and onion frying in olive oil, but for the most part he imagined himself a man coming home to a ghost town, a place where homes and shops remained but the inhabitants had long ago vanished.

The bakery where he had met with Shamron was closed. He walked a few paces to No. 2899. A small sign on the door read COMUNITÀ EBRAICA DI VENEZIA. Gabriel rang the bell, and a moment later came the voice of a woman over an unseen intercom. "Yes, may I help you?"

"My name is Mario Delvecchio. I have an appointment to see the rabbi."

"Just a moment, please."

Gabriel turned his back to the door and surveyed the square. A moment stretched to two, then three. It was the war in the territories. It had made everyone jittery. Security had been tightened at Jewish sites across Europe. So far, Venice had been spared, but in Rome and in cities across France and Austria, synagogues and cemeteries had been vandalized and Jews attacked on the streets. The newspapers were calling it the worst wave of public anti-Semitism to sweep the continent since the Second World War. At times like these, Gabriel despised the fact that he had to conceal his Jewishness.

A buzzer finally sounded, followed by the click of an automatic lock giving way. He pushed back the door and found himself in a darkened passageway. At the end was another door. As Gabriel approached, it too was unlocked for him.

He entered a small, cluttered office. Because of the air of decline hanging over the ghetto, he had prepared himself for an Italian version of Frau Ratzinger—a formidable old woman shrouded in the black cloak of widowhood. Instead, much to his surprise, he was greeted by a tall, striking woman about thirty years old. Her hair was dark and curly and shimmering with highlights of auburn and chestnut. Barely constrained by a clasp at the nape of her neck, it spilled riotously about a pair of athletic shoulders. Her eyes were the color of caramel and flecked with gold. Her lips looked as though they were attempting to suppress a smile. She seemed supremely aware of the effect her appearance was having on him.

"The rabbi is at the synagogue for *Ma'ariv*. He asked me to entertain you until he arrives. I'm Chiara. I just made coffee. Care for some?"

"Thank you."

She poured from a stovetop espresso pot, added sugar without asking whether he wanted any, and handed the cup over to Gabriel. When he took it, she noticed the smudges of paint on his fingers. He had come to the ghetto straight from Tiepolo's office and hadn't had time to wash properly.

"You're a painter?"

"A restorer, actually."

"How fascinating. Where are you working?"

"The San Zaccaria project."

She smiled. "Ah, one my favorite churches. Which painting? Not the Bellini?"

Gabriel nodded.

"You must be very good."

"You might say that Bellini and I are old friends," Gabriel said modestly. "How many people show up for *Ma'ariv*?"

"A few of the older men, usually. Sometimes more, sometimes fewer. Some nights, the rabbi is alone up there in the synagogue. He believes strongly that the day he stops saying evening prayers is the day this community vanishes."

Just then the rabbi entered the room. Once again, Gabriel was surprised by his relative youth. He was just a few years older than

Gabriel, fit and vibrant, with a mane of silver hair beneath his black fedora and a trimmed beard. He pumped Gabriel's hand and appraised him through a pair of steel-rimmed eyeglasses.

"I'm Rabbi Zolli. I hope my daughter was a gracious host in my absence. I'm afraid she's spent too much time in Israel the last few years and has lost all her manners as a result."

"She was very kind, but she didn't say she was your daughter."

"You see? Always up to mischief." The rabbi turned to the girl. "Go home now, Chiara. Sit with your mother. We won't be long. Come, Signor Delvecchio. I think you'll find my office more comfortable."

The woman pulled on her coat and looked at Gabriel. "I'm very interested in art restoration. I'd love to see the Bellini. Would it be all right if I stopped by sometime to watch you work?"

"There she goes again," the rabbi said. "So straightforward, so blunt. No manners anymore."

"I'd be happy to show you the altarpiece. I'll call when it's convenient."

"You can reach me here anytime. *Ciao.*"

Rabbi Zolli escorted Gabriel into an office lined with sagging bookshelves. His collection of Judaica was impressive, and the stunning array of languages represented in the titles suggested that, like Gabriel, he was a polyglot. They sat in a pair of mismatched armchairs and the rabbi resumed where they had left off.

"Your message said you were interested in discussing the Jews who took shelter during the war at the Convent of the Sacred Heart in Brenzone."

"Yes, that's right."

"I find it interesting that you should phrase your question in that manner."

"Why is that?"

"Because I've devoted my life to studying and preserving the history of Jews in this part of Italy, and I've never seen any evidence to suggest that Jews were provided sanctuary at that particular convent. In fact, the evidence suggests quite the opposite occurred—that Jews requested sanctuary and were turned away."

"You're absolutely sure?"

"As sure as one can be in a situation like this."

"A nun at the convent told me that a dozen or so Jews were provided sanctuary there during the war. She even showed me the rooms in a cellar where they hid."

"And what is this good woman's name?"

"Mother Vincenza."

"I'm afraid Mother Vincenza is sadly mistaken. Or, worse, she's deliberately trying to mislead you, though I would hesitate to level such an accusation against a woman of faith."

Gabriel thought of the late-night call to his hotel room in Brenzone: *Mother Vincenza is lying to you, the same way she lied to your friend.*

The rabbi leaned forward and laid his hand on Gabriel's forearm. "Tell me, Signor Delvecchio. What is your interest in this matter? Is it academic?"

"No, it's personal."

"Then do you mind if I ask you a *personal* question? Are you Jewish?"

Gabriel hesitated, then answered the question truthfully.

"How much do you know about what happened here during the war?" the rabbi asked.

"I'm ashamed to say that my knowledge is not what it should be, Rabbi Zolli."

"Believe me, I'm used to that." He smiled warmly. "Come with me. There's something you should see."

THEY CROSSED the darkened square and stood before what appeared to be an ordinary apartment house. Through an open shade, Gabriel could see a woman preparing an evening meal in a small, institutional kitchen. In the next room, a trio of old women huddled round a flickering television. Then he noticed the sign over the door: CASA ISRAELITICA DI RIPOSO. The building was a nursing home for Jews.

"Read the plaque," the rabbi said, lighting a match. It was a memorial to Venetian Jews arrested by the Germans and deported during the war. The rabbi extinguished the match with a flick of his wrist and gazed through the window at the elderly Jews.

"In September of 1943, not long after the collapse of the Mussolini regime, the German Army occupied all but the southernmost tip of the Italian Peninsula. Within days, the president of the Jewish community here in Venice received a demand from the SS: hand over a list of all Jews still living in Venice, or face the consequences."

"What did he do?"

"He committed suicide rather than comply. In doing so, he alerted the community that time was running out. Hundreds fled the city. Many took refuge in convents and monasteries throughout the north, or in the homes of ordinary Italians. A few tried to cross the border into Switzerland but were turned away."

"But none at Brenzone?"

"I have no evidence to suggest that any Jews from Venice—or anywhere else, for that matter—were given sanctuary at the Convent of the Sacred Heart. In fact, our archives contain written testimony about a family from this community who requested sanctuary in Brenzone and were turned away."

"Who stayed behind in Venice?"

"The elderly. The sick. The poor who had no means to travel or pay bribes. On the night of December fifth, Italian police and Fascist gangs entered the ghetto on behalf of the Germans. One hundred and sixty-three Jews were arrested. Here, in the *Casa di Riposo,* they hauled the elderly from their beds and loaded them onto trucks. They were sent first to an internment camp at Fossoli. Then, in February, they were transferred to Auschwitz. There were no survivors."

The rabbi took Gabriel by the elbow and together they walked slowly around the edge of the square. "The Jews of Rome were rounded up two months earlier. At five-thirty on the morning of October sixteenth, more than three hundred Germans stormed the ghetto in a driving rainstorm—SS field police along with a Waffen SS Death's Head unit. They went house to house, dragging Jews from their beds and loading them into troop trucks. They were taken to a temporary detention facility at the barracks of the Collegio Militare, about a half mile from the Vatican. Despite the horrible nature of their work that night, some of the SS men wanted to see the dome of the great Basilica, so the convoy altered its route accordingly. As it moved past St. Peter's Square, the terrified Jews in the back of the trucks pleaded with the Pope to save them. All evidence suggests he knew full well what was taking place in the ghetto that morning. It was, after all, under his very windows. He did not lift a finger to intervene."

"How many?"

"More than a thousand that night. Two days after the roundup, the Jews of Rome were loaded onto rail cars at the Tiburtina station for the journey east. Five days after that, one thousand and sixty souls perished in the gas chambers at Auschwitz and Birkenau."

"But many survived, did they not?"

"Indeed, remarkably, four-fifths of Italian Jewry survived the war. As soon as the Germans occupied Italy, thousands immediately sought and were provided shelter in convents and monasteries, as well as in Catholic hospitals and schools. Thousands more were given shelter by ordinary Italians. Adolf Eichmann testified at his trial that every Italian Jew who survived the war owed his life to an Italian."

"Was it because of an order from the Vatican? Was Sister Vincenza telling me the truth about the papal directive?"

"That is what the Church wishes us to believe, but I'm afraid there is no evidence to suggest the Vatican issued instructions to Church institutions to offer shelter and comfort to Jews fleeing the roundup. In fact there *is* evidence to suggest that the Vatican issued no such order."

"What sort of evidence?"

"There are numerous examples of Jews who sought shelter in church properties and were turned away. Others were told they had to convert to Catholicism in order to stay. Had the Pope issued a directive to throw open the doors to Jews, no mere nun or monk would have dared to disobey him. The Italian Catholics who rescued Jews did so out of goodness and compassion—not because they were acting under the orders of their Supreme Pontiff. If they had waited for a papal directive to act, I'm afraid many more Italian Jews would have died at Auschwitz and Birkenau. There was no such directive. Indeed, despite repeated appeals from the Allies and

Jewish leaders around the world, Pope Pius never found it in his heart even to speak out against the mass murder of Europe's Jews."

"Why not? Why did he remain silent?"

The rabbi raised his hands in a helpless gesture. "He claimed that because the Church was universal, he could not be placed in the position of taking sides, even against a force as wicked as Nazi Germany. If he condemned the atrocities of Hitler, Pius said, he would also have to condemn any atrocities committed by the Allies. He claimed that by speaking out, he would only make matters worse for the Jews, though it is hard to imagine what could be worse than the murder of six million. He also saw himself as a statesman and diplomat, an actor in European affairs. He wanted to play a role in bringing about a negotiated settlement that would preserve a strong, anti-Communist Germany in the heart of Europe. I have my own theories as well."

"What are they?"

"Despite public professions of love for the Jewish people, I'm afraid His Holiness did not care much for us. Remember, he was raised in a Catholic Church that preached anti-Semitism as a matter of doctrine. He equated Jews with Bolshevism and bought into all the old hatreds that Jews were interested only in the material. Throughout the nineteen thirties, while he was the Secretary of State, the Vatican's official newspapers were filled with the same sort of anti-Semitic filth one might have read in *Der Stürmer*. One article in the Vatican journal *La Civiltà Cattolica* actually discussed the possibility of eliminating the Jews through annihilation. In my opinion, Pius probably felt the Jews were getting exactly what they deserved. Why should he risk himself, and more importantly his Church, for a people he believed were guilty of history's greatest crime—the murder of God himself?"

"Then why did so many Jews thank the Pope after the war?"

"The Jews who stayed in Italy were more interested in reaching out to Christians than raising uncomfortable questions about the past. In 1945, preventing another Holocaust was more important than learning the truth. For the shattered remnants of the community, it was simply a matter of survival."

Gabriel and Rabbi Zolli arrived back at their starting point, the *Casa Israelitica di Riposo,* and once more stood side by side staring through the window at the elderly Jews sitting before their television.

"What was it Christ said? 'Whatsoever you do to the least of my brothers'? Look at us now: the oldest continuous Jewish community in Europe, reduced to this. A few families, a few old people too sick, too near to death, to ever leave. Most nights I say *Ma'ariv* alone. Even on Shabbat, we have only a handful who bother to attend. Most are visitors to Venice."

He turned and looked carefully at Gabriel's face, as though he could see the telltale traces of a childhood spent on an agricultural settlement in the Jezreel Valley.

"What is your interest in this matter, Signor Delvecchio? And before you answer that question, please try to remember you are speaking to a rabbi."

"I'm afraid that falls into the category of an uncomfortable question that is better not asked."

"I feared you might say that. Just remember one thing. Memories are long in this part of the world, and things are not so good at the moment. The war, the suicide bombers. . . . It might not be best to stir up a hornets' nest. So tread carefully, my friend. For us."

·11·

ROME

L'EAU VIVE WAS ONE of the few places in Rome where Carlo Casagrande felt at ease without a bodyguard. Located on the narrow Via Monterone, near the Pantheon, its entrance was marked only by a pair of hissing gas lamps. As Casagrande stepped inside, he was immediately confronted by a large statue of the Virgin Mary. A woman greeted him warmly by name and took his overcoat and hat. She had skin the color of coffee and wore a bright frock from her native Ivory Coast. Like all the employees of L'Eau Vive, she was a member of the Missionary Workers of the Immaculate Conception, a lay group for women connected to the Carmelites. Most came from Asia and Africa.

"Your guest has arrived, Signor Casagrande." Her Italian was heavily accented but fluent. "Follow me, please."

The humble entrance suggested a dark, cramped Roman cham-

ber with a handful of tables, but the room into which Casagrande
was shown was large and open, with cheerful white walls and a
soaring open-beam ceiling. As usual, every seat was filled, though,
unlike other restaurants in Rome, the clientele was all male and almost exclusively Vatican. Casagrande spotted no fewer than four
cardinals. Many of the other clerics looked like ordinary priests,
but Casagrande's trained eye easily picked out the gold chains that
marked bishops and the purple piping that revealed the *monsignori*.
Besides, no simple priest could afford to eat at L'Eau Vive, not unless he was receiving support from a well-to-do relative back home.
Even Casagrande's modest Vatican salary would be pushed to the
breaking point by a meal at L'Eau Vive. Tonight was business, however, and the cost would be covered by his generous operational expense account.

The conversations fell virtually silent as Casagrande made his
way toward his usual corner table. The reason was simple. Part of
his job was to enforce the Vatican's strict code of silence. L'Eau Vive,
despite its reputation for discretion, was also a beehive of Curial gossip. Enterprising journalists had been known to don cassocks and
reserve tables at L'Eau Vive to try to pick up tasty morsels of Vatican scandal.

Achille Bartoletti stood up as Casagrande approached. He was
twenty years younger than Casagrande, at the peak of his personal
and professional power. His suit was restrained and carefully pressed,
his face tanned and fit, his handshake firm and proper in duration.
There was just enough gray in his full head of hair to make him
look serious but not too old. The tight mouth and the rows of small,
uneven teeth hinted at a cruel streak, which Casagrande knew was
not too far from the truth. Indeed, there was little the Vatican

security chief did not know about Achille Bartoletti. He was a man whose every move had been devoted to the advancement of his career. He had kept his mouth shut, avoided controversy, taken credit for the successes of others and distanced himself from their failures. If he had been a Curial priest instead of a secret policeman, he would have probably been pope by now. Instead, thanks in large measure to the generous patronage of his mentor, Carlo Casagrande, Achille Bartoletti was the director of the *Servizio per le Informazioni e la Sicurezza Democratica,* Italy's Intelligence and Democratic Security Service.

When Casagrande sat down, conversation at surrounding tables carefully resumed.

"You do make quite an entrance, General."

"God knows what they were talking about before I arrived. But you can rest assured the conversation will be less stimulating now."

"There's a lot of red in the room tonight."

"They're the ones I worry about the most, the Curial prelates who spend their days surrounded by supplicant priests who say nothing but 'Yes, Excellency. Of course, Excellency. Whatever you say, Excellency.'"

"Excellent, Excellency!" Bartoletti chimed in.

The security chief had taken the liberty of ordering the first bottle of wine. He poured Casagrande a glass. The food at L'Eau Vive was French, and so was the wine list. Bartoletti had selected an excellent Médoc.

"Is it my imagination, General, or do the natives seem more restless than usual?"

Casagrande thought: *Is it that obvious?* Obvious enough so that an outsider like Bartoletti could detect the electric crackle of instability in the air of L'Eau Vive? He decided any attempt to dismiss the question out of hand would be transparently deceptive and therefore a violation of the subtle rules of their relationship.

"It's that uncertain time of a new papacy," Casagrande said, with a note of judicial neutrality in his voice. "The fisherman's ring has been kissed and homage has been paid. By tradition, he's promised to carry on the mission of his predecessor, but memories of the Pole are fading very quickly. Lucchesi has redecorated the papal apartments on the *terzo piano*. The natives, as you call them, are wondering what's next."

"What *is* next?"

"The Holy Father has not divulged his plans for the Church to me, Achille."

"Yes, but you have impeccable sources."

"I *can* tell you this: He's isolated himself from the mandarins in the Curia and surrounded himself with trusted hands from Venice. The mandarins of the Curia call them the Council of Ten. Rumors are flying."

"What sort?"

"That he's about to launch a program of de-Stalinization to reduce the posthumous influence of the Pole. Major personnel changes in the Secretariat of State and Congregation for the Doctrine of the Faith are expected—and that's just the beginning."

He's also going to make public the darkest secrets in the Vatican Archives, thought Casagrande, though he didn't share this with Achille Bartoletti.

The Italian security chief leaned forward, eager for more. "He's not going to move on the Holy Trinity of burning issues, is he? Birth control? Celibacy? Women in the priesthood?"

Casagrande shook his head gravely. "He wouldn't dare. It would be so controversial that the Curia would revolt and his papacy would be doomed. *Relevancy* is the buzzword of the day in the Apostolic Palace. The Holy Father wants the Church to be relevant in the lives of one billion Catholics around the world, many of whom don't have enough to eat each day. The old guard has never been interested in relevance. To them, a word like 'relevance' sounds like *glasnost* or *perestroika,* and that makes them very nervous. The old guard likes obedience. If the Holy Father goes too far, there will be hell to pay."

"Speak of the devil."

The room fell silent again. This time Casagrande was not to blame. Looking up, he spotted Cardinal Brindisi making his way toward one of the private rooms at the back of the restaurant. His pale blue eyes barely seemed to acknowledge the murmured greetings of the lesser Curial officials seated around him, but Casagrande knew that Cardinal Brindisi's faultless memory had duly recorded the presence of each one.

Casagrande and Bartoletti wasted no time ordering. Bartoletti perused the menu as if it were a report from a trusted agent. Casagrande chose the first thing he saw that looked remotely interesting. For the next two hours, over sumptuous portions of food and judicious amounts of wine, they swapped intelligence, rumors, and gossip. It was a monthly ritual, one of the enormous dividends of Casagrande's move to the Vatican twenty years earlier. So high was his standing in Rome after crushing the Red Brigades that his word was like Gospel inside the Italian government. *What Casagrande wants, Casagrande gets.* The organs of Italian state security were now virtual arms of the Vatican, and Achille Bartoletti was one of his most important projects. The nuggets of Vatican intrigue that Casagrande tossed him were like pure gold. They were often used to impress and entertain his superiors, just like the private audiences with the Pope and the front-row tickets to the Christmas Midnight Mass in St. Peter's.

But Casagrande offered more than just Curial gossip. The Vatican possessed one of the largest and most effective intelligence services in the world. Casagrande often picked up things that escaped the notice of Bartoletti and his service. For example, it was Casagrande who learned that a network of Tunisian terrorists in Florence was planning to attack American tourists over the Easter holiday. The information was forwarded to Bartoletti, and an alert was promptly issued. No American suffered so much as a scratch, and Bartoletti earned powerful friends in the American CIA and even the White House.

Eventually, over coffee, Casagrande brought the conversation round to the topic he cared about most—the Israeli named Ehud Landau who had gone to Munich claiming to be the brother of Benjamin Stern. The Israeli who had visited the Convent of the Sacred Heart in Brenzone, and who had shaken Casagrande's surveillance men as though he were brushing crumbs from the white tablecloth at L'Eau Vive.

"I have a serious problem, Achille, and I need your help."

Bartoletti took note of Casagrande's somber tone and set his coffee cup back in its saucer. Had it not been for Casagrande's patronage and support, Bartoletti would still be a mid-level apparatchik instead of the director of Italy's intelligence service. He was in no position to refuse a request from Casagrande, no matter what the circumstances. Still, Casagrande approached the matter with delicacy and respect. The last thing he wanted to do was embarrass his most important protégé by making crass demands on their relationship.

"You know that you can count on my support and loyalty, General," Bartoletti said. "If you or the Vatican are in some sort of trouble, I will do anything I can to help."

Casagrande reached into the breast pocket of his suit jacket and produced a photograph, which he placed on the table and turned so Bartoletti could see it properly. Bartoletti picked up the photo and held it near the flame of the candle for a better view.

"Who is he?"

"We're not sure. He's been known to use the name Ehud Landau on occasion."

"Ehud? Israeli?"

Casagrande nodded.

"What's the problem?" Bartoletti asked, his eyes still on the photo.

"We believe he's intent on killing the Pope."

Bartoletti looked up sharply. "An assassin?"

Casagrande nodded slowly. "We've seen him a few times in St. Peter's, acting strangely during the Wednesday general audiences. He's also been present at other papal appearances, in Italy and abroad. We believe he attended an outdoor papal Mass in Madrid last month with the intention of killing the Holy Father."

Bartoletti held up the photo between his first two fingers and turned it so the image was facing Casagrande. "Where did you get this?"

Casagrande explained that one of his men had spotted the assassin in the Basilica a week earlier and had snapped the photograph outside in the square. It was a lie, of course. The picture had been taken by Axel Weiss in Munich, but Achille Bartoletti did not need to know that.

"We've received several threatening letters over the past few weeks—letters we believe were written by this man. We believe he constitutes a serious threat to the Holy Father's life. Obviously, we would like to find him before he gets an opportunity to make good on his threats."

"I'll create a task force first thing in the morning," Bartoletti said.

"Quietly, Achille. The last thing this pope wants is a public assassination scare so early in his papacy."

"You may rest assured that the hunt for this man will be conducted so silently it might seem that you yourself were in command."

Casagrande dipped his head, acknowledging the compliment from his young protégé. With an almost imperceptible flick of his wrist, he signaled for the check. Just then the hostess who had greeted Casagrande at the beginning of the evening walked to the center of the dining room with a microphone in her hand. Bowing her head, she closed her eyes and recited a brief prayer. Then the waitresses gathered around the statue of the Virgin and, with hands clasped, began singing "Immaculate Mary." Soon the entire restaurant had joined in. Even Bartoletti, the hard-bitten secret policeman, was singing along.

After a moment, the music died away, and the cardinals and bishops resumed their conversation, flush from the soaring hymn and good wine. When the check came, Casagrande snatched it before his dinner guest had a chance. Bartoletti issued a mild protest. "If memory serves, it's my turn this month, General."

"Perhaps, Achille, but our conversation has been especially fruitful tonight. This one is on the Holy Father."

"My thanks to the Holy Father." Bartoletti held up the photograph of the papal assassin. "And you can rest assured that if this man gets within a hundred miles of him, he'll be arrested."

Casagrande fixed a melancholy gaze on his dinner guest. "Actually, Achille, I would prefer he not be arrested."

Bartoletti frowned thoughtfully. "I don't understand, General. What are you asking me to do?"

Casagrande leaned forward across the table, his face close to the flame of the candle. "It would be better for everyone involved if he simply vanished."

Achille Bartoletti slipped the photograph into his pocket.

·12·

VIENNA

SECURITY AT THE VAGUELY NAMED Wartime Claims and Inquiries had always been strict, long before the war in the territories. Located in a former apartment building in Vienna's old Jewish Quarter, its door was virtually unmarked and heavily fortified, and the windows overlooking the destitute interior courtyard were bulletproof. The executive director of the organization, a man called Eli Lavon, was not paranoid, just prudent. Over the years, he had helped track down a half dozen former concentration-camp guards and a senior Nazi official living comfortably in Argentina. For his efforts he had been rewarded with a constant stream of death threats.

That he was Jewish was a given. That he was of Israeli origin was assumed because of his non-German family name. That he had worked briefly for Israel's secret intelligence service was known by no one in Vienna and only a handful of people in Tel Aviv, most

of whom had long since retired. During the Wrath of God operation, Lavon had been an *ayin,* a tracker. He had stalked members
of Black September, learned their habits, and devised ways of killing them.

Under normal circumstances, no one was admitted into the of-
fices of Wartime Claims and Inquiries without a long-scheduled
appointment and a thorough background check. For Gabriel, all
formalities were waived and he was escorted directly to Lavon's
office by a young female researcher.

The room was classic Viennese in its proportions and furnish-
ings: a high ceiling, polished wood floor, bookshelves bent beneath
the weight of countless volumes and files. Lavon was kneeling on
the floor, his back hunched over a line of aging documents. He was
an archaeologist by training and had spent years digging in the
West Bank before devoting himself fully to his present line of work.
Now he was gazing at a sheet of tattered paper with the same wonder he felt while examining a fragment of pottery five millennia old.

He looked up as Gabriel entered the room and greeted him with
a mischievous smile. Lavon cared nothing of his appearance, and
as usual he seemed to have dressed in whatever had been within
easy reach when he rolled out of bed: gray corduroy trousers and a
brown V-neck sweater with tattered elbows. His tousled gray hair
gave him the appearance of a man who had just driven at high speed
in a convertible. Lavon did not own a car and did almost nothing
quickly. Despite his security concerns, he was a dutiful rider of Vienna's streetcars. Public transport did not bother him. Like the
men he hunted, Lavon was skilled in the art of moving through city
streets unseen.

"Let me guess," Lavon said, dropping his cigarette into a coffee
cup and struggling to his feet like a man suffering chronic pain.

"Shamron pulled you in to investigate Beni's death. And now you're here, which means you've found something interesting."

"Something like that."

"Sit down," Lavon said. "Tell me everything."

SPRAWLED ON Lavon's overstuffed green couch, feet propped on the arm, Gabriel gave him a careful account of his investigation, beginning with his visit to Munich and concluding with his meeting with Rabbi Zolli in the ghetto of Venice. Lavon walked back and forth along the length of the room, trailing cigarette smoke like a steam engine. He moved slowly at first, but as Gabriel's story wore on, his pace increased. When he finished, Lavon stopped walking and shook his head.

"My goodness, but you've been a busy boy."

"What does it all mean, Eli?"

"Let's go back to the telephone call you received at the hotel in Brenzone. Who do you think it was?"

"If I had to guess, it was the handyman at the convent, an old fellow named Licio. He came into the room while Sister Vincenza and I were speaking, and I think he was following me through the town after I left."

"I wonder why he left an anonymous message instead of speaking to you."

"Maybe he was frightened."

"That would be the logical explanation." Lavon shoved his hands in his pockets and stared at the high ceiling. "You're sure about the name he told you? You're sure it was *Martin* Luther?"

"That's right. 'Find Sister Regina and Martin Luther. Then you'll know the truth about what happened at the convent.'"

Lavon unconsciously smoothed his unruly hair. It was a habit when he was thinking. "There are two possibilities that spring to mind. I suppose we can rule out a certain German monk who turned the Roman Catholic Church on its ear. That would narrow the field to one. I'll be right back."

He disappeared into an adjoining room. For the next several minutes, Gabriel was treated to the familiar sound of his old friend rifling through file cabinets and cursing in several different languages. Finally, he returned with a thick accordion file bound by a heavy metal clasp. He laid the file on the coffee table in front of Gabriel and turned it so he could read the label.

MARTIN LUTHER: GERMAN FOREIGN OFFICE, 1938–1943.

LAVON OPENED the file and removed a photograph, holding it up for Gabriel to see. "The other possibility," he said, "is *this* Martin Luther. He was a high-school dropout and furniture mover who joined the Nazi Party in the twenties. By chance, he met the wife of Joachim von Ribbentrop during the redecoration of her villa in Berlin. Luther ingratiated himself with Frau von Ribbentrop, then her husband. When Ribbentrop became foreign minister in 1938, Luther got a job at the ministry."

Gabriel took the photograph from Lavon and looked at it. A rodent of a man stared back at him: a slack face; thick glasses that magnified a pair of rheumy eyes. He handed the photo back to Lavon.

"Luther rose rapidly through the ranks of the Foreign Office, largely because of his slavish devotion to Ribbentrop. By 1940, he was chief of the *Abteilung Deutschland,* the Division Germany.

That made Luther responsible for all Foreign Office business connected to Nazi Party affairs. Included in Luther's *Abteilung Deutschland* was a department called D–Three, the Jewish desk."

"So what you're saying is that Martin Luther was in charge of Jewish matters inside the German Foreign Office."

"Precisely," Lavon said. "What Luther lacked in education and intelligence, he made up for in ruthlessness and ambition. He was interested in only one thing: increasing his own personal power. When it became clear to him that the annihilation of the Jews was a top priority of the regime, he set out to make certain that the Foreign Office wasn't going to be left out of the action. His reward was an invitation to the most despicable luncheon in history."

Lavon paused for a moment to leaf through the contents of the file. After a moment he found what he was looking for, removed it with a flourish, and laid it on the coffee table in front of Gabriel.

"This is the protocol from the Wannsee Conference, prepared and drafted by its organizer, none other than Adolf Eichmann. Only thirty copies were made. All were destroyed but one—copy number sixteen. It was discovered after the war during the preparation for the Nuremburg Trials and resides in the archives of the German Foreign Ministry in Bonn. This, of course, is a photocopy."

Lavon picked up the document. "The meeting was held in a villa overlooking the Wannsee in Berlin on January 20, 1942. It lasted ninety minutes. There were fifteen participants. Eichmann served as host and made sure his guests were well fed. Heydrich served as master of ceremonies. Contrary to popular myth, the Wannsee Conference was not the place where the idea of the Final Solution was hatched. Hitler and Himmler had already decided that the Jews of Europe were to be exterminated. The Wannsee Conference was more like a bureaucratic planning session, a discussion of how the various departments of the Nazi Party and German government could work together to facilitate the Holocaust."

Lavon handed the document to Gabriel. "Look at the list of participants. Recognize any of the names?"

Gabriel cast his eyes down the attendees:

GAULEITER DR. MEYER AND REICHSAMTLEITER DR. LEIBBRANDT,
    REICH MINISTRY FOR THE OCCUPIED EASTERN TERRITORIES
STAATSSEKRETÄR DR. STUCKART, REICH MINISTRY OF THE
    INTERIOR
STAATSSEKRETÄR NEUMANN, PLENIPOTENTIARY FOR THE FOUR
    YEAR PLAN
STAATSSEKRETÄR DR. FREISLER, REICH MINISTRY OF JUSTICE
STAATSSEKRETÄR DR. BÜHLER, OFFICE OF THE GENERAL
    GOVERNMENT
UNTERSTAATSSEKRETÄR DR. LUTHER, FOREIGN OFFICE

Gabriel looked up at Lavon. "Luther was at Wannsee?"

"Indeed, he was. And he got exactly what he so desperately wanted. Heydritch mandated that the Foreign Office would play a pivotal role in facilitating deportations of Jews from countries allied with Nazi Germany and from German satellites such as Croatia and Slovakia."

"I thought the SS handled the deportations."

"Let me back up a moment." Lavon leaned over the coffee table and placed his hands on the surface, as though it were a map of Europe. "The vast majority of Holocaust victims were from Poland, the Baltics, and western Russia—places conquered and ruled directly by the Nazis. They rounded up Jews and slaughtered them at will, without any interference from other governments, because there were no other governments."

Lavon paused, one hand sliding over the imaginary map to the south, the other to the west. "But Heydrich and Eichmann weren't satisfied with murdering only the Jews under direct German rule. They wanted *every* Jew in Europe—eleven million in all." Lavon tapped his right forefinger on the table. "The Jews in the Balkans"— he tapped his left forefinger—"and the Jews in Western Europe. In most of these places, they had to deal with local governments to pry the Jews loose for deportation and extermination. Luther's section of the Foreign Office was responsible for that. It was Luther's job to deal with the local governments on a ministry-to-ministry basis to make certain that the deportations went smoothly and all diplomatic niceties were adhered to. And he was damned good at it."

"For argument's sake, let's assume the old man was referring to this Martin Luther. What would he have been doing at a convent in northern Italy?"

Lavon shrugged his narrow shoulders. "It sounds to me as if the old man was trying to tell you that something happened at the convent during the war. Something that Sister Vincenza is trying to cover up. Something that Beni knew about."

"Something that got him killed?"

Lavon shrugged. "Maybe."

"Who would be willing to kill a man over a book?"

Lavon hesitated, taking a moment to slip the protocol of the Wannsee Conference back into the file. Then he looked up at Gabriel, eyes narrowed, and drew a deep breath.

"There was one government in particular that Eichmann and Luther were concerned about. It maintained diplomatic relations with both the Allies and Nazi Germany during the war. It had representatives in all of the countries where the roundups and deportations were taking place—representatives who could have made the task more difficult had they chosen to forcefully intervene. For obvious reasons, Eichmann and Luther considered it critical that this government not raise objections. Hitler considered this government so pivotal that he dispatched the second-ranking official at the Foreign Office, Baron Ernst von Weizäcker, to serve as his ambassador. Do you know which government I'm talking about, Gabriel?"

Gabriel closed his eyes. "The Vatican."

"Indeed."

"So who are the clowns that have been following me?"

"That's a very good question."

Gabriel crossed the room to Lavon's desk, lifted the receiver of the telephone, and dialed a number. Lavon did not need to ask who Gabriel was calling. He could see it in the determined set of his jaw and the tension in his hands. When a man is being stalked by an enemy he does not know, it is best to have a friend who knows how to fight dirty.

THE MAN STANDING on the steps of Vienna's famed Konzerthaus radiated open-air Austrian good looks and Viennese sophistication. Had anyone spoken to him, he would have replied in perfect German, with the lazy inflection of a well-heeled young man who had spent many happy hours sampling the Bohemian delights of Vienna. He was not Austrian, nor had he been raised in Vienna. His name was Ephraim Ben-Avraham, and he had spent his childhood in a dusty settlement deep in the Negev, a place far removed from the world in which he moved now.

He glanced casually at his watch, then surveyed the expanse of the Beethoven Platz. He was on edge, more so than usual. It was a simple job: Meet an agent, deliver him safely to the communications room of the embassy. But the man he was meeting was no ordinary agent. The Vienna station chief had made the stakes clear to Ben-Avraham before dispatching him. "If you fuck it up, Ari Shamron will track you down and strangle you with one of his patented death grips. And whatever you do, don't try to talk to the agent. He's not the most approachable of men."

Ben-Avraham stuck an American cigarette between his lips and ignited it. It was at that moment, through the dancing blue flame of his lighter, that Ben-Avraham saw the legend emerge from the darkness. He dropped his cigarette to the wet pavement and ground it out with the toe of his shoe, watching while the agent made two complete circuits of the square. No one was following him—no one but the disheveled little man with flyaway hair and a wrinkled coat. He was a legend too: Eli Lavon, surveillance artist extraordinaire. Ben-Avraham had met him once at the Academy when Lavon had been a guest lecturer at a seminar on man-to-man street work. He had kept the recruits up till three in the morning, telling war stories about the dark days of the Black September operation.

Ben-Avraham watched the pair in admiration for a moment as they drifted among the evening crowd like synchronized swimmers. Their routine was by the book, but it had a certain flair and precision that came from working together in situations where one misstep could cost one of them his life.

Finally, the young officer started down the steps toward his target. "Herr Mueller," he called out. The legend looked up. "So good to see you."

Lavon vanished as though stepping through a stage curtain. Ben-Avraham hooked his fingers inside the elbow of the legend and pulled him toward the darkened footpaths of the Stadt Park. They walked in circles for ten minutes, diligently checking their tail. He was smaller than Ben-Avraham expected, lean and spare, like a cyclist. It was difficult to imagine that this was the same man who had liquidated half of Black September—the same man who had walked into a villa in Tunis and gunned down Abu Jihad, the second-ranking leader of the PLO, in front of his wife and children.

The legend said nothing. It was as if he were listening for his enemies. His footfalls on the pavement of the pathways made no sound. It was like walking next to a ghost.

The car was waiting a block from the park. Ben-Avraham climbed behind the wheel and for twenty minutes wound his way around the city center. The station chief was right—he was not a man who invited small talk. Indeed the only time he spoke was to politely ask Ben-Avraham to extinguish his cigarette. His German had the hard edge of a Berliner.

Satisfied that no one was following, Ben-Avraham turned into a narrow street in northeast Vienna called the Anton Frankgasse. The building at No. 20 had been the target of numerous terror attacks over the years and was heavily fortified. It was also under constant surveillance by the Austrian secret services. As the car slipped into the entrance of the underground parking garage, the legend ducked below the dashboard. For an instant, his head pressed lightly against Ben-Avraham's leg. His scalp was burning, like a man in the grip of a death fever.

THE SECURE communications room was located in a soundproof glass cubicle two levels below ground. It took several minutes for the operator in Tel Aviv to patch the call through to Shamron's home in Tiberias. Over the scrambler, his voice sounded as if it was emanating from the bottom of a steel drum. In the background, Gabriel heard water running into a basin and the tinkle of cutlery against china. He could almost picture Shamron's long-suffering wife, Ge'ulah, washing dishes in the kitchen sink. Gabriel gave Shamron the same briefing he had given earlier to Lavon. When he finished, Shamron asked what he planned to do next.

"I thought I'd go to London and ask Peter Malone why Beni called him from a hotel in Brenzone."

"*Malone?* What makes you think he'll talk? Peter Malone is in business for himself. If he's actually got something, he'll sit on it harder than even poor Beni."

"I'm working on a subtle way to make my approach."

"And if he's not interested in opening his notebook to you?"

"Then I'll try a not-so-subtle approach."

"I don't trust him."

"He's the only lead I have at the moment."

Shamron sighed heavily. Despite the distance and the scrambler, Gabriel could hear an edgy rattle in his chest.

"I want the meeting done the right way," Shamron said. "No more wandering into situations blind and without backup. He gets surveillance before and after. Otherwise, you can wash your hands of this thing and go back to Venice to finish your Bellini."

"If you insist."

"Helpful suggestions are not my way. I'll contact London station tonight and put a man on him. Keep me informed."

Gabriel hung up the phone and stepped outside into the corridor. Ephraim Ben-Avraham was waiting. "Where now?" the young field man asked.

Gabriel looked at his watch. "Take me to the airport."

·13·

LONDON

ON HIS SECOND DAY in London, Gabriel visited a used bookstore in the Charing Cross Road at dusk and purchased a single volume. He tucked it beneath his arm and walked to the Leicester Square underground station. At the entrance he removed the well-worn dust jacket and tossed it into a rubbish bin. Inside the station, he bought a ticket from the automated dispenser and rode the long escalator down to the Northern Line platform, where he endured an obligatory ten-minute delay. He used the time to leaf through the book. When he found the passage he was looking for, he circled it in red ink and folded the page to mark the place.

The train finally grumbled into the station. Gabriel squeezed into the crowded carriage and wound his arm around a metal pole. His destination was Sloane Square, which required a change of trains at the Embankment. As the train jerked forward, he looked down at the faded gold lettering on the spine of the book. THE DECEIVERS: PETER MALONE.

Malone . . . one of the most dreaded names in London. Revealer of personal and professional misdeeds, destroyer of lives and careers. An investigative reporter for *The Sunday Times,* Malone's list of victims was long and diverse: two Cabinet ministers, the second-ranking official at MI5, a slew of crooked businessmen, even the editor-in-chief of a rival newspaper. During the past decade, he had also published a string of sensational biographies and political exposés. *The Deceivers* dealt with the exploits of the Office. It had caused something of a firestorm in Tel Aviv, largely because of its telling accuracy. It included the revelation that Ari Shamron had recruited a spy from the senior ranks of MI6. The crisis that followed, Shamron would later say, was the worst between the British and the Jews since the bombing of the King David Hotel.

Ten minutes later, Gabriel was walking through the streets of Chelsea in the gathering darkness, Malone's book under his arm. He crossed Cadogan Square and paused in front of the handsome white Georgian townhouse. Lights were burning in the second-floor windows. He climbed the steps to the front door, laid the book on a braided straw mat, then turned and walked quickly away.

Parked on the opposite side of the square was a gray commercial van of American manufacture. When Gabriel tapped on the blacked-out rear window, the door swung open, revealing a darkened interior lit only by the soft glow of an instrument panel. Sitting before the console was a reedy, rabbinical looking boy named Mordecai. He offered Gabriel a bony hand and pulled him inside. Gabriel closed the door and crouched next to him. The floor was littered with grease-spotted *panini* wrappers and empty Styrofoam cups. Mordecai had been living in the van for most of the past thirty-six hours.

"How many people in the house?" Gabriel asked.

Mordecai reached out and turned a knob. Over the speakers, Gabriel could hear the faint voice of Peter Malone talking to one of his assistants.

"Three," Mordecai said. "Malone and two girls."

Gabriel dialed Malone's number. The ringing of his office telephone sounded like a fire alarm over Mordecai's speakers. The surveillance man reached out and turned down the volume. After three rings, the reporter answered and identified himself by name in a soft Scottish brogue.

Gabriel spoke English and made no attempt to conceal his Israeli accent. "I just left a copy of your last book outside your door. I suggest you take a look at it. I'll call you back in exactly five minutes."

Gabriel rang off and rubbed a clear patch on the fogged glass of the window. The front door opened a few inches and Malone, turtle-like, poked out his head. It swiveled from side to side as he searched in vain for the man who had just telephoned. Then he bent down and scooped up the book. Gabriel looked at Mordecai and smiled. *Victory*. Five minutes later, he pressed the redial button on his phone. This time Malone answered on the first ring.

"Who are you?"

"Did you see the passage I circled in the book?"

"The Abu Jihad assassination? What about it?"

"I was there that night."

"For which side?"

"The good guys."

"So you're a Palestinian?"

"No, Abu Malone, I'm not a Palestinian."

"Who are you, then?"

"I'm the agent who was code-named Sword."

"Good Lord," Malone whispered. "Where are you? What do you want?"

"I want to talk to you."

"About what?"

"Benjamin Stern."

A long pause: "I have nothing to say to you."

Gabriel decided to push a little harder. "We found your telephone number among his things. We know you were working with him on his book. We think you might know who killed him and why."

Another long silence while Malone pondered his next move. Gabriel's use of the pronoun *we* was quite deliberate, and it had its intended effect.

"And if I *do* know something?"

"I'd like to compare notes."

"And what do I get in return?" Malone, ever the alert reporter, was going to make Gabriel sing for his supper.

"I'll talk to you about that night in Tunis," Gabriel said, then added: "And others like it."

"Are you serious?"

"Benjamin was my friend. I'd do almost anything to find the men who killed him."

"Then you have a deal." Malone's tone was suddenly brisk. "How do you want to go about this?"

"Are there assistants in the house?" Gabriel asked, though he knew the answer already.

"Two girls."

"Get rid of them. Leave the front door unlatched. When I see them go, I'll come inside. No tape recorders, no cameras, no fucking around. Do you understand me?"

Gabriel killed the connection before the reporter could answer, then slipped the telephone into his pocket. Two minutes later, the front door opened and a pair of young women stepped outside. When they were gone, Gabriel climbed out of the van and walked across the square toward the house. The front door was unlocked, just as he had instructed. He turned the latch and stepped inside.

THEY APPRAISED each other across the marble entrance hall like captains of opposing football teams. Gabriel could see why it was difficult to watch British television without seeing Malone's face—and why he was considered one of London's most eligible bachelors. He was trim and fine-boned, immaculately dressed in wool trousers and a cardigan sweater the color of claret wine. Gabriel, dressed in jeans and a leather jacket, his face concealed behind a pair of sunglasses and a ball cap, seemed a man from the wrong side of town. Malone did not offer Gabriel his hand.

"You can take off that ridiculous disguise. I'm not in the habit of betraying sources."

"If you don't mind, I prefer to keep it on."

"Suit yourself. Coffee? Something stronger?"

"No, thank you."

"My office is upstairs. I think you'll find it comfortable."

It was an old drawing room, long and rectangular, with floor-to-ceiling bookshelves and oriental carpets. In the center of the room were two antique library tables, one for Malone, another for his research assistants. Malone switched off the computer and sat down in one of the wing chairs next to the gas fire, motioning for Gabriel to do the same.

"I must say it is rather bizarre to actually be in the same room with you. I've heard so much about your exploits that I feel I actually *know* you. You're quite the legend. Black September, Abu Jihad, and countless others in between. Have you killed anyone lately?"

When Gabriel did not rise to the bait, Malone carried on. "While I find you morbidly fascinating, I must admit that I find the things you've done to be morally repugnant. In my opinion, a state which resorts to assassination as a matter of policy is no better than the enemy it's trying to defeat. In many respects, it's worse. You're a murderer in my book, just so you understand where I'm coming from."

Gabriel began to wonder whether he had made a mistake by coming here. He had learned long ago that arguments like this could never be won. He'd had too many just like it with himself. He sat very still, gazing at Peter Malone through his dark glasses, waiting for him to come to the point. Malone crossed his legs and picked a bit of lint from his trousers. It was a gesture that betrayed anxiety. This pleased Gabriel.

"Perhaps we should finalize the details of our arrangement before we proceed," Malone said. "I will tell you what I know about Benjamin Stern's murder. In return, you'll grant me an interview. Obviously, I've written about intelligence matters before, and I know the rules. I will do nothing to reveal your true identity, nor will I write anything that will compromise current operations. Do we have a deal?"

"We do."

Malone spent a moment gazing up at the recessed lighting, then looked down at Gabriel. "You're right about Benjamin. I was working with him on his book. Our partnership was supposed to be confidential. I'm surprised you were able to find me."

"Why did Benjamin come to you?"

Malone stood up and walked over to the bookshelves. He removed a volume and handed it to Gabriel. CRUX VERA: THE KGB OF THE CATHOLIC CHURCH.

"Benjamin had something big—something dealing with the Vatican and the war."

Gabriel held up the book. "Something dealing with Crux Vera?"

Malone nodded. "Your friend was a brilliant academic, but he didn't know the first thing about *investigating* a story. He asked me if I would work for him as a consultant and investigator in all matters dealing with Crux Vera. I agreed, and we negotiated compensation. The money was to be paid half in advance and half on completion and acceptance of the manuscript. Needless to say, I only received the first payment."

"What did he have?"

"Unfortunately, I wasn't privy to that information. Your friend played things very close to the vest. If I didn't know better, I would have thought he was one of your crowd."

"What did he want from you?"

"Access to material I'd gathered while writing the Crux Vera book. Also, he wanted me to try to track down two priests who worked at the Vatican during the war."

"What were their names?"

"Monsignors Cesare Felici and Tomaso Manzini."

"Did you ever find them?"

"I tried," Malone said. "What I discovered is that they were both missing and presumed dead. And there's something even more interesting than that. The detective from the Rome headquarters of the *Polizia di Stato* who was investigating the cases was removed by his superiors and reassigned."

"Do you know the investigator's name?"

"Alessio Rossi. But for God's sake, don't tell him I gave you his name. I have a reputation to protect."

"If you know so much, why haven't you written anything?"

"What I have now is a series of murders and disappearances which I believe are linked, yet I haven't a shred of hard evidence conclusively linking them in any way. The last thing I want to do is accuse the Vatican, or someone close to the Vatican, of murder without a damned solid case. Besides, no decent editor would touch it."

"But you have a theory about who might be behind it."

"What you have to remember is that we're talking about the Vatican," Malone said. "Men linked to that venerable institution have been involved in intrigues and plots for nearly two millennia. They play the game better than anyone, and in the past, religious fervor and battles over doctrine have induced them to commit the mortal sin of murder. The Church is riddled with secret societies and cliques who might be involved in something like this."

"Who?" Gabriel repeated.

Peter Malone flashed a television smile. "In my humble opinion, you hold the answer in your hand."

Gabriel looked down. CRUX VERA: THE KGB OF THE CATHOLIC CHURCH.

MALONE LEFT the room, returning a moment later with a bottle of Médoc and a pair of large crystal goblets. He poured two generous measures and handed one to Gabriel.

"Do you speak Latin?"

"Actually, we speak another ancient language."

Malone grinned at Gabriel over his wineglass and continued on. "Crux Vera is Latin for the True Cross. It is also the name of an ultra-secret order within the Roman Catholic Church, a sort of church within a church. If you look in the *Annuario Pontificio,* the Vatican yearbook, you'll find no mention of Crux Vera. If you ask the Vatican press office, you will be told that it is a fabrication, a sort of blood libel spread by the enemies of the Church in order to discredit it. But if you ask me, Crux Vera *does* exist, and I proved it in that book, regardless of what the Vatican says. I believe the tentacles of Crux Vera reach to the highest levels of the Vatican, and that its adherents occupy positions of power and influence around the globe."

"What is it exactly?"

"The group was created during the Spanish Civil War by an anti-Communist priest named Juan Antonio Rodriguez. Monsignor Rodriguez was very selective about the type of people he permitted to join. The vast majority of his recruits were laymen. Most were wealthy or politically connected: bankers, lawyers, industrialists, government ministers, spies, and secret policemen. You see, Rodriguez was never interested in the business of saving souls. In his opinion, that sort of thing could be left to ordinary parish priests. Rodriguez was interested in only one thing: protecting the Roman Catholic Church from its mortal enemies."

"And who were they?"

"The Bolsheviks," Malone said, then quickly added: "And the Jews, of course. Crux Vera spread quickly across Europe throughout the thirties. It established beachheads in France, Italy, Germany, the Balkans, and the Roman Curia itself. During the war, members of Crux Vera worked in the papal household and the Secretariat of

State. As Crux Vera expanded, so did Monsignor Rodriguez's mission. He was no longer satisfied simply with protecting the Church from its enemies. He wanted to return the Church to the position of absolute power and supremacy that it enjoyed during the Middle Ages. That remains the core mission of Crux Vera to this day: reversing the defeats of the Reformation and the Enlightenment and making the state subservient to the Church once again. They also want to undo what they view as the heretical reforms of the Second Vatican Council: Vatican Two."

"How do they intend to do that?"

"Crux Vera may have loathed the KGB, but in many ways, it is an exact replica; hence the title of my book. It wages a secret war against those it deems enemies and acts like a secret police force within the Church, enforcing strict adherence to doctrine and crushing dissent. Oh, the dissidents and reformers are allowed to vent their spleen now and again, but if they ever pose a real threat, Crux Vera will step in and help them see the light."

"And if they refuse to yield?"

"Let's just say that several people who have run afoul of Crux Vera have died under less-than-clear circumstances. Prelates who have dared to oppose Crux Vera have fallen victim to sudden heart attacks. Journalists who have tried to investigate the order have disappeared or committed suicide. So have members of Crux Vera who've tried to leave."

"How does a religious order justify the use of violence?"

"The priests of Crux Vera aren't the ones who are resorting to violence. The priests give guidance, but it's the laymen who actually do the dirty work. Inside the order, they're known as *milites Christi*— the soldiers of Christ. They're encouraged to engage in *pillería,* or dirty tricks, to achieve the goals of the order. *Pillería* can be anything from blackmail to murder. And when the act is done, the priests provide absolution in the secrecy of the confessional. By the way, *milites Christi* aren't permitted to confess to anyone but a Crux Vera priest. That way, unpleasant secrets stay inside the family."

"How do they feel about the current pope?"

"From what I hear, they're lukewarm, to say the least. Pope Paul VII talks about rebirth and renewal. To Crux Vera, those words mean reform and liberalization, and they get nervous."

"What makes you think Crux Vera was involved in Benjamin's murder?"

"They might have had a motive. If there's one thing Crux Vera detests, it's revelations of the Vatican's dirty laundry. The order sees itself first and foremost as a guardian of the Church. If your friend had proof of something damaging, he would have fallen into the category of enemy. And Crux Vera would have seen it as their duty to deal with him harshly—for the greater good of the Church, of course."

Malone finished his glass of wine and poured himself another. Gabriel's glass remained untouched. "If you've been talking to people, asking questions, poking your nose into affairs that don't concern you, it's quite possible you've already appeared on Crux Vera's radar. If they think you pose a threat, they won't hesitate to kill you."

"I appreciate your candor."

"And we had a deal." Malone picked up a notepad and a pen and suddenly the roles were reversed. "It's my turn to ask the questions now."

"Just remember the rules. If you betray me—"

"Don't worry; I'm also aware of the fact that Crux Vera is not the only secret organization to engage in *pillería*." Malone licked his forefinger and turned to a fresh page in his notebook. "My God, I have so many questions, I don't know where to begin."

GABRIEL SPENT the next two hours unenthusiastically holding up his end of the bargain. Finally, he saw himself out the front door of Peter Malone's house and struck out across Cadogan Square in a steady rain. On Sloane Street, he pulled his cellular phone from his pocket and dialed Mordecai in the surveillance van. "Keep monitoring him," Gabriel said. "If he goes anywhere, go with him."

PETER MALONE sat before the computer in his upstairs office, feverishly typing up his notes. He could not quite believe his good fortune. He had learned long ago that success was the result of a volatile combination of hard work and pure luck. Sometimes good stories just fell into one's lap. The difference between an average journalist and a great one is what he did next.

After an hour of steady work, his handwritten notes had been transformed into a pair of organized memos. The first dealt with the exploits of the agent code-named Sword. The second was an account of their discussion regarding Benjamin Stern. Whether it was his intention or not, the Israeli had just given Malone the hook he needed for his story. Israeli intelligence was investigating the murder of prominent historian Benjamin Stern. He would ring Tel Aviv in the morning, secure the mandatory denial from the drones at headquarters, then stitch together the other mysterious details he knew about the case. He had not told the Israeli everything he knew about Stern's murder, just as he was quite certain the Israeli had not shared all of his knowledge. That's the way the game was played.

It took an experienced reporter to know the difference between truth and misinformation, to sift through the silt to find the nuggets of gold. With a bit of luck, he might have a piece ready by the weekend.

He spent a few minutes double-checking the quotes. He decided he would call Tom Graves, his editor at *The Sunday Times,* and reserve some space on the front page. He reached out for the telephone, but before he could lift the receiver from the cradle, he was flung backward by a blow to the chest. He looked down and saw a small, rapidly spreading circle of blood on his shirt. Then he looked up and saw the man, standing five feet from his desk, gray-blond hair, colorless eyes. Malone had been so engrossed in his work that he had failed to hear him enter the house.

"Why?" the reporter whispered, blood in his mouth.

The killer tilted his head, as though puzzled, and stepped around the desk. "*Ego te absolvo a peccatis tuis,*" he said, fingers caressing the forehead. "*In nomine Patris et Filii et Spiritus Sancti. Amen.*"

Then he pointed the silenced gun at Malone's head and fired one last shot.

IN THE LEXICON of the Office, the device that the surveillance artist called Mordecai had placed in Malone's office was known as a "glass." Concealed within the electronics of the telephone, it provided coverage of Malone's calls as well as conversations taking place inside the room. It had allowed Mordecai to monitor Gabriel's conversation with Malone. He had also listened in as Malone sat at his desk after Gabriel's departure, tapping away at his computer.

Shortly after nine o'clock, Mordecai heard murmuring in a language he could not understand. For the next five minutes, he was treated to the sound of file drawers opening and closing. He assumed it was Malone, but when the front door opened and a tall broad-shouldered man emerged, Mordecai knew at once that something terrible had just taken place inside the house.

The man walked quickly down the steps and started across the square, directly toward the van. Mordecai panicked. The only weaponry he had was a directional microphone and a long-lens Nikon camera. It was the Nikon he reached for. As the man drew closer to the van, Mordecai raised it calmly to his eye and snapped off three quick shots.

The last one, he was convinced, was a keeper.

· 1 4 ·

ROME

VATICAN CITY STATE is the world's smallest country
and also the most sparsely populated. More than four thousand people work there each day, yet only four hundred or so actually live behind the walls. Cardinal Secretary of State Marco Brindisi
was one of them. His private apartment in the Apostolic Palace was
just one floor away from that of the Holy Father. While some prelates
found life in the epicenter of Vatican power the equivalent of living
in a gilded cage, Cardinal Brindisi truly relished it. His rooms were
glorious, his commute was exceedingly short, and a staff of priests
and nuns saw to his every need. If there was one drawback, it was
the proximity of the papal household. While inside the palace, there
was little the Cardinal could do to shield himself from the prying
eyes of the Pope's secretaries. The back room at L'Eau Vive was suit-

able for many of the cardinal's private assignations, though others, like the one scheduled for this evening, had to be held under more secure circumstances.

A Mercedes sedan was waiting in the San Damaso Courtyard outside the entrance of the Apostolic Palace. Unlike lesser Curial cardinals, Brindisi did not have to endure the luck of the draw in the Vatican motor pool. A Mercedes sedan and a driver were permanently assigned to him, along with a *Vigilanza* security man. Brindisi climbed into the back, and the car pulled away. It moved slowly along the Via Belvedere—past the Pontifical Pharmacy and the Swiss Guards' barracks—before slipping through St. Anne's Gate into Rome proper.

The car crossed the Piazza della Città, then turned into the entrance of an underground parking garage. The building above was a Vatican-owned residential complex where many Curial cardinals lived. There were several others like it scattered around Rome.

The car braked to a halt next to a gray Fiat van. As Brindisi climbed out, the van's rear door swung open and a man lowered himself to the ground. Like Brindisi, he was cloaked in a cassock, with a crimson simar and fascia. But unlike the secretary of state, he had no right to wear it. He was not a cardinal; in fact, he was not even an ordained priest. Cardinal Brindisi did not know the man's name, only that he had worked briefly as an actor before coming to work for the *Vigilanza*.

Brindisi's stand-in stepped out of the shadows and paused for an instant before the cardinal. As always, Brindisi felt a chill at the back of his neck. It was as if he were gazing into a mirror. The features, the round eyeglasses, the gold pectoral cross—the man had even learned to mimic the arrogant angle of Brindisi's zucchetto. A tepid smile flickered over the man's face, a precise imitation of Brindisi's own, then he said, "Good evening, Eminence."

"Good evening, Eminence," Cardinal Brindisi found himself repeating.

The impersonator nodded tersely, then climbed into the back of Brindisi's staff car and sped away. Father Mascone, Brindisi's private secretary, was waiting in the back of the van. "Please hurry, Eminence. It's not safe to stay here long."

The priest helped the cardinal into the back of the van and closed the door, then guided him onto an embroidered stool. The van sped back up the ramp and turned into the street. A moment later, it was heading across Rome toward the Tiber.

The priest unzipped a garment bag and removed several articles of clothing: a pair of gray trousers, a mock turtleneck pullover, an expensive tan blazer, a pair of black loafers. Cardinal Brindisi loosened his simar and began to undress. After a moment, he was naked except for his underwear and a spiked chain wrapped around his right thigh.

"Perhaps you should remove your cilice," the priest said. "It might show through your trousers."

Cardinal Brindisi shook his head. "My willingness to shed my vestments goes only so far, Father Mascone. I will wear my cilice tonight, regardless of whether or not it shows through"—he paused—"my trousers."

"Very well, Eminence."

With the priest's help, the cardinal quickly changed into the unfamiliar clothing. When he was fully dressed, he removed his distinctive spectacles and replaced them with a pair of slightly tinted eyeglasses. The transformation was complete. He no longer looked like a prince of the church, but like a well-to-do Roman male of ill repute, perhaps a man who put himself about with younger women.

Five minutes later, in a deserted square on the opposite side of the Tiber, the van came to a stop. The priest opened the door. Cardinal Secretary of State Marco Brindisi made the sign of the cross and stepped out.

IN MANY WAYS, Rome is a company town. Under normal circumstances, Marco Brindisi could not walk the Via Veneto without being recognized, even dressed in the simple black cassock of a parish priest. Tonight, however, he moved unnoticed, slicing his way through the buzzing crowds and past overflowing cafés as though he were just another Roman in search of a good meal and pleasant company.

The glory days of the Via Veneto had long since faded. It was still a lovely boulevard lined with plane trees, exclusive shops, and expensive restaurants, but the intellectuals and movie stars had long ago moved on in search of undiscovered delights. Now the crowd was mainly tourists and businessmen and pretty Italian teenagers careening about on motor scooters.

Marco Brindisi had never been seduced by the Via Veneto's *dolce vita,* even in the sixties, when he was a young Curial bureaucrat fresh from his Umbrian hill town, and it seemed even less appealing now. The snatches of table conversation drifting past his ears seemed so utterly trivial. He knew that some cardinals—indeed, even some popes—liked to walk about Rome in mufti to see how the other half lived. Brindisi had no desire to see how the other half lived. With few exceptions, he found the other half to be an immoral and uncouth rabble who would be far better off if they listened more to the teachings of the Church and less to the incessant blare of their televisions.

An attractive middle-aged woman in a low-cut dress shot him an admiring glance from a café table. Brindisi, playing the part, smiled back. As he walked on, the cardinal begged Christ's forgiveness and applied pressure to his cilice to increase the pain. He had heard the confessions of priests who had fallen victim to the temptation of sex. Priests who kept mistresses. Priests who had performed unspeakable acts with other priests. Brindisi had never known such temptations. The moment he entered the seminary, his heart was given over to Christ and the Virgin. Priests who could not keep their vows sickened him. He believed that any priest who could not remain celibate should be defrocked. But he was also a pragmatist, and he realized that such a policy would certainly decimate the ranks of the clergy.

The cardinal came to the intersection of the Via Veneto and the Corso d'Italia and glanced at his watch. He had arrived at precisely the scheduled time. A few seconds later, a car pulled to the curb. The rear door swung open, and Carlo Casagrande climbed out.

"Excuse me if I don't kiss your ring," Casagrande said, "but I don't think it would be appropriate under the circumstances. The weather is quite mild this evening. Shall we walk in the Villa Borghese?"

CASAGRANDE LED the cardinal across the broad boulevard, exposing the second-most powerful man in the Catholic Church to the bloodlust of Rome's drivers. Arriving safely at the other side, they strolled along a gravel footpath. Come Sunday, the park would be filled with screaming children and men listening to the soccer matches on portable radios. Tonight it was quiet except for the swish of traffic along the Corso. The cardinal walked as though he were still wearing crimson, with his hands clasped behind his back and his head down—a rich man who had dropped money and was making a halfhearted effort to find it. When Casagrande whispered that Peter Malone was dead, Brindisi murmured a brief prayer but resisted the impulse to conclude it with the sign of the cross.

"This assassin of yours is quite efficient," he said.

"Unfortunately, he's had a good deal of practice."

"Tell me about him."

"It's my job to protect you from things like that, Eminence."

"I don't ask out of morbid curiosity, Carlo. My only concern is that this matter is being dealt with in an efficient manner."

They came to the Galleria Borghese. Casagrande sat down on a marble bench in front of the museum and motioned for Brindisi to do the same. The cardinal made a vast show of brushing away the dust before gingerly settling himself on the cold stone. Casagrande then spent the next five minutes reluctantly reciting everything he knew about the assassin called the Leopard, beginning with his long and bloody association with left-wing and Palestinian terrorist groups, and concluding with his transformation into a highly paid professional killer. Casagrande had the distinct impression that the cardinal was enjoying his vicarious association with evil.

"His real name?"

"Not clear, Eminence."

"His nationality?"

"The prevailing sentiment among European security officials is that he is Swiss, although that too is a matter of some speculation."

"You've actually met this man?"

"We've been in the same room, Eminence. We've done business, but I still wouldn't say that I've actually met him. I doubt whether anyone truly has."

"Is he intelligent?"

"Highly."

"Educated?"

"There is evidence to suggest that he studied theology briefly at the University of Fribourg before he was lured away by the call of leftist violence and terror. There is also evidence to suggest that he attended a novitiate in Zurich when he was a young man."

"You mean to tell me this monster actually studied for the priesthood?" Cardinal Brindisi shook his head slowly. "I don't suppose he still considers himself a Catholic?"

"The Leopard? I'm not sure he believes in anything but himself."

"And now a man who once killed for the Communists works for Carlo Casagrande, the man who helped the Polish pope bring down the Evil Empire."

"Politics, as they say, does make for strange bedfellows." Casagrande stood up. "Come, let's walk."

They set out down a path lined with stone pine. The cardinal was taller than the security man by a narrow head. His vestments had the effect of softening his appearance. Dressed as he was now, in civilian clothing, Marco Brindisi was a hard, menacing figure. A man who instilled fear rather than trust.

They sat on a bench overlooking the Piazza di Siena. Casagrande thought of his wife, of sitting with her in this very spot and watching the horses parade around the oval track. He could almost smell the strawberries on her hands. Angelina had loved to eat strawberries and drink *spumanti* in springtime in the Villa Borghese.

Cardinal Brindisi shattered Casagrande's unsettling memory by raising the subject of the man known as Ehud Landau. The Vatican security man told the cardinal about Landau's visit to the Convent of the Sacred Heart in Brenzone.

"My God," the cardinal murmured beneath his breath. "How did Mother Vincenza hold up?"

"Apparently quite well. She told him the cover story we devised and saw him on his way. But the next morning, he returned to the convent and asked about Sister Regina."

"Sister Regina! This *is* a disaster. How could he have known?"

Casagrande shook his head. It was a question he had been asking himself since Mother Vincenza's second telephone call. How could he have known? Benjamin Stern's apartment had been thoroughly searched. Everything dealing with the convent had been removed and destroyed. Obviously, some piece of evidence had slipped through Casagrande's net and landed in the hands of his adversary from Israel.

"Where is he now?" the cardinal asked.

"I'm afraid I haven't a clue. I put a man on him in Brenzone, but he slipped away from him in Verona. He's obviously a trained professional. We haven't heard from him again since."

"How do you plan to deal with him?"

Casagrande turned his gaze from the ancient racetrack and looked into the pale eyes of the cardinal. "As secretary of state, you should be aware that the Security Office has identified a man it believes is intent on assassinating the Holy Father."

"So noted," the cardinal said formally. "What steps have you taken to make certain he does not succeed?"

"I brought Achille Bartoletti into the picture, and he has responded as you might expect. A task force has been formed, and a round-the-clock search for this man is now underway."

"I suppose that at some point the Holy Father will need to be told about this threat as well. Perhaps we can use this information to influence his decision about going to the ghetto next week."

"My thoughts exactly," Casagrande said. "Is our business concluded?"

"One more item, actually." The cardinal told Casagrande about the reporter from *La Repubblica* who was investigating the Holy Father's childhood. "Exposure of a Vatican deceit, even a harmless one, would not be a welcome development at this time. See if there's something you can do to put this meddlesome reporter in his place."

"I'll work on it," Casagrande said. "What did you say to the Holy Father?"

"I told him it might be helpful if he prepared a memorandum summarizing the unhappy details of his childhood."

"How did he respond?"

"He agreed, but I don't want to wait for him. I'd like you to pursue your own investigation. It's important that we learn the truth before it's printed in the pages of *La Repubblica*."

"I'll put a man on it right away."

"Very well," the cardinal said. "Now, I believe our business is concluded."

"One of my men will be trailing you. At the right moment, the van will appear. It will take you back to the Vatican—unless you'd like to walk back to the Via Veneto. We could have a glass of *frascati* and watch Rome go by?"

162

The cardinal smiled, never an encouraging development. "Actually, Carlo, I prefer the view of Rome from the windows of the Apostolic Palace."

With that, he turned and walked away. A moment later, he vanished into the darkness.

· 1 5 ·

NORMANDY, FRANCE

EARLY THE NEXT MORNING, Eric Lange crossed the English Channel on the Newhaven-to-Dieppe ferry. He parked his rented Peugeot in a public lot near the ferry terminal and walked to the Quai Henri IV for breakfast. In a café overlooking the harbor, he had brioche and *café au lait* and read the morning papers. There was no mention of the murder of British investigative journalist Peter Malone, nor had there been any news on the radio. Lange was quite certain the body had not yet been discovered. That would take place at approximately ten o'clock London time, when his research assistants arrived for work. The police, when they launched their investigation, would have no shortage of suspects. Malone had made many powerful enemies over the years. Any one of them would have been more than happy to end Malone's life.

Lange ordered more brioche and another bowl of coffee. He

found that he was in no hurry to leave. The long night of driving had left him drowsy, and the idea of spending the day traveling back to Zurich depressed him. He thought of Katrine, her secluded villa on the edge of a dense Norman forest, the pleasures that could be found in her enormous canopied bed.

He left a few euros on the table and walked along the quay to the *Poissonnerie,* Dieppe's old covered fish market. He moved from stall to stall, carefully examining the catch, chatting easily with the fishmongers in perfect French. He selected a pair of lovely sea bass and an assortment of shellfish. Then he left the market and headed for the Grand Rue, Dieppe's main shopping street. He bought bread from the *boulangerie* and several fresh farm cheeses from the *charcuterie*. His last stop was the *cave,* where he purchased a half-dozen bottles of wine and a Calvados, the famed apple brandy of Normandy.

He loaded the food into the backseat of the Peugeot and set out. The road hugged the edges of the cliffs, rising and falling with the contour of the coastline. Below lay a rocky beach. In the distance, a line of fishing boats was motoring in to port. He passed through a string of quaint fishing towns, devouring one of the baguettes while he drove. By the time he reached St-Valery-en-Caux, the car smelled strongly of shrimp and mussels.

A mile before St-Pierre, he turned onto a narrow local road and followed it inland through apple orchards and fields of flax. Just beyond the village of Valmont, he turned onto a narrow track lined with beech trees and followed it for a kilometer or so, until it dead-ended at a wooden gate. Beyond the gate stood a stone villa, concealed in the shadows of tall beech and elm. Katrine's red jeep was parked in the gravel drive. She would still be asleep. Katrine rarely found a reason to get out of bed before noon.

Lange climbed out, opened the gate, then drove onto the grounds. Without knocking, he tried the front door and found it locked. He had two options: bang until Katrine woke up or begin his visit with a bit of fun. He chose the latter.

The villa was shaped like a U and surrounded by a tangled garden. In summer it was a riot of color. Now, in the last days of winter, it was somber green. Beyond the garden rose the outer edges of the forest. The trees were bare, and the limbs lay motionless in the still of the morning. In the center of the house was a stone courtyard. Lange picked his way through a minefield of broken flowerpots, careful to make no sound, and started trying the latches on each of the six sets of French doors. The fifth was unlocked. *Silly Katrine,* thought Lange. He would teach her a lesson she wouldn't soon forget.

He let himself inside and padded across the shadowed sitting room to the staircase, then climbed up to Katrine's room. He peered inside. The curtains were drawn. Lange could see Katrine in the half-light, her hair strewn across the pillow, her bare shoulders poking from the top of a white duvet. She had the olive skin of a southerner and the blue eyes and blond hair of a Norman girl. The red highlights were a gift from a Breton grandmother, as was her explosive temper.

Lange eased forward, hand reaching for the spot beneath the blanket where her foot appeared to be. Just as he was about to seize her ankle, Katrine sat bolt-upright in bed, eyes wide, hands wrapped around a Browning nine-millimeter pistol. She squeezed off two quick shots, just as Lange had taught her. In the confines of the bedroom, the explosions sounded like cannon fire. Lange fell to the floor. The rounds sailed overhead, shattering the mirror in Katrine's stunning two-hundred-year-old armoire.

"Don't shoot, Katrine," Lange said, laughing helplessly. "It's me."

"Stand up! Let me see you!"

Lange slowly got to his feet, hands in plain sight. Katrine switched on the bedside lamp and gave him a long, fiery look. Then she drew back her arm and threw the gun at his head. Lange ducked and the gun fell harmlessly onto the pile of glass shards.

"You fucking bastard! You're lucky I didn't blow your head off."

"I wouldn't have been the first."

"I loved that mirror!"

"It was old."

"It was an antique, you asshole!"

"I'll buy you a new one."

"I don't want a new one—I want that one!"

"So we'll get it fixed."

"And how will I explain the bullet holes?"

Lange put his hand on his chin and made a show of thought. "Actually, that might be a problem."

"Of course it's a problem. Asshole!" She pulled the duvet over her breasts, as if aware of her nudity for the first time, and her anger at him began to soften.

"What are you doing here, anyway?"

"I was in the neighborhood."

She gazed at his face for a moment. "You've killed again. I can see it in your eyes."

Lange picked up the Browning, set the safety, and dropped the gun on the end of the bed. "I was working nearby," he said. "I need a day or two of rest."

"What makes you think you can drop in here whenever you please? I might have had another man here."

"You might have, but the odds were in my favor. You see, I

am aware that, with few exceptions, most men bore you to tears—intellectually and in that grand bed of yours. I am also aware that any man you bring here isn't likely to last long. Therefore, I felt it was well worth the gamble."

Katrine was trying desperately not to smile. "Why should I let you stay here?"

"Because I'll cook for you."

"Well, in that case, we should work up an appetite. Come to bed. It's too early to get up."

KATRINE BOUSSARD was quite possibly the most dangerous woman in France. After earning degrees in literature and philosophy from the Sorbonne, she had joined the French left-wing extremist group *Action Directe*. While the political aims of the group may have fluctuated wildly, its tactics remained consistent. Throughout the eighties, it carried out a blood-soaked rampage of assassinations, kidnappings, and bombings that left scores dead and a nation terrorized. Thanks to the instruction she received from Eric Lange, Katrine Boussard was one of the group's most accomplished killers. Lange had worked with her on two occasions: the 1985 assassination of a senior official in the French Ministry of Defense, and the 1986 assassination of a French auto executive. In each case, it was Katrine Boussard who applied the *coup de grace* to the victims.

Lange usually worked alone, but in the case of Katrine, he made an exception. She was a skilled operative, cold and pitiless in the field, and highly disciplined. She and Lange suffered from a similar affliction. Operational stress increased their desire for sex, and they had used each other's bodies to great effect. They were not lovers—they had both seen too much to believe in something as pedestrian as love. They were more like skilled craftsmen in pursuit of perfection.

Katrine had been blessed with a body that provided her inordinate pleasure in any number of places. As always, she responded readily to Lange's touch. Only when she was completely satiated did she turn her considerable skills upon Lange. She was a torturous lover, so in tune with Lange's body that each time he was about to lose control, she released him and left him to suffer without absolution. When he could stand no more, Lange took matters into his own hands, grasping Katrine by the hips and thrusting himself inside her from behind. It was closer to conquest than he would have preferred, but it was exactly how Katrine had planned it. As Lange reached his climax, his head rolled back and he shouted like a madman at the ceiling. Katrine was looking over her shoulder at him, watching him with a look of deep satisfaction, for she had beaten him once again.

When it was over, she lay with her head on his chest and her hair strewn across his stomach. Lange looked out the French doors at the trees on the edge of the forest. A storm had moved in from the channel, and the trees were bent by the wind. Lange toyed with Katrine's hair, but she did not stir. Because they had killed together, Lange could make love to her without inhibition and without the latent fear that he might reveal something of himself. He did not love Katrine, but he was fond of her. In fact, she was the only woman he truly cared for at all.

"I miss it so," she murmured.

"What's that, Katrine?"

"The fight." She turned her face to him. "Now I sit here in Valmont, living on the trust fund of a father I despise, and wait to grow old. I don't want to grow old. I want to fight."

"We were foolish children. Now we're wiser."

"And you kill for anyone, as long as the price is right, of course."

Lange put a finger on her lips. "I never had the benefit of a trust fund, Katrine."

"Is that why you're a professional assassin?"

"I have certain skills—skills that the marketplace demands."

"You sound like such a proper capitalist."

"Haven't you heard? The capitalists won. The forces of good have been crushed beneath the heel of profit and greed. Now you can eat at McDonald's and visit Euro Disney whenever you please. You've earned your quiet life and your beautiful villa. Sit back and enjoy the satisfaction of a noble defeat."

"You're such a hypocrite," she said.

"I prefer to think of myself as a realist."

"Who are you killing for?"

Men we once despised, he thought. Then he said: "You know the rules, Katrine. Close your eyes."

WHEN KATRINE was asleep, Lange slipped from the bed, dressed quietly, and went outside. He opened the trunk of the Peugeot and removed Peter Malone's laptop computer, then tucked it beneath his coat and trotted back into the villa through the rain. Inside, he made a fire of apple wood and settled himself on the comfortable couch in Katrine's sitting room. He lifted the computer's cover, switched on the power, and waited for it to boot up. Under his agreement with Carlo Casagrande, Lange was obliged to deliver the computer and the other things he had taken from Malone's office to a safe-deposit box in Zurich. While the computer was still in his possession, he had no qualms about taking a look for himself.

He opened Malone's documents folder and inspected the dates and times of the latest entries. In the final hour of his life, the reporter had created two new documents, one entitled ISRAELI ASSASSIN, the second labeled BENJAMIN STERN MURDER. Lange felt a lightness in his fingertips. Outside, the wind of the Channel storm sounded like a passing bullet train.

He opened the first file. It was a remarkable document. Shortly before Lange had entered Malone's flat, the investigative journalist had interviewed a man who claimed to be an Israeli assassin. Lange read the file with a certain professional admiration. The man had had quite a colorful and productive career: Black September, a couple of Libyans, an Iraqi nuclear scientist. *Abu Jihad* . . .

Lange stopped reading and looked out the French doors at the trees twisting in the storm. *Abu Jihad?* Had the killer of Abu Jihad truly been in Malone's apartment a few hours before Lange? If it was true, what on earth was he doing there? Lange was not a man who put much stock in coincidence. The answer, he suspected, could be found in the second document. He opened it and started to read.

Five minutes later, Lange looked up. It was worse than he had feared. The Israeli agent who had calmly walked into Abu Jihad's villa in Tunis and killed him was now investigating the murder of Professor Benjamin Stern. Lange wondered why the Jewish professor's death would be of interest to Israeli intelligence. The answer seemed simple: The professor must have been an agent of some sort.

He was furious with Carlo Casagrande. If Casagrande had told him that Benjamin Stern was connected to Israeli intelligence, he might very well have refused the contract. The Israelis unnerved him. They played the game differently than the Western Europeans and the Americans. They came from a tough neighborhood, and the shadow of the Holocaust hung over their every decision. It led them to deal with their adversaries in a ruthless and pitiless fashion. They had pursued Lange once before, after a kidnapping and ransom operation he had carried out on behalf of Abu Jihad. He had managed to slip through their fingers by taking the rather draconian step of killing all his accomplices.

Lange wondered whether Carlo Casagrande was aware of the Israeli's involvement—and if he was, why he hadn't hired Lange to deal with it. Perhaps Casagrande didn't know how to find the Israeli. Thanks to the documents on Peter Malone's computer, Lange did know how to find him, and he had no intention of waiting for orders from Casagrande to act. He had a slight advantage, a brief window of opportunity, but he had to move swiftly or the window would close.

He copied the two files onto a disk, then erased them from the hard drive. Katrine, wrapped in the duvet from her bed, came into the room and sat down at the other end of the couch. Lange closed the computer.

"You promised to cook for me," she said. "I'm famished."

"I have to go to Paris."

"*Now?*"

Lange nodded.

"Can't it wait until morning?"

He shook his head.

"What's so important in Paris?"

Lange looked out the window. "I need to find a man."

RASHID HUSSEINI did not look much like a professional terrorist. He had a round fleshy face and large brown eyes heavy with fatigue. His wrinkled tweed jacket and turtleneck sweater gave him the appearance of a doctoral student at work on a dissertation he could not quite finish. It wasn't far from the truth. Husseini lived in France on a student visa, though he rarely found time to attend his courses at the Sorbonne. He taught English at a language center in a dreary Muslim suburb north of Paris, did the odd bit of translation work, and occasionally wrote incendiary commentary for various left-wing French journals. Eric Lange was aware of the true source of Husseini's income. He worked for a branch of the Palestinian Authority few people knew about. Rashid Husseini—student, translator, journalist—was chief of European operations for the PLO's foreign intelligence service. Husseini was the reason Eric Lange had come to Paris.

Lange telephoned the Palestinian at his apartment on the rue de Tournon. An hour later, they met in a deserted brasserie in the Luxembourg Quarter. Husseini, a secular Palestinian nationalist of the old school, drank red wine. Alcohol made him talkative. He lectured Lange on the suffering of the Palestinian people. It was virtually identical to the diatribe he had inflicted on Lange in Tunis twenty years ago, when he and Abu Jihad were trying to seduce Lange into working for the Palestinian cause. The land and the olive trees, the injustice and the humiliation. "The Jews are the world's new Nazis," Husseini opined. "In the West Bank and Gaza, they operate like the Gestapo and the SS. The Israeli prime minister? He's a war criminal who deserves the justice of Nuremberg." Lange bided his time, stirring his coffee with a tiny silver spoon and nodding sagely at appropriate moments. He couldn't help but feel sorry for Husseini. The war had passed him by. Once it had been waged by men like Rashid Husseini, intellectuals who read Camus in French and screwed stupid German girls on the beaches of St. Tropez.

Now the old fighters had grown fat on handouts from the Europeans and Americans while children, the precious fruit of Palestine, were blowing themselves up in the cafés and markets of Israel.

Finally, Husseini threw his hands up in a helpless gesture, like an old man who knows he has become a bore. "Forgive me, Eric, but my passion always gets the better of me. I know you didn't come here tonight to talk about the suffering of my people. What is it? Are you looking for work?"

Lange leaned forward over the table. "I was wondering whether you might be interested in helping me find the man who killed our friend in Tunis."

Husseini's tired eyes came suddenly to life. "Abu Jihad? I was there that night. I was the first one to enter the study after that Israeli monster had done his evil work. I can still hear the screaming of Abu Jihad's wife and children. If I had the opportunity, I'd kill him myself."

"What do you know about him?"

"His real name is Allon—Gabriel Allon—but he's used dozens of aliases. He's an art restorer. Used his job as cover for his killings in Europe. An old comrade of mine named Tariq al-Hourani put a bomb beneath Allon's car in Vienna about twelve years back and blew up his wife and son. The boy was killed. We were never sure what happened to the wife. Allon took his revenge against Tariq a couple of years ago in Manhattan."

"I remember," Lange said. "That affair with Arafat."

Husseini nodded. "You know where he is?"

"No, but I think I know where he's going."

"Where?"

Lange told him.

"*Rome?* Rome is a big city, my friend. You're going to have to give me more than that."

"He's investigating the murder of an old friend. He's going to Rome to find an Italian detective named Alessio Rossi. Follow Rossi and the Israeli will fall into your lap."

Husseini jotted the name in a small, leather-bound notebook and looked up. *"Carabinieri? Polizia di Stato?"*

"The latter," said Lange, and Husseini wrote *PS* in the book.

The Palestinian sipped his wine and studied Lange a long moment without speaking. Lange knew the questions running through Husseini's mind. How did Eric Lange know where the Israeli assassin was going? And why did he want him dead? Lange decided to answer the questions before Husseini could ask them.

"He's after me. It's a personal matter. I want him dead, and so do you. In that respect, we have common interests. If we work together, the matter can be resolved in a way that suits us both."

A smile spread over Husseini's face. "You were always a very cool customer, weren't you, Eric? Never one to let your emotions get the better of you. I would have enjoyed working with you."

"Do you have the resources in Rome to mount a surveillance operation against a police officer?"

"I could follow the Pope himself. If the Israeli is in Rome, we'll find him. But that's all we're going to do. The last thing the movement needs at the moment is to engage in extracurricular activity on European soil." He winked. "Remember, we've renounced terrorism. Besides, the Europeans are the best friends we have."

"Just find him," said Lange. "Leave the killing to me."

PART THREE

✦

A
PENSIONE
IN ROME

✦

·16·

ROME

T HE ABRUZZI HAD FALLEN on hard times. Located in the San Lorenzo Quarter, between *Stazione Termini* train station and the Church of Santa Maria Maggiore, its mustard-colored façade looked as though it had been raked by machine-gun fire, and the lobby smelled of cat litter. Despite its tumbledown appearance, the little *pensione* suited Gabriel's needs perfectly. The headquarters of the *Polizia di Stato* was a short walk away, and unlike most *pensiones* in Rome each room in this one had a telephone. Most importantly, if Crux Vera was searching for him, the last place they would look was the Abruzzi.

The night manager was an overweight man with round shoulders and a florid face. Gabriel checked in under the name Heinrich Siedler and spoke to him in labored Italian with a murderous German accent. The manager appraised Gabriel with a pair of melancholy eyes, then jotted down his name and passport number in the hotel registry.

Gabriel crossed a cluttered common room, where a pair of Croatian teenagers was engaged in a ferocious ping-pong match. He trod silently up the soiled staircase, let himself into his room, and locked the door. He entered the bathroom. The rust stains in the sink looked like dried blood. He washed his face, then removed his shoes and collapsed onto the bed. He tried to close his eyes but could not. Too exhausted to sleep, he lay on his back, listening to the *TAP-A-TAP-A-TAP* of the table-tennis match downstairs, reliving the last twenty-four hours.

He had been traveling since dawn. Instead of flying directly from London to Rome, which would have required him to clear customs at Fiumicino Airport, he had flown to Nice. At the airport there he had paid a visit to the Hertz outlet, where a friend of the Office called Monsieur Henri had rented him a Renault sedan in such a way that it could never be traced back to him. From Nice, he drove toward Italy along the A8 *autoroute*. Near Monaco, he switched on the English-language Radio Riviera to catch a bit of news on the war in the territories and learned instead that Peter Malone had been found shot to death in his London home.

Parked at the side of the motorway, traffic hurtling past, Gabriel had listened to the rest of the report with his hands strangling the steering wheel and his heart banging against his ribs. Like a chess grandmaster, he had played out the moves and saw disaster looming. He had spent two hours inside the reporter's home. Malone had taken copious notes. Surely the Metropolitan Police had discovered those notes. Because of the intelligence connection, they had probably briefed MI5. There was a very good chance every major police force and security service in Europe was looking for the Israeli assassin codenamed Sword. *The safe thing to do?* Call Shamron on an emergency line, arrange a bolt-hole, and sit on the beach in Netanya until things cooled down. But that would entail surrendering the search for Benjamin's killers. And Malone's. He pulled back onto the *autoroute* and accelerated toward Italy. At the border, a drowsy guard admitted him into the country with a languid wave of his hand.

And now, after an interminable drive down the Italian peninsula, he found himself here, in his sour-smelling room at the Abruzzi. Downstairs, the table-tennis match had deteriorated into something of a new Balkan war. The shouts of the aggrieved party filled Gabriel's room. He thought of Peter Malone and wondered whether he was responsible for his death. Had he led the killers to him, or had Malone already been marked for elimination? Was Gabriel next on the list? As he drifted toward sleep, he heard Malone's warning careening about his memory: *"If they think you pose a threat, they won't hesitate to kill you."*

Tomorrow he would find Alessio Rossi. Then he would get out of Rome as quickly as possible.

GABRIEL SLEPT poorly and was awakened early by the ringing of church bells. He opened his eyes and blinked in the severe sunlight. He showered and changed into fresh clothing, then went downstairs to the dining room for breakfast. The Croatians were nowhere to be seen, only a pair of churchy American pilgrims and a band of noisy college students from Barcelona. There was a sense of excitement in the air, and Gabriel remembered that it was a Wednesday, the day the Holy Father greeted pilgrims in St. Peter's Square.

At nine o'clock, Gabriel returned to his room and placed his first call to Inspector Alessio Rossi of the *Polizia di Stato.* A switchboard operator put him through to the detective's voice mail. "My name is Heinrich Siedler," Gabriel said. "I have information regarding Father Felici and Father Manzini. You can reach me at the Pensione Abruzzi."

He hung up. *Now what?* He had no choice but to wait and hope the detective called him back. There was no television in the room. The bedside table had a built-in radio, but the tuning knob was broken.

After one hour of paralyzing boredom, he dialed the number a second time. Once again the switchboard officer transferred him straight to Rossi's voice mail. Gabriel left a second message, identical to the first, but with a faint note of urgency in his voice.

At eleven-thirty, he placed a third call to Rossi's number. This time he was put through to a colleague who explained that the inspector was on assignment and would not be back in the office until late afternoon. Gabriel left a third message and hung up.

He decided to use the opportunity to get out of the room. In the streets around the Church of Santa Maria Maggiore he checked his tail for signs of surveillance and saw nothing. Then he walked down the Via Napoleone III. The March air was crisp and clear and scented with woodsmoke. He ate pasta in a restaurant near the Piazza Vittorio Emanuele II. After lunch, he walked along the looming western façade of the *Stazione Termini,* then wandered among the classical edifices of Rome's government quarter until he found the headquarters of the *Polizia di Stato.* In a café across the street, he drank espresso and watched officers and secretaries filing in and out, wondering whether Rossi was among them.

At three o'clock, he started back toward the Pensione Abruzzi.

As he was crossing the Piazza di Repubblica, a crowd of about five hundred students entered the square from the direction of the Università Romana. At the head of the procession was an unshaven boy wearing a white headband. Around his waist were sticks of mock dynamite. Behind him a group of pseudo-mourners carried a coffin fashioned of cardboard. As they drew closer Gabriel could see that most of the demonstrators were Italian, including the boy dressed as a suicide bomber. They chanted "Liberate the land of Palestine!" and "Death to the Jews!"—not in Arabic but in Italian. A young Italian girl, no more than twenty, thrust a leaflet into Gabriel's hand. It depicted the Israeli prime minister dressed in the uniform of the SS with a Hitlerian toothbrush mustache, the heel of his jackboot crushing the skull of a Palestinian girl. Gabriel squeezed the leaflet into a ball and dropped it onto the square.

He passed a flower stall. A pair of *carabinieri* were flirting shamelessly with the girl who worked there. They looked up briefly as Gabriel strode by and stared at him with undisguised interest before turning their attention once more to the girl. It could have been nothing, but something about the way they looked at him made sweat run over Gabriel's ribs.

He took his time walking back to the hotel, careful to make sure no one was following him. Along the way, he passed a bored *carabiniere* on a motorcycle, parked in a patch of sunlight, watching the madness of a traffic circle with little interest. Gabriel seemed to intrigue him even less.

He entered the Pensione Abruzzi. The Spaniards had returned from the Wednesday audience in a state of great excitement. It seemed that one of them, a girl with a spiked haircut, had managed to touch the Pope's hand.

Upstairs in his room, Gabriel dialed Rossi's number.

"Pronto."

"Inspector Rossi?"

"Si."

"My name is Heinrich Siedler. I called earlier today."

"Are you still at the Pensione Abruzzi?"

"Yes."

"Don't call here again."

CLICK.

NIGHT FELL and with it came a Mediterranean storm. Gabriel lay on his bed with the window open, listening to the rain smacking against the paving stones in the street below while the conversation with Alessio Rossi played over and over in his head like a loop of audio tape.

"Are you still at the Pensione Abruzzi?"

"Yes."

"Don't call here again."

Clearly the Italian detective wished to speak with him. It was also clear that he wanted no more contact with Herr Siedler on his office telephone. Gabriel had no choice but to wait him out and hope Rossi would make the next move.

At nine o'clock the telephone finally rang. It was the night manager.

"There's a man here to see you."

"What's his name?"

"He didn't say. Shall I send him away?"

"No, I'll be down in a minute."

Gabriel hung up the phone and stepped into the corridor, locking the door behind him. Downstairs, he found the night manager seated behind the front desk. No one else was there. Gabriel looked at him and shrugged. The night manager pointed a sausage-like forefinger toward the common room. Gabriel entered but found the room deserted, except for the Croatian table-tennis players.

He went back to the front desk. The Italian threw his hands up in a gesture of surrender and turned his attention to a miniature black-and-white television. Gabriel climbed the stairs to his room. He unlocked the door and stepped inside.

He saw the blow coming, a glint of light on black metal, sweeping toward him in an arc, like a shimmering swath of wet paint across blank canvas. Too late, he raised his hands to shield his head. The butt of a pistol crashed against the base of his skull behind his left ear.

The pain was immediate. His vision blurred. His legs seemed suddenly paralyzed, and he felt himself corkscrewing downward. His attacker caught him and eased him soundlessly to the linoleum floor. He heard Peter Malone's warning one last time—*"If they think you pose a threat, they won't hesitate to kill you"*—and then only the sound of the table tennis match downstairs in the common room. *TAP-a-TAP-a-TAP* . . .

WHEN GABRIEL AWAKENED, his face was burning. He opened his eyes and found himself staring into a halogen bulb not more than an inch from his face. He closed his eyes and tried to turn his head. Pain shot through the back of his skull like a second blow. He wondered how long he had been out. Long enough for his attacker to bind his mouth and wrists with packing tape. Long enough for blood to dry against the side of his neck.

The light was so close he could see nothing more of the room.

He had the sense that he had not left the Abruzzi. This was confirmed when he heard shouting in Serbo-Croatian. He was on his own bed.

He tried to sit up. A gun barrel seemed to flow out of the light. It pressed against his breastbone and pushed him back onto the mattress. Then a face appeared. Heavy shadows beneath the eyes, stubble on the square chin. The lips moved, sound reached Gabriel's ears. In his delirium, it seemed like a film out of sync, and his brain required a moment to process and comprehend the words he had just heard.

"My name is Alessio Rossi. What the fuck do you want?"

·17·

ROME

T HE YOUNG MAN sitting astride the *motorino* on the Via Gioberti had an air of bored insolence typical of Roman teenagers. He was not bored, nor was he a teenager, but a thirty-year-old *Vigilanza* officer assigned to Carlo Casagrande's special section of the Vatican Security Office. His youthful appearance proved an asset in his present assignment: the surveillance of Inspector Alessio Rossi of the *Polizia di Stato.* The *Vigilanza* man knew only what he needed to know about Rossi. A troublemaker, the inspector. Poking his nose into places it didn't belong. At the end of each shift, the officer returned to the Vatican, then typed up a detailed report and left it on Casagrande's desk. The old general always read the Rossi reports the moment they came in. He had taken a special interest in the case.

Rossi had been acting suspiciously. Twice that day—once in the morning and again in the late afternoon—he'd driven an unmarked car from headquarters to the Via Gioberti and parked there. The *Vigilanza* man had observed Rossi staring at the Pensione Abruzzi like a man who suspected his wife was having an affair upstairs. After the second visit, the officer contacted an informant in Rossi's department, a pretty young girl who answered the telephones and handled the filing. The girl told him that Rossi had received several telephone calls that day from a guest at the Abruzzi offering information about a cold case. The guest's name? Siedler, the informant had answered. Heinrich Siedler.

The Vigilanza man had a hunch. He climbed off the *motorino* and entered the pensione. The night manager looked up from a pornographic magazine.

"Is there a man named Heinrich Siedler staying in this hotel?"

The night manager shrugged his heavy shoulders. The *Vigilanza* officer slid a pair of euro notes across the counter and watched them disappear into the manager's grubby paw.

"Yes, I believe we have a man called Siedler staying here. Let me check." He made a vast show of consulting the registry book. "Ah, yes, Siedler."

The man from the Vatican pulled a photograph from the pocket of his leather jacket and laid it on the counter. This produced a noncommittal frown from the night manager. His face brightened at the appearance of more money.

"Yes, that's him. That's Siedler."

The *Vigilanza* man scooped up the picture. "What room?"

THE APARTMENT on the Via Pinciana was too large for an old man living alone: vaulted ceilings, a spacious sitting room, a broad terrace with a sweeping view of the Villa Borghese. On nights when

Carlo Casagrande was tormented by memories of his wife and daughter, it seemed as cavernous as the Basilica. Had he still been a mere *carabinieri* general, the flat would have been well beyond his reach, but because the building was owned by the Vatican, Casagrande paid nothing. He felt no guilt about living well on the donations of the faithful. The flat served not only as his residence, but as his primary office as well. As a result, he took precautions that his neighbors did not. There was a *Vigilanza* man permanently at his door and another in a car parked on the Via Pinciana. Once a week, a team from the Vatican Security Office scoured the flat to make sure it was free of listening devices.

He answered the telephone on the first ring and immediately recognized the voice of the *Vigilanza* man assigned to the Rossi case. He listened in silence while the officer filed his report, then severed the connection and dialed a number.

"I need to speak to Bartoletti. It's an emergency."

"I'm afraid the director is unavailable at this time."

"This is Carlo Casagrande. Make him available."

"Yes, General Casagrande. Please hold."

A moment later, Bartoletti came on the line. Casagrande wasted no time on pleasantries.

"We have received information that the papal assassin is staying in room twenty-two of the Pensione Abruzzi in the San Lorenzo Quarter. We have reason to believe he is armed and very dangerous."

Bartoletti hung up. Casagrande lit a cigarette and began the wait.

IN PARIS, Eric Lange brought his cellular phone to his ear and heard the voice of Rashid Husseini.

"I think we may have found your man."

"Where is he?"

"Your Italian detective has been acting peculiar all day. He just went inside a pensione called the Abruzzi—a real shithole near the train station."

"What street?"

"The Via Gioberti."

Lange looked at his watch. There was no way to get to Rome tonight. He'd have to leave in the morning. "Keep him under surveillance," he said. "Call me if he moves."

"Right."

Lange rang off, then dialed Air France reservations and booked a seat on the seven-fifteen flight.

·18·

ROME

ROSSI PRESSED THE GUN against Gabriel's forehead and tore the packing tape from his mouth.

"Who are you?"

Greeted by silence, the policeman ground the barrel painfully into Gabriel's temple.

"I'm a friend of Benjamin Stern."

"*Christ!* That explains why they're looking for you."

"Who?"

"Everyone! *Polizia di Stato.* The *carabinieri.* They've even got the SISDE after you."

With the gun still firmly in place, Rossi removed a slip of facsimile paper from his jacket pocket and held it before Gabriel's eyes. Gabriel squinted in the harsh light. It was a photograph, grainy and obviously shot with a telephoto lens, but clear enough for him to see that the face of the subject was his own. He looked at the cloth-

191

ing he was wearing and realized it was the clothing of Ehud Landau. He searched his memory. *Munich . . . the Olympic Village . . .* Weiss must have been following him then too.

The photograph rose like a curtain and Gabriel found himself staring once more into the face of Alessio Rossi. The detective smelled of sweat and cigarettes. His shirt collar was damp and grimy. Gabriel had seen men under pressure before. Rossi was on the edge.

"This photo has been sent to every police station within a hundred miles of Rome. The Vatican Security Office says you've been stalking the Holy Father."

"It's not true."

The Italian finally lowered the gun. The spot on Gabriel's temple where the barrel had been pressed throbbed for several seconds. Rossi turned the light toward the wall and kept the gun in his right hand, resting against his thigh.

"How did you get my name?"

Gabriel answered truthfully.

"They killed Malone too," Rossi said. "You're next, my friend. When they find you, they're going to kill you."

"Who's *they*?"

"Take my advice, Herr Siedler, or whatever the fuck your name is. Get out of Italy. If you can leave tonight, so much the better."

"I'm not leaving until you tell me what you know."

The Italian tilted his head. "You're not really in a position to make demands, are you? I came here for one reason—to try to save your life. If you ignore my warning, that's your business."

"I need to know what you know."

"You need to leave Italy."

"Benjamin Stern was my friend," Gabriel said. "I need your help."

Rossi eyed Gabriel a moment, his gaze tense, then he rose and walked into the bathroom. Gabriel heard water running into the basin. Rossi returned a moment later holding a wet towel. He rolled Gabriel onto his side, unbound his wrists, and gave him the damp cloth. Gabriel cleaned the blood from the side of his neck while Rossi walked to the window and parted the pair of gauzy curtains.

"Who do you work for?" he asked, staring into the street.

"Under the circumstances, it's probably better that I don't answer that."

"Jesus Christ," Rossi murmured. "What on earth have I gotten myself into?"

The detective pulled a chair close to the window and took another long look into the street. Then he switched off the light and told Gabriel the story from the beginning.

MONSIGNOR CESARE FELICI, an elderly and long-retired priest, went missing from his room at the College of San Giovanni Evangelista one evening in June. When the monsignor didn't return by the following evening, his colleagues decided it was time to report the matter to the police. Because the college did not have Vatican territorial status, jurisdiction fell to Italian authorities. Inspector Alessio Rossi of the *Polizia di Stato* was assigned the case and went to the college early that evening.

Rossi had investigated crimes involving the clergy before and had seen the rooms of priests. Monsignor Felici's struck him as inordinately spartan. No personal papers of any kind, no diary, no letters from friends or family. Just a couple of threadbare cassocks, an extra pair of shoes, some underwear and socks. A well-fingered rosary. A cilice.

Rossi interviewed twenty people that first night. They all told similar stories. The day of his disappearance, the old monsignor had taken his usual afternoon stroll in the garden before going to the chapel for prayer and meditation. When he didn't appear for supper, the seminarians and other priests assumed he was tired or not feeling well. No one bothered to check on him until late that evening, when they discovered that he was gone.

The head of the college provided Rossi with a recent photograph of the monsignor, along with a brief biography. Felici was no pastoral priest. He'd spent virtually his entire career working inside the Vatican as a functionary in the Curia. His last assignment, according to the dean, was a staff position at the Congregation for the Causes of Saints. He'd been retired for twenty years.

Not much to go on, but Rossi had started cases with less. The next morning, he entered the missing priest's particulars on the *Polizia di Stato* database and distributed the photograph to police forces across Italy. Next he searched the database to see if any other clergy had vanished lately. Rossi had no hunches and no working theory. He just wanted to make certain there wasn't a nut running around the country murdering priests.

What Rossi discovered shocked him. Two days before Felici's disappearance, another priest had vanished—a Monsignor Manzini, who lived in Turin. Like Felici, Monsignor Manzini was retired from the Vatican. His last position was in the Congregation for Catholic Education. He lived in a retirement home for priests, and like Monsignor Felici, he seemed to have vanished without a trace.

The second disappearance raised a number of questions in Rossi's mind. Were the two cases linked? Did Manzini and Felici know each other? Had they ever worked together? Rossi decided it was time to talk to the Vatican. He approached the Vatican Security Office and requested the personnel files for each of the missing priests. The Vatican denied Rossi's request. Instead, he was given a memorandum that purported to summarize the Curial careers of each priest. According to the memorandum, both had worked in a series of low-level staff assignments, each more trivial than the last. Frustrated, Rossi asked one more question. Did they know each other? They may have bumped into each other socially, Rossi was told, but they had never worked together.

Rossi was convinced that the Vatican was hiding something. He decided to bypass the Security Office altogether and get the complete files for himself. Rossi's wife had a brother who was a priest assigned to the Vatican. Rossi pleaded for help, and the priest reluctantly agreed. A week later, Rossi had copies of the complete personnel files.

"Did they know each other?"

"One would assume so. You see, both Felici and Manzini worked in the Secretariat of State during the war."

"Which section?"

"The German desk."

ROSSI TOOK a long look into the street before continuing. About a week later he had received a response to his original request for reports of other missing clergy. This one didn't match the criteria perfectly, but the local police had decided to forward the report to Rossi anyway. Near the Austrian border, in the town of Tolmezzo, an elderly widow had vanished. Local authorities had given up the search, and she was now presumed dead. Why had her disappearance been brought to Rossi's attention? Because for ten years she had been a nun, before renouncing her vows in 1947 in order to marry.

Rossi decided to bring his superiors into the picture. He wrote up his findings and presented them to his section chief, then requested permission to press Vatican authorities for more information on the two missing priests. Request denied. The nun had a daughter living in France, in a town called Le Rouret in the hills above Cannes. Rossi requested authorization to travel to France to question her. Request denied. Word had come down from on high that there was no link between the disappearances and nothing to be found by poking around behind the walls of the Vatican.

"Who sent down the word?"

"The old man himself," Rossi said. "Carlo Casagrande."

"Casagrande? Why do I know that name?"

"General Carlo Casagrande was the chief of counterterrorism at *L'arma dei Carabinieri* during the seventies and eighties. He's the man who routed the Red Brigades and made Italy safe again. For that, he's something of a national hero. He works for the Vatican Security Office now, but inside the Italian intelligence and security community he's still a god. He's infallible. When Casagrande speaks, everyone listens. When Casagrande wants a case closed, it's closed."

"Who's doing the killing?" Gabriel asked.

The detective shrugged—*We're talking about the Vatican, my friend.* "Whoever's behind it, the Vatican doesn't want the matter pursued. The code of silence is being strictly enforced, and Casagrande is using his influence to keep the Italian police on a short leash."

"The nun who disappeared in Tolmezzo—what was her name?"

"Regina Carcassi."

Find Sister Regina and Martin Luther. Then you'll know the truth about what happened at the convent.

"And what was the name of the convent where she lived during the war, before she renounced her vows?"

"Someplace up north, I think." Rossi hesitated for a moment, searching his memory. "Ah, yes, the Convent of the Sacred Heart. It's on Lake Garda, in a town called Brenzone. Nice place."

Something in the street below caught Rossi's attention. He leaned forward and pulled aside the curtain, peering through the window intently. Then he leaped to his feet and seized Gabriel's arm.

"Come with me. *Now!*"

THE FIRST police officers poured through the front door of the pensione: two plainclothes *Polizia di Stato* followed by a half-dozen *carabinieri* with submachine guns across their chests. Rossi led the way across the common room, then down a short corridor to a metal door that opened onto a darkened interior courtyard. Gabriel could hear the police hammering up the stairs toward his empty room. They had successfully eluded the first wave. More were sure to follow.

Across the courtyard was a passageway leading to the street that ran parallel to the Via Gioberti. Rossi grabbed Gabriel by the forearm and pulled him toward it. Behind them, on the second floor of the pensione, Gabriel could hear the *carabinieri* breaking down his door.

Rossi froze as two more *carabinieri* came through the passageway at a run, weapons at the ready. Gabriel gave Rossi a shove and they started moving again. The *carabinieri* reached the courtyard and clattered to a stop. Immediately their submachine guns swung up to the firing position. Gabriel could see that surrender was not an option. He dived to the ground, landing heavily on his chest, as the first rounds scorched over his head. Rossi was not quick enough. A shot struck him in the shoulder and threw him to the ground.

The Beretta fell from his grasp and landed three feet from Gabriel's left hand. Gabriel reached out and pulled the gun to him. Without hesitating, he rose to his elbows and started firing. One *carabiniere* fell, then the other.

Gabriel crawled over to Rossi. He was bleeding heavily from a wound to his right shoulder.

"Where did you learn to shoot like that?"

"Can you walk?"

"Help me up."

Gabriel pulled Rossi to his feet, wrapped his arm around the Italian's waist, and shepherded him toward the passageway. As they passed the two dead *carabinieri,* Gabriel heard shouting behind him. He released his hold on Rossi and scooped up one of the submachine guns, then dropped to one knee and raked the side of the pensione with automatic fire. He heard screaming and saw men diving for cover.

Gabriel grabbed a spare magazine, rammed it into the weapon, and shoved Rossi's Beretta nine-millimeter into the waistband of his trousers. Then he hooked his arm through Rossi's left elbow and pulled him through the passageway. As they neared the street, two more *carabinieri* appeared. Gabriel fired instantly, blowing both men from their feet.

As they reached the pavement, Gabriel hesitated. From the left, a car was racing toward him, lights flashing, siren blaring. From the right, four men were approaching on foot. Across the street was the entrance of a *trattoria.*

As Gabriel stepped forward, shots erupted from inside the passageway. He lunged to his left, behind the cover of the wall, and tried to pulled Rossi toward him, but the Italian was hit twice in the back. He froze, his arms flung wide, his head back, as one final round tore through the right side of his abdomen.

There was nothing Gabriel could do for him now. He sprinted across the street and threw open the door of the restaurant. As he burst into the dining room with the machine gun in his hands, there was pandemonium.

In Italian, he shouted: "Terrorists! Terrorists! Get out! Now!"

Everyone in the room rose in unison and rushed toward the door. As Gabriel ran toward the kitchen, he could hear frustrated *carabinieri* screaming at the patrons to get out of the way.

Gabriel raced through the tiny kitchen, past startled cooks and waiters, and kicked open the back door. He found himself in a narrow alleyway, not four feet wide, foul-smelling and dark as a mineshaft. He slammed the door behind him and kept running. A few seconds later, the door flew open again. Gabriel turned and sprayed the alleyway with gunfire. The door slammed shut.

At the end of the alley, he came to a broad boulevard. To his right was the façade of the Church of Santa Maria Maggiore; to his left, the expanse of the Piazza Vittorio Emanuele. He dropped the submachine gun in the alley and crossed the street, weaving his way through the traffic. Sirens rang out from every direction.

He wound his way through a chain of narrow streets, then dashed across another busy boulevard, the Via Merulana, and found himself at the edge of the vast park surrounding the Colosseum. He kept to the darkened footpaths. *Carabinieri* units were already searching by flashlight, which made them easy to see and avoid.

Ten minutes later, Gabriel came to the river. At a public telephone on the embankment, he dialed the number he had never be-fore been forced to use. It was answered after one ring by a young woman with a pleasant voice. She spoke to him in Hebrew. It was the sweetest sound he had ever heard. He spoke a code phrase, then recited a series of numbers. There were a few seconds of silence while the girl punched the numbers into a computer.

Then she said: "What's wrong?"

"I'm in trouble. You need to bring me in."

"Are you hurt?"

"Not badly."

"Are you safe in your present location?"

"For the moment, but not for long."

"Call back in ten minutes. Until then, keep moving."

·19·

ROME

THE VIA GIOBERTI was ablaze with flickering blue emergency lights. Achille Bartoletti stepped out of the Pensione Abruzzi and spotted Carlo Casagrande's car amid the turmoil. The Italian security chief came over at an easy executive stroll and climbed into the backseat.

"Your assassin is damned good with a gun, General. I hope he never gets anywhere near the Holy Father."

"How many dead?"

"Four *carabinieri* killed, six others wounded."

"Dear God," Casagrande murmured.

"I'm afraid there's one other casualty—a *Polizia di Stato* detective named Alessio Rossi. Apparently he was inside the assassin's room when the *carabinieri* went in. For some reason, Rossi tried to escape with him."

Casagrande feigned surprise. The tone of Bartoletti's next question revealed that he did not find his performance altogether convincing. "Is there something about this affair you've neglected to tell me, General?"

Casagrande met Bartoletti's quizzical stare and slowly shook his head. "I've told you everything I know, Achille."

"I see."

Casagrande tried to quickly change the subject.

"What is Rossi's condition?"

"He's dead, too, I'm afraid."

"Was it the Israeli?"

"No, it appears he was shot by *carabinieri*."

"Is there anything in the room?"

"Just a change of clothes. No papers, no identification. Your man is good."

Casagrande looked up at the open window on the second floor of the pensione. He had hoped the matter could be handled quietly. Now he had to use the circumstances to his advantage.

"Based on his performance tonight, it is clear to me that this man is a professional."

"I cannot argue with that conclusion, General."

"As for Rossi, perhaps he was involved somehow in the conspiracy."

"Perhaps," Bartoletti said with little conviction.

"Whatever the circumstances, the Israeli must not be allowed to leave Rome."

"A hundred officers are looking for him right now."

"He won't stay in Rome long. He'll leave at the first opportunity. If I were you, I'd seal the city. Put a watch on every train station and bus terminal."

Bartoletti's expression betrayed that he didn't appreciate being treated like an incompetent who needed to be told how to mount a search for a fugitive. "I'm afraid this affair has little to do with the Vatican at this point, General Casagrande. After all, five *Italian* policeman were killed on *Italian* soil. We will conduct the search in the manner we see fit and inform the Vatican Security Office as events warrant."

The pupil has turned on his master, thought Casagrande. Such was the nature of all relationships like this. "Of course, Achille," he said submissively. "I meant no disrespect."

"None taken, General. But I wouldn't hold out much hope that this man is going to simply *vanish*. Speaking for myself, I'd like to know what Inspector Rossi was doing in his room. I would think you'd like to know that too."

Bartoletti climbed out of the car without waiting for a reply and walked briskly away. Casagrande's driver looked up into the rearview mirror.

"Back to the Via Pinciana, General?"

Casagrande shook his head. *"Il Vaticano."*

IN A SOUVENIR KIOSK near the Forum, Gabriel bought a dark blue hooded sweatshirt with the words *Viva Roma!* emblazoned across the chest. In a public toilet, he removed his shirt and stuffed it into a rubbish bin. Only then did he notice that a bullet had grazed his right side, leaving a bloody furrow below his armpit. He used toilet paper to wipe away the blood, then carefully pulled on the new sweatshirt. Rossi's Beretta was still wedged into the waist of his jeans. He went out and headed north toward the Piazza Navona.

He had made his second call on the emergency line. The same woman had answered the phone and had told him to go to the

Church of Santa Maria della Pace. Inside, near the confessionals, would be a man in a tan overcoat with a folded copy of *L'Osservatore Romano.* The agent would tell Gabriel where to go next.

His first responsibility now was to his rescuers. He had to be certain he was not leading them into a trap. As he wound his way through the warren of narrow streets and alleyways in the *Centro Storico,* he mingled with tourists and ordinary Romans, keeping clear of main thoroughfares. He could still hear the wail of police sirens in the distance but was confident no one was following him.

In the Piazza Navona, *carabinieri* were patrolling in pairs. Gabriel pulled up his hood and settled into a group of people watching a man play classical guitar next to a fountain. He looked up and saw that the northern end of the piazza was free of police. He turned, crossed the square, and followed a narrow alley to the entrance of the church. A beggar was sitting on the steps. Gabriel slipped past and went inside.

The smell of incense greeted him. He thought of Venice. The stillness of San Zaccaria. Just two weeks ago he was at peace, restoring one of the most important paintings in all of Italy. Now he was being hunted by every policeman in Rome. He wondered whether he would ever be allowed to go back to his old life again.

He paused before the basin of holy water, thought better of it, and cased forward into the nave. An old woman was on her knees before a bank of memorial candles. Opposite the doors of the confessional sat the man in the tan overcoat. On the pew was a copy of *L'Osservatore Romano* folded in half. Gabriel settled in next to him.

"You're bleeding," said the man in the overcoat. Gabriel looked down and saw that the side of his sweatshirt was indeed soaked with blood. "Do you need a doctor?"

"I'll be fine. Let's get out of here."

"Not me. I'm just the messenger."

"Where do I go?"

"There's a silver BMW motorcycle parked outside the church. The driver is wearing a crimson helmet."

Gabriel walked outside. The motorcycle was there. As Gabriel approached, the driver pressed the starter button and revved the engine into life. Gabriel threw his leg over the back and wrapped his arms around the driver's waist. The bike turned into traffic and sped in the direction of the river.

It did not take Gabriel long to realize that the agent driving the motorcycle was a woman: the hourglass hips, the narrow waist and slender blue-jeaned thighs, the bunch of hair poking from the bottom of the helmet. It was curly and smelled of jasmine and tobacco. He was certain he had smelled it before.

They raced along the Lungotevere. To his right Gabriel could see the dome of St. Peter's, looming over the Vatican Hill. Crossing the river, he hurled Alessio Rossi's Beretta into the black water.

They headed up the Janiculum Hill. At the Piazza Ceresi they turned into a steeply sloped residential street lined with stone pines and small apartment houses. The bike slowed as they approached an old palazzo that had been converted into a block of flats. The woman killed the engine and they coasted beneath an archway, coming to a stop in a darkened courtyard.

Gabriel dismounted and followed her into the foyer, then up two flights of stairs. She unlocked the door and pulled him inside. In the darkened entrance hall, she unzipped her leather riding jacket and removed her helmet. Her hair tumbled over her shoulders. Then she turned on the lights.

"You?" said Gabriel.

The girl smiled. It was Chiara, the rabbi's daughter from Venice.

✦   ✦   ✦

FOR THE second time that evening, Eric Lange's cellular telephone chirped softly on the bedside table of his Paris hotel room. He brought it to his ear and listened silently while Rashid Husseini told him about the gun battle at the Pensione Abruzzi. Obviously, Carlo Casagrande *did* know about Allon, and he had sent a mob of incompetent Italian policemen to do the job when it could have been handled quite easily by one good man with a gun. Lange's window of opportunity to deal with Allon himself may have just closed permanently.

"What are you doing now?" Lange asked.

"We're looking for him, along with half the police in Italy. There's no guarantee we're going to find him. The Israelis are good at getting their people out of tight spots."

"Yes, they are," said Lange. "In fact, I'd say the Rome station of the Israeli secret service is very busy tonight. They've got quite a crisis on their hands."

"Indeed, they do."

"Have you identified any of their personnel in Rome?"

"Two or three that we're sure of," Husseini said.

"It might be wise to follow them. With a bit of luck, they'll lead you straight to him."

"You remind me of Abu Jihad," Husseini. "He was brilliant too."

"I'm coming to Rome in the morning."

"Give me your flight information. I'll have a man meet you."

GABRIEL SPENT a long time in the shower washing his wound and scrubbing the blood from his hair. When he emerged, wrapped in a white towel, Chiara was waiting for him. She cleaned his wounds carefully and bound his abdomen in a heavy dressing. Lastly she gave him a shot of antibiotics and handed him a pair of yellow capsules.

"What's this?"

"Something for the pain. Take them. You'll sleep better."

Gabriel washed down the tablets with a swig of mineral water from a plastic bottle.

"I laid some clean clothes for you on the bed. Are you hungry?"

Gabriel shook his head and walked into the bedroom to change. He was suddenly unsteady on his feet. While he was on the run, being fed by nerves and adrenalin, he had not felt the pain. Now his side felt as though it had a knife in it.

Chiara had left a blue sweatsuit on the bed. Gabriel carefully pulled it on. It was for a man several inches taller, and he had to roll up the sleeves and cuff the pant legs. When he came out again, she was sitting in the living room watching a bulletin on the television. She took her eyes from the screen long enough to glance at him and frown at his appearance.

"I'll get you some proper clothes in the morning."

"How many dead?"

"Five," she said. "Several more wounded."

Five dead . . . Gabriel closed his eyes and fought off a wave of nausea. A burst of pain shot through his side. Chiara, sensing his distress, laid a hand on his face.

"You're burning," she said. "You need to sleep."

"I've always found sleep difficult at times like this."

"I understand—I think. How about a glass of wine?"

"With the painkillers?"

"It might help you."

"A small one."

She went into the kitchen. Gabriel aimed the remote at the television and the screen went black. Chiara returned and handed him a glass of red wine.

"Nothing for you?"

She shook her head. "It's my job to make sure you stay safe."

Gabriel swallowed some of the wine. "Is your name really Chiara Zolli?"

She nodded.

"And are you really the rabbi's daughter?"

"Yes, I am."

"Where are you posted?"

"Officially, I'm attached to Rome station, but I do a fair amount of traveling."

"What sort of work?"

"Oh, you know—a little of this, a little of that."

"And that routine the other night?"

"Shamron asked me to keep an eye on you while you were in Venice. Imagine my surprise when you walked into the community center to see my father."

"What did he tell you about our conversation?"

"That you were asking him a lot of questions about the Italian Jews during the war—and about the Convent of the Sacred Heart on the *Lago di Garda*. Why don't you tell me the rest?"

Because I don't have the strength, he thought. Then he said, "How long do I have to stay here?"

"Pazner will tell you everything in the morning."

"Who's Pazner?"

Chiara smiled. "You *have* been out of the game for a while. Shi-

mon Pazner is the head of Rome station. At the moment, he's trying to figure out how to get you out of Italy and back to Israel."

"I'm not going back to Israel."

"Well, you can't stay here. Shall I turn on the television again?
Every policeman in Italy is looking for you. But that's not my decision. I'm just a lowly field hand. Pazner will make the call in the
morning."

Gabriel was too weak to argue with her. The combination of the
painkillers and the wine had left him feeling heavy-lidded and numb.
Perhaps it was for the best. Chiara helped him to his feet and guided
him into the bedroom. As he lay down, pain shot through his side.
He settled his head carefully on the pillow. Chiara switched off the
light and sat in an armchair at the side of the bed, a Beretta in her lap.

"I can't sleep with you there."

"You'll sleep."

"Go into the other room."

"I'm not allowed to leave you."

Gabriel closed his eyes. The girl was right. After a few minutes,
he slipped into unconsciousness. His sleep was aflame with nightmares. He fought the gun battle in the courtyard for a second time
and saw *carabinieri* drenched in blood. Alessio Rossi appeared in his
room, but in Gabriel's dream he was dressed as a priest, and instead
of a Beretta it was a crucifix he aimed at Gabriel's head. Rossi's death,
with his arms flung wide and his side pierced by a bullet, Gabriel
saw as a Caravaggio.

Leah came to him. She stepped down from her altarpiece and
shed her robes. Gabriel stroked her skin and found that her scars had
been healed. Her mouth tasted of olives; her nipples, pressed against
his chest, were firm and cool. She took him inside her body and

brought him slowly to climax. As Gabriel released inside her, she asked him why he had fallen in love with Anna Rolfe. *It's you I love, Leah,* he told her. *It's you I'll always love.*

He awakened briefly; the dream was so real he expected to find Leah in the room with him. But when he opened his eyes, it was the face of Chiara he saw, sitting in her chair, watching over him, a gun in her hand.

·20·

ROME

SHIMON PAZNER ARRIVED at the safe flat at eight o'clock the next morning. He was a squat and powerfully built man, with hair like steel wool and acne scars on his broad cheeks. Judging from his unshaven face and the red rims around his eyes, it was a safe assumption that he had not slept. Wordlessly he poured himself a cup of coffee and dropped the morning newspapers on the kitchen table. The shootout in the San Lorenzo Quarter was the lead of each paper. Gabriel, still groggy from the painkillers, looked down at them but was powerless to summon an expression.

"You made quite a mess in my town." Pazner tipped half a cup of coffee down his throat and pulled a face. "Imagine my surprise when I get the flash that the great Gabriel Allon is on the run and needs to be pulled in. You'd think someone at King Saul Boulevard would have the common sense to inform the local station chief when Gabriel Allon is in town to take someone down."

"I didn't come to Rome to take anyone down."

"Bullshit!" Pazner snapped. "That's what you do."

Pazner looked up as Chiara entered the kitchen. She wore a toweling robe. Her hair, still wet from the shower, was combed straight back. She poured herself some coffee and sat down next to Gabriel at the table.

Pazner said, "Do you know what's going to happen if the Italians ever figure out who you are? It will destroy our relationship. They'll never work with us again."

"I know," Gabriel said. "But I didn't come here to kill anyone. They tried to kill *me*."

Pazner pulled out a chair and sat down, his thick forearms resting on the table. "What were you doing in Rome, Gabriel? And don't bullshit me."

When Gabriel informed Pazner that he was in Rome on a job for Shamron, the station chief tilted his round head back and emptied his lungs toward the ceiling. "*Shamron?* That's why no one at King Saul Boulevard knows what you're working on. For Christ's sake! I should have known the old man was behind this."

Gabriel pushed away the newspapers. He supposed he did owe Pazner an explanation. It had been reckless to come to Rome after the murder of Peter Malone. He'd underestimated the capabilities of his enemies and left Pazner with a colossal mess to clean up. He drank a cup of coffee to clear his head and told Pazner the story from the beginning. Chiara's gaze remained fixed on him the entire time. Pazner managed to remain calm for the first half of Gabriel's account, but by the end of the story he was smoking nervously.

"Sounds as if they were following Rossi," Pazner said. "And Rossi led them to you."

"He seemed to know he was under surveillance. He never left the window while he was in my room. He saw them coming for us, but it was too late."

"Was there anything in that room that could link you to the Office?"

Gabriel shook his head, then asked Pazner whether he'd ever heard of a group called Crux Vera.

"One hears all sorts of rumors about secret societies and Vatican intrigue in Italy," Pazner said. "Remember the P2 scandal back in the eighties?"

Vaguely, thought Gabriel. Quite by chance the Italian police had come across a document revealing the existence of a secret right-wing society that had wormed its way into the highest reaches of the government, military, and intelligence community. And the Vatican, apparently.

"I've heard the name Crux Vera," Pazner continued, "but I've never put much stock into it. Until *now,* that is."

"When do I get to leave?"

"We'll move you tonight."

"Where?"

Pazner inclined his head toward the east, and by the look of finality in his dark eyes, it was clear to Gabriel that he was referring to Israel.

"I don't want to go to Israel. I want to find out who killed Benjamin."

"You can't move anywhere in Europe now. You're blown. You're going home—*period.* Shamron isn't the chief any more. Lev is the chief, and he's not going to be brought down by one of the old man's adventures."

"How are you going to get me out of the country?"

"The same way we got Vanunu out. By boat."

"If I remember correctly, that was one of Shamron's *adventures* too."

Mordechai Vanunu had been a disgruntled worker at the Dimona atomic facility who revealed the existence of Israel's nuclear arsenal to a London newspaper. A female agent named Cheryl Ben-Tov lured Vanunu from London to Rome, where he was kidnapped and taken by small boat to an Israeli naval vessel lying in wait off the Italian coast. Few people outside the Office knew the truth about the episode: that Vanunu's defection and betrayal of Israeli secrets had been choreographed and manipulated by Ari Shamron as a way to warn Israel's enemies that they had no hope of ever bridging the nuclear gap, while at the same time leaving Israel with the ability to deny publicly that it possessed nuclear weapons.

"Vanunu left Italy in chains and under heavy sedation," Pazner said. "You'll be spared that indignity as long as you behave yourself."

"Where do we set sail?"

"There's a beach near Fiumicino that's perfect. You'll take a motor launch from there at nine o'clock. Five miles offshore, you'll meet an oceangoing motor yacht, crew of one. He's Office now, but for many years he captained a navy gunboat. He'll take you back to Tel Aviv. A few days at sea will be good for you."

"Who's taking me to the yacht?"

Pazner looked at Chiara. "She grew up in Venice. She's damned good with a boat."

"She *does* handle a motorcycle well," Gabriel said.

Pazner leaned forward across the table. "You should see her with a Beretta."

✦   ✦   ✦

ERIC LANGE arrived at Fiumicino airport at nine o'clock that morning. After clearing customs and passport control, he spotted Rashid Husseini's man standing in the terminal hall, clutching a brown cardboard sign that read TRANSEURO TECHNOLOGIES — MR. BOWMAN. He had a car waiting outside in the covered parking lot, a battered beige Lancia that he piloted with unwarranted caution. He called himself Aziz and spoke English with a faint British accent. Like Husseini, he had the air of an academic.

He drove to a faded apartment house at the base of the Aventine Hill and led Lange up a crumbling staircase that spiraled upward into the gloom. The flat was empty of furniture except for a television connected to a satellite dish on the tiny balcony. Aziz gave Lange a gun, a Makarov nine-millimeter with a silencer screwed into the barrel, then brewed Turkish coffee in the galley kitchen. They spent the next three hours sitting cross-legged on the floor like Bedouins, drinking coffee and watching the war in the territories on *al-Jazeera* television. The Palestinian chain-smoked American cigarettes. With each televised outrage he let loose a string of Arabic curses.

At two in the afternoon, he went downstairs to fetch bread and cheese from the grocer. He returned to discover Lange enthralled by a cooking program on an American cable channel. He brewed more coffee and changed the channel back to *al-Jazeera* without asking Lange's permission. Lange ate a bit of lunch, then made a pillow of his overcoat and stretched out on the bare floor for a nap. He was awakened by the purr of Aziz's cellular telephone. He opened his eyes to find the Arab listening intently and scribbling a note on a paper sack.

Aziz rang off and his gaze was drawn back to the television. An anchorman was offering breathless narration to a piece of video depicting Israeli soldiers firing into a crowd of Palestinian boys.

Aziz lit another cigarette and looked at Lange.

"Let's go kill the bastard."

BY SUNSET, Gabriel's wound hurt less and his appetite had returned. Chiara cooked fettuccini with mushrooms and cream, and they watched the evening news. The first ten minutes of the broadcast was devoted to the search for the papal assassin. Over video of heavily armed Italian security forces patrolling the nation's airports and borders, the correspondent described it as one of the largest manhunts in Italian history. When Gabriel's photograph appeared on the screen, Chiara squeezed his hand.

After supper, she put a clean dressing on his wound and gave him another shot of antibiotics. When she offered Gabriel something for the pain, he refused. At six-thirty they changed clothes. The forecast was for rain and rough seas, and they dressed appropriately: fleece underwear, waterproof outerwear, rubber boots over insulated socks. Pazner had left Gabriel a false Canadian passport and a Beretta nine-millimeter. Gabriel hid the passport in a zippered compartment of his coat and slipped the Beretta into a patch pocket within easy reach.

Pazner arrived at six o'clock. His thick face was set in a furrowed scowl and his movements were crisp and precise. Over a last cup of coffee, he calmly briefed them. Getting out of Rome would be the most dangerous part of the escape, he explained. The police had mounted rolling checkpoints and were making random stops all over the city. His businesslike demeanor helped to settle Gabriel's nerves.

At seven o'clock they left the flat. Pazner made a point of speaking a few words in excellent Italian during the descent down the staircase. Parked in the courtyard was a dark-gray Volkswagen delivery van. Pazner climbed into the front passenger seat; Gabriel and Chiara clambered through the side door into the cargo hold. The floor was cold to the touch. The driver started the engine and switched on the wipers. He wore a blue anorak, and the pale hands gripping the steering wheel were the hands of a pianist. Pazner called him Reuven.

The van jerked forward and passed through the arched entrance of the courtyard, then turned right and accelerated into traffic. Sprawled on the floor of the van, Gabriel could see nothing but the night sky and the reflections of passing headlights. He knew they were heading west. To avoid the checkpoints on Rome's main thoroughfares and the *autostrada,* Pazner had charted a course to the sea consisting of side streets and back roads.

Gabriel looked toward Chiara and found that she was staring at him. He tried to hold her gaze, but she looked away. He leaned his head against the wall and closed his eyes.

AZIZ HAD BROUGHT Lange up to date during the brief drive from the Aventine Hill to the old palazzo high atop the Janiculum. For several years, Palestinian intelligence had been aware that Shimon Pazner was an agent of the Israeli secret service. They had followed him from posting to posting, charted the course of his career. In Rome, where he was assumed to be the chief of station, he was under regular surveillance. Twice that day—once in the early morning and again in the late afternoon—Pazner had visited a flat in a converted palazzo on the Janiculum. PLO intelligence had long suspected that the property was an Israeli safe flat. The case was circumstantial, the connections tenuous, but given the circumstances, the chances seemed reasonable that Gabriel Allon, the killer of Abu Jihad, was inside.

Parked on the street, one hundred meters from the entrance of the old palazzo, Lange and Aziz had watched and waited. There were lights burning in only two of the flats facing the street, one on the second floor and the other on the top. In that flat, the shades were tightly drawn. Lange took note of the arriving tenants: a pair of boys on a *motorino;* a woman in a miniature two-seater Fiat; a middle-aged man in a belted raincoat who came by way of a city bus. A dark-gray Volkswagen delivery van, one man in the front, dressed in a blue windbreaker, that turned into the central courtyard.

Lange consulted his watch.

Ten minutes later, the van poked from the entrance of the courtyard and turned into the street. As it sped past their position, Lange noticed that there was now a second man in the front seat. He spurred Aziz into action with a sharp elbow to the ribs. The Palestinian started the engine, waited a decent interval, then swung a U-turn and followed after the van.

FIVE MINUTES after leaving the safe flat Shimon Pazner's cellular phone rang. He had taken the precaution of a chase car, a second team of agents whose job it was to make certain that the van was not being followed. A call from the team at this stage could mean one of two things. No sign of surveillance, proceed to the beach as scheduled. Or: trouble, take evasive action.

Pazner pressed the call button and raised the phone to his ear. He listened in silence for a moment, then murmured, "Take them out the first chance you get."

He punched the END button and looked at the driver. "We've got company, Reuven. Beige Lancia, two cars back."

The driver put his foot to the floor, and the van shot forward. Gabriel reached into his pocket and wrapped his hand around the comforting shape of the Beretta.

FOR LANGE, the rapid acceleration of the van provided confirmation that Gabriel Allon was inside. It also meant that they had been spotted, that the element of surprise had been lost, and that killing Allon would entail a high-speed chase followed by a shoot-out, something that violated nearly all of Lange's operational tenets. He killed by stealth and surprise, appearing where he was least expected and slipping quietly away. Gun battles were for commandos and desperados, not professional assassins. Still, he was loath to let Allon escape so easily. Reluctantly, he ordered Aziz to take up the chase. The Palestinian downshifted and pressed hard on the accelerator, trying to maintain contact.

Two minutes later, the interior of the Lancia was suddenly filled with blinding halogen light. Lange shot a look over his shoulder and saw the distinctive headlights of a Mercedes, a few inches from the rear bumper. The Mercedes moved left, so that its right front bumper was aligned with the left rear bumper of the Lancia.

Lange braced himself against the dash. The Mercedes accelerated hard, closing the gap between the two cars. The Lancia shuddered with the impact, then went into a violent clockwise spin. Aziz shouted and clung desperately to the wheel. Lange grabbed the armrest and waited for the car to roll.

It never did. After what seemed like an eternity, the Lancia came to a stop, facing the opposite direction. Lange turned around and glanced through the rear window in time to see the van and the Mercedes disappear below the crest of a hill.

NINETY MINUTES later, the van rolled to a stop in a carpark overlooking a windswept beach. The labored howl of a jumbo jet sinking out of the black sky provided proof that they were near the end of Fiumicino's busy runway. Chiara climbed out and walked down to the water's edge to see if it was clear. The van shuddered in the wind gusts. Two minutes later, she poked her head through the doors and nodded. Pazner shook Gabriel's hand and wished him luck. Then he looked at Chiara. "We'll wait here. Hurry."

Gabriel followed her along the rocky beach. They came to the boat, a ten-foot Zodiac, and dragged it into the frigid surf. The engine started without hesitation. Chiara guided the boat expertly out to sea, the stubby prow bucking over the wind-driven surf, while Gabriel watched the shoreline falling away and the coastal lights growing dim. Italy, a country he loved, a place that had given him peace after the Wrath of God operation. He wondered whether he would ever be allowed to go back again.

Chiara removed a radio from her jacket pocket, murmured a few words into the microphone, and released the TALK button. A moment later, the running lights of a motor yacht flickered on. "There," she said, pointing off the starboard side. "There's your ride home."

She changed the heading and opened the throttle, racing across the whitecaps toward the waiting vessel. Fifty yards from the yacht, she killed the engine and glided silently toward the stern. Then, for the first time, she looked at Gabriel.

"I'm coming with you."

"What are you talking about?"

"I'm coming with you," she repeated deliberately.

"I'm going to Israel."

"No, you're not. You're going to Provence to find the daughter of Regina Carcassi. And I'm going with you."

"You're going to put me on that yacht, and then you're going to turn around."

"Even with that Canadian passport, you can't go anywhere in Europe right now. You can't rent a car, you can't get on an airplane. You need me. And what if Pazner was lying? What if there are two men on that boat instead of just one?"

Gabriel had to admit she had point.

"You're a fool to do this, Chiara. You'll destroy your career."

"No, I won't," she said. "I'll tell them that you forced me to accompany you against my will."

Gabriel looked up at the motor yacht. It was growing larger by degrees. Honor was due. Chiara had picked the perfect time to spring her trap.

"Why?" he asked. "Why do you want to do this?"

"Did my father tell you that his grandparents were among the elderly Jews who were removed from that home in the ghetto and deported to Auschwitz? Did he tell you that they died there, along with all the others?"

"He didn't mention that."

"Do you know why he didn't tell you? Because even now, even after all these years, he can't bring himself to speak of it. He can recite the name of every Venetian Jew who died at Auschwitz, but he can't bring himself to talk about his own grandparents." She removed a Beretta from her jacket pocket and pulled the slide. "I'm coming with you to find that woman."

The Zodiac nudged against the stern of the motor yacht. Above them, a figure appeared on the deck and looked over the railing at them. Gabriel tied off the line and held the boat steady while Chiara pulled herself up the ladder. Then he followed after her. By the time he reached the deck, the captain was standing with his arms in the air and a look of utter disbelief on his face.

"Sorry," Gabriel said. "I'm afraid there's been a slight change in our itinerary."

CHIARA HAD BROUGHT a syringe and a bottle of sedative. Gabriel led the captain down to one of the staterooms below deck and bound his wrists and ankles with a length of line. The man struggled for a few seconds as Chiara pulled up his sleeve, but when Gabriel pressed his forearm against the man's throat, he relaxed and allowed Chiara to give him the injection. When he was unconscious, Gabriel checked the knots—tight enough to hold him, not tight enough to cut off the circulation to his hands and feet.

"How long is the sedative supposed to last?"

"Ten hours, but he's big. I'll give him another dose in eight."

"Just don't kill the poor bastard. He's on our side."

"He'll be fine."

Chiara led the way up to the bridge. A chart of the waters off Italy's western coast was spread on the table. She checked their position on the GPS display and quickly plotted a course. Then she powered up the engines and brought the yacht around to a proper heading. A moment later they were cruising north, toward the straits between Elba and Corsica.

She turned and looked at Gabriel, who was watching in admiration, and said, "We're going to need some coffee. Think you can handle that?"

"I'll do my best."

"Sometime tonight would be good."

"Yes, sir."

SHIMON PAZNER stood motionless on the beach, hands on his hips, shoes filled with seawater, trousers soaked to the knees, like a long-submerged statue being slowly revealed by the receding waters. He brought his radio to his lips and tried to raise Chiara one last time. Silence.

She should have been back an hour ago. There were two possibilities, neither pleasant. Possibility one? Something had gone wrong and they were lost. Possibility two? *Allon . . .*

Pazner hurled his radio into the surf in disgust, a look of pure loathing on his face, and trod slowly back to the van.

THERE WAS just enough time for Lange for Eric Lange to catch the night train for Zurich. He directed Aziz to a quiet side street adjacent to the rail lines feeding out of the *Stazione Termini* and told him to shut down the engine. Aziz seemed puzzled. "Why do you want to be dropped here?"

"At the moment every police officer in Rome is looking for Gabriel Allon. Surely, they're watching the train stations and airports. It's best not to show your face there unless it's absolutely necessary."

The Palestinian seemed to accept this explanation. Lange could see a train easing out of the station. He waited patiently to take his leave.

"Tell Hussein that I'll contact him in Paris when things have cooled down," Lange said.

"I'm sorry we weren't successful tonight."

Lange shrugged. "With a bit of luck, we'll get another chance."

The train was suddenly next to them, filling the car with a metallic screeching. Lange saw his chance. He opened the door and stepped out of the car. Aziz leaned across the front seat and called out, but his words were drowned out by the sound of the train.

"What?" Lange asked, cupping his ear. "I can't hear you."

"The gun," Aziz repeated. "You forgot to give me the gun."

"Ah, yes."

Lange removed the silenced Stechkin from his coat pocket and pointed it toward Aziz. The Palestinian reached out for it. The first shot pierced the palm of his hand before tearing into his chest cavity. The second left a neat circle above his right eye.

Lange dropped the gun on the passenger seat and walked into the station. The Zurich train was boarding. He found his compartment in the first-class sleeper carriage and stretched out in the comfortable berth. Twenty minutes later, as the train slipped through the northern suburbs of Rome, he closed his eyes and was immediately asleep.

·21·

TIBERIAS, ISRAEL

THE CALL FROM LEV did not awaken Shamron. Indeed, he had not closed his eyes since the first urgent flash from Rome that Gabriel and the girl were missing. He lay in bed, the telephone a few inches from his ear, listening to Lev's histrionics while Ge'ulah stirred softly in her sleep. The indignity of aging, he thought. Not long ago, Lev was a green recruit, and Shamron was the one who did the screaming. Now, the old man had no choice but to hold his tongue and bide his time.

When the tirade ended, the line went dead. Shamron swung his feet to the floor, pulled on a robe, and walked outside to his terrace overlooking the lake. The sky in the east was beginning to turn pale blue with the coming dawn, but the sun had not yet appeared over the ridge of the hills. He dug through the pockets of the robe, looking for cigarettes, hoping against hope that Ge'ulah hadn't found them. It filled him with a sense of great personal victory when his stubby fingers came upon a crumpled packet.

He lit one and savored the bite of the harsh Turkish tobacco on his tongue. Then he lifted his gaze and let it wander for a moment over the view. He never tired of it, this window on his private corner of the Promised Land. It was no accident the vista faced eastward. That way Shamron, the eternal sentinel, could keep watch on Israel's enemies.

The air smelled of a coming storm. Soon the rains would arrive, and once more the land would run with floodwater. How many more floods would he see? In his most pessimistic moments, Shamron wondered how many more the children of Israel would see. Like most Jews, he was gripped by an unwavering fear that his generation would be the last. A man much wiser than Shamron had called the Jews the ever-dying people, a people forever on the verge of ceasing to be. It had been Shamron's mission in life to rid his people of that fear, to wrap them in a blanket of security and make them feel safe. He was haunted by the realization that he had failed.

He scowled at his stainless-steel wristwatch. Gabriel and the girl had been missing for eight hours. It was Shamron's affair, but it was blowing up in Lev's face. Gabriel was getting closer to identifying the killers of Benjamin Stern, but Lev wanted no part of it. *Little Lev,* thought Shamron derisively. The craven bureaucrat. A man whose innate sense of caution rivaled the daring and audacity of Shamron.

"Do I need this, Ari?" Lev had screamed. "The Europeans are accusing us of behaving like Nazis in the territories, and now one of your old killers is accused of trying to assassinate the *Pope!* Tell me where I can find him. Help me bring him in before this thing destroys this beloved service of yours once and for all."

Perhaps Lev was right, though it pained Shamron to even consider such a thought. Israel had enough problems at the moment. The *shaheeds* were turning markets into bloodbaths. The thief of Baghdad was still trying to forge his nuclear sword. Perhaps now was not the best time to pick a fight with the Roman Catholic Church. Perhaps now was not the best time to go wading in old waters. The water was dirty and filled with unseen hazards, potholes and rocks, hidden brush where a man could become entangled and drown.

And then an image appeared in his thoughts. A muddy village outside Kraków. A rampaging crowd. Shop windows smashed. Homes set ablaze. Men beaten bloody with clubs. Women raped. *Christ-killers! Jewish filth! Kill the Jews!* A child's village, a young child's memories of Poland. The boy would be sent to Palestine to live with relatives on a settlement in the Upper Galilee. The parents would stay behind. The boy would join the Haganah and fight in Israel's war of rebirth. When the new state was putting together an intelligence service, the boy, now a young man, would be invited to join. In a shabby suburb north of Buenos Aires, he would become an almost mythical figure by seizing the throat of the man who had sent his parents, and six million others, to the camps of death.

Shamron found that his eyes were squeezed tightly shut and that his hands were gripping the top of the balustrade. Slowly, finger by finger, he relaxed his grip.

A line of Eliot ran through his head: *"In my beginning is my end."* *Eichmann* . . .

How had this puppeteer of death, this murdering bureaucrat who made the trains of genocide run on time—how had it come to pass that he was living quietly in a hardscrabble suburb of Buenos Aires when six million had perished? Shamron knew the answer, of course, for every page of the Eichmann file was engraved in his memory. Like hundreds of other murderers, he had escaped via "the convent route"—a chain of monasteries and Church properties stretching from Germany to the Italian port of Genoa. In Genoa, he had been given shelter by Franciscans and, through the auspices of Church charitable organizations was provided with false papers describing him as a refugee. On June 14, 1950, he emerged from the shelter of the Franciscan convent long enough to board the *Giovanna C,* bound for Buenos Aires. Bound for a new life in the New World, thought Shamron. The leader of the Church had not been able to find the words to condemn the murder of six million, but his bishops and priests had given comfort and sanctuary to the greatest mass killer in history. This was a fact that Shamron could never comprehend, a sin for which there was no absolution.

He thought of Lev's voice screeching down the secure line from Tel Aviv. *No,* thought Shamron, *I will not help Lev find Gabriel.* Quite the opposite, he was going to help him discover what happened in that convent by the lake—and who killed Benjamin Stern.

He walked back into the house, his step crisp and surefooted, and went to his bedroom. Ge'ulah was lying in bed watching television. Shamron packed a suitcase. Every few seconds, she would glance up from the screen and look at him, but she did not speak. It had been this way for more than forty years. When his bag was packed, Shamron sat on the bed next to her and held her hand.

"You'll be careful, won't you, Ari?"

"Of course, my love."

"You won't smoke cigarettes, will you?"

"Never!"

"Come home soon."

"Soon," Shamron said, and he kissed her forehead.

+ + +

THERE WAS an indignity to his visits to King Saul Boulevard that Shamron found deeply depressing. He had to sign the logbook at the security station in the lobby and attach a laminated tag to his shirt pocket. No longer could he use his old private elevator—that was reserved for Lev now. Instead, he crowded into an ordinary lift filled with desk officers and boys and girls from the file rooms.

He rode up to the fourth floor. His ritual humiliation did not end there, for Lev still had a few more ounces of flesh to extract. There was no one to bring him coffee, so he was forced to fend for himself in the canteen, coaxing a cup of weak brew from an automated machine. Then he walked down the hall to his "office"—a bare room, not much larger than a storage closet, with a pine table, a folding steel chair, and a chipped telephone that smelled of disinfectant.

Shamron sat down, opened his briefcase, and removed the surveillance photograph from London—the one snapped by Mordecai outside Peter Malone's home. Shamron sat over it for several minutes, elbows on the table, knuckles pressed to his temples. Every few seconds, a head would poke around the edge of the door and a pair of eyes would stare at him as if he were some exotic beast. *Yes, it's true. The old man is roaming the halls of Headquarters once more.* Shamron saw none of it. He had eyes only for the man in the photograph.

Finally, he picked up the telephone and dialed the extension for Research. It was answered by a girl who sounded as though she was barely out of high school.

"This is Shamron."

"Who?"

"Sham-*RON*," he said irritably. "I need the file on the Cyprus kidnapping case. It was 1986, if I remember correctly. That's probably before you were born, but do your best."

He slammed down the phone and waited. Five minutes later, a bleary-eyed boy called Yossi appeared in Shamron's ignoble door. "Sorry, boss. The girl is new." He held up a bound file. "You wanted to see this?"

Shamron held out his hand, like a beggar.

IT HAD not been one of Shamron's prouder moments. In the summer of 1986, Israeli Justice Minister Meir Ben-David set sail from Tel Aviv for a three-week Mediterranean cruise aboard a private yacht along with twelve other guests and a crew of five. On day nine of their holiday, in the harbor at Larnaca, the yacht was seized by a team of terrorists claiming to represent a group called the Fighting Palestinian Cells. A rescue attempt was ruled out, and the Cypriots wanted the messiness resolved as quickly and as quietly as possible. That left the Israeli government with no choice but to negotiate, and Shamron opened a channel of communication with the German-speaking team leader. Three days later, the siege ended. The hostages were released, the terrorists were granted safe passage, and a month later a dozen hardcore PLO killers were released from Israeli jails.

Publicly, Israel denied there had been a quid pro quo, though no one believed it. For Shamron, it had been a bitter herb indeed, and now, flipping through the pages of the file, he relived it all again. He came to a photograph, the one image they had managed to capture of the team leader. It was useless, really: a long-distance shot, grainy and muddled, a face concealed behind sunglasses and a hat.

He placed the picture beside the surveillance photograph from London and spent several minutes comparing them. *Same man?* Impossible to tell. He picked up the phone and rang Research again. This time Yossi answered.

"Yes, boss?"

"Bring me the file on the Leopard."

HE WAS AN ENIGMA, an educated guess, a theory. Some said he was German. Some said Austrian. Some Swiss. One linguist who listened to the tapes of his conversations with Shamron, which were conducted in English, theorized that he was from the Alsace-Lorraine. It was the West Germans who had hung the codename Leopard on him; he had done a good deal of killing there and they wanted him the most. A terrorist for hire. A man who would work for any group, any cause, as long as it conformed to his core beliefs: Communist, anti-Western, anti-Zionist. It was the Leopard who was believed to have been behind the hijacking in Cyprus and the Leopard who had murdered three other Israelis in Europe on behalf of PLO commando Abu Jihad. Shamron had wanted him dead. His wish had gone unfulfilled.

He leafed through the file, which was hopelessly thin. Here a report from the French service, here an Interpol dispatch, here a rumor of an alleged sighting in Istanbul. There were three photographs as well, though it was not clear whether any were really him. The shot from the yacht in Cyprus, a surveillance photo taken in Bucharest, another at Charles de Gaulle airport. Shamron laid the photo from London next to them and looked up at Yossi, who was watching over his shoulder.

"That one and that one, boss."

Shamron pulled the Bucharest shot out of the lineup and laid it next to London. Same angle, head-on, chin slightly to the left, obscuring half the face.

"I could be wrong, Yossi, but I think it's possible that these are the same man."

"Hard to say, boss, but the computer may be able to tell us for sure."

"Run them," Shamron said, then he picked up the files. "I want to keep these."

"You have to sign a chit."

Shamron looked at Yossi over spectacles.

Yossi said, "I'll sign the chit for you."

"Good boy."

Shamron reached for the telephone one last time and dialed Travel. When he finished with his arrangements, he placed the files in his briefcase and headed downstairs. *I'm coming, Gabriel,* he thought. *But where in God's name are you?*

·22·

THE
MEDITERRANEAN SEA

THE ROCKS OF CAP CORSE appeared at dawn.
Chiara guided the yacht around the tip of the island and set
it on a northwesterly heading. A line of gunpowder cloud stood before them, swollen with rain. The winds had increased by several
knots, and it was suddenly much colder. "The *mistral*," Chiara said.
"It's blowing hard today. I'm afraid the rest of the trip isn't going to
be so pleasant."

A ferry appeared off the port side, steaming out of L'Ile Rousse
toward the French coast. "That one's going to Nice," she said. "We
can follow his heading, then steer toward Cannes as we get closer
to the coastline."

"How long?"

"Five to six hours, maybe longer because of the *mistral*. Take the
wheel for a while. I'll go down to the galley and see if there's anything for breakfast."

"Make sure Sleeping Beauty is still with us."

"I will."

Breakfast consisted of coffee, toasted bread, and a lump of hard cheese. They barely had time to eat, because thirty minutes after rounding Cap Corse, the storm closed in. For the next four hours, the boat was battered by a steady onslaught of wind-driven swells rolling out of the north, and sheets of rain that reduced visibility to less than a hundred meters. At some point they lost track of the ferry. It was no matter; Chiara simply navigated by compass and GPS.

The rain quit at noon, but the wind blew ceaselessly. It seemed to grow stronger as they drew closer to the coast. Behind the storm was a mass of bitterly cold air, and for the last hour of the journey, the sun was in and out of the clouds, shining one minute, hidden the next. The color of the water changed with the sun, now gray-green, now deep blue.

Finally, directly off the prow, Cannes: the distinctive line of gleaming white hotels and apartment houses along *La Croisette*. Chiara guided them away from the *Croisette,* toward the Old Port at the other end of town. In the summer season, the promenades around the *Vieux Port* would be teeming with tourists and the harbor jammed with luxury yachts. Now, most of the restaurants were tightly shuttered and there were plenty of berths available in the harbor.

Chiara left Gabriel on the boat and walked a few blocks to the rue d'Antibes to rent a car. While she was away, Gabriel untied the hands and feet of the unconscious boat captain. Chiara had given him an injection four hours earlier, which meant he would remain unconscious for several more hours.

Gabriel went back up to the deck and waited for Chiara. A few minutes later, a Peugeot hatchback pulled into a parking space on the Quai St-Pierre. Chiara stepped out of the car long enough to wave in Gabriel's direction and slide over into the passenger seat. Gabriel climbed down off the boat and got behind the wheel.

"Any problems?" he asked.

She shook her head.

"We need clothes."

"Ah, shopping on the *Croisette*. Just what I need after spending all night and half the day on the damned boat. I can't decide between Gucci and Versace."

"I was thinking of something a little more ordinary. Maybe one of those nice places along the boulevard Carnot where the real people go to buy their clothes."

"Oh, how pedestrian."

"Exactly."

Gabriel wound his way across the old town, and a few minutes later they were heading north up the boulevard Carnot, the main thoroughfare linking the waterfront of Cannes to the inland towns. The *mistral* was howling; a few brave souls were out, backs bent, hands on their hats. The air was filled with dust and paper. After a few blocks, Gabriel spotted a small department store next to a bus stop. Chiara frowned. He pulled into an empty parking space, gave her a wad of cash, and recited his sizes. Chiara climbed out and walked the rest of the way.

Gabriel left the engine running and listened to the news. Still no sign of the suspected papal assassin. Italian police had stepped up security at the nation's airports and border crossings. He switched off the radio.

Chiara emerged from the store twenty minutes later, a bulging plastic sack swinging from each hand. The wind was at her back, blowing her hair over her face. Because of the bags of clothing, she was defenseless to do anything about it.

She tossed the bags into the backseat and got in. Gabriel headed up the boulevard Carnot. Ten minutes later, he came to a large traffic circle and followed the signs for Grasse. A four-lane highway stretched before them, rising up the slope of the hills toward the base of the Maritime Alps. Chiara reclined the seat, pulled off her fleece shirt, and shimmied out of the heavy waterproof pants. Gabriel kept his eyes fastened on the road. She dug through the bags of clothing until she found the clean underwear and bra she had bought for herself.

"Don't look."

"I wouldn't dream of it."

"Really? Why not?"

"Just hurry up and get some clothing on, please."

"That's the first time a man has ever said that to me."

"I can see why."

She swatted his arm and quickly changed into jeans, a sweater with a thick turtleneck, and fashionable black leather boots with square toes and thick heels. She looked very much like the attractive young woman he had seen for the first time in the ghetto in Venice. When she was finished, she sat up. "Your turn. Pull over and I'll drive while you change."

Gabriel did as she asked. From a purely fashion perspective, he did not fare as well: a pair of loose fitting blue cotton trousers with an elastic waist, a thick wool fisherman's sweater, a pair of tan espadrilles that scratched his feet. He looked like a man who spent his days idling in the town square playing *boule*.

"I look ridiculous."

"I think you look very handsome. More importantly, you can

walk through any town in Provence and no one will think you're anything but a local."

For ten minutes, Chiara navigated the winding road through olive trees and eucalyptus. They came to the medieval town of Valbonne. Gabriel directed her northward, to a town called Opio, and from Opio to Le Rouret. She parked outside a *tabac* and waited in the car while Gabriel went inside. Behind the counter was a dark-complected man with tightly curled hair and Algerian features. When Gabriel asked whether he knew an Italian woman called Carcassi, the clerk shrugged his shoulders and suggested that Gabriel speak to Marc, the bartender next-door at the *brasserie.*

Gabriel found Marc polishing glasses with a dirty towel. When he put the same question to him, the bartender shook his head. He knew of no one named Carcassi in the village, but there was an Italian woman who lived on the road that led to the entrance of the nature park. He tossed his towel over his shoulder and stepped outside to point Gabriel in the right direction. Gabriel thanked him and rejoined Chiara.

"That way," he said. "Across the main road, past the *gendarmerie,* then up the hill."

The road was narrow, little more than a one-lane paved track, and the grade of the hill was steep. There were villas among the olive and pepper trees. Some were modest homes owned by locals; others were opulent, well-tended, and shielded by hedges and high stone walls.

The villa where the Italian woman purportedly lived fell into the second category. It was a stately old estate house with a turret rising above the main entrance. The garden was a terraced affair, surrounded by a stone wall. There was no name on the daunting, iron gate.

When Gabriel pressed the button on the intercom, dogs began to bark. A few seconds later, a pair of Belgian shepherds came galloping from the back of the villa, teeth bared, barking fanatically. They charged the gate and snapped at Gabriel through the bars. He took a quick step back and put a hand on the door latch of the car. He did not like dogs to begin with, and not long ago he'd had a run-in with an Alsatian that had left him with a broken arm and several dozen stitches. He inched forward cautiously so as not to further incite the dogs and pressed the intercom button once again. This time he received a response: a woman's voice, barely audible above the wild barking.

"*Oui?*"

"Madame Carcassi?"

"My name is Huber now. Carcassi was my maiden name."

"Was your mother Regina Carcassi from Tolmezzo in the north of Italy?"

A moment's hesitation, then: "Who is this, please?"

The dogs, hearing the note of anxiety in their master's voice, began to bark even more ferociously. During the night, Gabriel had been unable to decide how to make his approach to the daughter of Regina Carcassi. Now, with the shepherds trying to tear his legs off and a gale-force wind beating down on him from the Alps, he had little patience for subterfuge and cover stories. He reached out and pressed the button once more.

"My name is Gabriel," he said, shouting over the commotion of the dogs. "I work for the government of Israel. I believe I know who killed your mother, and I believe I know why."

There was no response from the intercom, only the rapid snarling of the dogs. Gabriel feared he had taken it too far too quickly. He reached for the intercom button again but stopped himself when he saw the front door swing open and a woman step into the courtyard. She stood there a moment, black hair flying in the wind, arms folded beneath her breasts, then walked slowly across the courtyard and examined Gabriel through the bars of the gate. Satisfied, she looked down at the dogs and scolded them in rapid French. They stopped barking and trotted off, disappearing behind the villa. Then she reached into her coat pocket, produced the remote for the gate, and pressed it with her thumb. The gate slowly opened, and she gestured them to come inside.

SHE SERVED coffee and steamed milk in a rectangular sitting room with a terracotta floor and damask-covered furniture. The French doors rattled in the *mistral*. Several times Gabriel found himself looking at the doors to see if someone was trying to get in, but he saw only the elaborate garden writhing in the wind.

Her name was Antonella Huber, an Italian woman, married to a German businessman, living in the south of France—a member of that itinerant class of European wealthy who are comfortable in many countries and many cultures. She was an attractive woman, mid-forties, with dark shoulder-length hair and deeply tanned skin. Her eyes were nearly black and radiated intelligence. Her gaze was direct and without apprehension. Gabriel noticed the edges of her nails were soiled with clay. He glanced around the room and saw that it was decorated with ceramics. Antonella Huber was a skilled potter.

"I'm sorry about the dogs," she said. "My husband travels for his work, so I spend a great deal of time here alone. Crime is a major problem all along the Cote d'Azur. We were robbed a half-dozen times before we bought the guard dogs. Lately, we haven't had any problems."

"I can see why."

She managed a brief smile. Gabriel used the lull in the small talk to come to the point. He leaned forward in his chair, elbows on his knees, and gave Antonella Huber a selective account of the events that had brought him here. He told her that his friend, the historian Benjamin Stern, had discovered that something unusual had taken place at the Convent of the Sacred Heart in Brenzone during the war—the same convent where her mother had lived before renouncing her vows. He told her that his friend had been killed by someone who wanted that unusual event to remain a secret. He told her that her mother was not the only person to vanish without a trace in Italy. Two priests, Felici and Manzini, had disappeared around the same time. An Italian detective named Alessio Rossi believed the disappearances were linked, but he was ordered to close his investigation after Italian police came under pressure from a man named Carlo Casagrande, who worked for the Vatican Security Office. Antonella Huber remained motionless throughout Gabriel's presentation, her eyes locked on him, her hands folded across her knee. He had the distinct impression he was telling her nothing she did not already know or suspect.

"Your mother didn't renounce her vows simply in order to marry, did she?"

A long silence, then: "No, she didn't."

"Something happened at that convent, something that made her lose her faith and renounce her vows?"

"Yes, that's right."

"Did she discuss it with Benjamin Stern?"

"I begged her not to, but she ignored my warning and spoke to him anyway."

"What were you afraid of?"

"That she would be harmed, of course. And I was right, wasn't I?"

"Have you spoken to the Italian police?"

"If you know anything about Italian politics, you'd realize that the Italian police are not to be trusted in a matter like this. Wasn't Alessio Rossi one of the men who was killed in Rome the night before last? A papal assassin?" She shook her head slowly. "My God, they'll do anything to protect their dirty little secrets."

"Do you know why they killed your mother?"

She nodded and said, "Yes, I do. I know what happened in that convent. I know why my mother renounced her vows, and her faith, and why she was killed for it."

"Will you tell me?"

"It's probably better if I show you." She stood up. "Please wait here. I won't be a moment."

She left the room and walked upstairs. Gabriel sat back and closed his eyes. Chiara, seated next to him on the couch, reached out and laid her hand on his forearm.

When Antonella Huber returned, she was holding a stack of yellowed writing paper. "My mother wrote this the night before she married my father," she said, holding up the papers for Gabriel and Chiara to see. "She gave a copy of this to Benjamin Stern. This is the reason your friend was killed."

She sat down, placed the papers in her lap, and began to read aloud.

My name is Regina Carcassi, and I was born in Brunico, a mountain village near the Austrian border. I am the youngest of seven children and the only girl. Therefore, it was almost preordained that I become a nun. In 1937, I took my vows and became a member of the Order of Saint Ursula. I was sent to the Convent of the Sacred Heart, an Ursuline convent in the town of Brenzone on Lake Garda, and I took a position teaching in a local Catholic school for girls. I was eighteen years old.

I was very pleased with my assignment. The convent was a lovely place, an old castle located on the shores of the lake. When the war came, little about our life changed. Despite the shortages of food, we received shipments of supplies each month and always had enough to eat. Usually, we had some left over to disperse among the needy in Brenzone. I continued my teaching duties and administered to the needs of those unfortunate souls affected by the fighting.

One evening in March 1942, Mother Superior addressed us after our evening meal. She informed us that in three days' time, our convent was to be the site of an important meeting between Vatican authorities and a high-level delegation from Germany. The Convent of the Sacred Heart had been chosen because of its isolation and the beauty of its facilities. She told us that we should all be very proud that such an important gathering should be held in our home, and we all were indeed pleased. Mother Superior told us that the topic of the meeting was an initiative by the Holy Father to bring about a speedy end to the war. We were instructed, however, not to speak a word about the meeting to anyone outside the convent. Even discussion amongst ourselves was forbidden. Needless to say, none of us slept much that night.

We were all very excited about what the coming days would bring.

Because I grew up so near the Austrian border, I spoke fluent German and knew about German food and customs. Mother Superior asked me to oversee the preparations for the conference, and I eagerly agreed. I was informed that the men would share a meal, then would adjourn to discuss the business at hand. In my opinion, our dining room was far too plain for such an occasion, so I decided that the meal and the conference should take place in our common room. It was a lovely room, with a large stone fireplace and beautiful views of the lake and the Dolomites—a truly inspirational setting. Mother Superior agreed, and she permitted me to rearrange the furniture in the room as I saw fit. Dinner would be served at a large circular table next to one of the windows. For the meeting, a long rectangular table with a dark finish was set in front of the fireplace. I wanted everything to be perfect, and when I was finished, the room looked quite beautiful indeed. I was thrilled by the prospect that my work might have some role in bringing about an end to all the death and destruction the war had wrought.

The day before the meeting, a large shipment of food arrived: hams and sausages, breads and pastas, tins of caviar, bottles of fine wine and champagne—things most of us had rarely seen in our lifetimes, and certainly not since the war had begun. The next day, with the help of two other sisters, I prepared a meal that I believed would suit the palates of the men from Rome and the visitors from Berlin.

The delegates were scheduled to arrive at six in the evening, but it snowed heavily that day, and everyone was delayed. The men from the Vatican arrived first, at eight-thirty. There were three in all: Bishop Sebastiano Lorenzi of the Vatican Secretariat of State, and his two young assistants, Father Felici and Father Manzini. Bishop Lorenzi inspected the room where the meeting was to take place, then he led us to the chapel to celebrate Mass. Before leaving the chapel, he repeated Mother Superior's instruction that we never speak of the evening's events at the convent. He went on to say that anyone who violated his order would do so under the pain of excommunication. It seemed a rather needless warning to me, for none of us would ever disobey a direct request from a senior Vatican official, but I knew that the men of the Roman Curia took their obedience to the rules of secrecy very seriously.

The delegation from Germany did not arrive until nearly ten o'clock. They too were three: a driver who did not take part in the conference, an aide called Herr Beckmann, and the leader of the delegation, a man from the German Foreign Office named State Secretary Martin Luther. I would never forget that name. Imagine, a man called Martin Luther, visiting the Roman Catholic Convent of the Sacred Heart in Brenzone! At the time, it was quite a shock. So was the state secretary's appearance. He was a small, sickly looking man with thick spectacles that distorted the shape of his eyes. He seemed to be suffering from a terrible cold, because he kept rubbing his nose with a white handkerchief.

They immediately sat down to dinner. Herr Luther and Herr Beckmann commented on the beauty of the room, and I felt very proud of my accomplishment. I served the food and opened the first bottles of wine. It was a pleasant meal, and there was a good deal of laughter and camaraderie among the five men seated at the table. I had the impression that Herr Luther and Bishop

Lorenzi were well acquainted. Apparently, Mother Superior had neglected to tell them that I was from Brunico in the far north, because they spoke freely in German whenever I was in the room, surely out of the mistaken impression that I did not understand the language. I heard much interesting gossip about the affairs in Berlin.

The conference began at midnight. In Italian, Bishop Lorenzi said to me, "We have much work to do, Sister. Please keep the coffee coming. If you see an empty cup, fill it." By now, all the other sisters had gone to bed. I sat outside the common room, in the antechamber. After a few moments, our young kitchen boy appeared, dressed in pajamas. He was an orphan who lived in the convent. The sisters nicknamed him Ciciotto, little chubby one. The child had been awakened by nightmares. I invited him to sit with me. To help calm him, we recited the rosary.

The first time I entered the room, it became clear to me that the men were not discussing a negotiated settlement to the war. State Secretary Luther was in the process of handing round a memorandum to the other four men. As I poured coffee, I was able to see it quite well. It had two columns, and the columns were divided by a vertical line. On the left were the names of countries and territories, on the right were figures. At the bottom of the page was a tally.

Herr Luther was saying, "The program to bring about the final solution to the Jewish question in Europe is well under way. The document you have before you was presented to me at a conference in Berlin in January. As you can see, by our careful estimate, there are eleven million Jews in Europe at the moment. That estimate includes territory controlled by the Reich and its allies and in countries that remain neutral or allied with the enemy."

Herr Luther paused and looked at Bishop Lorenzi. "Does the girl speak German?"

"No, no, Herr Luther. She is a poor girl from the Garda region. Her only language is Italian, and even that she speaks like a peasant. You may speak freely in front of her."

I turned and left the room, pretending not to have heard the terribly insulting things the prelate had just said about me to the German. My face must have shown my embarrassment, because when I entered the antechamber, Ciciotto said, "Is something wrong, Sister Regina?"

"No, no, I'm fine. Just a little tired."

"Shall we continue to say the rosary, Sister?"

"You say it, my child. But softly, please."

The boy resumed the rosary, but after a few moments he fell asleep with his head resting on my lap. I cracked the door a few inches so I could hear what was being said inside the common room. Herr Luther was still speaking. This is what I heard that night, recorded to the best of my recollection and ability.

"Despite our best efforts to keep the evacuations secret, word unfortunately is beginning to trickle out. It is my understanding from our own ambassador to the Vatican that some of these reports are beginning to reach the ears of the Holy Father."

Bishop Lorenzi replied, "That is indeed the case, State Secretary Luther. I'm afraid news of the evacuations has indeed reached the Vatican. The British and Americans are putting enormous pressure on the Holy Father to speak out."

"May I speak bluntly, Bishop Lorenzi?

"That was the point of this gathering, was it not?"

"This program to settle the Jewish question once and for all is under way. The machinery is in place, and there is nothing His

Holiness can do to stop it. The only thing he can do is make matters worse for the Jews, and I know that is the last thing the Holy Father wishes to do."

"That is correct, Herr Luther. But how would a protest make matters worse for the Jews?"

"It is imperative that the roundups and deportations go smoothly and with a minimum of struggle and histrionics. The element of surprise is a critical factor. If the Holy Father issues a protest, accompanied by an explicit warning about what deportation to the east truly means for the Jews, then it will make the roundups messy and difficult affairs. It will also mean that many Jews will go into hiding and escape our forces."

"One cannot argue with the logic of that statement, Herr Luther."

At this point, I felt it was time for me to offer the delegates more coffee. I eased the boy's head off my lap, then knocked on the door and waited for Bishop Lorenzi to invite me to enter the room.

"More coffee, Your Grace?"

"Please, Sister Regina."

There was a pause in the conversation while I refilled their cups and exited the room. Then Herr Luther resumed. Once again I left the door ajar so that I could hear what was being said.

"There is another reason why it is critical that the Holy Father not raise his voice in protest. Many of those who assist us in this necessary endeavor happen to be good Roman Catholics. If the Pope condemns their behavior, or threatens them with excommunication, it might make them think twice about the work that they are doing."

"You may rest assured, Herr Luther, that the last thing the

Holy Father would do is excommunicate Roman Catholics at a time like this."

"I wouldn't presume to give the Church advice on how to run its affairs, but there are reasons why papal silence on this matter would be best for all involved, including the Holy See."

"I'd be interested to hear your learned opinion, Herr Luther."

"Look at that figure I have laid before you. Imagine, eleven million Jews! A figure almost beyond comprehension! We are dealing with them as quickly and efficiently as possible, but it is a difficult task we have set for the Reich. What would happen if, God forbid, Germany should lose this war to Stalin and his gang of Jewish Bolsheviks? Try to imagine what would happen if there were millions of displaced Jews in Europe at the end of the war, alive and dispossessed, clamoring for the right to emigrate to Palestine. The Zionists and their friends in Washington and London would have their day. It would be impossible to prevent the creation of a Jewish national home in Palestine. Jewish control of Nazareth. Jewish control of Bethlehem. Jewish control of Jerusalem. Jewish control of all the holy sites! If they have their own state, they would have the right, as the Vatican does, to send their diplomats around the world. Judaism, the ancient enemy of the Church, would be placed on a footing equal to that of the Holy See. The Jewish state would become a platform for global Jewish domination. That would be a true disaster for the Roman Catholic Church, a setback of unimaginable proportions, and it looms just over the horizon, unless we complete the annihilation of the Jewish race in Europe."

There was a long silence. I could not see inside, but in my mind, I tried to picture the scene. Bishop Lorenzi, I imagined, was fuming at so grotesque and monstrous a speech. He was preparing, in my imagination, to shatter the man from Berlin with a ringing condemnation of the Nazis and their war against the Jews. Instead, this is what I heard though the half-open door that night.

"As you know, Herr Luther, we members of Crux Vera have been very supportive of National Socialism and its crusade against the Bolsheviks. We have worked very quietly, yet diligently, to align the policies of the Vatican to meet our common goal: a world free of the Bolshevik menace. I cannot instruct the Pope what to say about this situation. I can only offer him my heartfelt advice, in the strongest possible terms, and hope that he accepts it. I can tell you this: At the moment, he is predisposed to say nothing about this matter. He believes a protest will only make the situation of German Catholics more tenuous. Furthermore, he has no love for the Jews, and he believes that in many respects they have brought this calamity upon themselves. Your thoughts on the future situation in Palestine give me a potent new weapon in my arsenal. I'm sure His Holiness will be very interested to hear about this. But at the same time, I beg of you to proceed in such a manner that you will not unintentionally force his hand. The Holy See would not want to be obliged to utter a word of disapproval."

"Obviously, I am very pleased to hear your remarks, Bishop Lorenzi. You have proven, once again, that you are a true friend of the German people and a trusted ally in our fight against Bolshevism and the Jews."

"And fortunately for you, Herr Luther, there is another true friend of the German people inside the Vatican—a man who outranks me significantly. He will listen to what I have to say. As for myself, I will be glad to be rid of them."

"I believe a toast is in order."

"As do I. Sister Regina?"

I entered the room. My legs were trembling.

"Bring us a bottle of champagne," the bishop said to me in Italian, then added: "No, Sister, make that two bottles. Tonight is a night for celebration."

A moment later, I returned with the two bottles. One of them exploded when I opened it, and champagne spilled onto the floor and my habit. "I told you she was a peasant girl," the bishop said. "She must have shaken it on the way."

The others had a good laugh at my expense, and once again, I had to smile and pretend as though I had not understood. I poured out the champagne and turned to leave, but Bishop Lorenzi took my arm. "Why don't you join us in a glass, Sister Regina?"

"No, I couldn't, Your Grace. It wouldn't be proper."

"Nonsense!" Then he turned to Herr Luther and, in German, asked whether it would be all right if I had a glass of champagne after all my hard work preparing the meal.

"Ja, Ja," shouted Herr Luther. "Indeed, I insist."

And so I stood there, in my stained habit, and I drank their champagne. And I pretended not to understand when they congratulated themselves on a very successful evening of work. And as they were leaving, I shook hands with the murderer named Luther and kissed the proffered ring of his accomplice, Bishop Lorenzi. I can still taste the bitterness on my lips.

In my own room, I painstakingly transcribed the conversation I had just overheard. Then I lay awake in my bed until dawn. It was a night of perfect agony.

I am writing this now on an evening in September in the year 1947. It is the eve of my wedding day, a day I never wanted. I

*am about to marry a man who I am fond of but whom I do not
truly love. I am doing it because it is easier this way. How can I
tell them the real reason I am leaving? Who would believe such
a story?*

*I have no plans to tell anyone about that night, no plans to
show anyone this document. It is a document of shame. The
deaths of six million weigh heavily upon my conscience. I had
knowledge, and I kept silent. Some nights they come to me, with
their emaciated bodies and ragged prison clothing, and they ask
me why I did not speak up in their defense. I do not have an ac-
ceptable answer. I was just a simple nun from the north of Italy.
They were the most powerful people in the world. What could I
have done? What could any of us have done?*

Chiara stumbled into the powder room. A moment later, Gabriel
could hear her being violently sick into the toilet. Antonella Huber
sat silently, her eyes blank and damp, staring out the French doors at
the garden, which was twisting in the wind. Gabriel stared at the
pages in her lap; at the careful, precise script of Sister Regina Carcassi. It had been a torturous thing to hear, but at the same time he
was overwhelmed by a swell of pride. An amazing document, those
few yellowed pages. It dovetailed perfectly with things he had learned
independently already. Had not Licio, the old man from the convent, told him about Sister Regina and Luther? Had not Alessio
Rossi told him about the mysterious disappearances of two priests
from the Germany desk of the Secretariat of State, Monsignors Felici and Manzini? Did not Sister Regina Carcassi place those same
two priests at the side of Bishop Sebastiano Lorenzi, official of the
Secretariat of State, member of Crux Vera, friend of Germany?

"And fortunately for you, Herr Luther, there is another true friend

of the German people inside the Vatican—a man who outranks me significantly."

Here was an explanation of the inexplicable. Why had Pius XII remained silent in the face of the greatest case of mass murder in history? Was it because Martin Luther convinced an influential member of the Secretariat of State, a member of the secret order known as Crux Vera, that a papal condemnation of the Holocaust would ultimately lead to the creation of a Jewish state in Palestine and Jewish control of Christian holy sites? If so, it explained why Crux Vera was so desperate to keep the meeting at Brenzone a secret, for it linked the order, and by extension the Church itself, to the murders of six million Jews in Europe.

Chiara came out of the bathroom, her eyes damp and raw, and sat down next to Gabriel. Antonella Huber turned her gaze from the garden, and her dark eyes settled on Chiara's face.

"You are Jewish, yes?"

Chiara nodded and lifted her chin. "I am from Venice."

"There was a terrible roundup in Venice, wasn't there? While my mother was safe behind the walls of the Convent of the Sacred Heart, the Nazis and their friends were hunting down the Jews of Venice." She turned from Chiara and looked at Gabriel. "And what about you?"

"My family came from Germany." He said nothing more. There was nothing else to be said.

"Could my mother have done something to help them?" She looked out the French doors once more. "Am I guilty too? Do I bear my mother's original sin?"

"I don't believe in collective guilt," Gabriel said. "As for your mother, there was nothing she could have done. Even if she had defied the orders of the bishop and leaked word of the meeting at

Brenzone, nothing would have changed. Herr Luther was right. The machinery was in place, the killing had begun, and nothing but the defeat of Nazi Germany was going to stop it. Besides, no one would have believed her."

"Maybe no one will believe her now."

"It's a devastating document."

"It's a death sentence," she said. "They'll just dismiss it as a forgery. They'll say you're out to destroy the Church. That's what they do. That's what they *always* do."

"I have enough corroborating evidence to make it impossible for them to dismiss it as a hoax. Your mother may have been powerless to do anything in 1942, but she's not powerless any longer. Let me have this—the one she wrote with her own hand. It's important that I have the original."

"You may have it on one condition."

"And that is?"

"That you destroy the people who murdered my mother."

Gabriel held out his hand.

·23·

LE ROURET,
PROVENCE

GABRIEL EASED AWAY from Antonella Huber's villa through the gathering darkness, accompanied by the savage barking of the Belgian shepherds. Chiara sat next to him, clutching the letter. At the bottom of the hill, he turned onto a two-lane highway and headed west toward Grasse. The day's last light lay on the ridgeline of the distant hills like a scarlet wound.

Five minutes later, he noticed the dark-gray Fiat sedan. The man behind the wheel was too careful. He stayed in his own lane at all times, and even when Gabriel allowed his speed to dip well below the limit, the Fiat remained several car-lengths off his rear bumper. No, thought Gabriel, this is not your average suicidal Frenchman behind the wheel.

He followed the highway into Grasse, then turned down the hill, into the old town center. It had been taken over long ago by Middle

Eastern immigrants, and for a moment Gabriel might have imagined he was in Algiers or Marrakech.

"Put away the letter."

"What's wrong?"

"We're being followed."

Gabriel made a series of quick turns and accelerations.

"Is he still there?"

"Still there."

"What do we do?"

"Take him for a ride."

Gabriel left the old town and made his way back up the hill to the main highway, the Fiat following closely behind. He sped through the center of town, then turned onto the N85, a highway that runs from Grasse high into the Maritime Alps. Ten seconds later the Fiat swerved into his rearview mirror. Gabriel pressed the accelerator to the floor and pushed the Peugeot hard up the steep grade.

Grasse gradually fell away. The road was winding, full of switchbacks and hairpin turns. To their right rose the scrub-covered slope of the mountain; to their left, a deep gorge, falling away toward the sea. The Peugeot had less power than Gabriel would have liked, and no matter how hard he pushed it, the Fiat sedan easily kept pace. Whenever a straight section of road stretched before him, he would lift his eyes into the rearview mirror and check on the Fiat: always there, a few car-lengths back. Once, he thought he could see the driver talking on a mobile phone. *Who do you work for? Who are you calling? And how in the hell did you find us?* Antonella Huber . . . They'd killed her mother. They probably had a man watching the villa.

Ten minutes later, the village of St-Vallier appeared before

them, quiet and tightly shuttered. Gabriel pulled over in the center
of town, next to a small square, and traded places with Chiara. The
Fiat parked on the opposite side of the square and waited. Gabriel
told Chiara to take the D5 toward St-Cézaire, then he took out the
Beretta nine millimeter he'd been given by Shimon Pazner in Rome.
The Fiat followed after them.

It was a long descent, winding and difficult in some sections,
straight and fast in others. Chiara drove the same way she'd handled the motor yacht, with skill and a certain easy confidence that
Gabriel couldn't help but find attractive.

"Did you take the defensive driving classes at the Academy?"

"Of course."

"Did you learn anything?"

"Number one in my group."

"Show me."

She downshifted and slammed the accelerator to the floor. The
Peugeot shot forward, engine screaming. She stayed in that gear,
foot to the floor, until the needle topped the red zone, then power-
shifted. Gabriel looked over at the speedometer and saw it inching
toward 180 kilometers per hour. Her rapid acceleration seemed to
catch the driver of the Fiat by surprise, but he recovered quickly
and soon was sitting in his usual place, twenty meters off their rear
bumper.

"Our friend is back."

"What do you want me to do?"

"Make him work. I want his nerves on edge."

During a long downhill straightaway, Chiara pushed the Peugeot above two hundred. Then she entered a winding section, expertly downshifting and breaking in and out of the turns. Obviously,

she had learned her lessons well at the Academy. The man in the Fiat was having trouble keeping pace. Twice, he nearly lost control in the turns.

At the rate of speed they were traveling, it did not take long to reach St-Cézaire. It was a medieval town, walled in places and split in half by the D5. Chiara slowed. Gabriel shouted at her to go faster.

"What if someone crosses the fucking road?"

"I don't care! Go faster, damn it!"

"Gabriel!"

They flashed through the darkened town in a blur. The driver of the Fiat did not have the courage to follow their lead, and slowed as he passed through the town. As a result, he emerged trailing them by some three hundred meters.

"That was fucking insane. We could have killed someone."

"Don't let him get any closer."

The road became a four-lane highway. On their left was a large nature area, famous for its caves and grottoes, and in the distance was a ridge of stark mountains, visible in the bright moonlight.

"Turn there!"

Chiara slammed on the brakes, throwing the Peugeot into a power slide. Then she simultaneously downshifted and hit the accelerator, sending them careening along a dirt track. Gabriel turned around and took another long look over his shoulder. The Fiat had made the turn and was racing after them.

"Kill the lights."

"I won't be able to see."

"Kill them now!"

She switched off the lights and instinctively eased off the gas, but Gabriel shouted at her to go faster, and soon they were plunging through the luminous glow of the moonlight. They entered a grove of scrub oak and umbrella pine. The track hooked sharply to the right. The headlights of the Fiat were nowhere to be seen.

"Stop!"

"Here?

"*Stop!*"

She slammed on the brakes. Gabriel threw open the door. The air was filled with a choking dust. "Keep going," he said, then leapt out and slammed the door shut.

Chiara did as she was told, continuing in the direction of the mountain ridge. A few seconds later, Gabriel could hear the Fiat speeding toward his position. He stepped off the track and knelt behind an oak, the Beretta in his outstretched hands. As the Fiat came hurtling around the corner, Gabriel fired several shots into the tires.

At least two exploded. The Fiat instantly lost control, bucking and fishtailing, before the centrifugal force of the turn threw it into a violent leftward roll. Gabriel lost count of how many times the car flipped over; a half-dozen at least, perhaps more. He rose to his feet and slowly walked toward the crumpled mass of steel, the Beretta at his side. Somewhere, a mobile phone was ringing.

He found the Fiat wheels-up, resting on its smashed roof. Bending down, he peered through a shattered window and saw the driver, lying on what was once the ceiling. His legs were twisted grotesquely, his chest crushed and bleeding severely. Still, he was conscious, and his hand seemed to be reaching for a gun lying a few inches beyond his fingertips. The eyes were focused, but the hand would not obey the commands of his brain. His neck was snapped, and he didn't realize it.

Finally, his eyes left the gun and settled on Gabriel.

"You were a fool to chase us like that," Gabriel said softly.

"You're an amateur. Your boss sent you on a suicide mission. Who's your boss? He's the man who did this to you, not me."

The man managed little more than a gurgle. He was looking at Gabriel but his gaze was somewhere else. He did not have long to live.

"You're not hurt too badly," Gabriel said gently. "Some cuts and scrapes. Maybe a broken bone or two. Tell me who you're working for, so I can call an ambulance."

The man's lips parted, and he emitted a sound. Gabriel leaned close so he could hear.

"*Casszzzz . . . Cassszzzzzz . . . . Zzzzzz. . . .*"

"Casagrande? Carlo Casagrande? Is that what you're trying to tell me?"

"*Cassszzzzzz . . . . zzzzzzz. . . .*"

Gabriel reached inside the dying man's jacket and gently patted around until he found a wallet. It was soaked with blood. As he dropped it into his pocket, he could hear the telephone ringing again. It had ended up somewhere in the backseat, by the sound of it. He peered through the opening where the rear window had once been and saw the phone, power light aglow, lying on the ground beneath the trunk. He stretched out his hand and took hold of it. Then he pressed the SEND button and brought it to his ear.

"*Pronto.*"

"What's going on up there? Where is he?"

"He's right here," Gabriel said calmly in Italian. "In fact, he's speaking with you right now."

Silence.

"I know what happened in that convent," Gabriel said. "I know about Crux Vera. I know that you killed my friend. Now, I'm coming for you."

"Where's my man?"

"He's not doing so well at the moment. Would you like a word with him?"

Gabriel placed the telephone on the ground a few inches from the dying man's mouth. As he stood up, he could see the lights of the Peugeot bouncing toward him along the track. Chiara braked to a halt a few yards from where he was standing. Walking back to the car, Gabriel could hear only one sound.

"Casszzzz . . . Cassszzzzz . . . Zzzzzzzz. . . ."

·24·

ST-CÉZAIRE,
PROVENCE

GABRIEL SEARCHED the dead man's wallet by the jade-colored glow of the dashboard lights. He found no driver's license and no formal identification of any kind. Finally, he discovered a business card, folded in half and tucked behind a photograph of a girl in a sleeveless dress. It was so old he had to switch on the overhead light in order to make out the faded name: PAULO OLIVERO, UFFICIO SICUREZZA DI VATICANO. He held it aloft for Chiara to see. She glanced at it, then returned her eyes to the road.

"What does it say?"

"That there's a high probability the man I just killed was a Vatican cop."

"Great."

Gabriel memorized the telephone number on the card, then

tore it to shreds and flicked it out the window. They came to the *autoroute*. When Chiara slowed for guidance, Gabriel directed her west, toward Aix-en-Provence. She lit a cigarette with the dashboard lighter. Her hand was shaking.

"Would you like to tell me where we're going next?"

"Out of Provence as quickly as possible," he said. "After that, I haven't decided."

"Am I allowed to offer an opinion?"

"I don't see why not."

"It's time to go home. You know what happened at the convent, and you know who killed Benjamin. There's nothing else you can do but dig yourself deeper into a hole."

"There's more," Gabriel said. "There has to be more."

"What are you talking about?"

He stared absently out his window. The landscape was stark and windswept, red dust in the air. He saw none of it. Instead, he saw Sister Vincenza, sitting on the very spot where Martin Luther and Bishop Lorenzi had sealed their contract of murder, telling him that Benjamin had come to the Convent of the Sacred Heart to hear about the Jews that had taken refuge there. He saw Alessio Rossi, stinking of fear, fingernails gnawed to the quick, telling him how Carlo Casagrande had forced him to abort his investigation of missing priests. He saw Sister Regina Carcassi, listening to Luther and Lorenzi calmly discuss why Pope Pius XII should remain silent in the face of genocide, while a child slept with his head in her lap, a rosary wrapped around his hand.

And finally he saw Benjamin, a boy of twenty, myopic and round-shouldered, brilliant and destined for academic greatness. He had wanted to be a part of the Wrath of God team as badly as

Gabriel had wanted to be released from it. Indeed, Benjamin had wanted to be an *aleph,* an assassin, but his methodical brain did not leave him with the skills necessary to point a Beretta at a man's face in a darkened alley and pull the trigger. It did give him all the tools necessary to be a brilliant support agent, and never once did he make an error—even at the end, when Black September and the European security services were breathing down their necks. This was the Benjamin Gabriel saw now, the Benjamin who would never stake his reputation on the word of a single source or document, no matter how compelling.

"Benjamin wouldn't have written a book implicating the Catholic Church in the Holocaust based only on Sister Regina's letter. He must have had something else."

Chiara swung to the side of the *autoroute* and applied the brakes. "So?"

"I worked with Benjamin in the field. I know how he thought, how his mind worked. He was careful to a fault. He had backup plans for his backup plans. Benjamin knew the book would be explosive. That's why he kept the contents so secret. He would have hidden copies of his important material in places his enemies wouldn't think to look." Gabriel hesitated, then added: "But places his friends *would* think to look."

Chiara stuffed her cigarette into the ashtray. "When I was at the Academy, we were taught how to walk into a room and find a hundred places to conceal something. Documents, weapons, anything at all."

"Benjamin and I did the course together."

"So where are we going?"

Gabriel lifted his hand and pointed straight ahead.

THEY DROVE in shifts, roughly two hours on, two hours off. Chiara managed to sleep during her rest periods, but Gabriel lay awake, the seat reclined, hands behind his head, staring up through the tinted glass of the moon roof. He passed the hours by mentally searching Benjamin's apartment for a second time. He opened books and desk drawers, closets and file cabinets. He planned expeditions into uncharted regions.

Dawn arrived, gray and forbidding, now a siege of torrential rain, now an avalanche of biting Rhone Valley wind. It never seemed to get properly light, and the headlights of the Peugeot stayed on all morning. At the German border, Gabriel felt a sudden fever when the guard seemed to take an extra moment scrutinizing the false Canadian passport that Pazner had given him in Rome.

They sped across a plain of sodden Swabian farmland, keeping pace with the high-speed traffic on the autobahn. In a town called Memmingen, Gabriel stopped for gas. Not far away was a shopping center with a small department store. He sent Chiara inside with a list. He fared better than he had in Cannes: two pairs of gray trousers, two button-down shirts, a black pullover sweater, a pair of black crepe-soled shoes, a quilted nylon raincoat. A second bag contained two flashlights and a pack of batteries, along with screwdrivers, pliers, and wrenches.

Gabriel changed in the car while Chiara drove the final miles to Munich. It was mid-afternoon by the time they arrived. The sky was low and dark, and it was raining steadily. Operational weather, Shamron would have called it. A gift from the intelligence gods. Gabriel's head was throbbing with exhaustion, and his eyes felt as though there was sand beneath the lids. He tried to remember the last time he'd had a proper night's sleep. He looked at Chiara and saw that she was hanging on to the steering wheel as though it were the only thing keeping her upright. A hotel was out of the question. Chiara had an idea.

JUST BEYOND the old city center, near the Reichenbachplatz, stands a rather drab, flat-fronted stucco building. Above the glass double doors is a sign. JÜDISCHES EINKAUFSZENTRUM VON MÜNCHEN: JEWISH COMMUNITY CENTER OF MUNICH. Chiara parked outside the front entrance and hurried inside. She returned five minutes later, drove around the corner, and parked opposite a side entrance. A girl was holding open the door. She was Chiara's age, heavy-hipped, with hair the color of a raven's wing.

"How did you manage this?" Gabriel asked.

"They called my father in Venice. He vouched for us."

The interior of the center was modern and lit by harsh fluorescent light. They followed the girl up a staircase to the top floor, where they were shown into a small room with a bare linoleum floor and a pair of matching twin beds made up with beige spreads. To Gabriel, it seemed rather like a sick ward.

"We keep it for guests and emergencies," the girl said. "You're welcome to use it for a few hours. Through that door is a bathroom with a shower."

"I need to send a fax," Gabriel said.

"There's one downstairs. I'll take you."

Gabriel followed her to a small office near the main reception area.

"Do you have a copier?"

"Of course. Right over there."

Gabriel removed Sister Regina Carcassi's letter from his jacket pocket and made a photocopy. Then he scribbled a few words on a separate piece of paper and handed them all to the girl. Gabriel recited the number from memory, and she fed the pages into the fax machine.

"Vienna?" she asked.

Gabriel nodded. He heard the squelch as the fax machine made contact with Eli Lavon's office, then watched the pages slip through the feeder tray one by one. Two minutes after the transmission was complete, the fax machine rang and spit out a single page with two hastily scrawled words.

Documents received.

Gabriel recognized the handwriting as Lavon's.

"Do you need anything else?"

"Just a few hours of sleep."

"That I can't help you with." She smiled at him for the first time. "Can you find your way back upstairs?"

"No problem."

When he returned to the guest room, the curtains were tightly drawn. Chiara lay on one of the beds, knees pulled to her chest, already asleep. Gabriel undressed and slid beneath the blanket on the second bed, quietly settling onto the creaking bedsprings so as not to wake her. Then he closed his eyes and tumbled into a dreamless sleep.

IN VIENNA, Eli Lavon stood over his fax machine, cigarette between his lips, squinting at the document pinched between the tips of his nicotine-stained fingers. He walked back to his office, where a man sat in the heavy afternoon shadows. Lavon waved the pages.

"Our hero and heroine have surfaced."

"Where are they?" asked Ari Shamron.

Lavon looked down at the fax and found the telephone number of the transmitting machine. "It appears they're in Munich."

Shamron closed his eyes. "Where in Munich?"

Lavon consulted the fax once more, and this time he was smiling when he looked up. "It looks as though our boy has found his way back to the bosom of his people."

"And the document?"

"I'm afraid Italian is not one of my languages, but based on the first line, I'd say he found Sister Regina."

"Let me see that."

Lavon handed the fax pages to Shamron. He read the first line aloud—*"Mi chiamo Regina Carcassi . . ."*—then looked up sharply at Lavon.

"Do you know anyone who speaks Italian?"

"I can find someone."

"Now, Eli."

WHEN GABRIEL WOKE, the darkness was complete. He raised his wrist to his face and focused his gaze on the luminous dial of his watch. Ten o'clock. He reached down toward the floor and groped through his clothing until he found Sister Regina's letter. He breathed again.

Chiara lay next to him. At some point she had left her own bed and, like a small child, crawled into his. Her back was turned to him, and her hair lay across his pillow. When he touched her shoulder, she rolled over and faced him. Her eyes were damp.

"What's wrong?"

"I was just thinking."

"About what?"

A long silence, broken by the blare of a car horn outside their window. "I used to pop into the Church of San Zaccaria while you were working. I'd see you up there on your scaffolding, hidden behind your shroud. Sometimes, I'd peer around the edge and see you staring at the face of the Virgin."

"Obviously, I'm going to have to get a bigger shroud."

"It's her, isn't it? When you look at the Virgin, you see the face of your wife. You see her scars." When Gabriel made no response, Chiara propped her head on her elbow and studied his face, running her forefinger down the length of his nose, as though it were sculpture. "I feel so sorry for you."

"I have no one to blame but myself. I was a fool to bring her into the field."

"That's why I feel sorry for you. If you could blame someone else, it might be easier."

She laid her head on his chest and was silent for a moment. "God, but I hate this place. *Munich.* The place where it all started. Did you know Hitler had a headquarters a few streets over?"

"I know."

"I used to think everything had changed for the better. Six months ago, someone put a coffin outside my father's synagogue. There was a swastika on the lid. Inside was a note. 'This coffin is for the Jews of Venice! The ones we didn't get the first time!'"

"It's not real," Gabriel said. "At least, the threat isn't real."

"It frightened the old ones. You see, they remember when it was real." She lifted her hand to her face and pushed a tear from her cheek. "Do you really think Beni had something else?"

"I'd stake my life on it."

"What else do we need? A bishop from the Vatican sat down with Martin Luther in 1942 and gave his blessing to the murder of millions. Sixty years later, Crux Vera killed your friend and many more to keep it a secret."

"I don't want Crux Vera to succeed. I want to expose the secret, and I need more than Sister Regina's letter in order to do that."

"Do you know what this will do to the Vatican?"

"I'm afraid that's not my concern."

"You'll destroy it," she said. "Then you'll go back to the Church of San Zaccaria and finish restoring your Bellini. You're a man of contradictions, aren't you?"

"So I've been told."

She lifted her head, resting her chin on his breastbone, and stared into his eyes. Her hair spilled over his cheeks. "Why do they hate us, Gabriel? What did we ever do to them?"

THE PEUGEOT was where they had left it, parked at the side entrance of the community center, glistening beneath a yellow streetlamp. Gabriel drove carefully through the wet streets. He skirted the city center on the Thomas Winner Ring, a broad boulevard encircling the heart of old Munich, then headed toward Schwabing on the Ludwigstrasse. At the entrance of a U-Bahn station, he saw a stack of blue fliers beneath the weight of a red brick. Chiara darted out, scooped up the papers, and brought them back to the car.

Gabriel twice drove past Adalbertstrasse 68 before deciding it was safe to proceed. He parked around the corner, on the Barer-strasse, and killed the engine. A streetcar rattled past, empty but for a single old woman gazing hopelessly through the fogged glass.

As they walked toward the entrance of the apartment house, Gabriel thought of his first conversation with Detective Axel Weiss. *The tenants are very casual about who they let in. If someone presses the intercom and says "advertisements," they're routinely buzzed in.*

Gabriel hesitated, then simultaneously pushed two buttons. A few seconds later a sleepy voice answered, *"Ja?"* Gabriel murmured the password. The buzzer howled, and the door unlocked. They stepped inside and the door closed automatically behind them. Gabriel opened and closed it a second time for the benefit of anyone who might be listening. Then he placed the stack of fliers on the ground and crossed the foyer to the staircase—quickly, in case the old caretaker was still awake.

They crept quietly up the stairs to the second-floor landing. The door to Benjamin's apartment was still marked with crime-scene tape, and an official-looking note on the door declared that it was off-limits. The makeshift memorial—the flowers, the notes of con-dolence—had been cleared away.

Chiara crouched and went to work on the lock with a slender metal tool. Gabriel turned his back to her and watched the stair-well. Thirty seconds later, he heard the lock give way, and Chiara pushed open the door. They ducked beneath the crime-scene tape and went inside. Gabriel closed the door and switched on his flash-light.

"Work quickly," he said. "Don't worry about making a mess."

He led her into the large room overlooking the street—the room Benjamin had used as his office. The beam of Chiara's flashlight fell across the neo-Nazi graffiti on the wall. "My God," she whispered.

"You start at that end," Gabriel said. "We'll search each room together, then we'll move to the next."

They worked silently but efficiently. Gabriel tore the desk to pieces, while Chiara pulled every book from its shelf and thumbed through the pages. *Nothing.* Next, Gabriel went to work on the furniture, removing slipcovers, pulling apart cushions. *Nothing.* He turned over the coffee table and unscrewed the legs to check for hollow compartments. *Nothing.* Together, they turned over the rug and searched for a slit where documents might be concealed. *Nothing.* Gabriel got down on all fours and patiently checked every floorboard to see if one of them had been loosened. Chiara removed the covers from the heating vents.

Hell!

At one end of the room was a doorway leading to a small antechamber. Inside, Benjamin had stored more books. Gabriel and Chiara searched the room together and found nothing.

Closing the door on the way out, Gabriel detected a faint sound, something unfamiliar; not the squeak of a dry hinge, but a rustle of some sort. He put his hand on the knob, then opened and closed the door several times in quick succession. Open, close, open, close, *open . . .*

The door was hollow, and it sounded as if there was something inside.

He turned to Chiara. "Hand me that screwdriver."

He knelt down and loosened the screws holding the latch to the door. When he finished, he separated the latch. Attached to one of them was a line of nylon filament, hanging into the interior of the door. Gabriel gently tugged on the filament, and up came a clear plastic bag with a zip-lock enclosure. Inside was a tightly folded batch of papers.

"My God," Chiara said. "I can't believe you actually found it!"

Gabriel pried open the Ziplock bag, then carefully removed the papers and unfolded them by the illumination of Chiara's flashlight. He closed his eyes, swore softly, and held the papers up for Chiara to see.

It was a copy of Sister Regina's letter.

Gabriel got slowly to his feet. It had taken more than an hour to find something they already had. How much longer would it take to find what they needed? He drew a deep breath and turned around.

It was then that he saw the shadow of a figure, standing in the center of the room amid the clutter. He reached into his pocket, wrapped his fingers around the butt of the Beretta, and quickly drew it out. As his arm swung up to the firing position, Chiara illuminated the target with the beam of her flashlight. Fortunately, Gabriel managed to prevent his forefinger from pulling the trigger, because standing ten feet in front of him, with her hands shading her eyes, was an old woman wrapped in a pink bathrobe.

THERE WAS a pathological neatness about Frau Ratzinger's tiny flat that Gabriel recognized at once. The kitchen was spotless and sterile, the dishes in her little china cabinet fastidiously placed. The knickknacks on the coffee table in her sitting room looked as though they had been arranged and rearranged by an inmate in an asylum—which in many respects, thought Gabriel, she was.

"Where were you?" he asked carefully, in a voice he might have used for a small child.

"First Dachau, then Ravensbruck, and finally Riga." She paused for a moment. "My parents were murdered at Riga. They were shot by the *Einsatzgruppen,* the roving SS death squads, and buried along with twenty-seven thousand others in a trench dug by Russian prisoners-of-war."

Then she rolled up her sleeve to show Gabriel her number—like the number that Gabriel's mother had tried so desperately to conceal. Even in the fierce summer heat of the Jezreel Valley, she would wear a long-sleeved blouse rather than allow a stranger to see her tattoo. Her mark of shame, she called it. Her emblem of Jewish weakness.

"Benjamin was afraid he would be killed," she said. "They used to call him at all hours and say the most horrible things on his telephone. They used to stand outside the building at night to frighten him. He told me that if anything ever happened to him, men would come—men from Israel."

She opened the drawer of her china cabinet and pulled out a white linen tablecloth. With Chiara's help, she unfolded it. Hidden inside was a legal-size envelope, the edges and flap sealed with heavy plastic packing tape.

"This is what you were looking for, yes?" She held it up for Gabriel to see. "The first time I saw you, I thought you might be the one, but I didn't feel I could trust you. There were many strange things taking place in that apartment. Men coming in the middle of the night. Policemen carting off Benjamin's belongings. I was afraid. As you might imagine, I still do not trust German men in uniform."

Her melancholy eyes settled on Gabriel's face. "You're not his brother, are you?"

"No, I'm not, Frau Ratzinger."

"I didn't think so. That's why I gave you the eyeglasses. If you were the man Benjamin was talking about, I knew you would follow the clues, and that eventually you would find your way back to me. I had to be certain you were the right man. Are you the right man, Herr Landau?"

"I'm not Herr Landau, but I *am* the right man."

"Your German is very good," she said. "You *are* from Israel, aren't you?"

"I grew up in the Jezreel Valley," Gabriel said, switching to Hebrew without warning. "Benjamin was the closest thing to a brother I ever had. I'm the man he would have wanted to see what's inside that envelope."

"Then I believe this belongs to you," she responded in the same language. "Finish your friend's work. But whatever you do, don't come back here again. It's not safe for you here."

Then she carefully placed the envelope in Gabriel's hands and touched his face.

"Go," she said.

PART FOUR

✦

A

SYNAGOGUE

BY THE RIVER

✦

·25·

VATICAN CITY

BENEDETTO FOÀ PRESENTED HIMSELF for work at the four-story office building near the entrance of Saint Peter's Square at the thoroughly reasonable Roman hour of ten-thirty. In a city filled with beautifully dressed men, Foà was clearly an exception. His trousers had long ago lost their crease, the toes of his black leather shoes were scuffed, and the pockets of his sport jacket had been misshapen by his habit of filling them with notepads, tape recorders, and batches of folded papers. The Vatican correspondent for *La Repubblica,* Foà did not trust a man who couldn't carry his possessions in his pockets.

He picked his way through a pack of tourists queued up outside the souvenir shops on the ground floor and tried to enter the foyer. A blue-uniformed guard blocked his path. Foà sighed heavily and rummaged through his pockets until he found his press credentials.

It was a wholly unnecessary ritual, for Benedetto Foà was the dean of the *Vaticanisti* and his face was as well known to the Press Office security staff as the one belonging to the Austrian bullyboy who ran the place. Forcing him to show his badge was just another form of subtle punishment, like banning him from the Pope's airplane for next month's papal visit to Argentina and Chile. Foà had been a naughty boy. Foà was on probation. He'd been placed on the rack and offered a chance to repent. One more misstep and they'd tie him to the stake and light a match.

The *Sala Stampa della Santa Sede,* otherwise known as the Vatican Press Office, was an island of modernity in a Renaissance sea. Foà passed through a set of automatic glass doors, then crossed a floor of polished black marble to his cubicle in the press room. The Vatican inflicted a vow of poverty on those it deemed worthy of permanent credentials. Foà's office consisted of a tiny Formica desk with a telephone and a fax machine that was forever breaking down at the worst possible time. His neighbor was a Rubenesque blonde from *Inside the Vatican* magazine called Giovanna. She thought him a heretic and refused his repeated invitations to lunch.

He sat heavily in his chair. A copy of *L'Osservatore Romano* lay on his desk, next to a stack of clippings from the Vatican News Service. The Vatican's version of *Pravda* and Tass. With a heavy heart, Foà began to read, like a Kremlinologist looking for hidden meaning in an announcement that a certain member of the Politburo was suffering from a heavy chest cold. It was the usual drivel. Foà pushed aside the papers and began the long deliberation about where to have lunch.

He looked at Giovanna. Perhaps this would be the day her stoicism crumbled. He squeezed his way inside her cubicle. She was hunched over a *bollettino,* an official press release. When Foà peered over her shoulder, she covered it with her forearm like a schoolgirl hiding a test paper from the boy at the next desk.

"What is it, Giovanna?"

"They just released it. Go get your own and see for yourself."

She shoved him into the hall. The touch of her hand on Foà's hip lingered as he made his way toward the front of the room, where a fierce-looking nun sat behind a wooden desk. She bore an uncomfortable resemblance to a teacher who used to beat him with a stick. She handed him a pair of *bollettini* joylessly, like a camp guard doling out punishment rations. Just to annoy her, Foà read them standing in front of the desk.

The first dealt with a staff appointment at the Congregation for the Doctrine of the Faith. Hardly anything the readers of *La Repubblica* cared about. Foà would leave that one for Giovanna and her cohorts at the Catholic News Service. The second was far more interesting. It was issued in the form of an amendment to the Holy Father's schedule on Friday. He had cancelled an audience with a delegation from the Philippines and instead would pay a brief visit to the Great Synagogue of Rome to address the congregation.

Foà looked up and frowned. *A trip to the synagogue announced two days before the fact? Impossible!* An event like that should have been on the papal schedule weeks ago. It didn't take an experienced Vatican hand to know something was up.

Foà peered down a marble-floored corridor. At the end was an open door giving onto a pompous office. Seated behind a polished desk was a forbidding figure named Rudolf Gertz, the former Austrian television journalist who was now the head of the Vatican Press Office. It was against the rules to set foot in the corridor without permission. Foà decided on a suicide run. When the nun wasn't looking, he leapt down the hall like a springbok. A few steps from

Gertz's door a burly priest seized Foà by his coat collar and lifted him off the floor. Foà managed to hold up the *bollettino*.

"What do you think you're playing at, Rudolf? Do you take us for idiots? How dare you drop this on us with two days' notice? We should have been briefed! Why's he going? What's he going to say?"

Gertz looked up calmly. He had a skier's tan and was groomed for the evening news. Foà hung there helplessly, awaiting an answer he knew would never come, for somewhere during his journey from Vienna to the Vatican, Rudolf Gertz seemed to have lost the ability to speak.

"You don't know why he's going to the synagogue, do you, Rudolf? The Pope is keeping secrets from the Press Office. Something is up, and I'm going to find out what it is."

Gertz raised an eyebrow—*I wish you the best of luck.* The burly priest took it as a signal to frog-march Foà back to the press room and deposit him at his cubicle.

Foà shoved his things into his coat pockets and headed downstairs. He walked toward the river along the Via della Conciliazione, the *bollettino* still crumpled in his fist. Foà knew it was a signal of cataclysmic events to come. He just didn't know what they were. Against all better judgment, he had allowed himself to be used in a game as old as time itself: a Vatican intrigue pitting one wing of the Curia against the other. He suspected that the surprise announcement of a visit to the Great Synagogue of Rome was the culmination of that game. He was furious that he'd been blindsided like everyone else. He'd made a deal. The deal, in the opinion of Benedetto Foà, had been broken.

He stopped in the piazza just outside the ramparts of the Castel Sant'Angelo. He needed to make a telephone call—a call that couldn't be made from his desk in the *Sala Stampa*. From a public telephone, he dialed a number for an extension inside the Apostolic Palace. It was the private number of a man very close to the Holy Father. He answered as though he were expecting Foà's call.

"We had an agreement, Luigi," Foà said without preamble. "You broke that agreement."

"Calm down, Benedetto. Don't hurl accusations that you'll regret later."

"I agreed to play your little game about the Holy Father's childhood in exchange for something special."

"Trust me, Benedetto, something very special will be coming your way sooner than you think."

"I'm about to be permanently banned from the *Sala Stampa* because I helped you. The least you could have done is warn me that this trip to the synagogue was coming."

"I couldn't do that, for reasons that will be abundantly clear to you in the coming days. As for your problems at the *Sala Stampa,* this too shall pass."

"Why is he going to the synagogue?"

"You'll have to wait until Friday, like everyone else."

"You're a bastard, Luigi."

"Please try to remember you're talking to a priest."

"You're not a priest. You're a cutthroat in a clerical suit."

"Flattery will get you nowhere, Benedetto. I'm sorry, but the Holy Father would like a word."

The line went dead. Foà slammed down the receiver and headed wearily back to the Press Office.

A SHORT distance away, in a barricaded diplomatic compound at the end of a tree-lined cul-de-sac called the Via Michle Mercati,

Aaron Shiloh, Israel's ambassador to the Holy See, was seated behind his desk, leafing his way through a batch of morning correspondence from the Foreign Ministry in Tel Aviv. A compact woman with short dark hair knocked on the doorjamb and entered the room without waiting for permission. Yael Ravona, Ambassador Shiloh's secretary, dropped a single sheet of paper on his desk. It was a bulletin from the Vatican News Service.

"This just came over the wire."

The ambassador read it quickly, then looked up. "The synagogue? Why didn't they tell us something like this was coming? It makes no sense."

"Judging from the tone of that dispatch, the Press Office and VNS were caught off-guard."

"Put in a call to the Secretariat of State. Tell them I'd like to speak with Cardinal Brindisi."

"Yes, ambassador."

Yael Ravona walked out. The ambassador picked up his telephone and dialed a number in Tel Aviv. A moment later, he said quietly: "I need to speak to Shamron."

AT THAT same moment, Carlo Casagrande was seated in the back of his Vatican staff car, speeding along the winding S4 motorway through the mountains northeast of Rome. The reason for his unscheduled journey lay in the locked attaché case resting on the seat next to him. It was a report, delivered to him earlier that morning, by the agent he had assigned to investigate the childhood of the Holy Father. The agent had been forced to resort to a black-bag operation—a break-in at the apartment of Benedetto Foà. A hurried search of Foà's files had produced his notes on the matter. A summary of those notes was contained in the report.

The Villa Galatina appeared, perched on its own mountain, glowering at the valley below. Casagrande glimpsed one of Roberto Pucci's guards high among the battlements, a rifle slung over his shoulder. The front gate was open. A tan-suited security man glanced at the SCV license plates and waved the car onto the property.

Roberto Pucci greeted Casagrande in the entrance hall. He was dressed in riding breeches and knee-length leather boots, and smelled of gunsmoke. Obviously, he had spent the morning shooting. Don Pucci often said that the only thing he loved more than his collection of guns was making money—and the Holy Mother Church, of course. The financier escorted Casagrande down a long, gloomy gallery into a cavernous great room overlooking the garden. Cardinal Marco Brindisi was already there, a thin figure perched on the edge of a chair in front of the fire, a teacup balanced precariously on his cassocked thigh. Light reflected off the lenses of the cardinal's small round spectacles, turning them to white discs that obscured his eyes. Casagrande dropped to one knee and kissed the proffered ring. Brindisi extended the first two fingers of his right hand and solemnly offered his blessing. The cardinal, thought Casagrande, had exquisite hands.

Casagrande sat down, worked the combination locks on his attaché, and lifted the lid. Brindisi held out his hand and accepted a single sheet of typescript on Vatican Security Office letterhead, then looked down and began to read. Casagrande folded his hands across his lap and waited patiently. Roberto Pucci paced the floor, a restless hunter looking for a target of opportunity.

A moment later, Cardinal Brindisi stood and took a few teetering steps toward the fireplace. He dropped the report on the flames and watched it curl and disintegrate, then turned and faced Casagrande and Pucci, his eyes hidden behind the two white discs of light. Brindisi's *uomini di fiducia*—his men of trust—awaited the verdict, though for Casagrande there was little suspense, because he knew the course that Brindisi would choose. Brindisi's Church was in mortal danger. Drastic measures were in order.

R OBERTO PUCCI was a perpetual target of the Italian intelligence services, and it had been many days since the Villa Galatina had been swept for listening devices. Before Cardinal Brindisi could pronounce his death sentence, Casagrande raised his finger to his lips and his eyes to the ceiling. Despite a cold rain, they walked in Don Pucci's garden, umbrellas overhead, like mourners following a horse-drawn coffin. The hem of the cardinal's cassock quickly became soaked. To Casagrande it seemed they were wading shoulder to shoulder in blood.

"Pope Accidental is playing a very dangerous game," Cardinal Brindisi said. "His initiative to throw open the Archives is simply a ploy to give him cover to reveal things he already knows. It is an act of unbelievable recklessness. I believe it's quite possible that the Holy Father is delusional or mentally unbalanced in some way. We have a duty, indeed a divine mandate, to remove him."

Roberto Pucci cleared his throat. "Removing him and killing him are two different things, Eminence."

"Not really, Don Pucci. The conclave made him an absolute monarch. We cannot simply ask the king to step aside. Only death can end this papacy."

Casagrande looked up at the row of cypress trees swaying in the gusty wind. *Kill the Pope?* Insanity. He turned his gaze from the trees and looked at Brindisi. The cardinal was studying him intently. The pinched face, the round spectacles—it was like being appraised by Pius XII himself.

Brindisi looked away. "Will no one rid me of this meddlesome priest? Do you know who spoke those words, Carlo?"

"King Henry the Second, if I'm not mistaken. And the meddlesome priest he was referring to was Thomas à Becket. Not long after he uttered those words, four of his knights stormed into the cathedral at Canterbury and cut Thomas down with their swords."

"Very impressive," said the cardinal. "Pope Accidental and Saint Thomas have much in common. Thomas was a vain, ostentatious man who did much to bring about his own demise. The same can surely be said of the Holy Father. He has no right to bypass the Curia and launch this initiative on his own. And for his sins, and his vanity, he must suffer the fate of Thomas. Send forth your knights, Carlo. Cut him down."

"If the Holy Father dies a violent death, he will become a martyr, just like Saint Thomas."

"So much the better. If his death is choreographed properly, this whole sordid affair might end in a way that suits our purposes quite nicely."

"How so, Eminence?"

"Can you imagine the wrath that will rain down on the heads of the Jews if the Holy Father is killed in a synagogue? Surely, an assassin with the skills of your friend can carry off something like that. Once he is gone, we will build a case against our papal assassin, the Israeli who settled in our midst and restored our precious works of art while he waited for his chance to murder the Holy Father. It is a remarkable story, Carlo—one the world's media will find difficult to resist."

"If not difficult to believe, Eminence."

"Not if you do your job correctly."

A silence hung over them, broken only by the crunch of their footsteps on the gravel pathway. Casagrande could not feel his feet touching the earth. He felt he was floating, viewing the scene from above: the ancient abbey; the labyrinth gardens; three men, the Holy Trinity of Crux Vera, calmly deliberating whether to murder a pope. He squeezed the handle of his umbrella, assessing whether it was real or merely an object in a dream. He wished it could carry him away, transport him to another time—a time before his faith and his obsession for revenge had caused him to behave with the same cruelty and depravity as his enemies. He saw Angelina, seated on a blanket in the shade of a stone pine in the Villa Borghese. He bent to kiss her, expecting to find the taste of strawberries on her lips, but instead he tasted blood. He heard a voice. In his memory, it was Angelina, telling him she wanted to spend the summer holiday in the mountains of the north. In reality it was Cardinal Brindisi, holding forth on why the murder of a pope would serve the interests of both the Church and Crux Vera. *How easily the cardinal speaks of murder,* thought Casagrande. And then he saw it all clearly. A Church in turmoil. A time for proven leadership. After the Holy Father's death, Brindisi would seize what the last conclave had denied him.

Casagrande marshaled his forces and proceeded carefully.

"If I may approach the issue from an operational standpoint, Eminence, killing a pope is not something that can be done on the spur of the moment. It takes months, perhaps years, to plan something like this." He paused, waiting for Brindisi to interrupt, but the cardinal kept walking, a man on a journey with a great distance still to go. Casagrande carried on. "Once the Holy Father leaves the territory of the Vatican, he will be under the protection of Italian police and security services. At the moment, they are on war footing because of our spurious papal assassin. There will be a wall around the Holy Father that will be impossible to penetrate."

"What you say is true, Carlo. But there are two important factors weighing heavily in our favor. You work for the Vatican Security Office. You have the ability to get a man close to the Holy Father whenever you please."

"And the second?"

"The man you will get close to the Holy Father is the Leopard."

"I doubt even the Leopard would accept an assignment like the one you're proposing, Eminence."

"Offer him money. That's what creatures like him respond to."

Casagrande felt as though he were hurling himself against the walls of the old abbey. He decided to make one final assault.

"When I came to the Vatican from the *carabinieri,* I swore a sacred oath to protect the pope. Now you are asking me to break that oath, Eminence."

"You also swore a sacred oath to Crux Vera and to me personally, an oath that binds you to absolute obedience."

Casagrande stopped walking and turned to face the cardinal. His spectacles were dotted with rain. "I had hopes of seeing my wife and daughter once again in the Kingdom of Heaven, Eminence. Surely the only thing that awaits the man who carries out this deed is damnation."

"You need not worry about confronting the fires of Hell, Carlo. I will grant you absolution."

"Do you really have such power? The power to cleanse the soul of a man who murders a pope?"

"Of course I do!" snapped Brindisi, as if he found the question blasphemous. Then his demeanor and his tone softened. "You're tired, Carlo. This affair has been long and difficult for all of us. But there is a way out, and soon it will be over."

"At what cost, Eminence? To us? To the Church?"

"He wants to destroy the Church. I want to save it. Who do you stand with?"

After a moment's hesitation, Casagrande said, "I stand with you, Eminence. And the Holy Mother Church."

"As I knew you would."

"I have just one question. Do you intend to accompany the Holy Father to the synagogue? I wouldn't want you to be anywhere near the Holy Father when this terrible deed is done."

"As I told the Holy Father when he asked me the same question, I intend to have a case of the flu on Friday that will not permit me to be at his side."

Casagrande seized the cardinal's hand and feverishly kissed his ring. The prelate extended his long fingers and made the sign of the cross over Casagrande's forehead. There was no love in his eyes; only coldness and a fierce determination. From Casagrande's vantage point, it seemed he was anointing a dead man.

CARDINAL BRINDISI departed for Rome first. Casagrande and Roberto Pucci remained behind in the garden.

"It doesn't take a terribly perceptive man to see that your heart is not in this, Carlo."

"Only a madman would relish the opportunity to murder a pope."

"What do you intend to do?"

Casagrande moved some gravel around with the toe of his shoe, then looked up at the cypress trees bending in the wind. He knew he was about to embark on a course that would ultimately lead to his own destruction.

"I'm going to Zurich," Casagrande said. "I'm going to hire an assassin."

·26·

VIENNA

ELI LAVON'S OFFICE looked like the command bunker of an army in fighting retreat. Open files lay scattered across the tabletops, and a map hung crookedly on the wall. There were ashtrays overflowing with half-smoked cigarettes and a wastepaper basket filled with half-eaten remnants of a dismal carryout meal. A cup of cold coffee was balanced precariously atop a stack of books. A silent television flickered unnoticed in the corner.

Lavon had clearly been expecting them. He had flung open the door before Gabriel had even pressed the buzzer and hauled them inside like guests late for a dinner party in their honor. He had waved the facsimile of Sister Regina's letter and peppered Gabriel with questions as he led him down the corridor. *Where did you find this? What were you doing back in Munich? Do you know the trouble you've caused? Half the Office is looking for you! My God, Gabriel, but you gave us a scare!*

Shamron had said nothing. Shamron had survived enough disasters to realize that in due time he would learn everything he needed to know. As Lavon berated Gabriel, the old man paced the floorboards before the window overlooking the courtyard. His reflection was visible in the bulletproof glass. To Gabriel, the mirror image seemed like another version of Shamron. Younger and more surefooted. Shamron the invincible.

Gabriel sat heavily upon Lavon's couch. With Chiara at his side, he produced the envelope Frau Ratzinger had given him in Munich and laid it on the file-strewn coffee table. Lavon shoved a pair of reading glasses onto his face and carefully removed the contents: a photocopy of two pages of single-spaced typescript. He looked down and began to read. After a moment, his face drained of color and the papers were trembling between his fingertips. He glanced up at Gabriel and whispered, "Unbelievable."

Lavon held it up for Shamron. "I think you'd better take a look at this, Boss."

Shamron paused long enough to scan the letterhead, then resumed his journey. "Read it to me, Eli," he said. "In German, please. I want to hear it in German."

REICH MINISTRY FOR FOREIGN AFFAIRS

To: SS–Obersturmbannführer Adolf Eichmann, RSHA IV B4
From: Unterstaatssekretär Martin Luther, Abteilung Deutschland, regarding the policy of the Holy See concerning Jewish matters

Berlin, March 30, 1942
64–34 25/1

My meeting with His Grace Bishop Sebastiano Lorenzi at the Convent of the Sacred Heart in northern Italy was an unqualified success. As you know, Bishop Lorenzi is the leading expert on relations between Germany and the Holy See inside the Vatican Secretariat of State. He is also a member of the orthodox Catholic society known as Crux Vera, which has been very supportive of National Socialism from the beginning. Bishop Lorenzi is very close to the Holy Father and speaks with him on a daily basis. They attended the Gregorian College together, and the bishop was a leading player during the negotiations over the Concordat reached between the Reich and the Holy See in 1933.

I have worked closely with Bishop Lorenzi for some time. It is my opinion that he agrees wholeheartedly with our policy toward the Jews, though, for obvious reasons, he cannot say so. He couches his positions regarding the Jews in theological terms, but in candid moments, he betrays his beliefs that they are a social and economic menace as well as heretics and mortal enemies of the Church.

During our meeting, which was held in the pleasant surroundings of a convent situated on the shores of Lake Garda, we discussed many aspects of our Jewish policy and why it must go forward unencumbered. Bishop Lorenzi seemed most impressed by my suggestion that failure to deal with the Jews in a timely and thorough manner could lead to the creation of a Jewish state in the Holy Land. To buttress my arguments, I quoted heavily from your 1938 memorandum on that topic, in which you argued that a Jewish state in Palestine would only increase the power of world Jewry in law and international relations, because a miniature state would permit the Jew to send ambassadors and delegates around the world to promote his lust for domination. In that respect, the Jew would be placed on equal footing with political Catholicism, something Bishop Lorenzi is eager to prevent at all costs. Nor does he, or the Holy Father, wish to see Jews controlling the sacred Christian sites of the Holy Land.

I made clear our position that a papal protest of the round-ups and deportations would be a clear violation of the Concordat. I also vigorously pressed my position that a papal protest would have profound and disastrous effects on our Jewish policy. Lorenzi, more than others, realizes the power possessed by the Holy See in this matter, and he is committed to making certain the Pope does not speak. With the help of Bishop Lorenzi, I believe the Holy Father will be able to weather the storm of pressure put on him by our enemies and will maintain his position of strict neutrality. In my opinion, our position with the Vatican is secure, and we can expect no meaningful resistance to our Jewish policies from the Holy See or from Roman Catholics under Reich control.

Shamron had stopped pacing and seemed to be studying his face in the glass. He took a long time lighting his next cigarette. Gabriel could see he was thinking four moves ahead. "It's been some time since we last spoke," he said. "Before we go any further, I think you need to explain how you came by these documents."

As Gabriel began his account, Shamron resumed his private journey before the window. Gabriel told him about his meeting in London with Peter Malone and how in France the following morning he learned of Malone's murder. He told him of his meeting with Inspector Alessio Rossi at the Pensione Abruzzi and the gun battle that left Rossi and four other men dead. He told him of his decision to hijack the motor yacht to continue his investigation rather than return to Israel.

"But you're forgetting something," Shamron interjected. He spoke with uncharacteristic gentleness, as though he were addressing small children. "I saw Shimon Pazner's field report. According to Pazner, you were followed as you left the safe flat—a pair of men in a beige Lancia sedan. The second team dealt with the Lancia, and you then proceeded without incident to the departure point on the beach. Is that correct?"

"I never saw the surveillance. I only heard what Pazner told me. The people in the Lancia might have been watching us, or they might have been a couple of ordinary Romans on their way to dinner who got the surprise of their life."

"They might have been, but I doubt it. You see, a short time later, a beige Lancia was discovered near the train station. Behind the wheel was a Palestinian named Marwan Aziz, a man known to be an agent of PLO intelligence. He'd been shot three times and was quite dead. And by the way, the Lancia's left rear bumper was damaged. Marwan Aziz was one of the men who was following you. I wonder where the second man went. I wonder whether he was the one who killed Aziz. But I digress. Please continue."

Intrigued by Shamron's revelations, Gabriel pressed forward. The boat journey to Cannes. The meeting with Antonella Huber at which she surrendered the letter written by her mother, the former Sister Regina Carcassi. The dying man he had left behind in the field outside St-Cézaire. The midnight search of Benjamin's flat and the near-fatal confrontation with his caretaker, Frau Ratzinger. Shamron ceased his pacing only once, when Gabriel admitted that he had actually threatened Carlo Casagrande. An understandable reaction, said the look on the old man's creased face, but hardly the behavior one would expect from an agent of Gabriel's training and experience.

"Which brings us to the obvious next question," Shamron said. "Is the document real? Or is it the Vatican equivalent of the Hitler diaries?"

Lavon held it up. "Do you see these markings? They're consistent with documents from the KGB archives. If I had to guess, the Russians came across this while they were cleaning out their archives after the collapse of the empire. Somehow, it reached Benjamin's hands."

"But is it a hoax?"

"Taken in isolation, it might be easy to dismiss as a clever forgery concocted by the KGB in order to discredit the Catholic Church. After all, they were at each other's throats throughout much of the century, especially during the reign of Wojtyła and the crisis in Poland."

Gabriel leaned forward, elbows on his knees. "But if it's read in concert with Sister Regina's letter and all the other things I've learned?"

"Then it's probably the single most damning document I've ever seen. A senior Vatican official discussing genocide with Martin Luther over dinner? The covenant at Garda? It's no wonder people are dying because of this. If this is made public, it will be the equivalent of a nuclear bomb going off in St. Peter's Square."

"Can you authenticate it?"

"I have a few contacts inside the old KGB. So does the quiet little man standing in the window over there. It's not something he likes to talk about, but he and his friends from Dzerzhinsky Square did quite a lot of business together over the years. I bet he could get to the bottom of this in a couple of days if he set his mind to it."

Shamron looked at Lavon as if to say it would take him no more than an afternoon.

"Then what would we do with the information?" asked Gabriel. "Leak it to *The New York Times*? A Nazi memorandum, via the KGB and Israeli intelligence? The Church would deny that the meeting ever took place and attack the messenger. Very few people would believe us. It would also poison relations between Israel and the Vatican. Everything John Paul the Second did to repair relations between Catholics and Jews would go up in flames."

Frustration showed on Lavon's face. "The conduct of Pope Pius and the Vatican during the war is a matter of state concern for the government of Israel. There are those in the Church who wish to declare Pius the Twelfth a saint. It is the policy of the Israeli government that no canonization should take place until all relevant documents in the Secret Archives have been released and examined. This material should be turned over to the Foreign Ministry in Tel Aviv and acted upon."

"It *should,* Elijah," said Shamron, "but I'm afraid Gabriel speaks the truth. That document is too dangerous to make public. What do you think the Vatican is going to say? 'Oh dear, how could this have happened? We're terribly sorry.' No, that's not how they'll react. They'll attack us, and it will blow up in our faces. Our relations with the Vatican are tenuous at best. There are many members of the Secretariat of State who would use any excuse—including our involvement in this affair—to sever them. For anything good to come out of this, it has to be handled delicately and quietly—from the inside."

"By you? Forgive me, Boss, but the words *delicate* and *quiet* don't leap into my mind when I think about you. Lev gave you and Gabriel permission to investigate Beni's death, not cause a firestorm in our relations with the Holy See. You should turn the material over to the Foreign Ministry and go back to Tiberias."

"Under normal circumstances, I might take your advice, but I'm afraid the situation has changed."

"What are you talking about, Boss?"

"The phone call I took earlier this morning was from Aaron Shiloh, our ambassador to the Holy See. It seems there's been an unexpected addition to the Holy Father's schedule."

"WHICH BRINGS us back to the gentlemen who followed you when you left the safe flat in Rome." Shamron sat down opposite Gabriel and placed a photograph on the table. "This photograph was taken in Bucharest fifteen years ago. Recognize him?"

Gabriel nodded. The man in the photograph was the assassin and terrorist-for-hire known only as the Leopard.

Shamron laid a second photograph on the table, next to the first. "This photograph was taken by Mordecai in London minutes after the murder of Peter Malone. Research ran the photographs through the face-recognition software. They're the same man. Peter Malone was murdered by the Leopard."

"And Beni?" asked Gabriel.

"If they hired the Leopard to kill Malone, it's quite possible they hired him to kill Beni, but we may never know for certain."

"Obviously, you have a theory about the dead Palestinian in Rome."

"I do," Shamron said. "We know the Leopard had a long and

fruitful association with Palestinian terror groups. The operation on Cyprus was testament to that. We also know that he'd reached a deal with Abu Jihad to carry out additional acts of terror against Israeli citizens. Fortunately, you cut short Abu Jihad's illustrious career and the Leopard's operations never came to pass."

"You think the Leopard renewed his relationship with the Palestinians in order to find me?"

"I'm afraid it does make a certain amount of sense. Crux Vera wants you dead, and so do many people within the Palestinian movement. It's quite possible that the Leopard was the second man in that Lancia—and that he was the one who killed Marwan Aziz."

Gabriel picked up the photographs and studied them carefully, as if they were a pair of canvases, one that had been authenticated and one that was thought to have been painted by the same artist. It was impossible to tell with the naked eye, but he had learned long ago that the face-recognition software in Research rarely made a mistake. Then he closed his eyes and saw different faces. The faces of the dead: *Felici . . . Manzini . . . Carcassi . . . Beni . . . Rossi. . . .* Lastly, he saw a man in a white cassock, entering a synagogue by the river in Rome. *A cassock stained with blood.*

He opened his eyes and looked at Shamron. "We need to get a message to this Pope that his life may be in grave danger."

Shamron folded his arms and lowered his chin to his chest. "And how shall we do that? Call Rome information and ask for the Pope's private number? Everything goes through channels, and the Curia is famous for its slowness. If our ambassador goes through the Secretariat of State, it could take weeks to arrange an audience with the Pope. If I try to get to him through the Vatican Security Office, we'll run straight into Carlo Casagrande and his Crux Vera goons. We need to find someone who can take us up the back staircase of the Apostolic Palace to see the Pope privately. And we need to do it before Friday. Otherwise, His Holiness might never leave the Great Synagogue of Rome alive—and that's the *last* thing we need."

A long silence hung over the room. It was broken by Gabriel. "I know someone who can get us in to see the Pope," he said calmly. "But you have to get me back into Venice."

·27·

ZURICH

CARLO CASAGRANDE STRODE the chandeliered hallway on the fourth floor of the Hotel St. Gotthard and presented himself at the door of Room 423. He glanced at his watch—7:20 P.M., the precise time he had been instructed to come—then knocked twice. A confident knock, firm enough to make his presence known, not enough to disturb the occupants of the neighboring rooms. From the other side of the door came a voice in Italian instructing Casagrande to enter the room. He spoke Italian well for a foreigner. The fact that it lacked even the hint of a German accent sent acid flooding into Casagrande's stomach.

He pushed open the door and stepped inside, pausing on the threshold. A wedge of light from the chandelier in the corridor illuminated a portion of the room, and for an instant Casagrande could see the outline of a figure seated in a wing chair. When the door swung shut, the darkness was complete. Casagrande inched forward through the gloom until his shin collided with an unseen coffee table. He was made to stand there, enveloped in black, for several painful seconds. Finally a powerful lamp burst on, like a searchlight in a guard tower, and shone directly into his face. He raised his hand and tried to shield his eyes from the glare. It felt like a needle in his cornea.

"Good evening, General." A seductive voice, like warm oil. "Did you bring the dossier?"

Casagrande held up the briefcase. The silenced Stechkin moved into the light and prodded him onward. Casagrande removed the file and laid it on the coffee table like an offertory. The beam of light tilted downward, while the hand holding the weapon lifted the cover of the dossier. *The light* . . . Suddenly Casagrande was standing on the pavement outside his apartment in Rome, viewing the mutilated bodies of Angelina and his daughter by the beam of a *carabinieri* flashlight. *"Death was instantaneous, General Casagrande. You can at least take comfort in the knowledge that your loved ones did not suffer."*

The light tilted suddenly upward. Too late, Casagrande tried to shield his eyes, but the beam found his retina, and for the next several seconds he had the sensation he was being swallowed by a giant, undulating orange sphere.

"So much for the Middle Ages being over," the assassin said. The dossier slid across the table toward Casagrande. "He's too heavily protected. This is an assignment for a martyr, not a professional. Find someone else."

"I need you."

"How can I be sure I won't be set up to take the fall, like that idiot from Istanbul? The last thing I want to do is spend the rest of my life rotting away in some Italian jail, begging a pope for forgiveness."

"I give you my word that you will not be used as a pawn or a patsy in some larger game. You will perform this service for me, then, with my help, you will be permitted to escape."

"The word of a murderer. How reassuring. Why should I trust you?"

"Because I would do nothing to betray you."

"Really? Did you know Benjamin Stern was an agent of Israeli intelligence when you hired me to kill him?"

My God, thought Casagrande. *How does he know?* He weighed the advantages of lying, but thought better of it. "No," he said. "I did not know that the professor was connected to them in any way."

"You should have." There was a sudden edge to his voice, the blade of a trench knife. "And did you know that an agent named Gabriel Allon is investigating his death, along with the activities of your little group?"

"I didn't know his name until this moment. Obviously, you've done some investigating of your own."

"I make it my business to know when someone is hunting me. I also know that Allon was at the Pensione Abruzzi in Rome meeting with Inspector Alessio Rossi when you sent an army of *carabinieri* in there to kill him. You should have come to me with your problems, General. Allon would be dead now."

How? How does this monster know about the Israeli and Rossi? How is such a thing possible? He's a bully, thought Casagrande. *Bullies like to be placated.* He decided to play the role of the appeaser. It was not a role that came naturally to him.

"You're right," he said, his tone conciliatory. "I should have come to you. Obviously, it would have been better for both of us. May I sit down?"

The light lingered on his face for a few more seconds, then it fell upon an armchair, a few inches from the spot where Casagrande was standing. He sat down and placed his hands on his knees. The light remained in his eyes.

"The question is, General, can I trust you enough to work for you again, especially on something like this?"

"Perhaps I can earn your trust."

"With what?"

"Money, of course."

"It would take a great deal of money."

"The figure I had in mind was substantial," Casagrande said. "A sum of money that most men would consider sufficient to live on for a very long time."

"I'm listening."

"Four million dollars."

"Five million," countered the assassin. "Half now, half on completion."

Casagrande squeezed his kneecaps, trying to conceal his rising tension. It was not like quarreling with Cardinal Brindisi. The Leopard's sanctions tended to be irrevocable.

"Five million," Casagrande said in agreement. "But you will be paid only *one* million of that in advance. If you choose to steal my money without fulfilling the terms of the contract, that's your business. If you want the remaining four million dollars—" Casagrande paused. "I'm afraid trust cuts both ways."

There was a long, uncomfortable silence, long enough for Casagrande to inch forward out of his chair and prepare to take his leave. He froze when the assassin said, "Tell me how it would be done."

Casagrande spoke for the next hour—a veteran policeman, calmly recounting the timeline of a rather mundane series of street crimes. All the while the light bored into his face. It was making him hot. His suit jacket was soaked with sweat and was clinging to his back like a wet blanket. He wished he'd turn the damned thing off. He'd rather sit in the dark with the monster than stare into the light any longer.

"Did you bring the downpayment?"

Casagrande reached down and patted the side of his attaché case.

"Let me see it."

Casagrande placed the attaché case on the table, opened it, and turned it so the assassin could see his money.

"Do you know what will happen to you if you betray me?"

"I'm certain I can imagine," Casagrande said. "But surely a downpayment of that magnitude is enough to demonstrate my good faith."

"Faith? Is that what leads you to perform this act?"

"There are some things you're not permitted to know. Do you accept the contract?"

The assassin closed the attaché case and it disappeared into the darkness.

"There's just one last thing," Casagrande said. "You'll need Security Office identification to get past the Swiss Guards and the *carabinieri*. Did you bring the photograph?"

Casagrande heard the rustle of fabric, then a hand appeared, holding a passport photo. Poor quality. Casagrande reckoned it had been made by an automated machine. He looked at the image and wondered whether it was truly the face of the killing machine known as the Leopard. The assassin seemed to sense his thoughts, for a few seconds later the Stechkin reappeared. It was pointed directly at Casagrande's heart.

"You wish to ask me a question?"

Casagrande shook his head.

"Good," the assassin said. "Get out."

·28·

VENICE

THE *ACQUA ALTA* LAPPED against the steps of the
Church of San Zaccaria as Francesco Tiepolo, dressed in an
oilskin coat and rubber knee-length boots, made his way ponder-
ously across the flooded square through the gathering dusk. He entered the church and sacrilegiously shouted out that it was time to
close up for the night. Adriana Zinetti seemed to float down from
her perch high atop the main altar. Antonio Politi yawned elabo-
rately and struck a series of contortionist yoga poses, all designed to
demonstrate to Tiepolo the harsh toll the day had taken on his young
body. Tiepolo looked toward the Bellini. The shroud remained in
place, but the fluorescent lamps were extinguished. With great effort, he resisted the impulse to scream.

Antonio Politi appeared at Tiepolo's side and laid a paint-
smudged paw on his heavy shoulder. "When, Francesco? When are
you going to get it through your head he's not coming back?"

When indeed? The boy wasn't ready for the Bellini masterpiece, but Tiepolo had no choice, not if the church was going to reopen to the public in time for the spring tourist season. "Give him one more day," he said, his gaze still fixed on the darkened painting. "If he's not back by tomorrow afternoon, I'll let you finish it."

Antonio's joy was tempered by his unreserved interest in the tall, striking creature making her way apprehensively across the nave. She had black eyes and a head of abundant, uncontrollable dark hair. Tiepolo knew faces. Bone structure. He'd bet his fee for the San Zaccaria project she was a Jewess. She seemed familiar to him. He thought he might have seen her once or twice in the church, watching the restorers working.

Antonio started toward her. Tiepolo thrust out a thick arm, blocking his path, and summoned a watery smile.

"Is there something I can help you with, signorina?"

"I'm looking for Francesco Tiepolo."

Deflated, Antonio skulked away. Tiepolo laid a hand on his chest—*You've found him, my treasure.*

"I'm a friend of Mario Delvecchio."

Tiepolo's flirtatious gaze turned suddenly cold. He folded his arms across his massive chest and glared at her through narrowed eyes. "Where in God's name is he?"

The woman said nothing, just reached out and handed him a slip of paper. He unfolded the note and read the words written there:

Your friend in the Vatican is in grave danger. I need your help to save his life.

He looked up and stared at her in disbelief.

"Who are you?"

"It's not important, Signor Tiepolo."

He held up the note in his big paw. "Where *is* he?"

"Will you help him save your friend's life?"

"I'll listen to what he has to say. If my friend is truly in some sort of danger, of course I'll help."

"Then you have to come with me."

"Now?"

"Please, Signor Tiepolo. I'm afraid we don't have much time."

"Where are we going?"

But she just seized him by the elbow and pulled him toward the door.

CANNAREGIO SMELLED of salt and the lagoon. The woman led Tiepolo across a bridge spanning the Rio di Ghetto Nuovo, then into the clammy gloom of the *sottoportego*. A figure appeared at the opposite end of the passageway, a small man with his hands thrust into the pockets of a leather jacket, surrounded by a halo of yellow sodium light. Tiepolo stopped walking.

"WOULD YOU mind telling me what the *fuck* is going on?"

"Obviously, you got my note."

"Interesting. But you must admit it was short on details, as well as one critical piece of information. How would you, an art restorer named Mario Delvecchio, know that the Pope's life is in danger?"

"Because restoration is something of a hobby for me. I have another job—a job that very few people know about. Do you understand what I'm trying to say to you, Francesco?"

"Who do you work for?"

"Who I work for is not important."

"It's *damned* important if you want me to help you get to the Pope."

"I work for an intelligence service. Not always, just under special circumstances."

"Like a death in the family."

"Actually, yes."

"Which intelligence service do you work for?"

"I would prefer not to answer that question."

"I'm sure you would, but if you want me to talk to the Pope, you're going to answer my questions. I repeat: What service do you work for? SISDE? Vatican intelligence?"

"I'm not Italian, Francesco."

"Not Italian! That's very funny, Mario."

"My name isn't Mario."

THEY WALKED the perimeter of the square, Gabriel and Tiepolo side by side, Chiara a few paces behind. It took a long time for Tiepolo to process the information he had just been given. He was a shrewd man, a sophisticated Venetian, politically and socially connected, yet the situation confronting him now was well beyond anything he had ever experienced. It was as if he had just been told that the Titian altarpiece in the Frari was a reproduction painted by a Russian. Finally, he drew a deep breath, a tenor preparing himself for the climactic passage of an aria, and twisted his head toward Gabriel.

"I remember when you came here as a boy. It was seventy-four or seventy-five, wasn't it?" Tiepolo's eyes were on Gabriel, but his memory was fixed on Venice, twenty-five years earlier, a little workshop filled with eager young faces. "I remember when you served your apprenticeship with Umberto Conti. You were gifted, even then. You were better than everyone else. You were going to be great one day. Umberto knew it. So did I." Tiepolo stroked his tangled beard with his big hand. "Did Umberto know the truth about you? Did he know you were an Israeli agent?"

"Umberto knew nothing."

"You deceived Umberto Conti? You should be ashamed of yourself. He *believed* in Mario Delvecchio." Tiepolo paused, checked his anger, lowered his voice. "He believed Mario Delvecchio would be one of the greatest restorers ever."

"I always wanted to tell Umberto the truth, but I couldn't. I have enemies, Francesco. Men who destroyed my family. Men who wish to kill me today for things that happened thirty years ago. If you think Italians have long memories, you should spend some time in the Middle East. We're the ones who invented the *vendetta,* not the Sicilians."

"Cain slew Abel, and east of Eden he was cast. And you were cast here, to our swampy island in the lagoon, to heal paintings."

It was a peace offering. Gabriel accepted it with a conciliatory smile. "Do you realize that in my profession I have just committed a mortal sin? I revealed myself to you, because I fear your friend is in grave danger."

"Do you really think they intend to kill him?"

"They've killed many people already. They killed my friend."

Tiepolo looked around at the vacant *campo.* "I knew John Paul the First as well—Albino Luciani. He was going to clean up the Vatican. Sell off the Church's assets, give the money to the poor people. Revolutionize the Church. He died after thirty-three days. A heart attack, the Vatican said." Tiepolo shook his head. "There was nothing wrong with his heart. He had the heart of a lion. The courage of one, too. The changes he planned to bring to the Church were going to make a lot of people angry. And so—"

He shrugged his massive shoulders, then he reached into his pocket, removed a mobile telephone, and quickly punched in a number from memory. He raised the phone to his ear and waited. When finally someone answered, he identified himself and asked for a man called Father Luigi Donati. Then he smothered the mouthpiece and whispered to Gabriel: "The Pope's private secretary. He was with him here in Venice for years. Very discreet. Fiercely loyal."

Evidently, it was Donati who came on the line next, because for the next five minutes, Tiepolo carried on an animated conversation, full of condescending remarks about Rome and the Curia. It was clear to Gabriel that Tiepolo had picked up a good deal of Church politics from his friend the Pope. When finally he brought the conversation around to the point, he did it with such subtlety and grace that to Gabriel it seemed both innocent and urgent at the same time. The artistic intrigue of Venice had taught Tiepolo many valuable lessons. He was a man capable of holding two conversations at the same time.

Finally, he killed the connection and slipped the telephone back into his pocket.

"Well?" said Gabriel.

"Father Donati is going to see the Pope."

FATHER LUIGI DONATI stared at the telephone for a long moment before deciding on his course of action, Tiepolo's words ringing in his ears. *I need to see the Holy Father. It is important*

I see the Holy Father before Friday. Tiepolo never spoke like that. His relationship with the Holy Father was strictly collegial—pasta and red wine and humorous stories that reminded the Pope of the good times in Venice before he had been made a prisoner of the Apostolic Palace. And why before Friday? What did Friday have to do with anything? Friday was the day the Holy Father would visit the synagogue. Was Tiepolo trying to tell him that there was a problem?

Donati stood abruptly and set out for the papal apartments. He brushed past a pair of the Pope's household nuns without so much as a word and entered the dining room. The Holy Father was entertaining a delegation of bishops from the American Midwest, and the conversation had come round to a topic His Holiness found revolting. He seemed relieved to see Donati stride into the room, even though Donati's demeanor was grim and businesslike.

The priest stood next to his master and bent slightly at the waist, so that he could speak directly into his ear. The bishops took their cue from Donati's tense appearance and looked away. When Donati finished, the Pope laid down his knife and fork and closed his eyes for a moment. Then he looked up, nodded once, and returned his attention to his guests.

"Now, where were we?" the Pope said as Donati strode from the room.

THEY PACED the length of the *campo* a half-dozen times waiting for the phone to ring. Tiepolo filled the empty, anxious minutes by peppering Gabriel with a hundred questions—about his work for Israeli intelligence, about his life and family, about what it was like for a Jew to be surrounded day and night by the images of

Christianity. Gabriel answered those he could and gently fended off those that strayed into uncomfortable waters. Still skeptical that Gabriel was indeed not an Italian, Tiepolo goaded him into speaking a few words of Hebrew. For the next several minutes he and Chiara carried on a lively conversation, mostly at Tiepolo's expense, until they were interrupted by the chirp of the Italian's cellular phone. He brought it to his ear, listened in silence for a moment, then murmured: "I understand, Father Donati."

He severed the connection and slipped the phone back into his pocket.

"Did he give you an answer?" asked Gabriel.

Tiepolo smiled.

·29·

ROME

IN THE NORTH OF ROME, near a lazy bend in the Tiber, lies a tidy little piazza where tourists rarely venture. There is an ancient church with a cracked belfry and a bus stop that few people use. There is a coffee bar and a small bakery that prepares bread on the premises, so that in the early morning the smell of flour and yeast mingles with the marshy scent of the river. Directly opposite the bakery is a teetering tenement block with a pair of potted orange trees marking the entrance. On the top floor, there is a large flat, from where it is possible to see the dome of St. Peter's Basilica in the distance. The flat is rented by a man who rarely uses it. He does so as a favor to his masters in Tel Aviv.

The building contained no lift, and to reach the flat it was necessary to navigate four gloomy flights of stairs. Chiara went first, followed by Gabriel and Francesco Tiepolo. Before she could slip her key into the lock, the door flew open and Shimon Pazner's square physique filled the frame. The memory of Gabriel and Chiara's flight from the beach was visible in the expression on his face. Had Ari Shamron and Eli Lavon not been standing six feet behind him, each puffing away on a Turkish cigarette, Gabriel was quite certain Pazner would have pounced. Instead, he was forced to silently hold his ground as Gabriel brushed past without a word and greeted Shamron. There would be no family quarrels tonight, not in front of an outsider. But one day, when Shamron was gone, Pazner would take his revenge. That's the way things always went in the Office.

Gabriel handled the introduction. "This is Francesco Tiepolo. Francesco, these are the guys. I won't insult you by giving them names, because they wouldn't be real in any case."

Tiepolo seemed to take this news in good humor. Shamron stepped forward and took over the proceedings. He shook Tiepolo's hand and looked up directly into his eyes for a long moment. Tiepolo could see he was being appraised for trustworthiness but made no sign that he found Shamron's undisguised scrutiny at all uncomfortable.

"I can't thank you enough for agreeing to help us, Signor Tiepolo."

"The Holy Father is a dear friend of mine. If any harm ever came to him, I would never be able to forgive myself, especially if I had been in a position to somehow prevent it."

"You may rest assured that our interests in this matter are in complete harmony." Shamron finally released Tiepolo's hand and looked at Shimon Pazner. "Bring him some coffee. Can't you see he's had a long journey?"

Pazner shot Gabriel an icy look and stalked off to the kitchen. Shamron ushered Tiepolo into the sitting room. The Venetian settled himself at the end of the couch, the rest gathered around him. Shamron wasted no more time on small talk.

"What time do you enter the Vatican?"

"I'm expected at the Bronze Doors at six o'clock this evening. Customarily, Father Donati greets me there and escorts me up to the third floor, to the papal apartments."

"Are you certain this man Donati is to be trusted?"

"I have known Father Donati as long as I have known the Holy Father. He is intensely loyal."

Shimon Pazner entered the room and handed Tiepolo a cup of espresso.

"It is important that the Pope and his aides feel comfortable," Shamron resumed. "We will meet with His Holiness under any circumstances of his choosing. Obviously, we would prefer a secure location, someplace where our presence will not be noted by certain elements of the Curia. Do you understand what I'm trying to say to you, Signor Tiepolo?"

Tiepolo raised the coffee to his lips and nodded vigorously.

"The information we wish to pass to the Holy Father is of a sensitive nature. If necessary, we will meet with a trusted aide, but we believe it would be best for the Pope to hear it with his own ears."

Tiepolo swallowed the espresso in a gulp and set the cup gently on the saucer. "It would be helpful to me if I had some idea of the nature of this information."

Shamron allowed his face to register discomfort, then he leaned forward. "It concerns the actions of the Vatican during the Second World War and a meeting that took place in a convent on Lake

Garda a long time ago. You'll forgive me, Signor Tiepolo, if I say no more."

"And the nature of the threat to his life?"

"We believe the threat to the Holy Father originates from forces inside the Church, which is why he needs to take additional steps to protect himself and those around him."

Tiepolo inflated his cheeks and expelled the air slowly. "You have one thing working to your advantage. Father Donati has told me on any number of occasions that he is concerned about the security around the Holy Father. So this will come as no surprise to him. As for the war—" Tiepolo hesitated, clearly choosing his words carefully. "Let me just say that it is a topic to which the Holy Father has given a great deal of thought. He calls it a stain on the Church. A stain that he is determined to remove."

Shamron smiled. "Obviously, Signor Tiepolo, we're here to help."

AT 5:45 P.M., a black Fiat sedan pulled up outside the entrance of the apartment house. Francesco Tiepolo settled himself in the backseat. Shamron and Shimon Pazner appeared briefly on the terrace and watched the car set out along the river toward the dome in the distance.

Fifteen minutes later, the Fiat deposited the Venetian at the entrance of St. Peter's Square. Tiepolo slipped through the metal guard barrier and made his way along Bernini's Colonnade as the bells of the Basilica tolled six o'clock. At the Bronze Doors, he presented his name and Italian identity card to the Swiss Guard. The Guard consulted a clipboard, then compared Tiepolo's face to the photograph on the identity card. Satisfied, he allowed Tiepolo to enter the Apostolic Palace.

Father Donati was waiting at the foot of the Scala Regia. As usual, he wore a grim expression, like a man perpetually bracing himself for bad news. He shook Tiepolo's hand coldly and led him upstairs to the papal apartments.

As always, Tiepolo was taken aback by the appearance of the papal study. It was a simple room—much too austere for so powerful a man, he thought—yet completely in keeping with the humble clergyman he had come to know and admire in Venice. Pope Paul VII was standing in the window overlooking St. Peter's Square, a white figure posed against the crimson drapery. He turned as Tiepolo and Father Donati entered the room and managed a fatigued smile. Tiepolo fell to his knees, kissing the fisherman's ring. Then the Pope took Tiepolo by the shoulders and guided him to his feet. He seized the Venetian by his biceps and squeezed, seemingly drawing strength from the bigger man.

"You look well, Francesco. Obviously life in Venice continues to treat you well."

"Until yesterday, Holiness, when I learned about a threat to your life."

Father Donati sat down, carefully crossed one leg over the other, and smoothed the crease of his trousers—a busy chief executive, eager to move the proceedings along. "All right, Francesco," Donati said. "Enough of the dramatics. Have a seat and tell me exactly what in God's name is going on."

POPE PAUL VII was scheduled to dine that evening with a delegation of visiting bishops from Argentina. Father Donati telephoned the leader of the delegation, a prelate from Buenos Aires, and told him that unfortunately His Holiness was under the weather and would not be able to host the meal. The bishop promised to pray for the Holy Father's speedy recovery.

At nine-thirty, Father Donati stepped into the corridor outside the papal study and confronted the Swiss Guard standing watch. "The Holy Father wishes to walk in the gardens to meditate," Donati said briskly. "He'll be leaving in just a few moments."

"I thought His Holiness was ill this evening," the Swiss Guard replied innocently.

"How His Holiness is feeling is none of your concern."

"Yes, Father Donati. I'll notify the Guards in the garden that His Holiness is coming."

"You will do no such thing. The Holy Father would like to meditate in peace."

The Swiss Guard stiffened. "Yes, Father Donati."

The priest walked back to the study, where he found Tiepolo helping the Pope into a long fawn overcoat and brimmed hat. With the coat buttoned, only the fringe of his white soutane was visible.

There are a thousand rooms in the Vatican and countless miles of corridors and staircases. Father Donati had made it his business to learn every inch of them. He led the Pope past the Swiss Guard, then spent the next ten minutes winding his way downward through the labyrinthine passageways of the ancient palace—here a murky shoulder-width tunnel with a dripping arched ceiling, here a flight of stone steps, rounded by time, slick as ice.

Finally, they came to a darkened underground garage. A small Fiat sedan was waiting. The Vatican SCV license plates had been replaced by normal Italian tags. Francesco Tiepolo helped the Pope into the backseat and joined him there. Father Donati climbed behind the wheel and started the engine.

The Pope could not hide his alarm at this development. "When was the last time you drove a car, Luigi?"

"To be honest, Holiness, I can't recall. It was certainly before we came to Venice."

"That was eighteen years ago!"

"May the Holy Spirit protect us on our journey."

"And all the angels and saints," added the Pope.

Donati forced the car into gear and guided it timidly up a winding, darkened ramp. A moment later, the car emerged into the night. The priest hesitantly pushed the accelerator toward the floor and sped along the Via Belvedere toward St. Anne's Gate.

"Duck down, Holiness."

"Is that really necessary, Luigi?"

"Francesco, please help His Holiness conceal himself!"

"I'm sorry, Holiness."

The big Venetian grabbed the Pope by the lapels of his overcoat and pulled him down into his lap. The Fiat sped past the Pontifical Pharmacy and the Vatican Bank. As they approached St. Anne's Gate, Father Donati switched on his headlights and sounded his horn. A stunned Swiss Guard leapt out of the path of the speeding car. Father Donati made the sign of the cross as the car flashed through the gate and entered Rome proper.

The Pope looked up at Tiepolo. "May I sit up now, Francesco? This is most undignified."

"Father Donati?"

"Yes, I think it's safe now."

Tiepolo helped the Pope sit up and straightened his overcoat.

IT WAS CHIARA, standing on the terrace of the safe flat, who spotted the Fiat entering the piazza. The car stopped in front of the building and three men climbed out. Chiara ducked into the sitting room. "There's someone here," she said. "Tiepolo and two other men. I think one of them might be him."

A moment later there was a sharp knock. Gabriel quickly crossed the room and pulled open the door. He was greeted by the sight of Francesco Tiepolo and a priest in clerical suit, flanking a small man in a long overcoat and a fedora hat. Gabriel stepped aside. Tiepolo and the priest ushered the man into the safe flat.

Gabriel closed the door. As he turned around, he saw the little man remove his fedora and hand it to the priest. Perched on his head was a white zucchetto. Next, he removed the fawn overcoat, revealing a soutane of brilliant white.

His Holiness Pope Paul VII said: "I'm told that you gentlemen have some important information you'd like to impart to me. I'm all ears."

· 30 ·

ROME

THE DOOR OF THE FLAT opened to Lange's touch, just as the Italian had said it would. He closed it again and pushed the deadbolt into place before switching on the lights. He was greeted by the sight of a single room with a bare floor and water-marked walls. There was a steel bed—more like a cot than a real bed—with a wafer-thin mattress. No pillow, a scratchy woolen blanket folded at the foot, stains. *Piss? Semen?* Lange could only guess. It was not unlike the room in Tripoli, where he had once spent a feverish fortnight waiting for his guide from the Libyan secret service to take him to the training camps in the south. There were distinct differences about this place, though, namely the large carved-wood crucifix hanging above the bed, adorned with a rosary and a length of dried palm leaf.

Next to the bed was a small chest. Lange wearily pulled open the drawers. He found underpants, balled black socks, and a dog-eared breviary. With some trepidation he ventured into the bathroom: a rust-stained basin with twin taps, a mirror that barely cast a reflection, a toilet with no seat.

He opened the closet. Two clerical suits hung from the rod. On the floor was a pair of black shoes, well worn but polished, the shoes of a poor man who took care of his appearance. Lange pushed the shoes out of the way with the toe of his loafer and saw the loose floorboard. He bent down and pried it up.

Reaching into the small space, he found a bundle of oilcloth. He unfolded the cloth: a Stechkin pistol, a silencer, two magazines of nine millimeter ammunition. Lange rammed one magazine into the butt and slipped the Stechkin into the waistband of his trousers. The silencer and the second magazine he rewrapped in the oilcloth.

He reached into the compartment a second time and found two more items: a set of keys to the motorcycle parked outside the apartment house, and a leather billfold. He opened the billfold. Inside was a Vatican Security Office identification badge, quite obviously the real thing. Lange looked at the name—MANFRED BECK, SPECIAL INVESTIGATIONS DIVISION—then at the photograph. It was the one he had given Casagrande in the hotel room in Zurich. It was not him, of course, but the vague resemblance could easily be enhanced with a bit of preparation.

Manfred Beck, Special Investigations Division . . .

He returned the billfold to the compartment, then replaced the floorboard and covered it with the shoes. He looked around at the barren, lonely room. A priest's room, this. A sudden memory overtook him: a winding cobblestone street in Fribourg, a young man in a black cassock drifting through the mist rising from the river Saane. A young man in crisis, Lange remembered. A tormented man. A man who could not bear the acute loneliness of the life that lay ahead of him. A man who wanted to be on the front lines. How odd that the path he had chosen had resulted in a life more lonely than a parish priest's. How odd that it had led him back here, to this desperate room in Rome.

He went to the window and pushed open the glass. The wet night air washed over his face. The *Stazione Termini* stood in the distance, about a half-kilometer away. Directly across the street lay a straggly, unkempt park. A woman was making her way along the puddled walkway. A streetlamp briefly caught the Breton red highlights in her hair. Something made her look up at the open window. Training. Instinct. *Fear.* Seeing his face, she smiled, and started across the road.

·31·

ROME

ARI SHAMRON HAD DECIDED that there would be no misleading the Vicar of Christ. Gabriel was to tell him everything, with no regard for protecting sources or methods. He also ordered Gabriel to give the account chronologically, for Shamron, a man who had briefed a half-dozen prime ministers, knew the value of a good story. He believed that the dirty details of how intelligence was acquired often made the conclusions more credible to the target audience—in this case the Supreme Pontiff of the Roman Catholic Church.

They settled themselves in the sitting room. The Pope sat in a comfortable armchair, knees together, hands folded. Father Donati sat next to him, a notebook open on his lap. Gabriel, Shamron, and Eli Lavon squeezed shoulder to shoulder on the couch, separated from the Pope and his secretary by a low coffee table and a pot of tea that no one touched. Chiara and Shimon Pazner stood watch on the balcony. Francesco Tiepolo, his work complete, kissed the papal ring and left for Venice in the back of an Office car.

Gabriel spoke to the Pope in his native tongue, while Father Donati took furious notes. Every few minutes, Donati would interrupt Gabriel by raising his silver pen and peering at him over his half-moon spectacles. Then he would force Gabriel to backtrack in order to clarify some seemingly mundane detail, or quibble with Gabriel on a point of translation. If it conflicted with what was written in his notebook, he would make a vast show of expunging the offending passage. When Gabriel recounted his conversation with Peter Malone—and the words "Crux Vera" were mentioned for the first time—Donati shot a conspiratorial glance at the Pope, which the Pontiff pointedly ignored.

For his part, the Pope remained silent. Sometimes his gaze was focused on his intertwined fingers; sometimes his eyes would close, as though he were at prayer. Only the deaths seemed to stir him from his reverie. With each killing—Benjamin Stern, Peter Malone, Alessio Rossi and the four *carabinieri* in Rome, the Crux Vera operative in the south of France—the Pope made the sign of the cross and murmured a few words of prayer. He never once looked at Gabriel or even at Father Donati. Only Shamron could capture his attention. The Pope seemed to find kinship with the old man. Perhaps it was the closeness of their age, or perhaps the Pope saw something reassuring in the fissures and ravines of Shamron's rugged face. But every few minutes, Gabriel would notice them staring at each other over the coffee table, as though it were a chasm of time and history.

Gabriel handed Sister Regina's letter to Father Donati, who then read it aloud. The Pope wore an expression of grief on his face, his

eyes tightly closed. To Gabriel it seemed like a remembered pain—
the pain of an old wound being torn open. Only once did he open
his eyes, at the point Sister Regina wrote of the boy sleeping on her
lap. He looked across the divide at Shamron, holding his gaze for a
moment, before closing his eyes once more and returning to his private agony.

Father Donati handed the letter back to Gabriel when he was
finished. Gabriel told the Pope of his decision to return to Munich
to search Benjamin's apartment a second time and of the document
Benjamin had entrusted to the old caretaker, Frau Ratzinger.

"It's in German," Gabriel said. "Would you like me to translate
it, Your Holiness?"

Father Donati answered the question for the Pope. "The Holy
Father and I both speak German fluently. Please feel free to read
the document in its original language."

The memorandum from Martin Luther to Adolf Eichmann
seemed to cause the Pope physical pain. At the halfway point, he
reached out and took Father Donati's hand for support. When
Gabriel finished, the Pope bowed his head and joined his hands beneath his pectoral cross. When he opened his eyes again, he looked
directly at Shamron, who was holding Sister Regina's account of
the meeting at the convent.

"A remarkable document, is it not, Your Holiness?" Shamron
asked in German.

"I'm afraid I would use a different word," the Pope said, answering him in the same language. "'Shameful' is the first word
that comes to mind."

"But is it an accurate account of the meeting that took place at
that convent in 1943?"

Gabriel looked first at Shamron, then at the Pope. Father Donati opened his mouth to object, but the Pope silenced him by gently placing a hand on his secretary's forearm.

"It's accurate except for one detail," said Pope Paul VII. "I wasn't really sleeping on Sister Regina's lap. I'm afraid I just couldn't bear to say another decade of the rosary."

A N D T H E N he told them the story of a boy—a boy from a poor village in the mountains of northern Italy. A boy who found himself orphaned at the age of nine, with no relatives to turn to for support. A boy who made his way to a convent on the shores of a lake, where he worked in the kitchen and befriended a woman named Sister Regina Carcassi. The nun became his mother and his teacher. She taught him to read and write. She taught him to appreciate art and music. She taught him to love God and to speak German. She called him *Ciciotto*—little chubby one. After the war, when Sister Regina renounced her vows and left the convent, the boy left too. Like Regina Carcassi, his faith in the Church was shaken by the events of the war, and he found his way to Milan, where he scratched out an existence on the streets, picking pockets and stealing from shops. Many times, he was arrested and beaten up by police officers. One night he was beaten nearly to death by a gang of criminals and left for dead on the steps of a parish church. He was discovered in the morning by a priest and taken to a hospital. The priest visited him each day and saw to the bills. He discovered that the filthy street urchin had spent time in a convent, that he could read and write and knew a great deal about Scripture and the Church. He convinced the boy to enter the seminary and study for the priesthood as a way to escape a life of poverty and prison. The boy agreed, and his life was forever changed.

Throughout the Pope's account, Gabriel, Shamron, and Eli Lavon sat motionless and enthralled. Father Donati looked down at his notebook but his hands were still. When the Pope finished, a deep silence hung over the room, broken finally by Shamron.

"What you must understand, Your Holiness, is that it was not our intention to uncover the information about the Garda covenant or your past. We only wanted to know who killed Benjamin Stern and why."

"I am not angry with you for bringing me this information, Mr. Shamron. As painful as these documents are, they must be made public, so that they can be examined by historians and ordinary Jews and Catholics alike and placed in their proper context."

Shamron laid the documents in front of the Pope. "We have no desire to make them public. We leave them in your hands to do with them what you will."

The Pope tilted his head down at the papers, but his gaze was distant, his eyes lost in thought. "He was not as wicked as his enemies have made him out to be, our Pope Pius the Twelfth. But unfortunately, neither was he as virtuous as his defenders, the Church included, have claimed. He had his reasons for silence—fear of dividing German Catholics, fear of German retaliation against the Vatican, a desire to play a diplomatic role as a peacemaker—but we must face the painful fact that the Allies wanted him to speak out against the Holocaust and Adolf Hitler wanted him to remain silent. For whatever reason—his hatred of Communism, his love of Germany, the fact that he was surrounded by Germans in his papal household—Pius chose the course Hitler wanted, and the shadow of that choice hangs over us to this day. He wanted to be a statesman when what the world needed most was a priest—a man in a cassock to shout at the murderers at the top of his lungs to stop what they were doing, in the name of God and all that was decent."

The Pope looked up and studied the faces before him—first Lavon, then Gabriel, then finally Shamron, where his gaze lingered longest. "We must face the uncomfortable fact that silence was a weapon in the hands of the Germans. It allowed the roundups and deportations to go forward with a minimum of resistance. There were hundreds, perhaps thousands, of Catholics who took part in rescuing Jews. But had the priests and nuns of Europe received in- structions or simply the blessing from their pope to resist the Holo- caust, many more Catholics would have sheltered Jews, and many more Jews would have survived the war as a result. Had the Ger- man episcopacy spoken up against the murder of Jews early on, it is possible that the Holocaust might never have reached its feverish pitch. Pope Pius knew that the wholesale mechanized murder of the European Jews was under way, but he chose to keep that infor- mation largely to himself. Why did he not tell the world? Why did he not even tell his bishops in the countries where roundups were taking place? Was he honoring a covenant of evil reached on the shores of a lake?"

The Pope reached for the pot in the center of the table. When Father Donati leaned forward to help him, he raised his hand, as if to say His Holiness still knew how to pour a cup of tea. He spent a moment reflectively stirring in the milk and sugar before resuming.

"I'm afraid the behavior of Pius is only one aspect of the war that needs examination. We must face the uncomfortable truth that, among Catholics, there were many more killers than there were rescuers. Catholic chaplains ministered to the very German forces committing the slaughter of the Jews. They heard their confessions and provided them the sacrament of Holy Communion. In Vichy

France, Catholic priests actually helped French and German forces round up Jews for deportation and death. In Lithuania, the hierarchy actually forbade priests to rescue Jews. In Slovakia, a country ruled by a priest, the government actually *paid* the Germans to take away their Jews to the death camps. In Catholic Croatia, clergymen actually took part in the killings themselves. A Franciscan nicknamed Brother Satan ran a Croatian concentration camp where twenty thousand Jews were murdered." The Pope paused to sip his tea, as though he needed to remove a bitter taste from his mouth. "We must also face the truth that after the war, the Church sought leniency for the murderers and helped hundreds escape justice altogether."

Shamron stirred restlessly in his seat but said nothing.

"Tomorrow, at the Great Synagogue of Rome, the Catholic Church will begin to confront those questions honestly for the first time."

"Your words are compelling, Your Holiness," said Shamron, "but it might not be safe for you to venture across the river and say them aloud in a synagogue for the world to hear."

"A synagogue is the only place for these words to be spoken—especially the synagogue in the Roman ghetto, where the Jews were rounded up beneath the very windows of the Pope without so much as a murmur of protest. My predecessor went there once to begin this journey. His heart was in the right place, but I'm afraid many segments of the Curia were not with him, and so his journey stopped short of its destination. I will finish it for him, tomorrow, in the place where he started it."

"It appears you have something else in common with your predecessor, Holiness," Shamron said. "There are elements within the Church—quite probably here in Rome—who do not support a candid examination of the Vatican's role in the Holocaust. They have proven themselves willing to commit murder to keep the past a secret, and you should act on the assumption that your life is now in danger as well."

"You're referring to Crux Vera?"

"Does such an organization exist within the Church?"

The Pope and Father Donati exchanged a long look. Then the Pope's gaze settled once more on Shamron. "I'm afraid Crux Vera does indeed exist, Mr. Shamron. The society was allowed to flourish during the thirties and throughout the Cold War because it proved to be an effective weapon in the fight against Bolshevism. Unfortunately, many of the excesses committed in the name of that fight can be laid directly at the feet of Crux Vera and its allies."

"And now that the Cold War is over?" asked Gabriel.

"Crux Vera has adapted with the times. It has proved itself a useful tool for maintaining doctrinal discipline. In Latin America, Crux Vera has battled the adherents of liberation theology, sometimes resorting to ghastly violence to keep rebellious priests in line. It has waged a ceaseless fight against liberalism, relativism, and the tenets of the Second Vatican Council. As a result, many of those inside the Church who support the goals of Crux Vera have turned a blind eye to some of its more unseemly methods."

"Is Crux Vera also engaged in an effort to keep unpleasant Church secrets from coming to light?"

"Without a doubt," answered Father Donati.

"Is Carlo Casagrande a member of Crux Vera?"

"I suppose that in your line of work he would be known as the director of operations."

"Are there other members inside the Vatican itself?"

This time it was the Pope who answered Gabriel's question. "My secretary of state, Cardinal Marco Brindisi, is the leader of Crux Vera," the Pope said gloomily.

"If you know Brindisi and Casagrande are members of Crux Vera, why do you allow them to keep their jobs?"

"Was it not Stalin who said keep your allies close but your enemies closer?" A smile flashed over the Pope's face, then quickly evaporated. "Besides, Cardinal Brindisi is untouchable. If I tried to move against him, his allies in the Curia and the College of Cardinals would revolt and the Church would be hopelessly divided. I'm afraid that, for now, I'm stuck with him and his henchmen."

"Which brings us back to my original point, Holiness. Your security is being handled by men who oppose you and your mission. Under the circumstances, I think it would be wise for you to postpone your visit to the synagogue until a safer moment presents itself."

Then Shamron laid a file on the table and opened it—the dossier on the assassin codenamed the Leopard that he had taken from King Saul Boulevard. "We believe this man is working for Crux Vera. He is without a doubt one of the world's most dangerous assassins. We're virtually certain he was the man who killed Peter Malone in London. We suspect he also killed Benjamin Stern. We must assume that he will now try to kill you."

The Pope looked at the photographs, then at Shamron. "What you must remember, Mr. Shamron, is that I am under the protection of these men wherever I am, inside the Vatican walls or beyond them. The threat to me is the same whether I am standing in the papal apartments or in the Great Synagogue of Rome."

"Point taken, Holiness."

Father Donati leaned forward. "Once the Holy Father steps beyond the walls of the Vatican, onto Italian soil, his security is augmented by Italian police. Thanks to the false papal-assassin plot engineered by Carlo Casagrande, security for tomorrow's event at the synagogue will be unprecedented. We believe that it is safe enough for His Holiness to make the appearance."

"And what if this man is a member of the Pope's security contingent?"

"The Holy Spirit will protect me during this journey," the Pope replied.

"With all due respect, Holiness, I would feel better if someone else was looking over your shoulder as well."

"You have a suggestion, Mr. Shamron?"

"I do, Holiness." Shamron put a rough hand on Gabriel's shoulder. "I'd like Gabriel to accompany you and Father Donati into the synagogue. He's an experienced officer who knows a thing or two about this sort of business."

The Pope looked at Father Donati. "Luigi? Surely, this can be accomplished, can it not?"

"It *can,* Holiness. But there is one problem."

"You're referring to the fact that Carlo Casagrande has portrayed Mr. Allon as a papal assassin?"

"I am, Holiness."

"Obviously, the situation will have to be handled carefully, but if there's one person the Swiss Guards will listen to, it's me." He looked at Shamron. "I will make this pilgrimage to the ghetto as scheduled, and you will be at my side, protecting me, as we should have been at yours sixty years ago. Quite fitting, don't you think, Mr. Shamron?"

Shamron gave a curt nod and an iron smile. Indeed, it was.

TWENTY MINUTES LATER, the arrangements for the morning complete, Father Donati and the Pope left the safe flat and sped along the river toward the Vatican. At St. Anne's Gate, the car braked to a halt. Father Donati lowered his window as a Swiss Guard stepped out of his sentry post.

"Father Donati? What in the world is—"

The guardsman fell silent as Pope Paul VII leaned into view. Then the Swiss Guard snapped to attention.

"Holiness!"

"No one must know about this," the Pope said evenly. "Do you understand me?"

"Of course, Holiness!"

"If you tell anyone—even your superiors—that you've seen me tonight, you'll have to answer to me. And I promise you, it won't be a pleasant experience."

"I won't say a word, Holiness. I swear."

"I hope so, young man—for *your* sake."

The Pope leaned back in his seat. Father Donati raised his window and sped toward the Apostolic Palace. "I'm not sure that poor fellow is ever going to get over that," he said, suppressing laughter.

"Was that really necessary, Luigi?"

"I'm afraid so, Holiness."

"God forgive us," the Pope said. Then he added: "For everything we've done."

"It will all be over soon, Holiness."

"I pray you're right."

·32·

ROME

ERIC LANGE DID NOT sleep well that night. A rare bout of conscience? Nerves? Perhaps it was the furnacelike heat of Katrine's body nestled against him on the tiny cot. Whatever the reason, he awoke at three-thirty and lay there, wide-eyed, Katrine pressing against his ribs, until the first gray shreds of light entered the window of Carlo Casagrande's hateful room.

He swung his legs out of the bed and crept naked across the bare floor to the window, parted the net curtains, and peered down into the street. His motorcycle was there, parked outside the entrance of the tenement house. There were no signs of surveillance. He released the curtain and it fell back into place. Katrine stirred, wrestled with the blanket, then rolled over and slept on.

Lange brewed a pot of espresso on the electric ring and drank several cups before entering the bathroom. He spent the next hour there, carefully grooming and altering his appearance. He darkened his hair with dye, transformed his gray eyes to brown with a pair of contact lenses. Lastly, he added eyeglasses, black-rimmed and cheap-looking, the spectacles of a priest. When he finished, the face staring back at him in the fogged glass was that of a stranger. He compared it to the photograph on the badge Casagrande had prepared for him: *Manfred Beck, Special Investigation Division, Vatican Security Office*. Satisfied, he went back into the main room.

Katrine was still sleeping. Lange padded across the floor, a towel around his waist, and opened the dresser drawer. He slipped on underwear and a pair of the threadbare socks, then went to the closet and opened the door. Black shirt and Roman collar, black trousers, black suit-jacket. Finally, he stepped into the shoes and carefully knotted the laces.

He walked back to the bathroom and stared at himself for a long time in the mirror, slowly transforming himself into the man in the black suit, an actor assuming the role. An assassin, wrapped in a priest's garments; the man he might have been, concealing the man he was. He slipped the Stechkin into the waistband of his trousers and looked at himself one last time. Priest. Revolutionary. Killer. *Which one are you, old man?*

He poured the last of the coffee into a cup and sat down at the edge of the bed. Katrine opened her eyes and recoiled, hands reflexively padding the bedding for a weapon. When Lange gently touched her leg, she froze, a hand over her breast as she tried to gather herself.

"My God, Eric. I didn't recognize you."

"That's the point, my dear." Lange handed her the cup of coffee. "Get dressed, Katrine. We haven't much time."

+ + +

CHIARA WAS brewing coffee in the kitchen of the safe flat when the telephone rang. She recognized the voice of Father Donati.

"I'll be there in a minute or two. Send him down."

Chiara hung up as Gabriel came into the room. He was wearing a gray suit, white shirt, and dark tie, all compliments of Shimon Pazner's Rome station. Chiara brushed a bit of lint from his sleeve.

"You look very handsome." Then she added: "A bit like an undertaker, but handsome."

"Let's hope not. Who was on the phone?"

"Father Donati. He's on his way."

Gabriel swallowed a cup of coffee and pulled on a tan raincoat. Then he kissed Chiara on the cheek and held her in his arms for a moment.

"You will be careful, won't you, Gabriel?"

A car horn sounded outside. When Gabriel tried to pull away, Chiara held him tightly for a moment, refusing to let him leave. When Father Donati honked the horn again, this time with more urgency, she released her hold on him. Gabriel kissed her one last time.

He slipped his Beretta into a shoulder holster and walked downstairs. A gray Fiat sedan with Vatican plates stood outside the entrance. Father Donati sat behind the wheel, dressed in a clerical suit and a black raincoat. Gabriel climbed into the passenger seat and closed the door. Donati turned toward the Tiber embankment.

It was a gray morning, low, dark clouds, a gusty wind making whitecaps on the river. The priest was hunched over the wheel, eyes wide, foot heavy on the accelerator. Gabriel squeezed the armrest, thinking that it was a miracle the Pope had made it back to the Vatican alive last night.

"Drive much, Father Donati?"

"Last night was the first time in about eighteen years."

"I wouldn't have guessed."

"You're a terrible liar, Mr. Allon. I thought people in your line of work were supposed to be good at deception."

"How's the Holy Father this morning?"

"He's quite well, actually. Despite the events of last night, he managed to get a few hours of sleep. He's looking forward to his journey across the river."

"I'll be happy when it's over and he's safely back in the papal apartments."

"That makes two of us."

As they sped along the Tiber, Father Donati briefed Gabriel on the security arrangements. The Pope would travel to the synagogue in his usual armor-plated Mercedes limousine, accompanied by Donati and Gabriel. Immediately surrounding the Pope would be a ring of plainclothes Swiss Guards. As always, Italian police and security forces would provide a second cordon of protection. The route from the Vatican to the old ghetto would be lined by *carabinieri* traffic units and closed to all other traffic.

The square dome of the Great Synagogue rose before them, a towering structure of pale gray stone and aluminum, Persian and Babylonian in its architectural design. The extreme height of the structure, coupled with its unique façade, made it stand out from the surrounding ocher-colored baroque buildings. The effect was intentional. The community that built the synagogue a hundred years earlier had wished to make it easily visible to the men on the other side of the Tiber—the men behind the ancient walls of the Vatican.

A hundred meters from the synagogue, they came to a police

checkpoint. Father Donati lowered his window, flashed his Vatican identification, and exchanged a few words in Italian with an officer. A moment later, they pulled into the courtyard at the front of the synagogue and braked to a halt. Before Father Donati could shut down the engine, they were set upon by a *carabiniere* with an automatic weapon slung over his shoulder. Gabriel liked what he saw so far.

They climbed out of the Fiat. Gabriel could not help but feel the shadow of history hanging over the place. Rome was the oldest Diaspora settlement in Western Europe, and Jews had been living in its center for more than two thousand years. They had come to this place long before the fisherman named Peter from the Galilee. They had seen the assassination of Caesar, witnessed the rise of Christianity and the fall of the Roman empire. Vilified by popes as murderers of God, they had been ghettoized on the banks of the Tiber, humiliated, and ritually degraded. And on a night in October 1943, a thousand were rounded up and sent to the gas chambers and ovens of Auschwitz, while a pope on the other side of the river said nothing. In a few hours' time, Pope Paul VII, a witness to the sins of the men in the Vatican, would come here to atone for the past. *If he lives long enough to accomplish his mission.*

Father Donati seemed to sense Gabriel's thoughts, for he placed a hand gently on his shoulder and pointed toward the river. "The protesters will be kept behind barricades over there, next to the embankment."

"Protesters?"

"We're not expecting anything terribly large. Just the usual lot." Donati shrugged helplessly. "The birth-control crowd. Women in the priesthood. Gays and lesbians. That sort of thing."

They climbed the steps of the synagogue and went inside. Fa-

ther Donati seemed perfectly at ease. He sensed Gabriel was looking at him, and he smiled confidently in response.

"When we were still in Venice, it was my job to build better relations between the patriarch and the Jewish community there. I'm
quite comfortable in a synagogue, Mr. Allon."

"I can see that," Gabriel said. "Tell me how the ceremony will
unfold."

The papal procession would form at the entrance of the synagogue, Father Donati explained. The Pope would walk up the center aisle accompanied by the chief rabbi, and take a seat next to him
in a gilded chair on the *bimah*. Father Donati and Gabriel would
trail the Holy Father during the walk to the front of the synagogue,
then take their position in a special VIP section, a few feet from the
Pope. The chief rabbi would make a few introductory remarks, then
the Holy Father would speak. In a break with usual protocol, an advance text of the Pope's remarks would not be released to the Vatican
press corps. The speech was bound to provoke an immediate reaction among the reporters, but no one would be permitted to leave
their seat until the Pope had completed his remarks and left the
synagogue.

Gabriel and the priest walked to the front of the synagogue, the
spot where they would be standing during the Pope's remarks. A
carabiniere with a bomb-sniffing dog straining at its leash was making steady progress up the left side of the hall. A second dog team
was working the opposite side. A few meters from the *bimah,* a handful of television cameramen were setting up their equipment on a
raised platform under the watchful gaze of an armed security man.

"What about the other entrances to the synagogue, Father
Donati?"

"They've all been sealed. There's only one way in and out now, and that's the main entrance." Donati looked at his watch. "I'm afraid we haven't much time, Mr. Allon. If you're satisfied, we should be getting back to the Vatican."

"Let's go."

FATHER DONATI waved his Vatican ID badge at the Swiss Guard standing watch at St. Anne's Gate. Before the guard could question the identity of the man in the passenger seat, the priest pushed his foot to the floor and sped along the Via Belvedere toward the Apostolic Palace.

Father Donati left the car in the San Damaso Courtyard, hustled Gabriel around the security checkpoints, and headed upstairs toward the papal apartments. Gabriel's feet felt light on the marble floor, his pulse quickened. He thought of Shamron, standing in the half-light of the Campo di Ghetto Nuovo, summoning him to find the men who had murdered Benjamin Stern. Now his search had brought him here, to the epicenter of the Roman Catholic Church.

At the entrance to the papal apartments, they slipped past a Swiss Guard and went inside. Father Donati led him into the study, where the Pope was seated at his desk, working through a stack of morning correspondence. He looked up at Gabriel as he entered the room and smiled warmly.

"Mr. Allon, so good of you to come." With the tip of his pen, he pointed toward the seating area next to the fireplace. "Please make yourself comfortable. Father Donati and I have a few things to attend to before we leave."

Gabriel did as the Pope instructed. He reached into the breast pocket of his jacket and removed the photographs of the assassin known as the Leopard. Gabriel started from the beginning and worked his way forward. In each picture, the assassin looked re-markably different. Some of the changes had been achieved through plastic surgery, others through more prosaic means, such as hats, wigs, and eyewear.

Gabriel returned the photographs to his pocket and looked across the study toward the little man in white, hunched over a stack of papers at his desk. He felt his spirits sink. If the Leopard had come to Rome to kill the Pope, it would be almost impossible to stop him. And based on the photographs in his pocket, Gabriel was quite cer-tain he would never see him coming.

LANGE SANITIZED the flat while Katrine showered and dressed. With a wet cloth, he meticulously wiped down every sur-face that he had touched in the room. Doorknobs, the dresser top, bathroom fixtures, the electric ring, the coffee pot. Then he placed his extra clothing in a plastic rubbish bag, along with his toiletries. Satisfied that he had erased every trace of himself from the flat, he sat on the edge of the bed, careful not to touch anything.

Katrine came out of the bathroom. She wore blue jeans, lace-up leather boots, and a bomber-style jacket. Her hair was pulled back tightly against her scalp, her eyes covered by a pair of sunglasses. She looked very beautiful. The average *carabiniere* would find her ter-ribly distracting. Lange was counting on that.

He stood up, slipped the Stechkin into his trousers, and buttoned his jacket. Then he pulled on a cheap black nylon raincoat, the kind worn by half the clerics in Rome, and picked up the bag of rubbish.

They walked downstairs. Lange held the rubbish bag in one hand, and with the other he drew the collar of his raincoat tight to conceal the clerical suit underneath.

Outside, he mounted the motorcycle and started the engine. Katrine climbed on the back and wrapped her arms around his waist. He eased forward, turned the bike east toward the ancient center of Rome, and opened the throttle. Along the way he dropped the keys to the flat down a sewer. The bag of rubbish he handed to a garbage collector, who tossed it into the back of his truck and wished Lange a pleasant morning.

·33·

VATICAN CITY

THE POPE WAS SCHEDULED to begin his remarks at eleven A.M. At ten-thirty, he left the papal study, accompanied by Father Donati and Gabriel. In the hall outside the papal apartments, they encountered a detail of plainclothes Swiss Guard. The chief of the detail was a towering Helvetian named Karl Brunner. This was the moment Gabriel was dreading most, his first confrontation with the Swiss Catholic noblemen sworn to lay down their lives if necessary to protect the Pope.

When Brunner spotted Gabriel, his hand slipped inside the jacket of his blue suit and came out with a pistol. He rushed forward, pushing the Pope aside with a sweeping forearm, and seized Gabriel by the throat. Gabriel fought every survival instinct and allowed himself to be brought down by the Swiss Guard. Not that there was much he could do about it. Karl Brunner outweighed him by at least fifty pounds and was built like a rugby player. The hand around

Gabriel's throat was like a steel vise. He landed on his back, with Brunner falling on his chest. He kept his hands in plain sight and allowed the security man to tear the Beretta from his shoulder holster. Brunner tossed the gun away and pointed his own weapon at Gabriel's face while two other members of the detail pinned Gabriel firmly to the floor.

The rest of the detail had formed a protective cocoon around the Pope and was hustling him down the corridor. He ordered them to release him, then hurried to Karl Brunner's side. Brunner pushed the Pope away and shouted at him to get back.

"Let him up, Karl," the Pope said.

Brunner got to his feet while his two men kept Gabriel pinned to the floor. He reached into his pocket and produced a copy of the security alert with Gabriel's photograph and held it up for the Pope to see.

"He's an assassin, Holiness. He's come here to kill you."

"He's a friend, and he's come here to protect me. It's all a misunderstanding. Father Donati will explain everything. Trust me, Karl. Let him up."

THE MOTORCADE sped through St. Anne's Gate, then turned into the Via della Conciliazione for the run to the river. The Pope closed his eyes. Gabriel looked at Father Donati, who leaned over and whispered into Gabriel's ear that His Holiness always passed the time in motorcades by praying.

A motorcycle outrider moved into position a few feet from the Pope's window. Gabriel looked carefully at his face, at the hinge of his jaw and the shape of the cheekbones showing beneath the visor. Mentally, he compared the features to those of the man in the photographs, as if he were authenticating a painting, comparing the brushstrokes of a master to those in a newly discovered work. The faces were similar enough to make Gabriel reach into his jacket and put his hand on the butt of his Beretta. Father Donati noticed this. The Pope, who was still praying with his eyes tightly closed, was oblivious.

As the motorcade turned onto the Lungotevere, the outrider dropped back a few meters. Gabriel felt his tension subside. The street had been cleared of traffic, and there were only a few knots of onlookers here and there along the river. Evidently, the sight of a papal motorcade in this part of Rome did not arouse much interest.

The journey passed quickly: three minutes by Gabriel's calculation. The dome of the synagogue appeared before them, and soon they were rushing past the mob of protesters. The motorcade stopped in the front courtyard. Gabriel stepped out of the car first, blocking the half-open door with his body. The chief rabbi stood on the steps of the synagogue, flanked by a delegation from Rome's Jewish community. Around the limousine stood the security men: Italian and Vatican, some plainclothes, some in uniform. To the right of the steps, the Vatican press corps strained against a yellow rope. The air was filled with the rumble of the motorcycles.

Gabriel scanned the faces of the security men, then the reporters and photographers. A dozen might have been the assassin in disguise. He poked his head into the back of the car and looked at Father Donati. "This is the part that worries me most. Let's be quick about it." When he stood upright, he found himself staring into the bluff face of Karl Brunner.

"This part is my job," Brunner said. "Step out of the way."

Gabriel did as he was told. Brunner helped the Pope out of the car. The rest of the Swiss Guard detail closed in. Gabriel found himself in a sea of dark suits, the Pope, clad in his sparkling white cassock, clearly visible in the center.

The motorcycles went silent. On the steps of the synagogue, the Pope embraced the chief rabbi and a few of the delegates. It was quiet, except for the distant chanting of the protesters and the cicada-like whirring of the news cameras. Gabriel stood behind Karl Brunner, whose left hand was resting on the small of the Pope's back. Gabriel looked around him, eyes alert, searching for anything out of the ordinary. A man pushing his way forward. An arm swinging upward.

There was a commotion behind them. Gabriel turned in time to see a trio of *carabinieri* wrestling a man to the ground, but it was only a protester carrying a sign that read FREE CHINESE CATHOLICS!

The Pope turned around as well. At that instant Gabriel caught his eye. "Please go inside, Holiness," Gabriel murmured. "There are too many people out here."

The Pope nodded and turned to his host. "Well, Rabbi, shall we get on with it?"

"Yes, Your Holiness. Please, come inside. Let me show you *our* place of worship."

The rabbi led the Pope up the stairs. A moment later, much to the relief of Gabriel and Father Donati, the leader of the world's one billion Catholics was safely inside the synagogue.

AT THE entrance to St. Peter's Square, Eric Lange climbed off the motorbike. Katrine slid forward, taking hold of the handlebars. Lange turned and started walking.

The square was filled with pilgrims and tourists. *Carabinieri* paced the edge of the colonnade. Lange headed toward the Apostolic Palace, his walk crisp and purposeful, his pace quick but controlled. Passing the towering Egyptian obelisk, he drew several long breaths to slow his heart rate.

A few paces from the palace, a *carabiniere* stepped in his path.

"Where do you think you're going?" he asked Lange in Italian, staring at him with a pair of stubborn brown eyes.

"*Portone di Bronzo,*" Lange replied.

"You have an appointment inside?"

Lange removed his wallet and flashed the identification badge. The *carabiniere* took a step backward. "I'm sorry, Father Beck. I didn't realize."

Lange put the wallet away. "Tell me your name, young man."

"It's Mateo Galeazzi."

Lange looked directly into the policeman's eyes. "I'll be sure to put in a good word for you inside. I know General Casagrande will be pleased to know that the *carabinieri* are maintaining good order out here in the square."

"Thank you, Father."

The *carabiniere* actually dipped his head and held out his hand for Father Beck to proceed. Lange almost felt sorry for the boy. In a few minutes, he would be on his knees, begging forgiveness for allowing an assassin to enter the palace.

At the Bronze Doors, Lange was stopped again, this time by a Swiss Guard in full Renaissance regalia, a dark-blue cloak draped over his shoulders. Once again, Lange produced the ID badge. The Swiss Guard ordered Lange to register with the officer at the permission desk, just inside the door to the right. There, Lange presented his identification to another Swiss Guard.

"Who are you here to see?"

"That's none of your business," Lange said coldly. "This is a security review. If you feel it's necessary, you may tell Casagrande that I have entered the palace. If you tell anyone else—such as your friends who are standing watch at the moment—I'll deal with you personally."

The Swiss Guard swallowed hard and nodded. Lange turned around. The Scala Regia rose grandly before him, lit by vast iron lamps. Lange climbed the stairs slowly, like a man performing a job he secretly loathed. He paused once to look down at the permission desk, where the Swiss Guard was eyeing him intently. At the top of the stairs, he came to a set of glass doors and was challenged again. Before the Swiss Guard could say a word, Lange had his badge out. The guard took one look at it and nearly tripped over himself to get out of the way.

Amazing, Lange thought. Casagrande's scheme was working better than he imagined possible.

Next he found himself in a gloomy interior courtyard known as the Cortile di San Damaso. Above him soared the loggias of the Apostolic Palace itself. He passed beneath a stone archway, came to a staircase, and climbed quickly upward, footsteps echoing on the marble. Along the way, he passed three more Swiss Guards, but there were no more challenges. This deep inside the palace, Lange's clerical suit and Roman collar were identification enough.

On the top floor, he came to the entrance of the papal apartments. A Swiss Guard stood there, halberd in hand, blocking Lange's path. Lange held the ID badge in front of his face.

"I need to see Father Donati."

"He's not here at the moment."

"Where is he?"

"He's with the Holy Father." He hesitated, then added: "At the synagogue."

"Ah, yes, of course. I'm sure Father Donati would appreciate knowing that you told a complete stranger his whereabouts."

"I'm sorry, Father, but you—"

Lange cut him off. "I need to leave something for Father Donati. Can you take me to his office?"

"As you know, Father Beck, I'm not allowed to leave this post under any circumstances."

"Very good," Lange said with a conciliatory smile. "At least you got *something* right. Please point me in the direction of the good father's office."

The Swiss Guard hesitated for a moment, unsure of himself, then told Lange the way. The papal apartments were deserted but for a single nun in gray habit, busy with a feather duster. She smiled at Lange as he walked past the entrance to Father Donati's office and entered the next room.

He closed the door behind him and stood for a moment while his eyes adjusted to the gloom. The heavy curtains were drawn, obscuring the view of St. Peter's Square, and the room was in deep shadow. Lange moved forward, across the simple Oriental carpet, toward the wooden desk. He stood next to the high-backed chair and ran his palm over the pale plush covering while he surveyed the desk. It was too simple for so powerful a man. Too severe. A blotter, a cylindrical container for his pens, a pad of lined paper for jotting down his thoughts. A white telephone with an old-fashioned rotary dial. Looking up, he noticed a painting of the Madonna. She seemed to be peering at Lange through the shadows.

He reached into the breast pocket of his clerical suit, removed an envelope, and dropped it on the blotter. It landed with a muffled metallic thump. He took one last look around the study, turned, and walked quickly out.

At the entrance of the *appartamento,* he paused to glare sternly at the Swiss Guard. "You'll be hearing from me," Lange snapped, then he turned and disappeared down the corridor.

THE DESK in the office of Secretary of State Marco Brindisi was quite different from the austere one in the papal study. It was a large Renaissance affair with carved legs and gold inlay. Those who stood before it tended to be uncomfortable, which suited Brindisi's purposes nicely.

At the moment, he sat alone, fingers formed into a bridge, eyes focused somewhere in the middle distance. A few minutes earlier, from his window overlooking St. Peter's Square, he had seen the Pope's motorcade speeding toward the river along the Via della Conciliazione. By now he was probably inside the synagogue.

The cardinal's gaze settled on the bank of television screens on the wall opposite his desk. His goal was to restore the Church to the power it had enjoyed during the Middle Ages, but Marco Brindisi was very much a man of the modern age. Gone were the days when Vatican bureaucrats wrote their memoranda on parchment with quill and ink. Brindisi had spent untold millions upgrading the machinery of the Vatican Secretariat of State in order to make the bureaucracy of the Church run more like the nerve center of a modern nation. He tuned the television to BBC International. A flood in Bangladesh, thousands killed, hundreds of thousands homeless. He jotted a minute to himself to make a suitable donation through Vatican charitable organizations to ease the suffering in any way possible. He switched on a second television and tuned it to RAI, the main Italian network. The third television he set to CNN International.

He had made good on his threat not to accompany the Pope on this disgraceful journey. As a result he was now supposed to be working on a benign-sounding letter of resignation, one that would cause the Holy See no embarrassment and raise no uncomfortable questions for the rabble in the Vatican press corps to ponder in their infantile columns. Had he any intention of resigning, his letter would have stressed a deep desire to return to pastoral duties, to tend to a flock, to baptize the young and anoint the sick. Any *Vaticanisti* with a bit of intelligence would recognize such a letter as deception on a grand scale. Marco Brindisi had been raised, educated, and nurtured to wield bureaucratic power within the Curia. The notion that he would willingly yield his authority was patently absurd. No one would believe such a letter, and the cardinal had no intention of writing it. Besides, he thought, the man who had ordered him to write it did not have long to live.

Had he started a letter of resignation, it would have raised uncomfortable questions in the days after the Pope's assassination. Had the two most powerful men in the Church experienced a falling out in recent weeks? Did the Cardinal Secretary of State have something to gain by the Pope's death? No letter of resignation, no questions. Indeed, thanks to a series of well-placed leaks, Cardinal Brindisi would be portrayed as the Pope's closest friend and confidant in the Curia, a man who admired the Pope immensely and was much beloved in return. These press clippings would capture the attention of the cardinals when they gathered for the next conclave. So would Marco Brindisi's smooth and adept handling of Church affairs in the traumatic days after the Pope's assassination. At such a time, the conclave would be reluctant to turn to an outsider. A man of the Curia would be the next pope, and the Curial candidate of choice would be Secretary of State Marco Brindisi.

His dreamlike trance was shattered by an image on RAI: Pope Paul VII, entering the Great Synagogue of Rome. Brindisi saw a different image: Beckett standing on his altar at Canterbury. The murder of a meddlesome priest.

Send forth your knights, Carlo. Cut him down.

Cardinal Marco Brindisi turned up the volume and waited for news of a pope's death.

· 34 ·

ROME

THE ROME CENTRAL SYNAGOGUE: Eastern and ornate, stirring in restless anticipation. Gabriel took his place at the front of the synagogue, his right shoulder facing the *bimah,* his hands behind his back, pressed against the cool marble wall. Father Donati stood next to him, tense and irritable. The vantage point provided him perfect sightlines around the interior of the chamber. A few feet away sat a group of Curial cardinals, dazzling in crimson cassocks, listening intently as the chief rabbi made his introductory remarks. Just beyond the cardinals stirred the fidgety denizens of the Vatican press corps. The head of the press office, Rudolf Gertz, appeared nauseated. The rest of the seats were filled with ordinary members of Rome's Jewish community. As the Pope finally rose to speak, a palpable sense of electricity filled the hall.

Gabriel resisted the temptation to look at him. Instead, his eyes scanned the synagogue, looking for someone or something that seemed out of place. Karl Brunner, standing a few feet from Gabriel, was doing the same thing. Their eyes met briefly. Brunner, Gabriel decided, was no threat to the Pope.

The Pope expressed his gratitude to the rabbi and the community at large for inviting him to speak here this day. Then he remarked on the beauty of the synagogue and of the Jewish faith, stressing the common heritage of Christians and Jews. In a term borrowed from his predecessor, he referred to Jews as the elder brothers of Roman Catholics. It is a special relationship, this bond between siblings, the Pope said—one that can pull apart if not tended to properly. Too often over the past two thousand years, the siblings had quarreled, with disastrous consequences for the Jewish people. He spoke without a text or notes. His audience was spellbound.

"In April 1986, my predecessor, Pope John Paul the Second, came to this synagogue to bridge the divide between our two communities and to begin a process of healing. Over these past years, much has been accomplished." The Pope paused for a moment, the silence hanging heavy in the hall. "But much work remains to be done."

A round of warm applause swept over the synagogue. The cardinals joined in. Father Donati elbowed Gabriel and leaned close to his ear. "Watch them," he said, pointing to the men in red. "We'll see if they're clapping in a few minutes."

But Gabriel kept his eyes on the crowd as the Pope resumed. "My brothers and sisters, God took John Paul from us before he could complete his work. I intend to continue where he left off. I intend to shoulder his burden and carry it home for him."

Again the Pope was interrupted by applause. *How brilliant,* Gabriel thought. He was portraying his initiative as merely a continuation of the Pole's legacy rather than something radically new.

Gabriel realized that the man who liked to portray himself as a simple Venetian priest was a shrewd tactician and political operator.

"The first steps of the journey of reconciliation were easy compared with the difficult ones that lie before us. The last steps will be hardest of all. Along the way, we may be tempted to turn back. We must not. We must complete this journey, for Catholics and Jews alike."

Father Donati touched Gabriel's arm. "Here we go."

"In both our religions, we believe that forgiveness does not come easily. We Roman Catholics must make an honest confession if we are to receive absolution. If we have murdered a man, we cannot confess to taking the Lord's name in vain and expect to be forgiven." The Pope smiled, and laughter rippled through the synagogue. Gabriel noticed that several of the cardinals seemed not to find the remark humorous. "On Yom Kippur, the Jewish day of atonement, Jews must seek out those they have wronged, make an honest confession of sin, and seek forgiveness. We Catholics must do the same. But if we are to make an honest confession of sin, we must first know the truth. That is why I am here today."

The Pope paused for a moment. Gabriel could see him looking at Father Donati, as if gathering strength, as if saying there was no turning back now. Father Donati nodded, and the Pope turned once more to the audience. Gabriel did the same thing, but for a very different reason. He was looking for a man with a gun.

"This morning, in this magnificent synagogue, I am announcing a new review of the Church's relationship with the Jewish people and the Church's actions during the Second World War, the darkest period in Jewish history, the time in which six million were lost to the fires of the Shoah. Unlike previous examinations of this

terrible time, *all* relevant documents contained in the Vatican Secret Archives, regardless of their age, will be made available to a
panel of scholars for review and evaluation."

The Vatican press corps was in tumult. A few of the reporters
were whispering into cellular phones; the rest were scribbling wildly
on notepads. Rudolf Gertz sat with his arms folded and his chin
resting on his chest. Evidently, His Holiness had neglected to tell
his chief spokesman that he intended to make a bit of news today.
The Pope had already entered uncharted territory. Now he was
about to go even further.

"The Holocaust was not a Catholic crime," he resumed, "but far
too many Catholics, lay and religious alike, took part in the murder
of Jews for us to ignore. We must acknowledge this sin, and we
must beg forgiveness."

There was no applause now, just stunned and reverential silence.
To Gabriel, it seemed that no one seated in the synagogue could
believe that words such as these were being spoken by a Roman
pontiff.

"The Holocaust was not a Catholic crime, but the Church sowed
the seeds of the poisonous vine known as anti-Semitism and provided the water and nourishment those seeds needed to take root
and thrive in Europe. We must acknowledge this sin, and we must
beg forgiveness."

Gabriel thought he could detect unrest among the cardinals. Dark
looks, heads shaking, shoulders rising and falling. He looked at Father Donati and whispered, "Which one is Cardinal Brindisi?"

The priest shook his head. "He's not here today."

"Why not?"

"He said he was under the weather. Truth is, he'd rather be
burned at the stake than listen to this speech."

The Pope pressed on. "The Church could not have halted the Shoah, but it is quite possible we could have lessened its severity for many more Jews. We should have put geopolitical interests aside and shouted our condemnation from the top of our mighty basilica. We should have excommunicated those members of our Church who were among the murderers and the enablers. After the war, we should have spent more time caring for the victims instead of tending to the perpetrators, many of whom found sanctuary in this blessed city on their way to exile in distant lands."

The Pope spread his arms wide. "For these sins, and others soon to be revealed, we offer our confession, and we beg your forgiveness. There are no words to describe the depth of our grief. In your hour of greatest need, when the forces of Nazi Germany pulled you from your houses in the very streets surrounding this synagogue, you cried out for help, but your pleas were met by silence. And so today, as I plead for forgiveness, I will do it in the same manner. In silence."

Pope Paul VII lowered his head, folded his hands beneath his pectoral cross, and closed his eyes. Gabriel looked at the Pope in disbelief, then glanced around the synagogue. He was not alone. Mouths hung open throughout the audience, including the usually cynical press corps. Two of the cardinals had joined the Pope in prayer, but the rest seemed as stunned as everyone else.

For Gabriel, the sight of the Pope in silent prayer on the altar of the synagogue meant something else. He had spoken. His initiative could not be undone, even if he were not alive to see it through. If Crux Vera had intended to kill him, they would have done so *before* he made his remarks. Killing him after the fact would only make him a martyr. The Pope was safe, at least for the time being. Gabriel had only one concern now—getting him safely back inside the papal apartments.

A movement caught Gabriel's eye—an arm in motion—but it was only Karl Brunner, raising his right hand and touching his earpiece. Immediately his demeanor changed. His shoulders squared, and he seemed to be leaning forward on the balls of his feet. Blood rushed to his face, and his eyes were suddenly alive and on the move. He raised his wrist to his lips and mouthed a few words into the microphone concealed in his shirt cuff. Then he took a quick step toward Father Donati.

The priest leaned forward and said, "Is something wrong, Karl?"

"There's an intruder at the Vatican."

AFTER LEAVING the papal apartments, Eric Lange walked downstairs one level to the office of the Vatican Secretary of State. In the antechamber he encountered Father Mascone, Cardinal Brindisi's trusted private secretary.

Lange said, "I'd like to see the cardinal, please."

"That's impossible." Father Mascone shuffled some papers and bristled visibly. "Just who in God's name do you think you are marching in here and making demands like that?"

Lange reached into his pocket and in a fluid motion withdrew the silenced Stechkin. Father Mascone murmured, "Mother Mary, pray for me."

Lange shot him through the center of the forehead and walked quickly around the desk.

GABRIEL AND Father Donati scampered down the steps of the synagogue. The papal limousine stood outside, glistening from a light drizzle, surrounded by several *carabinieri* straddling idle motorcycles. Father Donati approached the closest officer and said, "There's an emergency at the Vatican. We need a motorbike."

The *carabiniere* shook his head. "I can't, Father Donati. It's completely against regulations. I could be fired if I let you take my motorcycle."

Gabriel put a hand on the officer's shoulder. In Italian, he said: "*Il papa* has personally dispatched us on this mission. Do you really wish to refuse a direct request from His Holiness?"

The *carabiniere* quickly dismounted the motorcycle.

Gabriel took the handlebars and swung his leg over the saddle. Father Donati climbed on the back.

"Can you drive one of these things?"

"Hold on."

Gabriel turned onto the deserted Lungotevere and opened the throttle full. As he raced north toward the Vatican, he could hear Father Donati reciting the Lord's Prayer in his ear.

MARCO BRINDISI stood in the center of the room before a bank of television screens. His arms were spread wide, his palms were open, his face seemed to have drained of blood. In his rage, the red zucchetto had fallen from his pate and lay on the carpet at his feet.

"Will no one silence this heretic?" the cardinal screamed. "Damn you, Carlo! Cut him down! Where is your man?"

"I'm right here," Eric Lange said calmly.

Cardinal Brindisi turned his head a few degrees and took note of the man in a humble clerical suit who had slipped silently into his office.

"Who are you?"

Lange's arm swung up, the Stechkin in his hand.

"Would you like to make a last confession, Eminence?"

The cardinal narrowed his eyes. "May the fires of hell consume your soul."

He closed his eyes and prepared himself for death.

Lange indulged him.

He pulled the trigger three times in rapid succession. The Stechkin spit fire but emitted no sound. Three shots struck the cardinal in the chest, forming a perfect triangle over his heart.

As the cardinal collapsed onto his back, Lange stepped forward and stared into the lifeless eyes. He placed the tip of the silencer against the prelate's temple and fired one last shot.

Then he turned and walked calmly out.

· 35 ·

VATICAN CITY

I T T O O K T H R E E M I N U T E S for Gabriel to reach the entrance of St. Peter's Square. As he skidded to a halt at the metal barricades, a startled *carabiniere* leveled his automatic weapon and braced himself for assault. Father Donati waved his Vatican badge.

"Put your gun down, you idiot! I'm Luigi Donati, the Pope's private secretary. We have an emergency. Move the barricade!"

"But—"

"Move it! *Now!*"

The *carabiniere* lifted a section of the barricade, creating a passage wide enough for a motorcycle. Gabriel nosed through and started across the crowded square. Startled tourists leapt out of the way to safety, screaming insults at him in a half-dozen languages.

By the time they reached the Bronze Doors, the Swiss Guard had dispensed with his halberd and was holding a Beretta pistol in his outstretched hands. He lowered the gun when he saw that it truly was Father Donati on the back of the motorcycle.

"We were told there was an intruder," Donati said.

The Swiss Guard nodded. "Now there's been a report of a shooting inside the palace."

In another life, Father Luigi Donati must have been a track star or a footballer. With his long legs and lean build, he bounded up staircases three steps at a time and charged down hallways like a sprinter hurtling toward the finish line. Gabriel was doing all he could do just to keep the cleric in sight.

It took less than two minutes to reach Cardinal Brindisi's apartment on the second floor of the palace. Several Swiss Guards were already there, along with a trio of Curial priests. The body of Father Mascone was slumped over the desk in the antechamber in a pool of blood.

"My God, but this thing has gone too far," murmured Father Donati. Then he bent over the body of the dead priest and administered last rites.

Gabriel entered the study and found a nun bowed over the body of Cardinal Brindisi. Father Donati followed a moment later, his face ashen. He walked wearily across the room, then collapsed to the floor next to the nun, oblivious to the fact that he was kneeling in blood.

FROM HER position at the end of the colonnade, Katrine Boussard had seen everything: the arrival of the two men on motorcycle, the confrontation between the *carabiniere* and the priest who claimed to be the Pope's secretary, the mad race across the square. Clearly they knew something was taking place inside the palace. She started the engine, gazed across the square toward the Bronze Doors, and waited.

LANGE'S HOPES of slipping quietly out of the Vatican were all but gone. The entrance hall of the palace was filled with Swiss Guards and Vatican police, and it appeared as though the Bronze Doors had been sealed. Obviously someone had ignored his warnings and sounded an alarm. Lange would have to use other means of escaping. In a hasty attempt to alter his appearance, he removed his eyeglasses and shoved them into his pocket. Then he headed calmly toward the Bronze Doors.

A Swiss Guard put a hand on his chest. "No one in or out for the time being."

"I'm afraid I can't be detained," Lange said calmly. "I need to leave at once for a pressing appointment."

"Orders are orders, Monsignor. There's been a shooting. No one can leave."

"A shooting? In the Vatican? Dear God."

For the benefit of the Swiss Guard, Lange made the sign of the cross before reaching inside the jacket of his clerical suit and drawing the Stechkin. The Swiss Guard fumbled in his Renaissance costume, trying desperately to remove his own weapon, but before he could bring it into play Lange shot him twice in the chest.

A scream filled the hall as Lange lunged toward the Bronze Doors. A Swiss Guard stepped into his path, a Beretta in his outstretched hands. He hesitated; Lange was surrounded by shouting clerics and Vatican bureaucrats. The man who spent eight hours a day holding a halberd didn't have the nerve to fire into a crowd and risk innocent casualties. Lange had no such worries. The Stechkin swung up, and he blew the Swiss Guard from his feet.

Lange sprinted through the Bronze Doors. A *carabiniere* walked toward him, gun leveled on his hip, shouting at him in Italian to lay down his weapon. Lange turned and fired. The *carabiniere* fell to the paving stones of St. Peter's.

What he saw next was something out of his nightmares: a half dozen *carabinieri,* running across the square directly toward him, automatic weapons drawn. There would be no shooting his way out of this. *Come on, Katrine. Where are you?*

Standing a few feet away was a woman, an American girl by the look of her, about twenty-five years old, too terrified to move. Lange closed the distance between himself and the girl in three powerful strides, then seized her hair and pulled her to his body. The *carabinieri* skidded to a stop. Lange placed his Stechkin against the side of the girl's head and started dragging her across the square.

GABRIEL HEARD screaming outside the window of Cardinal Brindisi's office. He parted the heavy curtains and looked down. The square was in turmoil: *carabinieri* running with weapons drawn, tourists scurrying for cover in the colonnade. And walking across the center of the square was a man in a clerical suit, holding a gun to the head of a woman.

KATRINE BOUSSARD saw him too, though from a different vantage point: her position at the end of Bernini's Colonnade. As the square erupted into chaos, the *carabiniere* who had opened the barricade to the two men on motorcycle left his position and ran toward the palace. Katrine kicked the bike into gear and rolled forward, then she turned through the gap in the fence and started across the square.

Lange saw her coming. When she was a few feet away he pushed the American girl to the ground, climbed on the bike in front of Katrine took hold of the handlebars, then turned the bike around and headed for the edge of St. Peter's Square. A *carabiniere* was sprinting along the barricade, trying to close the breach before the bike arrived. Lange took aim and squeezed off the last two rounds in his magazine. The *carabiniere* tumbled to the pavement.

Lange sped through the opening in the barricade and leaned the bike south. A moment later, they were gone.

ST. PETER'S SQUARE was in chaos. Clearly, the first priority of the police would be to secure the area and tend to the victims rather than pursue the man who had wreaked the havoc. Gabriel knew it would take only a matter of seconds for a trained professional to disappear into the labyrinth of Rome. Indeed, he had done it once himself. In a moment, the Leopard, the man who had murdered Benjamin and countless others, would be gone forever.

The motorcycle Gabriel and Father Donati had ridden from the synagogue was where they had left it, resting on its kickstand a few meters from the Bronze Doors. Gabriel still had the keys in his pocket. He climbed into the saddle and roared across the square.

Rounding the end of the colonnade, he turned right, as the assassin had done, and was immediately confronted with a decision. He could continue along the perimeter of the city state or turn to the left, toward the southern end of the sprawling Janiculum Park. As Gabriel slowed to make his decision, a tourist with a camera around his neck stepped forward and shouted at him in French: "Are you looking for the priest with a gun?"

The Frenchman pointed down the Borgo Santo Spirito, a narrow cobbled street lined with Vatican office buildings and souvenir shops selling religious articles. Gabriel turned left and opened the throttle. It made sense. If the assassin followed this route of escape, he could disappear into the open spaces of the park. From there he could make his way to the tangled streets of Trastevere in a matter of minutes. From Trastevere he could cross the river to the residential districts of the Aventine Hill.

After a hundred meters, Gabriel banked to the right and sped along the façade of a dusty palazzo. He came to a busy piazza near the river, swerved to the right, and headed up an access ramp leading into the park. At the top of the ramp was a traffic circle outside the entrance of an underground bus terminal. Gabriel thought he saw the assassin for the first time, a motorcyclist dressed in black, with a female passenger on the back. The bike accelerated around the circle and disappeared into the park. Gabriel sped after it.

The roadway was lined with broad gravel walkways and towering umbrella pine. It ran along the spine of the hill and rose gradually, so that after a few seconds Gabriel felt as though he was floating above the city. As he neared the Piazzale Garibaldi, he saw a flash in the heavy traffic, a motorcycle knifing dangerously between cars, a man in black at the handlebars. Entering the chaos of the massive piazzale, Gabriel briefly lost sight of the bike; then he spotted it again, turning onto a smaller road that led down the hill toward Trastevere. Gabriel leaned the bike hard and fought his way through the traffic, ignorning the symphony of horns and curses, and followed after him.

The descent out of the park was a steep series of switchbacks and hairpin turns. The *carabinieri* motorcycle had more power than the assassin's, and Gabriel did not have the added weight and balance problems of a passenger. He closed the distance quickly, and was soon about thirty meters behind.

Gabriel reached inside his coat and drew the Beretta. He maneuvered the weapon into his left hand and twisted hard on the throttle with his right. The bike roared forward. The woman glanced over her shoulder, then turned and took awkward aim at him with an automatic pistol.

Gabriel barely heard the sound of the shots over the drone of the motorcycles. One of the rounds pierced the windscreen. The bike bucked from the impact. Gabriel's hand slipped from the throttle. The Leopard began to pull away. Gabriel managed to get his hand back on the throttle. With agonizing slowness, he gradually closed the gap.

LANGE TOOK his eyes off the street long enough to glance into his rearview mirror at the man pursuing him. Dark hair, olive skin, narrow features, a look of sheer determination in his eyes. Was he Gabriel Allon? The agent codenamed Sword who had coldly walked into a villa in Tunis and assassinated one of the most heavily protected men on the planet? The man whom Casagrande had promised would not be a problem? Lange hoped someday to repay the favor.

For now he focused his thoughts on the task at hand: finding some avenue of escape. A car was waiting across the river on the

Aventine Hill. To get there, he needed to navigate the maze of Trastevere. He was confident he could lose the Israeli there—if they survived that long.

He thought of his home in Grindelwald, of skiing beneath the face of the Eiger and bringing women home to his enormous bed. Then he pictured the alternative: rotting in an Italian jail, subsisting on rancid food, never touching a woman again for the rest of his life. Anything was better—even death.

He opened the throttle full and drove perilously fast. The streets of Trastevere lay before him. Freedom. He glanced into the rearview mirror and saw that the Israeli had closed the gap and was preparing to fire. Lange tried to increase his speed, but couldn't. It was Katrine. Her weight was slowing him down.

Then he heard the gunshots, felt the rounds shearing past him. Katrine screamed. Her grip on his pelvis weakened. "Hold on!" Lange said, but there was little conviction in his voice.

He left the park and entered Trastevere, racing along a street lined with faded tenement houses. Then he turned into a smaller street, narrow and cobblestoned, cars parked on both sides. At the head of the street rose the spire of a Romanesque church, a cross on top, like the site of a rifle. Lange made for it.

Katrine's grip was slackening. Lange glanced over his shoulder. There was blood in her mouth and her face was the color of chalk. He looked into the mirror. The Israeli was about thirty meters behind, no more, and making up ground quickly.

Lange murmured, "Forgive me, Katrine."

He grabbed her wrist and twisted it until he could feel the bones cracking. Katrine screamed and tried to grab hold of his torso, but with only one hand it was futile.

Lange felt the weight of her body tumbling helplessly off the back of the bike. The sound of her body striking cobblestones was something he would never forget.

He did not look back.

THE WOMAN fell diagonally across the street. Gabriel had less than a second to react. He squeezed the brakes in a vise-grip but realized that the powerful motorcycle was not going to stop in time. He leaned hard to the left and laid the bike on the cobblestones. His head slammed to the pavement. As he slid along the street, skin was torn from his body. At some point he saw the bike cartwheel into the air.

He came to rest atop the body of the woman and found himself staring into a pair of beautiful lifeless eyes. He lifted his head and saw the Leopard roar up the street and vanish into a church steeple.

Then he blacked out.

IN THE turmoil of St. Peter's Square, no one took notice of the old man making his way slowly across the timeworn paving stones. He glanced at a dying Swiss Guard, his vibrant uniform stained with blood. He paused briefly near the body of a young *carabiniere*. He saw a young American girl, screaming in the arms of her mother. In a few minutes, the horror would be amplified when news of the cardinal's assassination was made public. The stones of St. Peter's, awash in blood. A nightmare. Worse than that day in 1981, when the Pole was nearly killed. *I have wrought this,* thought Casagrande. *It is my doing.*

He slipped through the colonnade and made for St. Anne's Gate. He thought of what lay ahead. The inevitable exposure of the conspiracy. The unmasking of Crux Vera. How could Casagrande explain that he had actually saved the life of the Pope? Indeed, that he had saved the life of the Church itself by killing Cardinal Brindisi? The blood in St. Peter's was necessary, he thought. It was a cleansing blood. But no one would believe him. He would die in shame, a disgraced man. A murderer.

He stopped outside the door of the Church of St. Anne. A Swiss Guard was standing watch. He had been hastily called to duty and was dressed in jeans and a windbreaker. He seemed surprised to see Casagrande climbing slowly up the steps.

"Is there anyone inside?" Casagrande asked.

"No, General. We cleared the church as soon as the shooting began. The doors are locked."

"Unlock them, please. I need to pray."

The tiny nave was in darkness. The Swiss Guard remained near the door, watching curiously as Casagrande made his way forward and fell to his knees in front of the altar. He prayed feverishly for a moment, then reached into his coat pocket.

The Swiss Guard sprinted forward up the center aisle, screaming, "No, General! Stop!" But Casagrande seemed not to hear him. He placed the gun in his mouth and pulled the trigger. A single shot echoed throughout the empty church. He remained balanced upon his knees for a few seconds, long enough for the Swiss Guard to hope that the general had somehow missed. Then the body slumped forward and collapsed onto the altar. Carlo Casagrande, savior of Italy, was dead.

PART FIVE

✦

A
CHURCH
IN VENICE

✦

·36·

ROME

THERE ARE ROOMS on the eleventh floor of the Gemelli Clinic that few people know. Spare and spartan, they are the rooms of a priest. In one there is a hospital bed. In another there are couches and chairs. The third contains a private chapel. In the hallway outside the entrance is a desk for the guards. Someone stands watch always, even when the rooms are empty.

In the days following the shootings at the Vatican, the rooms were occupied by a patient with no name. His injuries were severe: a fractured skull, a cracked vertebra, four broken ribs, abrasions and lacerations over much of his body. Emergency surgery relieved the life-threatening pressure caused by swelling of the brain, but he remained deep in a coma. Because of the terrible wounds on his back, he was placed on his stomach, his head turned toward the window. An oxygen mask obscured the swollen face. The eyelids, darkened by bruises, remained tightly closed.

There was a great deal of evidence to suggest he was a man of some importance. Father Luigi Donati, the papal secretary, called several times a day to check on his progress. A pair of bodyguards stood watch outside his door. Then there was the striking fact that he was in the room at all, for the suite on the eleventh floor of the Gemelli is reserved for only one man: the Supreme Pontiff of the Roman Catholic Church.

For the first four days, there were only two visitors: a tall, striking woman with long curly hair and black eyes, and an old man with a face like desert stone. The girl spoke Italian, the old man did not. The nursing staff assumed, wrongly as it turned out, that he was the patient's father. The visitors made a base camp in the sitting room and never left.

The old man seemed concerned about the patient's right hand, which struck the nursing staff as odd, since his other injuries were much more serious. A radiologist was summoned. X rays were taken. An orthopedic specialist concluded that the hand had come through the accident remarkably intact, though she did take note of a deep scar in the webbing between the thumb and forefinger, a recent wound that had never healed properly.

On the fifth day, a prie-dieu was placed at the bedside. The Pope arrived at dusk, accompanied by Father Donati and a single Swiss Guard. He spent an hour kneeling over the unconscious man, his eyes closed in prayer. When he was finished, he reached down and gently stroked the hand.

As the Pope rose to his feet, his gaze fell upon the large carved-wood crucifix above the bed. He stared at it for a moment before extending his fingers and making the sign of the cross. Then he leaned close to Father Donati and whispered into his ear. The priest reached over the bed and gently removed the crucifix from the wall.

Twenty-four hours after the Pope's visit, the right hand began to move; the same motion, over and over again; a tap followed by three swift stroking movements. *Tap, stroke, stroke, stroke . . . Tap, stroke, stroke, stroke . . .*

This development caused much debate among the team of doctors. Some dismissed it as spasmodic in nature. Others feared it was the result of a seizure. The tall girl with black eyes told them it was neither spasm or seizure. "He's just painting," she assured them. "He's coming back to us soon."

The next day, one week after his arrival, the patient with no name briefly regained consciousness. He opened his eyes slowly, blinking in the sunlight, and looked quizzically at the old man's face, as if he did not recognize him.

"Ari?"

"We've been worried about you."

"I hurt everywhere."

"I don't doubt it."

He raised his eyes toward the window. "*Yerushalayim?*"

"Rome."

"Where?"

The old man told him. The injured man smiled weakly beneath the oxygen mask.

"Where's . . . Chiara?"

"She's here. She never left."

"Did I . . . get him?"

But before Shamron could answer, Gabriel's eyes closed and he was gone once more.

·37·

VENICE

I T WOULD BE A MONTH before Gabriel was fit enough to return to Venice. They settled in a canal house in Cannaregio, with four floors and a tiny dock with a skiff. The entrance, flanked by a pair of ceramic pots overflowing with geraniums, opened onto a quiet courtyard that smelled of rosemary. The security system, installed by an obscure electronics firm based in Tel Aviv, was worthy of the Accademia.

Gabriel was in no condition to resume his battle with the Bellini. His vision remained blurred, and he could not stand for long without becoming dizzy. Most nights, he was awakened by a pounding headache. Seeing his back for the first time, Francesco Tiepolo thought he looked like a man who had been flayed. Tiepolo appealed to the superintendent in charge of Venice's churches to delay the reopening of San Zaccaria for another month so that Signor Delvecchio could recover from his unfortunate motorcycle accident. The superintendent suggested in turn that Tiepolo scale the scaffolding himself and finish the Bellini on time. *The tourists are coming, Francesco! Am I supposed to hang a sign on the Church of San Zaccaria that says closed for remodeling?* In a highly unusual development, the Vatican intervened in the dispute. Father Luigi Donati fired off a blistering e-mail to Venice, expressing the wishes of the Holy Father that Signor Delvecchio be permitted to complete the restoration of the Bellini masterpiece. The superintendent quickly reversed his ruling. The next day, a box of Venetian chocolates arrived at the house, along with a note wishing Gabriel a speedy recovery.

While Gabriel healed, they behaved as typical Venetians. They ate in restaurants no tourists could find, and after supper each night they walked in the Ghetto Nuovo. Some nights, after *Ma'ariv,* Chiara's father would join them. He would press them gently on the nature of their relationship and sound out Gabriel on his intentions. When it had gone on long enough, Chiara would swat him gently on the shoulder and say, "Papa, *please.*" Then she would take each man by the arm, and they would stroll the *campo* in silence, the soft evening air on their faces.

Gabriel never left the ghetto without first pausing at the Casa Israelitica di Riposo to gaze through the windows at the old ones watching their evening television. His stance never varied: right hand on his chin, left hand supporting his right elbow, head tilted slightly down. Chiara could almost imagine him perched atop his scaffolding, staring at a damaged painting, a brush between his teeth.

WITH LITTLE else to do that spring but wait for Gabriel to heal, they followed developments at the Vatican with intense interest. As promised, Pope Paul VII set in motion his initiative by appointing a panel of historians and experts to reevaluate the role of the Vatican during the Second World War, along with the Church's long history of anti-Semitism. There were twelve members in all: six Catholics, six Jews. Under the rules established at the outset, the historians would spend five years analyzing countless documents contained in the Vatican Secret Archives. Their deliberations would be conducted in the utmost secrecy. At the end of five years, a report would be written and forwarded to the pope for action, whoever the pope might be. From New York to Paris to Jerusalem, the response from the world's Jewish community was overwhelmingly positive.

One month after convening, the commission submitted its first request for documents to the Secret Archives. Among the items contained in the initial batch was a memorandum written by Bishop Sebastiano Lorenzi of the Secretariat of State to His Holiness Pope Pius XII. The memo, once thought destroyed, contained details of a secret meeting that took place at a convent on Lake Garda in 1942. Members of the commission, true to the guidelines, said nothing about it in public.

The Pope's initiative was quickly overshadowed, however, by what became known in the Italian press as the Crux Vera affair. In a series of incendiary exposés, Benedetto Foà, the Vatican correspondent for *La Repubblica,* revealed the existence of a secret Catholic society that had infiltrated the highest levels of the Holy See, the Rome government, and Italy's financial world. Indeed, according to Foà's shadowy sources, the tentacles of Crux Vera reached across Europe to the United States and Latin America. Cardinal Marco Brindisi, the slain Vatican secretary of state, was named as leader of Crux Vera, along with the reclusive financier Roberto Pucci and the former chief of the Vatican Security Office, Carlo Casagrande. Pucci issued a denial of the accusation through his lawyers, but not long after Foà's article appeared, a Pucci-owned bank suffered a liquidity crisis and collapsed. The bank failure revealed the Pucci empire to be a financial house of cards, and within weeks it was a smoldering ruin. Pucci himself fled his beloved Villa Galatina and took up exile in Cannes.

As for the Vatican, publicly it clung to its theory that the gunman who wreaked havoc was a religious madman with no ties to any country, terrorist organization, or secret society. It strenuously denied the existence of a clandestine group called Crux Vera and reminded the *Vaticanisti* at every turn that secret societies and lodges were strictly forbidden by the Church. Still, it soon became apparent to the press corps and all those who followed Vatican affairs that Pope Paul VII was in the process of cleaning house. More than a dozen senior members of the Roman Curia were reassigned to pastoral duties or were retired, including the doctrinaire head of the Congregation for the Doctrine of the Faith. Following the appointment of a replacement for Marco Brindisi, there were wholesale staff changes in the Secretariat of State. Press office chief Rudolf Gertz returned to Vienna.

Ari Shamron monitored Gabriel's recovery from Tel Aviv. Against Lev's wishes, Shamron managed to tunnel his way back into King Saul Boulevard to head up what eventually became known as Team Leopard. The sole purpose of the group was to locate and neutralize the elusive terrorist thought to be responsible for the murder of Benjamin Stern and countless others. Shamron seemed rejuvenated by the new assignment. Those closest to him noticed a marked improvement in his appearance.

Unfortunately for those drafted onto his team, better health brought the return of his fiery temper, and he drove himself and his underlings to the point of exhaustion. No lead, no piece of gossip, was deemed too small to ignore. There was a suspected sighting of the Leopard in Paris and another in Helsinki. There was a report that Czech police suspected the Leopard was behind a murder in Prague. His name surfaced in Moscow in connection with the murder of a senior intelligence official. An Office agent in Baghdad heard rumors that the Leopard had just signed a contract to work for the Iraqi secret service.

The clues were tantalizing, but eventually they all proved fruitless. In spite of the setbacks, the old man pleaded with his team not to lose faith. Shamron had his own theory about how the Leopard would be found. It was money that fueled him, Shamron told his team, and it would be money that would bring him down.

ONE WARM evening in the last days of May, a soccer ball bounded toward Gabriel as he walked in the Campo di Ghetto Nuovo with Chiara. He released her hand and lunged toward the moving ball with three swift steps. "Gabriel! Your head!" she shouted, but he did not listen. He drew back his foot and met the ball with a solid *thump* that echoed off the façade of the synagogue. It sailed through the air in a graceful arc and landed in the hands of a boy, about twelve years old, with a *kippah* clipped to his head of curly hair. The child stared at Gabriel for a moment, then smiled and ran off to rejoin his friends. Returning home, Gabriel telephoned Francesco Tiepolo and told him he was ready to go back to work.

HIS PLATFORM was as he had left it: his brushes and his palette, his pigment and his medium. He had the church to himself. The others—Adriana, Antonio Politi, and the rest of the San Zaccaria team—had completed their work and moved on long ago. Chiara never left the church while Gabriel was inside. With his back to the door, framed by the majestic altarpiece, he made an inviting target, so she sat at the base of his scaffolding while he worked, her dark eyes fixed on the door. She made only one demand—that he remove the shroud—and uncharacteristically he agreed.

He worked long hours, longer than he would have preferred under normal circumstances, but he was determined to finish as quickly as possible. Tiepolo stopped by once a day to bring food and check on his progress. Some days he would linger for a few minutes to keep Chiara company. Once he even hauled his lumbering frame up the scaffolding to consult with Gabriel on a difficult section of the apse.

Gabriel worked with renewed confidence. He had spent so much time studying Bellini and his works that some days he could almost feel the presence of the master standing next to him, telling him what to do next. He worked from the center outward—the Madonna and child, the saints and the donors, the intricate background. He thought about the case in much the same way. As he worked, he was troubled by two questions that ran incessantly through his subconscious. Who had given Benjamin the documents on the Garda covenant in the first place? And why?

ONE AFTERNOON late in June, Chiara looked up and saw him standing on the edge of the scaffolding, right hand on his chin, left hand supporting his right elbow, head tilted slightly down. He stood motionless for a long time, ten minutes by Chiara's watch, his eyes traveling the length and breadth of the towering canvas. Chiara took the scaffolding in hand and shook it once, the way Tiepolo always did. Gabriel looked down at her and smiled.

"Is it finished, Signor Delvecchio?"

"Almost," said he distantly. "I just need to talk to him one more time."

"What on earth are you talking about?"

But Gabriel made no reply. Instead, he knelt down and spent the next several minutes cleaning his brushes and palette and packing away his pigments and medium in a flat rectangular case. He climbed off the scaffolding, took Chiara by the hand, and walked out of the church for the last time. On the way home, they stopped by Tiepolo's office in San Marco. Gabriel told him that he needed to see the Holy Father. By the time they arrived home in Cannaregio, a message was waiting on the answering machine.

Bronze Doors, tomorrow evening, eight o'clock. Don't be late.

·38·

VATICAN CITY

GABRIEL CROSSED ST. PETER'S SQUARE at dusk. Father Donati met him at the Bronze Doors. He shook Gabriel's hand solemnly and remarked that he looked much better than he had the last time they had met. "The Holy Father is expecting you," Father Donati said. "It's best not to keep him waiting."

The priest led Gabriel up the Scala Regia. A five-minute walk along an archipelago of looming corridors and darkened courtyards brought them to the Vatican Gardens. In the dusty sienna light it was easy to spot the Pope. He was walking along a footpath near the Ethiopian College, his white soutane glowing like an acetylene torch.

Father Donati left Gabriel at the Pope's side and drifted slowly back toward the palace. The Pope took Gabriel's arm and led him along the pathway. The evening air was warm and soft and heavy with the scent of pine.

"I'm pleased to see you looking so well," the Pope said. "You've made a remarkable recovery."

"Shamron is convinced it was your prayers that brought me out of the coma. He says hell testify to the miracle of the Gemelli Clinic at your beatification proceedings."

"I'm not sure how many in the Church will support my canonization after the commission has finished its work." He chuckled and squeezed Gabriel's bicep. "Are you pleased with the restoration of the San Zaccaria altarpiece?"

"Yes, Holiness. Thank you for intervening on my behalf."

"It was the only just solution. You started the restoration. It was fitting that you complete it. Besides, that altarpiece is one of my favorite paintings. It needed the hands of the great Mario Delvecchio."

The Pope guided Gabriel onto a narrow pathway leading toward the Vatican walls. "Come," he said. "I want to show you something." They headed directly toward the spire of Vatican Radio's transmission tower. At the wall, they mounted a flight of stone steps and climbed up to the parapet. The city lay before them, rustling and stirring, dusty and dirty, eternal Rome. From this angle, in this light, it was not so different from Jerusalem. All that was missing was the cry of the muezzin, calling the faithful to evening prayer. Then Gabriel's eye traveled down the length of the Tiber, to the synagogue at the entrance of the old ghetto, and he realized why the Pope had brought him here.

"You have a question you wish to ask me, Gabriel?"

"I do, Holiness."

"I suspect you want to know how your friend Benjamin Stern got the documents about the covenant at Garda in the first place."

"You're a very wise man, Holiness."

"Am I? Look at what I have wrought."

The Pope was silent for a moment, his gaze fixed on the towering synagogue. Finally he turned to Gabriel. "Will you be my confessor, Gabriel—metaphorically speaking, of course?"

"I'll be whatever you want me to be, Holiness."

"Do you know about the seal of confession? What I tell you here tonight must never be repeated. For a second time, I place my life in your hands." He looked away. "The question is, whose hands are they? Are they the hands of Gabriel Allon? Or are they the hands of Mario Delvecchio, the restorer?"

"Which would you prefer?"

The Pope looked across the river once more, toward the synagogue, and leaving Gabriel's question unanswered, he began to speak.

THE POPE told Gabriel of the conclave, the terrible night of agony at the Dormitory of St. Martha, when, like Christ in the Garden of Gethsemane, he had begged God to let this cup pass from his lips. How could a man with knowledge of the terrible secret of the Garda covenant be chosen to lead the Church? What would he do with such knowledge? The night before the final session of the conclave, he summoned Father Donati to his room and told the priest he would refuse the papacy if chosen. Then, for the first time, he told his trusted aide what had happened at the convent by the lake that night in 1942.

"Father Donati was horrified," the Pope said. "He believed that the Holy Spirit had chosen me for a reason, and that reason was to confess the secret of the Garda covenant and cleanse the Church.

But Father Donati is a very clever man and a skilled operative. He knew the secret had to be revealed in such a way that it would not destroy my papacy in its infancy."

"It had to be revealed by someone other than you."

The Pope nodded. *Indeed.*

Father Donati went looking for Sister Regina Carcassi. In retrospect, it was probably Father Donati's relentless search of Church records that alerted the hounds of Crux Vera. He found her living alone in a village in the north. He asked about her memories of that night in 1942, and she gave him a copy of a letter—a letter she had written the night before her wedding. Father Donati then asked whether she would be willing to speak publicly. Enough time had passed, Regina Carcassi said. She would do whatever Father Donati asked.

As powerful as Sister Regina's letter was, Father Donati knew he needed more. There had been rumors inside the Curia for years that the KGB had been in possession of a document that had the power to inflict serious damage on the Church. According to the rumor mill, the document was almost leaked during the showdown with the Polish pope, but calmer heads inside the KGB prevailed, and it remained buried in the KGB archives. Father Donati traveled secretly to Moscow and met with the chief of the KGB's successor, the Russian Foreign Intelligence Service. After three days of negotiation, he took possession of the document. Captured by advancing Russian forces in the final days of the war, it was a memorandum written by Martin Luther to Adolf Eichmann about a meeting at a convent on Lake Garda.

"When I read it, I knew the battle that lay ahead would be a difficult one," the Pope said. "You see, the document contained two ominous words."

"Crux Vera," said Gabriel, and the Pope nodded in agreement.
Crux Vera.

Father Donati began searching for the right man to bring these
documents to the attention of the world. A man of passion. A man
whose past work made him above reproach. Father Donati settled
on an Israeli Holocaust historian attached to Ludwig-Maximilian
University in Munich: Professor Benjamin Stern. Father Donati traveled to Munich and met with him secretly at his flat on the Adalbertstrasse. He showed Professor Stem the documents and promised full
cooperation. Senior Vatican officials, who for obvious reasons could
not be named, would attest to their authenticity. At the time of pub-
lication, the Vatican would refrain from public attacks on the book.
Professor Stern accepted the offer and took possession of the documents. He secured a contract for the work from his publisher in
New York and a leave of absence from his department at Ludwig-
Maximilian. Then he began his work. At Father Donati's suggestion, he did so under the utmost secrecy.

Three months later, the trouble began. Father Cesare Felici disappeared. Two days after that, Father Manzini vanished. Father
Donati tried to warn Regina Carcassi, but it was too late. She too disappeared. He traveled to Munich to meet with Benjamin Stern and
warn him that his life was in grave danger. Professor Stern promised to take precautions. Father Donati feared for the professor's life
and for his own stratagem. Skilled operative that he was, he began
to prepare a backup plan.

"And then they killed Benjamin," Gabriel said.

"It was a terrible blow. Needless to say, I felt responsible for his
death."

Father Donati was outraged by the murder, the Pope resumed.
He vowed to use the secret of the Garda covenant to destroy Crux

Vera—or, better still, to force Crux Vera to destroy itself. He hastily scheduled the appearance at the synagogue. He whispered secrets into the ears of known Crux Vera members—secrets he knew would eventually reach Carlo Casagrande and Cardinal Brindisi. He enlisted Benedetto Foà of *La Repubblica* to ask questions about the Pope's childhood at the press office, which was run by Rudolf Gertz, a member of the society.

"Father Donati was waving a red flag in front of the bull," Gabriel said. "And *you* were the red flag."

"That's right," the Pope replied. "He was hoping he could goad Crux Vera into an act so repulsive that he could use it as justification to destroy them once and for all, and purge the group's influence from the Curia."

"A tale as old as time," Gabriel said. "A Vatican intrigue, with your life hanging in the balance. And it worked out better than Father Donati could have hoped. Carlo Casagrande sent his assassin against Cardinal Brindisi and then killed himself. Then Father Donati rewarded Benedetto Foà by giving him the dirt on Crux Vera. The group is discredited and disgraced."

"And the Curia is free of its poisonous influence, at least for the moment." The Pope took hold of Gabriel's hand and looked directly into his eyes. "And now I have a question for you. Will you grant me forgiveness for the murder of your friend?"

"It's not mine to give, Holiness."

The Pope lifted his gaze toward the river. "Some nights, when the wind is right, I swear I can still hear it. The rumble of the German trucks. The pleading for the Pope to do something. Sometimes now, when I look at my hands, I see blood. The blood of Benjamin. We used him to do our dirty work. It is because of us that he is dead." He turned and looked at Gabriel. "I need your forgiveness. I need to sleep."

Gabriel looked into his eyes for a moment, then nodded slowly. The Pope raised his right hand, fingers extended, but stopped himself. He placed his palms on Gabriel's shoulders and pulled him to his breast.

FATHER DONATI saw him out. At the Bronze Doors, he handed Gabriel an envelope. "Somehow, the Leopard managed to get into the papal study before he killed Cardinal Brindisi. He left this on the Pope's desk. I thought you might like to see it."

Then he shook Gabriel's hand and disappeared into the palace once more. Gabriel crossed the deserted expanse of St. Peter's Square as the bells of the Basilica tolled nine o'clock. An Office car was waiting near St. Anne's Gate. There was still time to catch the night train for Venice.

He opened the envelope. The short, handwritten note was a photocopy. The nine-millimeter bullet was not.

This could have been yours, Holiness.

Gabriel crushed the note into a tight ball. A moment later, crossing the Tiber, he tossed it into the black water. The bullet he slipped into his jacket pocket.

⋆39⋆

GRINDELWALD, SWITZERLAND: FIVE MONTHS LATER

THE SNOWS HAD COME EARLY. Overnight, a November gale had swept over the spires of the Eiger and the Jungfrau and left a half-meter of downy powder on the slopes below Kleine Scheidegg. Eric Lange pushed himself clear of the chairlift, the last of the day, and floated gracefully down the slope through the lengthening shadows of late afternoon.

At the bottom of the slope, he turned off the trail and entered a stand of pine. The sun had slipped behind the massif, and the grove was deep in shadow. Lange navigated by memory, picking his way effortlessly between the trees.

His chalet appeared, perched at the edge of the wood, staring out over the valley toward Grindelwald. He skied to the back entrance, removed his gloves, and punched the security code into the keypad located next to the door.

He heard a sound. Footfalls on new snow. He turned and saw a man walking toward him. Dark-blue anorak, short hair, gray at the temples. Sunglasses. Lange ripped open his ski jacket and reached inside for his Stechkin. It was too late. The man in the blue anorak already had a Beretta aimed at Lange's chest, and he was walking faster now.

The Israeli . . . Lange was sure of it. He knew the way they were trained to kill. Advance on the target while shooting. Keep shooting until the target is dead.

Lange seized the grip of the Stechkin and was trying to bring it into play when the Israeli fired—a single shot, which struck Lange perfectly in the heart. He toppled backward into the snow. The Stechkin slipped from his fingers.

The Israeli stood over him. Lange braced himself for the pain of more bullets, but the Israeli just pushed his sunglasses onto his forehead and stood there, watching Lange curiously. His eyes were a brilliant shade of green. They were the last thing Lange ever saw.

HE HIKED down the valley through the gathering dusk. The car was waiting for him, parked at the edge of a rocky stream. The engine turned over as he approached. Chiara leaned across the passenger seat and pushed open the door. Gabriel climbed in and closed his eyes. *For you, Beni,* he thought. *For you.*

AUTHOR'S NOTE

The Confessor is a work of fiction. The cardinals and clergy, spies and assassins, secret policemen and secret Church societies portrayed in this novel are products of the author's imagination or have been used fictitiously. Any resemblance to any person, living or dead, is entirely coincidental. The Convent of the Sacred Heart in Brenzone does not exist. Martin Luther of the German Foreign Ministry was present at the Wannsee Conference, but the actions attributed to him in *The Confessor* are wholly fictitious. Pope Pius XII reigned from 1939 until his death in 1958. His public silence in the face of the annihilation of Europe's Jews, despite repeated Allied requests to speak out, is, in the words of Holocaust scholar Susan Zuccotti, a fact that is "rarely contested, nor can it be." So is the sanctuary and aid given by Church officials to Adolf Eichmann and other prominent Nazi murderers after the defeat of the Third Reich.

Defenders of Pius XII, including the Vatican itself, have portrayed him as a friend of the Jews whose tireless, quiet diplomacy saved hundreds of thousands of Jewish lives. His critics have portrayed him as a calculating politician who, at best, displayed a callous and near-criminal indifference to the plight of the Jews, or, at worst, was actually complicit in the Holocaust.

A more complete portrait of Pope Pius XII might be drawn from documents concealed in the Vatican Secret Archives, but more than a half-century after the end of the war, the Holy See still refuses to open its repository of records to historians in search of the truth. Instead, it insists that historians may review only the eleven volumes of archival material, mainly wartime diplomatic traffic, published between 1965 and 1981. These records, known as *Actes et Documents du Saint Siège relatifs à la Seconde Guerre Mondiale,* have contributed to many of the unflattering historical accounts of the war—and these are the documents the Vatican is *willing* to let the world see.

What other damning material might reside in the Secret Archives? In October 1999, in a bid to calm the controversy swirling about its beleaguered Pope, the Vatican created a commission of six independent historians to assess the conduct of Pius XII and the Holy See during the war. After reviewing those documents already made public, the commission concluded: "No serious historian could accept that the published, edited volumes could put us at the end of the story." It submitted to the Vatican a list of forty-seven questions, along with a request for supporting documentary evidence from the Secret Archives—records such as "diaries, memoranda, appointment books, minutes of meetings, draft documents" and the personal papers of senior wartime Vatican officials. Ten months passed without a response. When it became clear the Vatican had no intention of releasing the documents, the commission disbanded, its work unfinished. The Vatican angrily accused the three *Jewish* members of "clearly incorrect behavior" and of waging a "slanderous campaign" against the Church, though it leveled no such accusations against the three Catholic members. According to sources quoted by *The Guardian* newspaper, access to the Secret Archives "was blocked by a cabal led by the Vatican's secretary of state, Cardinal Angelo Sodano." Cardinal Sodano, it was suggested, opposes opening the Archives because it would set a terribly dangerous precedent and leave the Vatican vulnerable to other historical investigations, such as the relationship between the Holy See and the murderous military regimes of Latin America.

Clearly, there are those within the Church who would like the Vatican to offer a more complete accounting of its wartime actions, coupled with a more energetic admission of guilt for the Church's persecution of the Jews. Archbishop Rembert Weakland of Milwaukee appears to be one of them. "We Catholics through the centuries acted in a fashion contrary to God's law toward our Jewish brothers and sisters," Archbishop Weakland told Congregation Shalom in Fox Point, Wisconsin, in November 1999. "Such actions harmed the Jewish community through the ages in both physical and psychological ways."

The archbishop then made the following remarkable statement: "I acknowledge that we Catholics—by preaching a doctrine that the Jewish people were unfaithful, hypocritical and God-killers—reduced the human dignity of our Jewish brothers and sisters and created attitudes that made reprisals against them seem like acts of conformity to God's will. By doing so, I confess that we Catholics contributed to the attitudes that made the Holocaust possible."

ACKNOWLEDGMENTS

This novel, like the previous two books in the series, *The Kill Artist* and *The English Assassin,* could not have been written without the guidance, support, and friendship of David Bull. Unlike the fictitious Gabriel Allon, David is truly one of the world's finest art restorers. His encyclopedic knowledge of art history, along with his experiences working in the restoration community of Venice, proved invaluable and inspirational and for that I am eternally in his debt. He answered all my questions, no matter how tedious, read my manuscript for accuracy, and never failed to make me laugh.

Fred Francis, the award–winning NBC News correspondent, shared his experiences behind the walls of the Vatican and his memories of the turbulent years when Italy was caught in the grips of Red Brigades terror. Brian Ross, the brilliant ABC News investigative reporter, regaled me with stories about covering the less seemly side of the Vatican, including his infamous encounter with Cardinal Joseph Ratzinger, which resulted in Brian's actually being slapped by the Inquisitor. Columnist E. J. Dionne, who covered the Vatican for *The New York Times,* allowed me to pick his agile and analytical mind, as did Daniel Jonah Goldhagen. My cousins Axel Lorka and Stacey Blatt generously and humorously recounted their days at Adalbertstrasse 68, which allowed me to bring "an apartment in Munich" to life. Italian law enforcement authorities, who cannot be named, helped me to get the details of the country's security and police agencies as accurate as possible. A special thanks to the Israeli officials in Rome who lent me assistance as well.

One of my dearest friends, journalist and author Louis Toscano, read my manuscript and, as always, made marked improvements. Columnist and MSNBC commentator Bill Press shared his memories of the School of Theology at the University of Fribourg and proofread my manuscript for accuracy on all things Catholic. Rabbi Mindy Portnoy of Temple Sinai in Washington, D.C., was an advisor and friend and managed to change my life for the better along the way.

The evidence of Europe's new anti-Semitism is all too visible in Rome, where members of the Jewish community pray each evening in a synagogue surrounded by heavily armed *carabinieri* units. Like the Jews of Venice, they treated me kindly and provided me with experiences I will never forget. My tour guide in Venice, Valentina Ronzan of the *Museo Ebraico di Venezia,* showed me corners of the ancient ghetto no history book could reveal.

While writing *The Confessor,* I consulted dozens of books, articles, and websites dealing with the papacy of Pope Pius XII, the Shoah, and the history of the Roman Catholic Church. Among those writers whose work proved especially helpful were John Cornwell,

Susan Zuccotti, Garry Wills, David I. Kertzer, James Carroll, Michael Phayer, Gitta Sereny, Guenter Lewy, Michael Novak, Ronald Rychlak, Robert S. Wistrich, Kevin Madigan, Carl Bernstein, Thomas Reese, Daniel Jonah Goldhagen, Mark Aarons and John Loftus, Peter Hebblethwaite, and Tad Szulc. Without their meticulous scholarship, it would not have been possible for me to construct this work of fiction.

I am fortunate to be represented by the finest agent in the business, Esther Newberg of International Creative Management, and as always her friendship, encouragement, and editorial suggestions were invaluable. Her talented assistant, Andrea Barzvi, was always there when I needed her. Also, a heartfelt thanks to the unbelievable team of professionals at Penguin Putnam: Carole Baron, Dan Harvey, Marilyn Ducksworth, and especially my editor, Neil Nyren, whose brilliant suggestions and steady hand made *The Confessor* a better book. His contribution was enormous, matched only by my gratitude.

Finally, I would be remiss if I did not acknowledge my wife, Jamie, who listened patiently while I fleshed out my ideas, skillfully edited my early drafts, and helped me find the essence of the story when it eluded me. She made this one possible, and everything else for that matter.